Grasmere, 2010

Selected Papers from
The Wordsworth Summer Conference

GW00493664

Grasmere, 2010

Selected Papers from
The Wordsworth Summer Conference

compiled by Richard Gravil on behalf of
The Wordsworth Conference Foundation

HEB ☼ Humanities-Ebooks, LLP

© The Wordsworth Conference Foundation, 2010

Copyright is asserted by the Foundation on behalf of the contributing authors who retain all rights of further publication and distribution.

Cover photograph showing Ullswater in November (the Ebook) or January (the Paperback) © Richard Gravil

First published by *Humanities-Ebooks, LLP,*
Tirril Hall, Tirril, Penrith CA10 2JE

The Ebook is available to individual purchasers exclusively from http://www.humanities-ebooks.co.uk
and to libraries from http://www.MyiLibrary.com.

The paperback is available exclusively from Lulu.com

ISBN 978-1-84760-185-8 Ebook
ISBN 978-1-84760-186-5 Paperback

Contents

Foreword

The Wordsworth Summer Conference, founded in 1970 by Richard Wordsworth, the son of Gordon Wordsworth and great-great-grandson of the poet, enjoyed its 40th anniversary in 2010. This souvenir selection of lectures and papers from the anniversary conference is the third such collection to be published on behalf of the Wordsworth Conference Foundation. All three are available in pdf form to libraries from MyiLibrary.com, and to individuals from humanities-ebooks, and from Lulu.com in paperback.

Several of the essays in this volume (those by Ken Johnston, Anthony Harding and Daniel Robinson among them) will appear also, with variations, in a special conference issue of *The Wordsworth Circle*, Volume XLII, No 1, edited by Marilyn Gaull early in 2011. Together, the two publications are designed to ensure wider circulation for approximately half of the 48 presentations at the 2010 conference.

One apology is necessary. The compiler's contribution was not in fact presented at the 2010 conference. It derives from of a lecture at the 2009 Winter School on 'Paradise Regained? Wordsworth's *Recluse* Project' and is included here to make a trio of essays (with those of Ken Johnston and Anthony Harding) contributing to recent critical reassessments of *The Excursion*.

I am delighted to announce that the next Wordsworth Summer Conference will be directed by Nicholas Roe, and its dates are 1–11 August, 2011. For details please visit the Foundation's website, http://www.wordsworthconferences.org.uk.

Richard Gravil, *1 December 2010*

Simon Bainbridge

'The Power of Hills': Romantic Mountaineering

I. Romantic Mountaineers

On 9 August 1802, Samuel Taylor Coleridge returned to his Keswick home at the end of his famous nine-day 'circumcursion' of the more remote parts of the Lake District, a vigorous tour that had included a ground-breaking ascent of Scafell and had left the poet's trousers in tatters and his boots in need of repair. That evening Coleridge wrote an excited account of his adventures to Robert Southey in which he made the first recorded use of the verb 'mountaineering', writing that he had 'Spent the greater part of the next Day mountaineering'.[1] Coleridge was using a new word for a new activity; the ascending of mountains for pleasure, rather than for economic or military purposes, was a pursuit that had originated in Britain in the previous few decades. And while Coleridge was the first to use 'mountaineer' as a verb, the noun was also in the process of transformation. Long used to define 'a person who is native to or lives in a mountainous region', 'mountaineer' was also coming to mean 'a person who engages in or is skilled at mountain climbing'.[2] In 1792, for example, the pioneering mountain climber and travel writer Captain Joseph Budworth described his guide Partridge in *A Fortnight's Ramble to the Lakes* as 'so bold a mountaineer, he can go any where that a

1 Samuel Taylor Coleridge, *Collected Letters of Samuel Taylor Coleridge*, 6 vols., ed. Earl Leslie Griggs (Oxford: Clarendon Press, 1956-71), II. 452. 'Mountaineer, v.', *Oxford English Dictionary Online*, Draft Revision June 2010.

2 'Mountaineer, *n* and *adj*', *OED Online*, Draft Revision June 2010. The examples cited for the latter definition by the *OED Online*, dating from 1860 and after, are much later than those I discuss here.

sheep can; and I dare say thinks every person can do the same'.[1] Here Partridge's identity as one from a mountainous region is also being used to describe his skill and ability at a particular activity. By the third edition of *Rambles*, when Budworth recounts what he claims to be the first ascent of Pike o' Stickle for pleasure in 1797, he tests the applicability of the word to himself, describing how he and his guide 'started like hardy mountaineers'.[2] William Wordsworth plays on the word's emergent double meaning in *The Prelude* when he describes himself and Robert Jones as 'mountaineers'; both come from mountainous regions and both are intent upon climbing peaks.[3] By 1837, when Wordsworth describes himself as 'an Islander by birth,/ A Mountaineer by habit',[4] the word has become capable of referring specifically to an individual who participates in mountain climbing rather than one who lives in mountainous regions.

In the Romantic period, then, we see the emergence of a new activity—mountaineering—and a new identity—the mountaineer— and both, I want to argue in this essay, are crucial to Romanticism, to the writers' senses of their identities and to their literary outputs. While the mountain has long been recognised as a key symbol in the writing of the period, there has been surprisingly little critical analysis of the links between the physical activity of mountaineering and Romantic literature.[5] Yet, almost all the major male Romantic poets were active

1 Joseph Budworth, *A Fortnight's Ramble to the Lakes. By a Rambler* (London: Joseph Palmer, 1792), 159.

2 Joseph Budworth, *A Fortnight's Ramble to the Lakes*, third edition (London: John Nicols, 1810), 266.

3 William Wordsworth, *The Prelude, 1799, 1805, 1850*, ed. Jonathan Wordsworth, M. H. Abrams, and Stephen Gill (New York and London: W.W. Norton and Company, 1979), 202. Unless otherwise stated, all further references are to the 1805 *Prelude* and are cited by book and line number within parenthesis in the text.

4 'Musings Near Aquapendente. April 1837', *Sonnets Series and Itinerary Poems, 1820-1845*, ed. Geoffrey Jackson (Ithaca and London: Cornell University Press, 2004), 742.

5 The major study of the change in the aesthetic response to mountains is Marjorie Hope Nicolson, *Mountain Gloom and Mountain Glory: The Development of the Aesthetics of the Infinite* (Ithaca, New York: Cornell University Press, 1959). For an excellent wide-ranging analysis of the culture of mountains and mountaineering, see Robert Macfarlane, *Mountains of the Mind: A History of a Fascination* (London: Granta Books, 2004).

mountaineers at some point in their lives, or were keen to present themselves as such, and it is worth briefly recounting their climbing histories and detailing how the poets themselves saw these as linked to their identities as writers.

William Wordsworth, as we have seen, was a self-proclaimed 'mountaineer', both a 'Child of the mountains' (*Prelude* X. 1006) who felt that the mountainous region in which he grew up was the ideal classroom for a poet's education, and an active climber of mountains throughout his life. The highlights of his climbing career included his schoolboy scrambling for bird's eggs on Yewbarrow crags, his 1790 Tour of the Alps, his 1791 summiting of Wales's highest peak, Snowdon, and his 1805 ascent with Humphry Davy and Walter Scott of Helvellyn, a mountain he continued to climb for the rest of his life, including an ascent in 1840 when he was aged 70. A fitting illustration of Wordsworth's mountaineering identity is Benjamin Robert Haydon's painting *Wordsworth on Helvellyn*, which can be seen in the Wordsworth Trust Museum.

While Wordsworth was a lifelong mountaineer, Coleridge—who Molly Lefebure has called the 'patron saint of fellwalkers' in her excellent essay 'The First of the Fellwalkers'[1]—had his own brief but glorious golden age of mountaineering, from the so-called 'picturesque' tour of the Lake District he undertook with Wordsworth in November 1799, which included an ascent of Helvellyn, until his departure for Malta in early 1804. During this period Coleridge's climbing exploits included the first known traverse of the ridge that runs from Keswick to Grasmere, by ways of the Dodds and Helvellyn; the exploration of the mountains in the Newlands Valley, including his completion of what is now know as the Coledale horseshoe, again a first; the 'circumcursion' of the Lake District, including the first recorded ascent of Scafell and the famous life-threatening descent of Broad Stand; and his scramble up Moss Force in Buttermere. Unlike Wordsworth, Coleridge never made it to the Alps, but he did plan such a trip, carefully designing a nailed boot for the purpose.

Wordsworth and Coleridge are going to be key figures in this

1 Molly Lefebure, 'The First of the Fellwalkers', *Cumberland Heritage* (London: Gollancz, 1970), 131–47.

paper, but while second-generation Romantics may not have been quite as dedicated or outstanding mountaineers, they still felt the need to participate in mountain climbing, or at least present themselves as doing so. Mountains are, of course, a key feature of Percy Shelley's poetry—we think of *Alastor*, 'Mont Blanc' and *Prometheus Unbound*—though other than 'Lines Written Among the Euganean Hills', which makes excellent poetic use of an elevated viewpoint, Shelley writes mainly from below and seems to lack the ambition to ascend to summits that characterises the other poets and their works (Mont Blanc, for him, remains a symbol of the unascendable, even though its summit had been reached in 1786 and it was the subject of John Keats's climbing fantasies). All the same, Shelley was keen to present himself as a mountaineer in both senses of the word, and while he had visited the Mer de Glace and Boisson glacier near Chamonix in 1816, he rather overstated his mountain experience in the 'Author's Preface' to *The Revolt of Islam* when writing that 'I have been familiar from boyhood with mountains and lakes, and the sea, and the solitude of forests: Danger, which sports upon the brink of precipices, has been my playmate. I have trodden the glaciers of the Alps, and lived under the eye of Mont Blanc'.[1] These activities, Shelley states, are part of an 'education peculiarly fitted for a poet', illustrating both Wordsworth's influence and the increasing perceived link between the sublime experience and poetic production.

John Keats too saw mountaineering adventure as crucial preparation for the poetic role. He described his planned pedestrian tour of 1818 through Northern England and Scotland, which was 'to make a sort of Prologue to the Life I intend to pursue', as follows:

> I will clamber through Clouds and exist. I will get such an accumulation of stupendous recollections that as I walk through the suburbs of London I may not see them—I will stand upon Mount Blanc and remember this coming Summer when I intend to straddle ben Lomond—with my Soul![2]

1 Percy Shelley, *Poetical Works*, ed. Thomas Hutchinson, corr. G. M. Matthews (Oxford: Oxford University Press, 1970), 34.

2 John Keats, *Letters of John Keats, A New Selection*, ed. Robert Gittings (Oxford: Oxford University Press, 1970), 83.

While Keats never made it to Mont Blanc, and the high price of a guide deterred him from tackling Ben Lomond, his tour took him through the Lake District, which, with its 'magnitude of mountains' was the place where, he declared, 'I shall learn poetry', and where he climbed Skiddaw, having earlier been frustrated by mist in an attempt to climb Helvellyn.[1] Travelling North to Scotland, despite suffering from a sore throat Keats climbed Ben Nevis, which as he noted in his letter to his brother Tom is 'the highest Mountain in Great Britain', 4300 feet above his starting point at sea level.[2] 'Imagine the task of mounting 10 Saint Pauls without the convenience of Stair cases' he told Tom, providing a strikingly Cockney perspective on the effort involved.[3]

Both Walter Scott and Lord Byron suffered from physical disabilities that limited their mountaineering careers, but they nevertheless undertook significant climbs. As we have seen, Scott ascended Helvellyn with Wordsworth in 1805 and his writing, particularly his account of Fitz-James scrambling in the Trossachs in the opening to *The Lady of the Lake*, had a strong influence on the development of Scottish mountaineering. Like Shelley, Byron overstated his achievements in early poems such as 'When I rov'd a young Highlander' in which he claims to have 'clim'd thy steep summit, Oh Morven of snow' but in poems such as this and 'Lachin Y Gair' he is keen to present himself as an 'active mountaineer' in both senses of the word.[4] Byron frequently places his heroes on mountain summits—we think of Manfred on the Jungrau or Napoleon in *Childe Harold's Pilgrimage III* as the embodiments of the figure who 'ascends to mountain-tops'[5]—and during his 1816 Alpine tour he did himself ascend what he believed to be the 7,000 feet Wengernalp, though John Clubbe has argued convincingly that the peak was in fact the Lauberhorn (8,111 feet).[6]

1 Keats, *Letters*, 103
2 Keats, *Letters*, 145.
3 Keats, *Letters*, 145.
4 Lord Byron, *The Complete Poetical Works*, 7 vols., ed. Jerome J. McGann (Oxford: Clarendon Press, 1980-1993), I. 47.
5 Byron, *Complete Poetical Works*, II. 92.
6 See John Clubbe, 'Byron in the Alps: The Journal of John Cam Hobhouse 17–29 September 1816', in John Clubbe and Ernest Giddey, *Byron et la Suisse:*

Mountaineering, then, was an important activity for all the major male Romantic poets, except Blake, though his famous notebook jotting 'Great things are done when men and mountains meet'[1] might be taken as a motto for this essay. All these writers participated in the emergent activity, and the role of the 'mountaineer' was one to which they all aspired and frequently claimed. In the rest of this essay, I will place their experiences and writing within a broader account of the rise of mountaineering to explain why they should be so keen to engage in it, and to be seen engaging in it, and to consider how they helped define and question mountaineering as an emerging practice and discourse.

II. The Rise of Mountaineering

Mountaineering in Britain develops out of the picturesque tour popular in the second half of the eighteenth century. While fellwalking and mountaineering as emergent activities are often set against picturesque travel, characterised as only interested in low-level views, the possibility of ascending to summits was inherent within the picturesque from its origins. In his *Guide to the Lakes* of 1778, a founding text of the picturesque tour, Thomas West advocated the Lake District over the Alps as a travel destination because, though 'the tops of the highest Alps are inaccessible, being covered with everlasting snow', the Lake District mountains 'are all accessible to the summit' and, moreover, they 'furnish prospects no less surprising [and] with more variety than the Alps themselves'.[2] West's *Guide* offers no advice on how to ascend to these summits, but his well-known 'stations' or viewpoints can be surprisingly elevated. For example, his fourth station at Derwentwater is Castle Crag, a very steep peak in the so-called 'Jaws of Borrowdale' which is just under 1000 feet high and requires quite a demanding climb to gain what West describes as

Deux Études (Genève: Librairie Droz, 1982), 24–6.

1 William Blake, *The Complete Poetry and Prose of William Blake*, ed. David V. Erdman and Harold Bloom (Berkeley and Los Angeles, California: University of California Press, 2008), 511.

2 Thomas West, *A Guide to the Lakes* (London: Richardson and Urquhart, 1778), 6.

'a most astonishing view'.[1]

Alongside the proliferation of written guides such as West's that encouraged tourists to ascend to summits, the closing decades of the eighteenth century saw the development of a rudimentary infrastructure of roads, accommodation and human guides that supported the efforts of those who wished to climb. Though Budworth was a pioneer with his first civilian ascents of Helm Crag in 1792 and the Langdale Pikes in 1797, even by the time of his first visit to the Lake District there had emerged a nascent guiding culture, focused on the three most accessible high mountains: Skiddaw, Helvellyn and Coniston 'Old Man'. While visiting Coniston, for example, Budworth and his companion were approached by a figure in 'harvest dress' and were 'soon convinced, by certain shrewd remarks, [that] he wished to officiate as guide' up the 'Old Man'.[2]

As early as 1798 this nascent summit fever had become a target for satire. In the comic parody of picturesque tourism *The Lakers*, the heroine Veronica's plans to climb Skiddaw are frustrated by bad weather but she comments 'I must go up whether it is fine or not. My tour would be absolutely incomplete without an account of a ride up Skiddaw'.[3] As this illustrates, before the start of the nineteenth century summiting had become a standard feature of a visit to the Lakes, though Veronica intended to ascend Skiddaw by pony, as many tourists would have done. Semi-organised mountain trips of the sort a real-life Veronica would have taken were often rather sociable events. Led by a local guide, usually a farmer, shepherd or innkeeper, many people climbed as part of a group or small party, like Keats who went up Skiddaw, 'with two others, very good sort of fellows'.[4] These trips often began very early in the morning—Keats was up at four to ascend Skiddaw and five for Ben Nevis—and seem to have involved drinking fairly copious amounts of brandy, rum and whisky, supplied by the guide. Exploring summits beyond the most popular ones remained rare, however, and the desire to do so could disconcert even the local guides. Budworth recounts how having scrambled

1 West, *Guide*, 97.
2 Budworth, *Fortnight's Ramble* (1792), 111.
3 James Plumptre, *The Lakers. A Comic Opera* (London: W. Clarke, 1798), 27.
4 Keats, *Letters*, 108.

over the rocks to reach the summit of Pike o' Stickle in Langdale, his guide Paul Postlethwaite turned to him and said, in a broad Cumbrian accent:

> *P.P.* Ith' neome oh fackins, wot a broughtin yoa here?
> *Ramb*[ler]. Curiosity, Paul.
> *P.P.* I think yoa mun be kurious enuff: I neor cum here bu after runnaway sheop, an I'me then so vext at um, I cud throa um deawn th' Poike.[1]

III. The View from the Top

Postlethwaite's question was a version of the one regularly asked of mountaineers, and one they have frequently asked themselves: why climb? The primary reason offered by most early mountaineers for ascending was the view or prospect they hoped to gain, which is often presented as the reward for the effort of ascending. In her account of climbing Scafell Pike that was included in her brother William's *Guide to the Lakes*, Dorothy Wordsworth comments that 'Scawfell and Helvellyn [are] the two Mountains which will best repay the fatigue of ascending them'.[2] This economy of physical expenditure and visual reward is well captured by Keats's account of his Skiddaw climb: 'we had fagged & tugged nearly to the top, when at half past six there came a mist upon us & shut out the view; we did not however lose anything by it, we were high enough without mist, to see the coast of Scotland; the Irish sea; the hills beyond Lancaster; & nearly all the large ones of Cumberland and Westmoreland, particularly Helvellyn & Scawfell'.[3] Keats here expresses no interest in summiting Skiddaw or disappointment at having failed to do so; the achievement of the view provides the culmination of his efforts. Much summit literature, like Keats's letter, is concerned with identifying the various sights and places that can seen. Mountain climbing creates a compelling visual fusion of the familiar and the strange,

1 Budworth, *Fortnight's Ramble* (1810), 269.
2 William Wordsworth, *Guide to the Lakes*, ed, by Ernest de Sélincourt with a preface by Stephen Gill (London: Lincoln Frances, 2004), 111.
3 Keats, *Letters*, 108.

enabling the viewer to see new places, or to identify known places but to see them in new ways. (The pleasure in identification and naming of landscape we see in much of this early mountaineering literature continues today and is perhaps best illustrated by the enduring popularity of Alfred Wainwright's seven-volume *Pictorial Guide to the Lakeland Fells*.)

In considering this early mountaineering writing, we need to appreciate just how extraordinary and novel a view from 3,000 feet would have been for these Romantic-period climbers, unfamiliar with air-travel, aerial photography or even the high-rise buildings that have made the sensations of altitude more familiar in the centuries since.[1] When Keats writes to his brother Tom about his experience on Ben Nevis that 'I do not know whether I can give you an Idea of the prospect from a large Mountain top',[2] he reminds us that this was an entirely new visual experience and one that was difficult to capture in language. For Keats, as for others, summit views were unprecedented and unrivalled. He described the chasms on Ben Nevis as 'the most tremendous places I have ever seen',[3] while Coleridge wrote that 'of all earthly things which I have beheld, the view *of* Sca'fell and *from* Sca'fell (*both* views from it's own summit) is the most heart-exciting'.[4] Moreover, the new sensations and experiences produced by mountaineering came not only from the grand and sublime but also from the exquisitely beautiful. For example, at the culmination of a wonderful description of Scafell Pike's summit, Dorothy Wordsworth identifies a visual sensation available to only the very few who reach that remote spot, writing that 'flowers, the most brilliant feathers, and even gems, scarcely surpass in colouring some of these masses of stone, which no human eye beholds, except the shepherd or traveller be led thither by curiosity: and how seldom must this happen!'[5]

Mountaineering enabled these early climbers to see new things, prospects on an unprecedented scale and colours of unsurpassable

1 On this general point, see Macfarlane, *Mountains of the Mind*, 143-4.
2 Keats, *Letters*, 147.
3 Keats, *Letters*, 147.
4 Coleridge, *Collected Letters*, II. 846.
5 Wordsworth, *Guide*, 110.

beauty. Ascent also produced new ways of seeing, frequently as a result of the combination of elevation, geography and weather conditions, perhaps allied to a predisposition on the climber's part for a transformation of vision. When Keats climbed Ben Nevis he was again unlucky with the mist, which, as he described, formed 'as it appeard large dome curtains which kept sailing about, opening and shutting at intervals here and there and everywhere'.[1] But the poet was not disappointed by these atmospheric conditions, finding in them an alternative way of seeing. He continues: 'so that although we did not see one vast wide extent of prospect all round we saw something perhaps finer—these cloud-veils opening with a dissolving motion and showing us the mountainous region beneath as through a loop hole—these Mouldy [*probably for* cloudy] loop holes ever varrying and discovering fresh prospect east, west north and South'.[2] There is something characteristically Keatsian about the way the poet enjoys having his vision shaped by atmospheric conditions. Whereas Wordsworth in one mountaineering poem describes the climbing process as 'Obtaining ampler boon, at every step / Of visual sovereignty' ('Musings Near Aquapendente', ll. 39–40),[3] Keats seems to feel no need to assert the power of his own eye or self over nature or the landscape beneath. As he says later in the same letter, on a Mountain 'the most new thing of all is the sudden leap of the eye from the extremity of what appears a plain into so vast a distance'[4]; Keats's eye is tricked by the strangeness of the place it finds itself, but the poet relishes this new visual sensation, which is itself only one of a number of new sensations.

Wordsworth himself, of course, was similarly deprived of the experience of seeing 'one vast wide extent of prospect all round' on his two most famous mountaineering experiences, the crossing of the Alps in Book 6 of *The Prelude* and the summiting of Snowdon with which he concludes his epic autobiography. In this masterwork, Wordsworth repeatedly climbs high, but by doing so he gains insight rather than far sight. He is rarely, if indeed ever, rewarded for his 'climbing toil' with a prospect of an actual landscape, instead what

1 Keats, *Letters*, 146.
2 Keats, *Letters*, 146–7.
3 Wordsworth, *Sonnet Series*, 744.
4 Keats, *Letters*, 147.

he sees is an internal 'prospect'—the 'prospect' of his own mind or soul[1]—and what is revealed to him is not the sublimity or beauty of the landscape but the power of his imagination. The Snowdon and Alps incidents in *The Prelude* are very well known, and need no further comment from me other than to emphasise that it is specifically through the process of mountain climbing that Wordsworth learns the poem's key lessons.

Wordsworth emphasises the importance of mountaineering to his ambitious poetic project by conceiving *The Prelude* as a mountain that the reader too must climb if they are to experience the same revelation. He frequently calls upon the metaphor of mountain climbing when describing his own poetic activity, for example invoking the figure of the chamois hunter when he describes how he has 'tracked the main essential power—/ Imagination—up her way sublime' (XIII. 289–90). But perhaps Wordsworth's mountaineering conception of his poetic task is best seen in Book 3 when he announces the exciting new theme for his epic, his own inner life. He begins the passage: 'And here, O friend, have I retraced my life/ Up to an eminence' and ends: 'Enough, for now into a populous plain / We must descend' (III. 168–196). By adopting such a framework of ascent and descent for the key statement of his new found epic purpose, Wordsworth illustrates the extent to which the concept as well as the activity of mountaineering structures one of the key texts of Romanticism.

IV. Wordsworth and Sublime Elevation

As the language of many of these examples has already suggested, mountain climbing gave access to both sublime objects and sublime experiences. A change in altitude could produce a change in the self, and physical elevation could lead to spiritual elevation, ideas neatly summed up by Wordsworth in a draft for his poem 'View from the Top of Black Comb':

> Let him—who, having wandered by the side
> Of Lakes and Rivers entertains a wish
> By lofty place to elevate his soul

1 Wordsworth, *The Prelude*, II. 371.

—Ascend on some clear morning to the top
Of huge Black-comb...[1]

Here mountain climbing becomes an almost instantaneous means of elevating both one's self and one's soul, a development of the discourse of the sublime that was most influentially codified by Edmund Burke in his *A Philosophical Enquiry into the Origin of our Ideas of the Sublime and the Beautiful* of 1757. It was in terms of the sublime that Wordsworth's friend Thomas Wilkinson justified a lifetime of climbing, opening his memoir *Tours to the British Mountains* of 1825 by stating 'From early life I have been an admirer of the sublime in Nature. Mountains and their accompaniments are amongst the finest specimens of the sublime. Hence, when circumstances allowed, I availed myself of the opportunity of exploring their recesses and ascending their summits'.[2] For the Quaker Wilkinson, the sublimity of mountains was specifically religious; he comments that 'Mountains may be said to be among the most conspicuous and imperishable monuments of the Creator's power that we behold'.[3] We can find variations on this idea that mountain climbing gives access to God or the divine throughout the period, perhaps most notably in the Wanderer of Wordsworth's *The Excursion* who feels his faith 'on the tops / Of the high mountains'.[4]

In other mountaineering accounts of the period we encounter a more secular sublime, one concerned with the power of the self rather than the Creator. In his *Remarks on Local Scenery and Manners of Scotland during the Years 1799 and 1800*, for example, the future editor of *The Times* and Hazlitt's brother-in-law to be, John Stoddart, describes standing on Ben Lomond's summit and feeling 'a degree of surprise arising almost to terror' (a pleasurable experience of terror is, of course, central to Burke's definition of the sublime). Contrary

1 William Wordsworth, *Shorter Poems, 1807–1820*, ed. Carl H. Ketcham (Ithaca: Cornell University Press, 1989), 347.
2 Thomas Wilkinson, *Tours to the British Mountains* (London: Taylor and Hessey, 1824), v.
3 Wilkinson, *Tours*, vi.
4 William Wordsworth, *The Excursion*, ed. Sally Bushell, James A. Butler, and Michael C. Jaye (Ithaca and London: Cornell University Press, 2007), Book I, lines 215–248.

to the group mentality of many of the organised summit excursions I've discussed above, Stoddard argues that 'In such a situation, the most sublime sensations cannot be felt, unless you are alone. A single insulated being, carrying his view over these vast, inanimate masses, seems to feel himself attached to them, as it were, by a new kind of bond; his spirit dilates with magnitude, and rejoices in the beauty of the terrestrial objects'.[1] Here, the sublime experience of mountain climbing leads to an expansion and empowering of the self, magnified and isolated from others. Stoddart goes on to give an archetypal statement of how climbing can produce a sense of transcendence and seem to open up new modes of being:

> It was a bright, lovely day, and I stood contemplating with admiration a beautiful vale, with its glittering lake, rich woods, and numerous buildings. Gradually, a thick mist rolled, like a curtain, before it, and took away every object from my view. I was left alone, on the mountain top, far above the clouds of the vale, the sun shining full upon my head; it seemed as if I had been suddenly transported into a new state of existence, cut off from every meaner association, and invisibly united with the surrounding purity and brightness.[2]

Stoddart's account of his summit experience during a cloud inversion might seem like a prototypical description of the Romantic Mountaineer, paralleling Wordsworth's description of himself on Snowdon, Byron's image of Manfred on the Jungfrau, or Casper David Friedrich's *The Wanderer in the Mist*. Loss of bodily vision becomes revelation and corporeal ascending becomes disembodied ascension as Stoddart achieves transcendence, rising above the physical earth and every-day care into an otherworldly state of 'purity and brightness'. As a result, Stoddart's self-representation might seem an example of the issues of power and gender politics inherent within Romanticism and mountaineering, both of which have been accused of a self-glorifying elevation of the male protagonist over Nature, the feminine, and the everyday.

1 John Stoddart, *Remarks on Local Scenery and Manners of Scotland during the Years 1799 and 1800*, 2 vols. (London: W. Miller, 1801), I. 236.

2 Stoddart, *Remarks*, I. 237.

In response to such arguments, I want to argue that many writers of this period were already aware of these issues of gender and power politics inherent in climbing high, and that they were themselves engaged in debating mountaineering's moral and ethical dimensions. There are many examples that could be looked at here, including Keats's resistance to the rhetoric of the sublime or Byron's use of the Chamois Hunter in *Manfred* to interrogate his own earlier representation of the Napoleonic individual 'who ascends to mountain-tops' in Childe Harold III[1] (the dialogue between Manfred and the Chamois Hunter stages a dramatic confrontation between the two different kinds of mountaineer I was outlining in this paper's opening). But here I'd like to focus on Wordsworth, who is the poet most frequently cited as the major exponent of the Romantic conquest of Nature but who I think actually provides the most sustained examination of the power and gender politics of mountaineering throughout his career.

At times in Wordsworth's poetry mountain climbing can certainly produce the self-elevation and empowering vision that we saw in Stoddart. As mentioned above, for example, in the relatively late poem 'Musings near Aquapendente. April, 1837', Wordsworth describes climbing Helvellyn as a process of 'Obtaining ampler boon, at every step / Of visual sovereignty'.[2] Here, ascending grants a form of dominion over all that the poet surveys, and elsewhere Wordsworth links the power of elevated vision with more explicitly political forms of power. A particularly important mountain for Wordsworth was Black Combe, at the very Southern end of the Lake District, which he climbed in 1811 and which he considered gave the fullest view of Britain, as he states in the opening of his 'View from the Top of Black Comb':

> This Height a minist'ring Angel might select:
> It is a spot from which the amplest range
> Of unobstructed prospect may be seen
> That British ground commands: (ll. 1–4)[3]

1 Byron, *Complete Poetical Works,* 117.
2 Wordsworth, *Sonnet Series*, 744.
3 Wordsworth, *Shorter Poems*, 99

What is particularly important for Wordsworth about Black Combe's summit is that on a clear day you can see all four countries of the United Kingdom, so the view offers a visual equivalence to what the poet hopes will be a united nation at a time when Great Britain is at war with France. Wordsworth ends the poem by combining the mountain tropes of prospect and revelation to emphasise this geographical expression of Britain's national identity.

> Of Nature's works,
> In earth, and air, and earth-embracing sea,
> A revelation infinite it seems;
> Display august of man's inheritance,
> Of Britain's calm felicity and power! (ll. 18–22)

Here a view becomes symbolic of national power, and there are other instances in the period when climbing a mountain becomes a performance of national identity, as when Wordsworth, Southey and their two families celebrated the defeat of Napoleon at Waterloo in 1815 with a party on top of Skiddaw.

At other times in Wordsworth's poetry, however, it is the mountain that retains power, even once it has been climbed. In 'To ———, On Her First Ascent to the Summit of Helvellyn' of 1816, Wordsworth celebrates the feelings of 'awe, delight' and 'amazement' that the unnamed lady climber experiences when gazing from 'the watch towers of Helvellyn' (ll.3-4).[1] While the poem beautifully captures the euphoria that reaching a summit can produce, it resists any sense that summiting may be a triumph or a conquest, instead emphasising a recognition of what in the final stanza the poet terms 'the power of hills':

> For the power of hills is on thee,
> As was witnessed through thine eye
> Then, when old Helvellyn won thee
> To confess their majesty! [2]

Here it is the hills that reign sovereign over the eye, which can only

1 Wordsworth, *Shorter Poems*, 221–2.
2 Wordsworth, *Shorter Poems*, 221–2.

pay its tribute. Similarly, in a poem that has been the subject of much critical scrutiny, 'Lines Written with a slate pencil at the base of Black Comb', Wordsworth shows how an attempt to impose a scientific understanding on the mountain meets with failure.

A final example of Wordsworth's interrogation of the tropes of mountaineering is the opening to his poem of 1817, 'To the Same', one of the 'Odes to Lycoris'. In this poem, Wordsworth strikingly captures how the changes in visual perspective achieved by ascending can alter the individual's relationship with the world he or she has risen above. But here the poet is critical of the sense of elevation above, and distance from, everyday care that can come with altitude:

> Enough of climbing toil! —Ambition treads
> Here, as mid busier scenes, ground steep and rough,
> Or slippery even to peril! and each step,
> As we for most uncertain recompense
> Mount tow'rd the empire of the fickle clouds,
> Each weary step, dwarfing the world below,
> Induces, for its old familiar sights,
> Unacceptable feelings of contempt,
> With wonder mixed—that Man could e'er be tied,
> In anxious bondage, to such nice array
> And formal fellowship of petty things!
> —Oh! 'tis the *heart* that magnifies this life,
> Making a truth and beauty of her own;
> And moss-grown alleys, circumscribing shades,
> And gurgling rills, assist her in the work
> More efficaciously than realms outspread,
> As in a map, before the adventurer's gaze—
> Ocean and Earth contending for regard. [1]

Wordsworth offers a striking alternative to the 'egotistical sublime'[2] with which Keats famously associated him, rejecting the 'visual sovereignty' of mountain top prospects and arguing that climbing produces '*unacceptable* feelings of contempt' (my emphasis) for the world that

1 Wordsworth, *Shorter Poems*, 253–5.
2 Keats, *Letters*, 157.

the climber has risen above. He implies that the gaining of an elevated position is an attempt to control and subordinate landscape akin to map reading. Interestingly, 'adventurer' is a word Wordsworth frequently used for Napoleon, so there is a suggestion here that summiting and map making are attempts to conquer nature, part of, or akin to, an inherently imperial or colonial project. In place of this rejected sublime often seen to characterise 'masculine Romanticism', Wordsworth embraces the heart, aligning it with the feminine and the beautiful—'tis the *heart* that magnifies this life, / Making a truth and beauty of her own'. Whereas the changing perspectives produced by ascent result in a diminishing or shrinking of the perceived landscape and the sense of the everyday, the heart 'magnifies this life', making possible what the poet presents as a proper appreciation of truth and beauty. In these lines, one of mountaineering's earliest practitioners offers a powerful critique of the potential gender and power politics of this emerging activity.

Coleridge and the Joys of Ascent

So far I have discussed Romantic mountaineering in what might be described as Romantic terms, focusing on issues of vision, insight, elevation, revelation and transcendence. In the final section of this paper, however, I want to stress the importance of climbing as an embodied activity and one whose excitements and satisfactions are linked to a sense of danger or fear that goes beyond Burke's notion that terror can be pleasurable only if experienced from a position of safety.

Nearly all mountaineering writing of the period stresses what Wordsworth terms 'climbing toil', the physical effort required to reach the top (the main exception here is Byron, whose heroes' positions on the summit is more of a symbolic location than the result of physical labour). Keats, for example, gives an amusing evocation of the exertions required to summit Ben Nevis, writing to Tom that:

> I have said nothing yet of out [*for* our] getting on among the loose stones large and small sometimes on two sometimes on three, sometimes four legs—sometimes two and stick, sometimes three

> and stick, then four again, then two <,> then a jump, so that we kept on ringing changes on foot, hand, Stick, jump boggl<e>, s[t]umble, foot, hand, foot, (very gingerly) stick again, and then again a game at all fours.[1]

The staccato rhythms of Keats's prose enacts the awkwardness of his movement on the mountain; for him, climbing was not a physically enjoyable experience, as is obvious from the conclusion of his account: 'I felt it horribly— 'T was the most vile descent—shook me all to pieces'.[2] For other climbers—perhaps fitter, more experienced, and in better health than Keats, who was suffering from a sore throat at the time of his climb—the physical demands of mountaineering were integral to the fulfilment it offered. Wordsworth has a wonderfully rich vocabulary for his movement in the mountains, an environment in which he hurries, plods, toils, climbs, clambers and scrambles, bounds like the roe, pants with an eager pace, hangs 'by knots of grass / and half inch fissures in the slippery rock', or 'greedy in the chase', roams 'from hill to hill, from rock to rock, / Still craving combinations of new forms' (*The Prelude*, 1. 343–4; 11.190–1). Yet for no-one was this pleasure in the kinds of movement demanded by a mountain environment as important as it was for Samuel Taylor Coleridge, whose notebooks and letters exude a captivating pleasure in ascending and descending, seen in his account of his crossing of the Helvellyn ridge from Keswick to Grasmere in August 1800: 'the evening now lating, I had resolved to pass [the top]; but Nature twitched me at my heart strings—I ascended it— thanks to her'.[3] Coleridge registers his frequent changes of altitude with a joyful relish, noting of his tour up Saddleback earlier the same month that [I] 'mount & mount & mount, the vale now fronting me as I stand ... —ascend again & again leave the precipices & tents behind me, descend Northward, and ascend, & thence see the Tarn'.[4] While Keats

1 Keats, *Letters*, 147.
2 Keats, *Letters*, 148.
3 Samuel Taylor Coleridge, *The Notebooks of Samuel Taylor Coleridge*, 3 double vols., ed. Kathleen Coburn (London: Bollingen Series and Routledge & Kegan Paul, 1957–73), I. entry 798. References to the notebooks are hereafter cited by volume and entry number
4 Coleridge, *Notebooks*, I. 784.

suffers repeatedly from that demoralising curse of novice climbers, the false summit—the mistaken belief that the next peak is the mountain top, only to discover another one beyond it, and another beyond that, seemingly *ad infinitum*—Coleridge seeks out extra summits to climb; on his high-level walk from Keswick to Grasmere, for example, he retraces his tracks by 3 furlongs because he is 'determined to wind up to the very top'.[1] And writing as he climbs, Coleridge's notebook form enables him to capture the immediacy of his elation on reaching the summit: 'I went, my face still toward Wasdale, Ennerdale, Buttermere, &c till I reached the very top, then, & not till then turned my face, and beheld (O Joy for me!) Patterdale and Ulswater'.[2] 'Joy' is, of course, a key word in Coleridge's thinking and writing and it is an emotion that he felt and articulated most strongly in the mountains.

Like Keats, Coleridge registers the bodily effects of climbing, but he does so with a satisfied curiosity: 'descended / as I bounded down, noticing the moving stones under the moss, hurting my feet'.[3] As this comment might suggest, Coleridge's engagement with mountain climbing was one that embraced its potential hazards. A feeling of exhilaration is common in Romantic-period accounts of climbing; Keats, for example, describes how on Skiddaw 'All [of his party] felt on arising into the cold air, that same elevation, which a cold bath brings—I felt as If I were going to a Tournament',[4] while a sense of the peril of mountain environments is central to a real understanding of Wordsworth's education 'by beauty and by fear' in *The Prelude* (II. 306). But Coleridge comes increasingly to search out risk for its own sake on the mountains and, in the process, to understand his reasons for doing so.

Coleridge thrilled in the sublimity of mountain landscapes, particularly relishing the sensation of looking down from a height into voids and chasms. On the top of Scafell, for example, he exclaims:

1 Coleridge, *Notebooks*, I. 798.
2 Coleridge, *Notebooks*, I. 798.
3 Coleridge, *Notebooks*, I. 798.
4 Keats, *Letters*, 108.

> But O! what a look down just under my Feet! The frightfullest Cove that might ever be seen / huge perpendicular Precipices, and one Sheep upon it's only Ledge, that surely must be crag! ... Just by it & joining together, rise two huge Pillars of bare lead-colored stone ... their height & depth is terrible.[1]

For Coleridge, the sublime wasn't experienced from a place of safety, as recommended by Burke. He knew that the Lake District cliffs and precipices that he loved exploring were dangerous; in his notebook account of his 1799 tour he recalls how 'A little beyond Scale Force a man, named Jerome Bowman, slipped, broke his leg, & crawled on his hands & knees up and down Hill 3 miles to that cottage in Sycamores ... he died soon after, his wounds festering'.[2] Coleridge himself had near death experiences on several occasions, describing how he 'almost broke my neck' when descending Carrock Fell in October 1800.[3] By August 1802 the poet was courting the risk inherent in such descents, as his famous account of his scramble off the summit of Scafell via Broad Stand illustrates. Choosing a descent route at random, Coleridge found himself dropping from ledge to ledge until he reached a point where he estimated the drop was 'twice my own height, & the Ledge at the bottom was [so] exceedingly narrow, that if I dropt down upon it I must of necessity have fallen backward & of course killed myself'.[4] At this point, his limbs all in a tremble, Coleridge lay on his back 'in a state of almost prophetic Trance & Delight', before eventually identifying a route down.

By the end of August 1802, Coleridge was reflecting on his perilous mountaineering adventures and starting to articulate their role for him. Writing to Sara Hutchinson, he describes an ascent of the waterfall Moss Force near Buttermere:

> [I] climbed up by the waterfall as near as I could, to the very top of the Fell—but it was so craggy—the Crags covered with spongy soaky Moss, and when bare so jagged as to wound one's hands fearfully—and the Gusts came so very sudden & strong, that the

1 Coleridge, *Letters*, II. 840.
2 Coleridge, *Notebooks*, I. 540.
3 Coleridge, *Notebooks*, I. 828.
4 Coleridge, *Letters*, II. 842.

> going up was slow, & difficult & earnest—& the coming down, not only all that, but likewise extremely dangerous. However, I have always found this *stretched & anxious* state of mind favourable to depth of pleasurable Impression, in the resting Places & *lownding* Coves.[1]

The physical danger of mountain climbing intensified Coleridge's relationship with the world around him once he had returned to a place of safety. And it is this sense of increasing what he terms 'the Intensity of the feeling of Life' that lies at the centre of Coleridge's greatest statement of his mountaineering identity and activity, written in January 1803, one of the greatest pieces of mountaineering literature:

> In simple earnest, I never find myself alone within the embracement of rocks & hills, a traveller up an alpine road, but my spirit courses, drives, and eddies, like a Leaf in Autumn: a wild activity, of thoughts, imaginations, feelings, and impulses of motion, rises up from within me—a sort of *bottom-wind*, that blows to no point of the compass, & comes from I know not whence, but agitates the whole of me; my whole Being is filled with waves, as it were, that roll & stumble, one this way, & one that way, like things that have no common master. I think, that my soul must have pre-existed in the body of a Chamois-chaser; the simple image of the old object has been obliterated—but the feelings, & impulsive habits, & incipient actions, are in me, & the old scenery awakens them. The farther I ascend from animated Nature, from men, and cattle, & the common birds of the woods, & fields, the greater becomes in me the Intensity of the feeling of Life; Life seems to me then a universal spirit, that neither has, nor can have, an opposite. God is every where, I have exclaimed, & works everywhere; and where is there *room* for Death? In these moments it has been my creed, that Death exists only because Ideas exist / that Life is limitless Sensation; that Death is a child of the organic senses, chiefly of the Sight; that Feelings die by flowing into the mould of the Intellect, & becoming Ideas; & that Ideas passing forth into action re-instate themselves again in

1 Coleridge, *Letters*, II. 853.

> the world of Life. And I do believe, that Truth lies inveloped in these loose generalizations. —I do not think it possible, that any bodily pains could eat out the love & joy, that is so substantially part of me, towards hills, & rocks, & steep waters![1]

This is a rich and complex passage which sees in mountaineering an activity that combines reason, imagination, emotion and bodily activity. In seeing himself as a chamois hunter reincarnated, Coleridge illustrates how the role of mountaineer that he was himself inventing offered him a coherent and satisfying identity, one which seemed literally to make available the meaning of life. Yet if this letter finds the mountaineering role a fulfilling one, it was not one which could be sustained, given Coleridge's need to make money. Moreover, I think we can also see a less positive element to the attractions of the role at other points in Coleridge's writing, as when he muses in his notebooks in August 1802 as follows:

> A gentle Madman that would wander still over the Mountains by the lonely Tairns <Lakes>—the like never seen since the crazy Shepherd, who having lost almost all his sheep in a long hard snow was repulsed or thought himself treated coldly by his Sweet-heart—& so went a wanderer seeking his Sheep for ever/ in storm & snow especially.[2]

Whether Coleridge is writing autobiography or the plan for another poem is unclear, but this entry presents an alternative version of the mountaineer to the purposeful figure of the chamois hunter. Here the mountaineer is a kind of outcast, an ancient mariner-like figure who has lost both his economic role and his relationship to other humans. Rather than an activity through which one realises life in all its intensity, mountaineering becomes a form of escapism for one who has lost not only a meaningful place in the world but also his mind. Like Wordsworth's climbing poetry, Coleridge's notebook entry illustrates that even as mountaineering was being invented it was seen as deeply ambivalent, both embracing life while simultaneously fleeing from it; an ambivalence that has persisted in the way the activity has con-

1 Coleridge, *Letters*, II. 916.
2 Coleridge, *Notebooks*, I. 1214.

tinued to be perceived over the past two centuries.

In Coleridge we have, if not the first, then certainly one of the most important British pioneers of both mountaineering and mountaineering literature, a form of writing that has now become a genre in itself. Unlike Wordsworth, who was able to incorporate mountaineering within his own vocational identity, Coleridge found it impossible to reconcile his activities as a mountaineer with his professional life; similarly, he was unable to use the materials in his prose mountaineering writing as the basis for a major poem, as he had planned. But in his wonderful notebooks and letters, we now recognise the outstanding writings of the first age of mountaineering, the greatest articulation of an activity which I hope I have shown was integral not only to the history but also to the literature of the Romantic age.

Peter F. Spratley

Wordsworth's Walking Aesthetic

Those assembled in this room on the fortieth anniversary of the least sedentary conference in the world, will have the fullest appreciation of the following: Wordsworth and walking go hand in hand. Pedestrians and wanderers of all kinds are scattered throughout the literary landscape of the late eighteenth and early nineteenth centuries, and while the peripatetic activities of Rousseau, Hazlitt, De Quincey, Thelwall, Coleridge and others are essential to an understanding of the newly emerging walking culture during the Romantic era, it is invariably Wordsworth who occupies the central position in this group. There are two main reasons for this. Firstly, we know from biographical evidence that Wordsworth was not merely a frequent, but a *prolific* walker. De Quincey famously calculated that the poet had 'traversed a distance of 175 to 180,000 English miles' all conducted on legs which were, as De Quincey claims, 'pointedly condemned by all the female connoisseurs in legs that I ever heard lecture on that topic'.[1] Secondly, Wordsworth's poetry is full of representations of walking. His landscapes are peopled by wanderers, pedlars and vagrants; characters who are defined by their pedestrian mode of travel, whether that is through desire or necessity. *The Prelude*, with its sense of onward progression, interrupted by tangential detours and wandering digressions, is presented as an epic walk along a path that is, in Robin Jarvis's words 'sometimes direct, but more often circuitous'.[2] Throughout his poetry, but particularly here, Wordsworth continually

1 Thomas De Quincey, *Recollections of the Lakes and the Lake Poets,* ed. David Wright (Harmondsworth: Penguin, 1970), 53–54.

2 Robin Jarvis, *Romantic Writing and Pedestrian Travel* (Basingstoke: Macmillan, 1997), 119.

draws upon peripatetic metaphors in order to understand his passage through life. We see him 'pacing', 'stepping' and 'rambling' through his childhood, moving along to the point at which, upon returning home in the early hours after a night of 'dancing, gaiety and mirth',[1] his vocation as poet is chosen for him:

> —I made no vows, but vows
> Were then made for me; bond unknown to me
> Was given, that I should be, else sinning greatly,
> A dedicated spirit. (*P*: IV, 341–44)

It is no coincidence, but is instead entirely necessary, that this moment of insight comes upon him while he is walking. 'On I walked / In blessedness, which even yet remains' (344–5) he concludes. We must acknowledge that for Wordsworth, more so than any other poet, walking is not merely a mode of travel, or form of recreational pursuit. It is instead a mode of existence, and it is through walking that Wordsworth locates himself in the world.

Critical approaches to Wordsworth's pedestrianism tend to focus on the relationship between his real *physical* acts of walking in the world, and the poetic representations of walking. This is what I will do here, although I shall be considering a very specific aspect of this intersection. I am drawn to an interesting phrase in Robin Jarvis's book on Romantic walking. He says that 'walking generates writing' (Jarvis, 89). I interpret this, with reference to Wordsworth, in two ways. It certainly corresponds with a particular strain in Wordsworth criticism that sees the poet's actual acts of walking—the literal movement of foot after foot upon solid earth—as the germ of the creative act. Later, I will briefly return to this popular idea of Wordsworth composing out of doors while walking, the 'crunch and scuffle of the gravel working like a metre' in Seamus Heaney's words[2], but for now, I want to focus on how else we might understand Jarvis's 'walk-

1 William Wordsworth, *The Prelude* (1805), IV, 320. All quotations from Wordsworth's poetry are cited from *William Wordsworth: The Major Works,* ed. Stephen Gill (Oxford: Oxford University Press, 2000).

2 Seamus Heaney, 'The Makings of a Music: Reflections on Wordsworth and Yeats' in *Preoccupations: Selected Prose1968–1978* (London: Faber, 1984), 65.

ing generates writing'. For it is not only the corporeal conditions of Wordsworth's walking that influence his writing: the psychological and ideological preconditions of the walking experience influence the location of the pedestrian act, and in turn, shape the manner in which it is presented in the poetry.

Rebecca Solnit rightly designates Wordsworth's 1790 European walking tour with Robert Jones as a pivotal moment in his young life. In considering the social and cultural significance of the tour, she stresses that 'travel has its rogue and rebel aspects—straying, going out of bounds, escaping'.[1] This tour was an early act of rebellion, leaving behind supposedly important university work to embrace Revolutionary France and sublime, republican Switzerland, with its Rousseau associations. While Wordsworth's political mind was still in its embryonic stage at this time, it is significant that he avoided the traditional destination of the young Grand Tourist from the privileged classes—Italy—and instead pursued a path that took in mountain scenery and radicalism. The essence of this heady trip is bound up in that phrase of Solnit's: walking 'out of bounds'. Ten years later when Wordsworth and Dorothy settled in Grasmere and set about building their home—their termination and last retreat—Wordsworth returned to those bounds, and a new walking aesthetic emerged. This dichotomy—the early boundless walk of the itinerant and the later enclosed walk of the dweller—is what I want to explore here. This inevitably comes back to the familiar tension between public and private realms in Wordsworth, and I suggest that we can perhaps establish a perspective on the poet's political shift through a reading of his changing pedestrian practices. Furthermore, as is often the case with Wordsworth, much of this interpretative work is reliant upon the unstable evidence provided by the poet himself. Wordsworth's accounts of his pedestrian practices are driven by a self-mythologizing incentive that sees him self-consciously construct— often retroactively—a particular pedestrian identity to accord with a particular stage of the developing poetic mind.

Part way into Book XII of *The Prelude* comes an iconic hymn of praise to walking; but it is a mode of walking in a very specific physi-

1 Rebecca Solnit, *Wanderlust: A History of Walking* (London: Verso, 2002), 107.

cal space: the pathways of the people. He says:

> I love a public road: few sights there are
> That please me more; such object hath had power
> O'er my imagination since the dawn
> Of childhood, when its disappearing line,
> Seen daily afar off, on one bare steep
> Beyond the limits which my feet had trod,
> Was like a guide into eternity,
> At least to things unknown and without bound.
> (*P*: XII, 145–52)

This is a road 'without bounds' that goes 'beyond the limits' and there is a semblance of the picturesque traveller's delight in the aesthetic appeal of the disappearing line fading into eternity. But the real emotional pull of the road in this account becomes clear a few lines later, when Wordsworth explains how it can *teach*, through its potential to stage moments of human interaction:

> —The lonely roads
> Were schools to me in which I daily read
> With most delight the passions of mankind,
> There saw into the depth of human souls. (163–6)

Wordsworth celebrates the *public* road because it offers him periods of precious solitude combined with the opportunity for chance meetings with others; others who are also, significantly, travelling on foot. The encounter with the discharged soldier is one such meeting. While the recalling of this event was later incorporated into Book IV of *The Prelude*, the original discrete poem of 1798 opens in a direct manner, similar to the passage from Book XII: 'I love to walk / Along the public way' ('The Discharged Soldier' 1-2). Wordsworth's wanderings lead him to the soldier, they walk together and converse with one another before they part at a cottage door, Wordsworth leaving him in the care of the benevolent resident. The experience is brief, but is a quintessential Wordsworthian moment of awakening and insight. It is just one of numerous instances where the act of walking instigates communal and social sympathy. Wordsworth's compassionate engagement with the common man and his plight is made possible because he purposely seeks out a public space in which to walk. As Rebecca Solnit argues, walking in this manner in the late eighteenth century expresses 'an unconventionality and a willingness to identify and be identified with the poor' (Solnit, 109). This mode of walking, a particular feature of the 1790s, connects him to the world of men in a way that travelling in a carriage cannot. In many of the poems written during this period, and in the later poems that recall this time, Wordsworth portrays himself as someone who wilfully pursues these public pedestrian encounters so that he may be seen as a 'man walking with men', a democratic gesture analogous to the familiar 'man speaking to men'. For at this time of course, Wordsworth himself was a homeless, uprooted itinerant, and so held an outcast status similar to his fellow pedestrians. This early walking aesthetic is therefore a political gesture, allied to Wordsworth's youthful radicalism. It is a manifestation of the Rousseau / Thelwall inheritance, what Solnit calls the 'trinity of radical politics, love of nature, and pedestrianism' (109).

While this stage of Wordsworth's political thinking was at its most acute in 1793, and still in evidence later in the decade, with the portrayal of the disenfranchised wanderers of *Lyrical Ballads*, it was the tours of Revolutionary France at the beginning of the decade that fostered the early walking aesthetic. The preface to *Descriptive Sketches*, written in 1792 and recalling the 1790 tour with Jones, romanticizes their mode of travel, highlighting the democratic principles of freedom, virtue and simplicity that walking engenders. They were not 'two companions lolling in a post chaise', but 'two travellers plodding slowly along the road, side by side, each with his little knapsack of necessaries upon his shoulders' (qtd. in Jarvis, 97). Here, Wordsworth and Jones are equals, their needs frugal, and as travellers with no absolute fixed route or destination, their walk is without limits or bounds. A year later, when Wordsworth returns to France, he seeks to understand the Revolution and engage with it emotionally by *walking* through it:

> The Arcades I traversed in the Palace huge
> Of Orleans, coasted round and round the line
> Of Tavern, Brothel, Gaming-house, and Shop,

Great rendezvous of worst and best, the walk
Of all who had a purpose, or had not. (*P*: IX, 50–4)

Wordsworth locates himself among the people by *walking* through their experiences: he is the emerging democrat and travelling pedestrian.

A very different voice occupies the 'Sonnets Dedicated to Liberty' of 1802, a group of poems that see Wordsworth realign his political perspectives. In the third of the sequence, written when Wordsworth was back in France during the Peace of Amiens, he remembers his peripatetic travels with Jones, but the sense of joy and virtue that can be seen in other accounts of the tour, is absent:

Jones! when from Calais southward you and I
Travelled on foot together; then this Way,
Which I am pacing now, was like the May
With festivals of new-born Liberty.
('To a Friend, Composed near Calais', 1–4)

That glorious public way is now firmly in the past and in its place is a solitary greeting of "'*Good morrow Citizen*!" a hollow word, / As if a dead man spake it!' (11-12). Clearly, the change here owes a great deal to the altered political climate: this is post-Terror, England and France are at war, and Wordsworth is torn emotionally between the two countries for both personal and political reasons. But the change in tone is also due to Wordsworth's new social and domestic situation in Grasmere, one which is sustained by a new walking aesthetic. The *Prelude* accounts of Wordsworth in France during the early 1790s were written in 1804, when he was the rooted dweller of Dove Cottage, and they are designed to paint the younger poet as a free, wandering man of the people. However, other poems composed during the Grasmere years have a different agenda, and portray another type of poetic persona entirely. We are consistently made aware of Wordsworth's attempt to represent his shifting and developing identity, and as I argue here, he does this by foregrounding his changing walking strategies.

The moment of transition is easy to pinpoint, and falls at the very end of the eighteenth century: Wordsworth and Dorothy's 1799 winter walk to Grasmere. This is the walk of two itinerant wanderers, apart from one another for much of their youth, now coming home to finally establish a settled domestic existence that will be nurtured by cultivating a bounded, self-sustaining mode of pedestrianism. The initial walk to Grasmere is described in some depth in a long letter Wordsworth wrote to Coleridge on Christmas Eve, 1799. The letter combines details of the siblings' new home—the chimneys, the garden, neighbours, mountain views and so on—with an extended account of their pedestrian journey through the Yorkshire Dales and into their Lakeland vale. The walk and the home-making are united and seem dependent upon one another. Their journey was not easy. At one point they walk 'three miles in the dark and two of them over hardfrozen road to the great annoyance of our feet and ancles (sic)'.[1] It is as if this long walk, a kind of final journey to their terminus, is *preparation* for dwelling. *Home at Grasmere*, written in 1800, is perhaps the clearest portrayal of Wordsworth's shift from wanderer to dweller, and it centralises the act of walking in the process of cultivating rooted domesticity. He describes how he arrived with Dorothy—or in the poem, Emma—'on foot' and how they:

> might in that hallowed spot to which our steps
> Were tending, in that individual nook,
> Might even thus early for ourselves secure,
> And in the midst of these unhappy times,
> A portion of the blessedness which love
> And knowledge will, we trust, hereafter give
> To all the Vales of earth and all mankind.
> (*Home at Grasmere,* 250–6)

In rediscovering the vale by travelling on foot, Wordsworth becomes conscious that the act of pedestrianism can represent something different from what it has done previously, and within the vale, he can practise a new, but no less meaningful and nourishing strategy of walking. Once he is safely within the vale after his final lengthy journey there, his walking is characterised by enclosure and bounds, some-

1 Wordsworth, qtd in Colette Clark ed. *Home at Grasmere: Extracts from the Journal of Dorothy Wordsworth and from the poems of William Wordsworth* (Harmondsworth: Penguin, 1960), 20.

thing distinct from the limitless wandering of youth. Wordsworth's walks in Grasmere see him possess the land by treading and retreading familiar spaces, within circumscribed limits. He celebrates this as a way of forging regional, familial and private identity, instead of public, political and worldly identity. We see this clearly in *Home at Grasmere*. 'Embrace me, then, ye Hills, and close me in' (129), he declares. Toward the beginning of the poem, Wordsworth remembers looking down upon Grasmere vale as a schoolboy, and fancifully imagining what it would be like to live there. He then provides a sweeping description of the kind of walking aesthetic that Grasmere can offer:

> I seemed to feel such liberty was mine,
> Such power and joy; but only for this end,
> To flit from field to rock, from rock to field,
> From shore to island, and from isle to shore,
> From open place to covert, from a bed
> Of meadow-flowers into a tuft of wood,
> From high to low, from low to high, yet still
> Within the bounds of this huge Concave; here
> Should be my home, this Valley be my World. (35–43)

These lines show Wordsworth rejoicing in his ability to roam within his native valley, genuinely free, and not at all compromised by the 'bounds of [the] huge Concave'. It is spiritually fulfilling because it fosters a sense of place, roots him in his surroundings, and ensures that he does not risk being cast adrift as he was in the 1790s. Anne Wallace has termed this kind of Wordsworthian walking 'excursive walking'. She sees it as 'an agent of home-making and nation-building' because it involves a journey outwards but always 'relocation at the walk's origins, [and this] counters the threat of wandering with a promise of return'.[1]

The ideological core of this new mode of walking can be discerned in a sonnet of 1802, one of Wordsworth's best known, 'Nuns fret not at their Convent's narrow room'. The poem is ostensibly a defence

1 Anne Wallace, *Walking, literature and English culture: the origins and uses of peripatetic in the nineteenth century* (Oxford: Clarendon, 1993), 120.

of the sonnet and a rejection of the myth that the form's tight metrical rules limit poetic freedom. However, the poem has a larger point beyond simply prosodic matters. It is a paean to the benefits of restraint and self-imposed boundaries, and expresses a dominant strain of Wordsworth's thinking at this time. For the poem works towards its final assertion that Wordsworth enjoys functioning within limits because he has felt 'the weight of too much liberty' ('Nuns fret not', 13). Wordsworth retreats from the French Revolution because it was the harmful *excess* of civil freedoms that brought about their eventual dissolution. *The Recluse* remained unwritten while more and more short poems, like sonnets, were written, since the *excessive* liberty of epic blank verse served as a hindrance rather than a help to Wordsworth's creativity. In the same way, Wordsworth now felt that his early boundless walks gave him 'too much liberty', leaving him directionless and uprooted. The circumscribed walks in Grasmere allow him to *dwell*.

The famous gravel path of Rydal Mount is perhaps the clearest image of Wordsworth's self-imposed bounded walks, and this returns us to the idea of Wordsworth composing outdoors, his pedestrianism generating poetry. Commenting on Wordsworth's compositional techniques, Lady Beaumont once remarked that 'in wet weather he takes out an umbrella, chuses [sic] the most sheltered spot, and there walks backwards and forwards, and though the length of his walk be sometimes a quarter or half a mile, he is as fast bound within the chosen limits as if by prison walls'.[1] His spatial restriction, combined with the regularity of bipedal motion, feed his creativity. In an essay entitled 'The Makings of a Music' Seamus Heaney writes of Wordsworth's composition that 'the continuity of the thing was what was important, the onward inward pouring out, up and down the gravel path…the automatic, monotonous turns and returns of the walk, the length of the path acting like the length of the line' (Heaney, 65). He sees Wordsworth 'to-ing and fro-ing like a ploughman up and down a field' (65). Anne Wallace sees this kind of walking as an extension of Virgilian georgic, with a pedestrian metaphor replacing

1 Lady Beaumont, qtd. in Andrew Bennett, *Wordsworth Writing* (Cambridge: Cambridge UP, 2007), 25.

the agricultural one (Wallace, 120). This is what bounded walks are all about: cultivating the land and forging an emotional connection with it.

All of these ideas—the limited space, the retreading of steps, and the fostering of communal bonds—are in evidence in one of Wordsworth's most important walking poems, 'When first I journeyed hither', and it is with this that I want to briefly conclude. Wordsworth recalls his early days at Grasmere and how in a cold and stormy season, he sought out the shelter and seclusion of a 'sequestered nook' (9), a densely packed grove of trees. He is attracted to the grove because it is an enclosed space, a smaller scale version of the homely narrow room of Grasmere vale, or indeed the liberating 'scanty plot of ground' ('Nuns fret not', 11) he finds in the sonnet. However, while the nook is initially inviting for Wordsworth, he cannot fully connect with the space, a cause for some frustration. The reason for this is that the trees are so closely crowded together, that he can find no space in which to walk:

> —I in vain
> Between their stems endeavoured to find out
> A length of open space where I might walk
> Backwards and forwards long as I had liking
> In easy and mechanic thoughtlessness. (34–8)

With the attempt at walking *backwards and forwards*, we have the familiar motion of the bounded walk. Wordsworth is striving to recreate the gravel path: the hypnotic retreading generating poetry, the continuous, repetitive momentum of the ploughman, rooting himself in the land. It is noteworthy here that this is, like the gravel path at Rydal Mount, a specific cultivation of *private* paths and walkways, far removed from the *public* roads and streets of Paris. Yet this is no solipsistic rejection of the world or social retreat. Wordsworth walks in this manner to *animate* the space, to forge bonds of regional and familial affection. For while his initial 'inability to walk in the grove also frustrates his settlement in Grasmere' (Wallace, 130), he is able to overcome this through the 'finer eye' and 'heart more wakeful' ('When first I journeyed hither', 67, 68) of his brother John. John comes to stay with Wordsworth and Dorothy and visits the grove himself. When Wordsworth later returns there, he finds 'a hoary pathway traced around the trees / And winding on with such an easy line' (57–8). Thinking at first that he inexplicably failed to see the path on earlier visits, he soon realises that John—bringing with him his own methods of enclosed walking, practised on the deck of his ship at sea—traced the path with his own steps. With John later back at sea, 'pacing to and fro' the Vessel's deck' (108), Wordsworth sets about retracing his brother's steps in the grove, knowing that by 'timing my steps to thine' (113) they can walk together even though they are separated by thousands of miles. There is no actual physical meeting of the brothers described in the poem, but by reanimating the space that the other has just left, the brothers are spiritually connected. As Markus Poetzsch has argued, 'they are able to maintain solitude while forging a conversational space: a grove that becomes a pedestrian palimpsest'.[1] What Wordsworth seems to suggest in this poem is that a truly engaged mode of walking—performed as labour, as cultivation—does not simply exist in the here and now; it can forge connections across time and space. Open-ended walking cannot do this, which is perhaps why Wordsworth experiences a disjunction between his itinerant self in 1790, and his mindset of 1802, writing the liberty sonnets. Anne Wallace writes that in 'When first I journeyed hither', walking 'places John in the landscape, in name [since Wordsworth later names the grove after him], in material trace, and in Wordsworth's own memory, and enables William's physical and metaphorical home-making' (Wallace, 132). We can say that the enclosed space in the grove was empty, derelict. It is brought to life by John's walk and sustained by his brother's walk. The *retreading* is the important thing, and surely, that is why we are all here, in Grasmere, this week: to walk in Wordsworth's footsteps.

1 Markus Poetzsch, 'Palimpsest Walks and the Practice of Wordsworthian Recollection', unpublished conference paper, 2010.

Gary Harrison

The Poetics of Acknowledgment: John Clare[1]

In a recent book that he describes as a 'field guide to nature poems', John Felstiner asks 'Can Poetry Save the Earth'?[2] 'Can poems help, when the times demand environmental science and history, government leadership, corporate and consumer moderation, nonprofit activism, local initiatives'? (xiii) Felstiner's answer arises from an assortment of sometimes impressionistic readings of poems from an eclectic group of poets: from the usual suspects such as William Wordsworth, John Clare, Walt Whitman, Gerard Manley Hopkins, Robert Frost, Robinson Jeffers and Gary Snyder to perhaps more unlikely candidates including the Hebrew Psalmists, Maxine Kumin, A. R. Ammons, George Oppen, and Denise Levertov. Conceding that in a world of global environmental catastrophe poetry can do 'next to nothing', Felstiner settles upon poetry's ability to make us 'look again' and 'see anew'; like artists, poets 'make things matter by getting them right'; 'a poem like a painting catches life for the ear or eye, stills what's ongoing in human and nonhuman nature' (14). While not discounting the power of poetic defamiliarization to reset our relationship to the world, I'd like to complicate the problematic notion that poetry recalibrates our perception of the world, and to suggest instead–or in addition–that poetry may re-orient our *disposition* to the world. It may do so not so much by presenting us with

1 I wish to thank Richard Gravil and Nicholas Roe for their kind invitation for me to present this paper as a lecture at the 40th Anniversary Wordsworth Summer Conference 2010; I am also grateful to those at the conference who attended my lecture and whose comments have helped shape my further thinking about the poetics of acknowledgment.

2 John Felstiner, *Can Poetry Save the Earth? A Field Guide to Nature Poems* (New Haven & London: Yale University Press, 2009), xiii.

mimetic acts of representation, but by presenting us with sympathetic acts of affective engagement with and in the world. That is, poetic acts of engagement with the world invite readers into the emotional and intellectual complex of an exemplary attunement to nature. To illustrate what I mean, I will appeal to French sociologist and philosopher Pierre Bourdieu's notion of 'habitus' and American philosopher Stanley Cavell's notion of 'acknowledgment' to emphasize poetic language's important function of recalibrating our *feel* for the world of living things that must remain to us in some sense mysterious and unknowable. John Clare, the quintessential English poet of place, provides my primary source of evidence, though I will draw lines of connection from Clare to some others.

In his brilliant, often vexing, excursion through the fields of nature writing and ecological criticism, *Ecology without Nature*, Timothy Morton observes that nature writing typically aims to dissolve the division between the human subject and the natural world. 'Ecological writing wants to undo habitual distinctions between nature and ourselves. It is supposed not just to describe, but also to provide a working model for a dissolving of the difference between subject and object, a dualism seen as the fundamental philosophical reason for human beings' destruction of the environment' (63–64).[1] Furthermore, nature writing, dominated by what he calls ecomimesis, attempts to 'present an original, pristine nature not "infected" with the consciousness, the mentality, or the desire of the perceiver, unless it is deemed to be "natural"' (68). The burden of *Ecology without Nature*, at least in part, is to demonstrate that both the fusion of subject and object and the presentation of an untainted nature are false, because impossible, goals. Any description of the natural world no matter what its rhetorical force is always already compromised in the subjective apperception of the writer or speaker, as well as in the linguistic and cultural codes that enable any articulation or representation of nature. For example, while arguing that ecological writing essentially carries out a referential project that 'aims to render the object world', Lawrence Buell in *The*

1 Timothy Morton, *Ecology without Nature: Rethinking Environmental Aesthetics* (Cambridge, MA & London: Harvard University Press, 2007), 63–64.

Environmental Imagination recognizes that ecological criticism must take into account the impossibility of that end.[1] Using Henry David Thoreau as his primary example, Buell argues that effective ecocentric writing should demonstrate both 'facticity', defined as 'fidelity to the evidence' derived from direct experience and study of the objective world, and defamiliarization, a certain poetic displacement that, to invoke Wordsworth's Preface, casts over the ordinary 'a certain colouring of imagination' (Buell 96).[2] Buell recognizes that 'verbalizations . . . are not replicas but equivalents of the world of objects, such that writing in some measure bridges the abyss that inevitably yawns between language and the object world' (98). Thus even the most precise descriptive language can only situate us in a verbal 'near equivalent'—what Francis Ponge called an *adéquation*—of that world.[3] Morton goes so far as to say that 'Some nature writers think that they are receiving a direct transmission from nature, when in fact they are watching a mirror of the mind' (Morton 68). He wants us to 'admit that all we can sense of nature is an echo of our "sounding out" of it' (68).

I want to suggest here that so far as we admit the inadequacy, but necessity, of representation, and so far as we admit the possibility of offering a sense of our 'sounding out' of the world, we may fruitfully recast the ecocritical project from the irresolvable subject/object dilemma to the perhaps more promising one of seeking in poetry exemplary modes of attunement or disposition towards the world. That is, we might worry less about place and more about emplacement; less about reference, more about reverence. As I will argue, reverence—which I will associate here with *habitus* and acknowledgmen—hifts the critical project of reading nature poetry, such as that of John Clare, Gary Snyder, Mary Oliver, Geoffrey Hill, or Seamus Heaney from a poetics of *place* to a poetics of *acknowledgment*.

1 Lawrence Buell, *The Environmental Imagination: Thoreau, Nature Writing, and the Formation of American Culture* (Cambridge, MA: Harvard University Press, 1995), 99.

2 William Wordsworth, Preface to *Lyrical Ballads*, *William Wordsworth*, ed. Stephen Gill, The Oxford Authors (1984; rpt. Oxford and New York: Oxford University Press, 1998), 595–615, 597.

3 See Buell, *Environmental Imagination*, 98.

Part I: Habitus

I will begin by defining what I mean by habitus, a term I adapt from the work of Pierre Bourdieu. In *The Environmental Imagination* Lawrence Buell recognizes that even when pursuing a referential project, ecocentric texts must invoke, in order to elicit, 'environmental codes of manners' (109). We might describe these environmental manners as 'ecocentric competence' or, following Buell, 'environmental proficiency' (107). Bourdieu's notion of habitus, however, provides I think a richer, more comprehensive rubric under which to comprehend this condition of possibility for or disposition towards acting in the world. Throughout *In Other Words* Bourdieu uses the analogy of the 'feel for the game' to clarify what he means by habitus, a system of dispositions that enables adaptive moves, strategies, and tactics in the face of contingencies that 'no rule, however complex, can foresee'.[1] Thus, habitus equates to a kind of intuition that guides our actions in the world, but which also undergoes subtle changes resulting from our actions and experiences. Habitus encompasses the whole of an individual's experience and, as he puts it in *Outline of a Theory of Practice*, 'brings into play a whole body of wisdom, sayings, commonplaces, ethical precepts … and, at a deeper level, the unconscious principles of the ethos which … determines "reasonable" and "unreasonable" conduct for every agent' in everyday life.[2] Habitus accounts for those kinds of behaviour that 'can be directed towards certain ends without being consciously directed to these ends, or determined by them' (*In Other Words* 10). One may prefer to think of habitus as what Paul Woodruff calls "virtue," defined as 'the capacity to have certain feelings and emotions' that are 'cultivated over time through experience, use, and training'.[3] Virtue, in this broad sense, 'inclines those who have it to doing the right thing' at the right time (Woodruff 61-62).

1 Pierre Bourdieu, *In Other Words: Essays Towards a Reflexive Sociology*, trans. Matthew Adamson (Stanford: Stanford University Press, 1990), 9.

2 Pierre Bourdieu, *Outline of a Theory of Practice*, trans Richard Nice, ed. Jack Goody, Cambridge Studies in Social Anthropology 16 (Cambridge: Cambridge University Press, 1977), 77.

3 Paul Woodruff, *Reverence: Renewing a Forgotten Virtue*. (Oxford: Oxford University Press, 2001), 24.

Doing the right thing at the right time also has a spatial component, as geographer Edward Casey explains when recruiting Bourdieu's habitus to help explain the sense of place. For Casey, habitus comprehends the 'indispensable dimension of the body's role in implacing human beings' that forms the basis of our actions in and towards the world.[1] As the 'mediatrix of place and self', habitus disposes us to certain ways of being in the world, of inhabiting and relating to the place world (686).[2] In his work, Casey distinguishes between *habitus*, the 'durable disposition' ('On Habitus' 686) that motivates our acts in the world, and *habitation*, the bodily–and I would add poetic–acts by which we make the spaces we inhabit into meaningful places. While I will not say much about 'habitation' in this essay, habitus and habitation operate hand in hand, so for Clare and poets like him, writing itself is an act of habitation, an act of bringing meaning to and making meaning from places which otherwise would might be overlooked or neglected. Hence, Clare's act of writing itself is an inhabiting that acknowledges the natural world and assigns it a value which, as we know from the writing of Wordsworth with regard to the Lake District, Henry David Thoreau to Walden, or Robinson Jeffers to Point Reyes, enables those places to hold value for others–at least, for those others with like dispositions.

The interaction between habitus and habitation, of course, is key to understanding the dynamics of place. In Lawrence Buell's phrase: 'humanity *qua* geographer is *Homo faber*, the environment's constructor, and the sense of place is necessarily always a social product and not simply what is "there"' (*Environmental Imagination* 77). Jonathan Bate claims that 'Clare's self and his poetry were shaped as much by environment as by heredity. To understand him, we need to know his native place' (42).[3] But what more must we consider than the native place itself to account for Clare's astonishing love for Helpston

1 Edward Casey, 'Between Geography and Philosophy: What Does It Mean to Be in the Place-World'? *Annals of the Association of American Geographers* 91.4 (December 2001), 716–23, 717.

2 Edward Casey, 'On Habitus and Place: Responding to My Critics', *Annals of the Association of American Geographers* 91.4 (December 2001), 683–93, 686.

3 Jonathan Bate, *John Clare: A Biography* (New York: Farrar, Straus and Giroux, 2003), 42.

and its environs? While Kentucky farmer and writer Wendell Berry acknowledges that his work 'originates in part in actual experience of an actual place: its topography, weather, plants, and animals; its language, voices, and stories', he cautions against environmental determinism.[1] The 'influence of this place alone,' he continues, 'cannot account for the fiction and the other work I have written here' (41). Moreover, as Bob Heyes warns, 'nothing in Clare's writings can be taken at face value, as a straightforward description of the external world or of his personal experiences. It could be argued that Clare's poems are no more a description of rural Northamptonshire than Keats's poems are an account of life in Hampstead. In both cases the connection to the external world is there, but it is subtle and elusive, not simple and straightforward as many who have written on Clare seem to suppose'.[2] The same can be said of Clare's natural history prose writings, which Alan Vardy describes as 'a series of beautifully delineated moments of perception and description—what we might call poetic field notes'.[3]

Like Gilbert White's *Natural History of Selborne*, Clare's natural history prose letters describe with sensuous immediacy the flora and fauna of Helpston and give us a sense of the rare combination of scientific curiosity and poetic delight that Clare brings to his experience of a dynamic natural world. Clare's habits of close observation and precise description, combined with a strong feeling for nature, though, result not just from his childhood practices of reading the fields, but also from his reading of books and his conversation with others. Complicating the notion of Clare as a naïve observer of the natural world, Alan Vardy, Paul Chirico, and Douglas Chambers, among others, have recently shown how Clare brought book learning to his botanizing. In his autobiographical writings Clare himself attributes the increasing sophistication of his naturalist investigations not only to his reading of John Hill's *The Family Herbal* (1812), James Lee's

1 Wendell Berry, 'Imagination in Place', *The Way of Ignorance and Other Essays* (Berkeley: Counterpoint, 2005), 39–51, 41.

2 Robert Heyes, "'Looking to Futurity': John Clare and Provincial Culture", Ph.D. Thesis, Birkbeck College, University of London, 1999), 28.

3 Alan Vardy, *John Clare, Politics and Poetry* (Houndmills and New York: Palgrave / Macmillan, 2003), 135.

Botany (1776), and Robert Bloomfield's *Poems*, but to his friendships with amateur naturalists Edmund Tyrell Artis, archeologist and antiquarian, and Joseph Henderson, head gardener at Burghley, who shared books and compared notes with Clare.[1]

From Artis and Henderson, among others, Clare accumulated technical knowledge about the classification and habits of plants and animals. Thus, on those days when Clare went a' botanizing, as he often did, as Douglas Chambers reminds us, '"botanizing" would mean 'a careful attention to what is there, with all its literary and cultural associations'. Chambers observes that Clare's names for plants are associated not only with the oral tradition and folk wisdom of his childhood but with the lexicon of pre-Linnean botanists (249).[2] Thus, even at their most precise, Clare's observations blend the immediacy of experience with the intermediacy of culture. Chirico sums it up plainly: 'despite himself, Clare is not able to write of an authentic nature without acknowledging the intermediate, constructive function of artistic representation' (61). As a self-conscious poet and informed if amateur naturalist, Clare wrought his cultural understandings in such a way as to enhance his objective descriptions of the natural world, to infuse them with childhood memories, a complex of past and present feelings, and with intertextual references to poets such as Thomson and Bloomfield, among many others.

The sum of Clare's direct and indirect experiences of nature and culture constitutes the habitus or virtue that manifests itself in Clare's poetry as a particularly powerful sense of ecolocation, an acute awareness of and knowledge about the ambient environment and the interdependent relations among things within that environment. That habitus or virtue also embodies the socio-cultural complex of structures of thought and feeling–and of course poetry is a part of that complex of embodied experience–that give him the capacity to be

1 See Jonathan Bate, *John Clare: A Biography*; Alan Vardy, *John Clare, Politics and Poetry*; and Paul Chirico,, *John Clare and the Imagination of the Reader*. (Houndmills, Basingstoke, Hampshire and New York: Palgrave/Macmillan, 2007).

2 Douglas Chambers, '"A love for every simple weed": Clare, botany and the poetic language of lost Eden', *John Clare in Context*, ed. Hugh Haughton, Adam Phillips, and Geoffrey Summerfield. (Cambridge: Cambridge University Press, 1994), 238–58, 250.

and act in the world. My argument is that Clare's descriptive poetry, even as it pursues the most representational project, stems from and makes present that feel, disposition, or intuition for being in the world that I believe may be of greatest concern for ecocriticism. In 'Feeling into Words' Seamus Heaney captures this very notion when he describes the moment when he first found that his poetry captured not just ideas and feeling, but his feel. He writes that '"Digging", in fact, was the name of the first poem I wrote where I thought my feelings had got into words, or to put it more accurately, where I thought my *feel* had got into words'.[1] Heaney distinguishes between craft, which can be learned, and technique, which, in his words, 'involves not only a poet's way with words, his management of metre, rhythm and verbal texture; it involves also a definition of his stance towards life, a definition of his own reality' (47). That stance, that feel, that habitus, that virtue, may well give us the most promising purchase on ecological and nature writing.

I think what moves us most, at least me most, in Clare's work is the sense of being in the presence of a sympathetic consciousness that delights in the very existence of ordinary stuff in an ordinary world. In this respect, Clare fits Coleridge's description of genius in chapter four of *Biographia Literaria*, where he observes that 'it is the prime merit of genius, and its most unequivocal mode of manifestation, so as to represent familiar objects as to awaken in others a kindred feeling concerning them, and that freshness of sensation which is the constant accompaniment of mental no less than of bodily convalescence' (49).[2] While Clare's poetry has been praised (and blamed) for its accurate depiction of the natural world–its facticity, Jonathan Bate gets to the heart of the matter when he asks us to understand Clare's poetry 'as an experiencing of the world, rather than a description of it'.[3] In poems such as "The Nightingale's Nest" we find the combi-

1 Seamus Heaney, 'Feeling into Words', *Preoccupations: Selected Prose 1968-78* (New York: Noonday Press, 1980), 41–60, 41.

2 Samuel Taylor Coleridge, *Biographia Literaria, or Biographical Sketches of My Literary Life and Opinions*, ed. George Watson (1965; rpt. London and New York: J. M. Dent and E. P. Dutton, 1975), 49.

3 Jonathan Bate, *The Song of the Earth* (Cambridge, MA: Harvard University Press, 2000), 167.

nation of feeling and disposition towards the world that promises to elicit similar responses from others, as well as those physical descriptions of the natural world that constitute and give readers a sense of Clare's ecolocation, the dynamic interplay between habitus and habitation.

'The Nightingale's Nest', to which I'll return later, shows us this interplay between an active attunement to the world and respect, or reverence, for the living things of that world.

> Up this green woodland ride lets softly rove
> And list the nightingale—she dwelleth here
> Hush let the wood gate softly clap—for fear
> The noise may drive her from her home of love (213)[1]

As he does so often, Clare here uses indexical signs to put the reader directly into the experience, and his apprehension of the bird is visual and auditory. Respect for the nightingale's home comes from the injunction to close the gate quietly to avoid disturbing the home, another indication of Clare's conscious gesture to acknowledge the simple dignity of the nightingale's existence. As Hugh Haughton has noted, the poem, which he reads as a tribute to the idea of home itself, emphasizes the integrity of the home place of both bird and poet. As readers 'our access to this world is only made possible by the fact of [Clare's] being on home territory too':[2]

> For here Ive heard her many a merry year
> At morn and eve nay all the live long day (213)

Moreover, the poet has earned familiarity with the nightingale's nest by 'creeping on hands and knees through matted thorns / To find her nest' (213).

We find such moments of intimate familiarity and interplay between

1 John Clare, 'The Nightingale's Nest,' *John Clare*, ed. Eric Robinson and David Powell, The Oxford Authors (Oxford: Oxford University Press, 1984), 213-15. Unless otherwise noted, quotations from John Clare's poetry are from this edition. I do not add '[sic]' to mark Clare's idiosyncratic spellings or punctuation.

2 Hugh Haughton, '"Progress and Rhyme: "The Nightingale's Nest" and Romantic Poetry', *John Clare in Context*, ed. Hugh Haughton, Adam Phillips, and Geoffrey Summerfield. (Cambridge: Cambridge University Press, 1994), 51–86, 60.

habitus and habitation throughout Dorothy Wordsworth' journals as well, especially at those moments when sight and insight combine to ignite a lucid instant of affective engagement with birds or flowers, prospects or sky, particular places and familiar landmarks. The daffodil passage of 15 April 1802 is no doubt most well known, so let me cite from 20 June 1802:

> We lay upon the sloping Turf. Earth and sky were so lovely that they melted our very hearts. The sky to the north was of a chastened yet rich yellow, fading into pale blue and streaked and scattered over wit steady islands of purple melting away into shades of pink. It made my heart feel like a vision to me. (139)[1]

Here Dorothy Wordsworth animates the painterly facticity of the scene and blends observation with capacious feeling, thus giving heightened significance to her and her readers' experience. For such active and affective seeing, Dorothy Wordsworth, like John Clare, was particularly disposed. What we take away from these texts is both a sense of the world and a sense of the writers' reverent disposition to that world. The latter, I suggest, is what we as readers should attend to most carefully, for it is the habitus, not the habitat, that we may incorporate into our own repertoire of living interdependently with others.

Writing of the place sense of the Western Apache, anthropologist Keith Basso offers a description of the way the Apache sense of place devolves from a similar give and take between habitus and habitation. In *Wisdom Sits in Places: Notes on a Western Apache Landscape*, Basso shows that the sense of place among the Apache is 'both roundly reciprocal and incorrigibly dynamic. As places animate the ideas and feelings of persons who attend to them, these same ideas and feelings animate the places on which attention has been bestowed, and the movements of this process–inward toward facts of the self, outward toward aspects of the external world, alternately both together–cannot be known in advance. When places are actively sensed, the physical landscape becomes wedded to the landscape of the mind, to the roving imagination, and where the mind

1 Dorothy Wordsworth, *Journals of Dorothy Wordsworth*, ed. Mary Moorman, 2nd ed. (1958; rpt. Oxford: Oxford University Press, 1971), 139.

may lead is anybody's guess'.[1] Basso describes this emplacement as a process of interanimation, which even among the Apache not everyone achieves equally–and some not at all. Clare recognizes this interanimation between place and idea in his poetics of acknowledgment, and he too recognizes that place itself does not bestow this gift upon everyone:

> Taste is from heaven
> A inspiration nature cant bestow
> Tho natures beautys where a taste is given
> Warms the ideas of the soul to flow
> With that enchanting 'thusiastic glow
> That throbs the bosom when the curious eye
> Glances on beautious things that give delight
> Objects of earth or air or sea or sky
> That bring the very senses in the sigh
> To relish what it sees – but all is night
> To the gross clown – natures unfolded book
> As on he blunders never strikes his eye
> Pages of lanscape tree and flower and brook
> Like bare blank leaves he turns unheeded bye[2]

'Taste' here designates that disposition to receive with a giving eye and blessing heart, the facility unbidden to see in particular objects of the world beauty and delight. Recognizing that this disposition comes not just from being in the presence of worldly things, Clare contrasts the man of taste to the 'gross clowns' who pass through beauty every day with their eyes closed for lack of imagination. For such people, the dynamic reciprocity between mind and place, no matter what their familiarity with these places, must go wanting. Clare confirms Buell's caveat that 'grounding in place patently does not guarantee ecocentrism' or a sense of place, since place is 'by definition perceived or felt space, space humanized, rather than the material world taken on its own terms' (*Environmental Imagination* 253).

1 Keith H. Basso, 'Wisdom Sits in Places', *Senses of Place*, ed. Steven Feld and Keith H. Basso (Santa Fe: School of American Research Press, 1996), 53–90, 55.

2 John Clare, 'On Taste', *John Clare*, ed. Robinson and Powell, 45.

Elsewhere in Clare this faculty enabling the marriage between the physical landscape and the landscape of the mind takes the form of what I see as a version of 'wise passiveness'. We see this facility, for example, in 'Pastoral Poesy', where Clare writes:

> An image to the mind is brought,
> Where happiness enjoys
> An easy thoughtlessness of thought,
> & meets excess of joys
>
> The world is in that little spot
> With him—& all beside
> Is nothing all a life forgot
> In feelings satisfied
>
> & such is poesy; its power
> May varied lights employ,
> Yet to all mind[s] it gives the dower
> Of self-creating joy.
>
> & whether it be hill or moor,
> I feel where e'er I go
> A silence that discourses more
> Then any tongue can do. (291–92)[1]

Clare's wise passiveness takes us to Wordsworth, who may still be one of our best theorists–if not poets–of place. Wordsworth understands the dynamic reciprocity and dual agency that takes place between nature and mind in everyday life, and in artistic production:

> 'What then does the Poet? He considers man and the objects that surround him as acting and re-acting upon each other, so as to produce an infinite complexity of pain and pleasure; he considers man in his own nature and in his ordinary life as contemplating this with a certain quantity of immediate knowledge, with certain convictions, intuitions, and deductions which by habit become of the nature of intuitions [this acquired intuition is what

1 John Clare, 'Pastoral Poesy', *John Clare: The Midsummer Cushion*, ed. Kelsey Thornton and Anne Tibble (1979; rpt. Ashington, Northumberland: Carcanet, 1990), 291–94.

> Bourdieu means by habitus]; he considers him as looking upon this complex scene of ideas and sensations, and finding every where objects that immediately excite in him sympathies which, from the necessities of his nature, are accompanied by an overbalance of enjoyment' (Preface 605–606).

Here is the interrelationship between habitus and habitation that I have been describing, couched in an embodied poetics of place and acknowledgment wherein things and practices, convictions and intuitions, lead to habits—a second nature—that regulate but do not overdetermine the poet's understanding of and responses to his or her immediate environment. This interplay of knowing–or attempting to know–and imagining is what I will in the next section call the distance between knowledge and acknowledgement, the index of John Clare's particular habitus—a predisposition to acknowledge the ordinary stuff of the world as familiar partners in a joyful life of mutual interdependence. To characterize Clare's habitus I want to focus in the last part of my discussion upon the concept of 'acknowledgment' advanced by the American philosopher Stanley Cavell.

Part II. Acknowledgment

In *The Natural Contract*, Michel Serres reads Francisco de Goya's *Riña a garrotazos* (*Fight with Sticks*) as a visual metaphor for the struggle between nature and culture. One of Goya's so-called Black Paintings, the painting shows in the foreground two peasant men mired up to their knees in what appears to be quicksand; the antagonists face each other intently in the heat of battle, each with a cudgel raised for an imminent exchange of blows. For Serres, the two combatants, totally absorbed in their mutual struggle, remain oblivious to their surroundings and to the bog into which they are sinking. Their gaze fixed upon each other, the fighters completely ignore the grip the bog has upon them. Neither do they take into account the negative consequences their actions have upon the place where they are fighting. In Serres's analysis, the bog represents what he calls the world-wide system of objects and living things upon which humanity is dependent and of which it is a part; because of the men's refusal to take that world-wide world into account, it will eventually and menacingly rebound from its subordinated position as a neglected third term and become a forceful combatant with which the men (perhaps or perhaps not putting down their own differences) will have to reckon.

The world-wide world, nature in an inclusive sense, widely suffers both from the 'collateral damage' of our objectification of nature as a backdrop for human action and as an exploitable resource–both stemming from our refusal to acknowledge the bond we hold with the earth. In Serres's words, 'to defend or attack other men, we have laid waste the landscape without thinking about it, and we were preparing to destroy the whole Earth'.[1] As a remedy to this condition of indifference, Serres adduces the value of what he calls the 'natural contract', which means 'above all the precisely metaphysical recognition, by each collectivity, that it lives and works in the same global world as all the others' (46).

This deliberate metaphysical recognition of the other, the claims of the other, and the implication of the self in the condition of the other, is consistent with Stanley Cavell's understanding of 'acknowledgment' as a mode of recognition. For Cavell, acknowledgement involves a reflexive move, whereby our recognition of the other entails an equally important recognition of our relation to the other. In describing Leontes' eventual acceptance of Hermione in *The Winter's Tale*, for example, Cavell notes that 'For her to return to him is for him to recognize her; and for him to recognize her is for him to recognize his relation to her; in particular to recognize what his denial of her has done to her, hence to him'.[2] The worldwide world, that is, the natural world, may be Hermione, Leontes' wrongly abandoned wife, or Perdita, his wrongly abandoned daughter–both of whom Leontes must learn to acknowledge; and, indeed, those subplots of *The Winter's Tale* could loosely serve as a sort of parable for our relationship with nature, whose death has been as widely reported, as its

1 Michel Serres, *The Natural Contract*, trans. Elizabeth MacArthur and William Paulson (Ann Arbor: The University of Michigan Press, 1995), 50.

2 Stanley Cavell, 'Othello and the Stake of the Other', *Disowning Knowledge in Seven Plays of Shakespeare*, 2nd ed. (Cambridge: Cambridge University Press, 2007), 125–42, 125.

resurrection or return has been promised. To accept the misreported death of nature, as in the case of Leontes with Hermione, or not to acknowledge our kinship with nature, as in the case of Leontes with Perdita, is to bring undue suffering upon ourselves and other living things because of our stubborn neglect to recognize and take responsibility for our relationship to the environment. To rectify these hurtful dispositions, according to Cavell, we need to learn to acknowledge the other—to exercise our sympathetic imagination, which he defines as 'the capacity for making connections, seeing or realizing possibilities' for connection that may then determine our actions.[1]

For Paul Woodruff, imagination and will are the agencies by means of which we are enabled to express capacities 'in the language of behavior' (159). The work of John Clare and other writers like him involves its readers in a *poesis* that stems from and enacts a language of sympathetic behavior. His poetry displays a self-consciously moral relationship with the world from which example readers can learn to transform their own capacities for acknowledging and revering the world as an equal partner in the living community of which we are a part. Such a *poesis* as *synthesis*, of course, revives a Romantic poetics where imagination is the agency that 'marks the before unapprehended relations of things' and excites 'rational sympathy'—to adduce two concepts from Shelley's *A Defence of Poetry* and Wordsworth's Preface, respectively.[2] The end of this vitally metaphoric poesis, for Cavell (as for Serres), is to bring into the jurisdiction of our social contract, the relations of our moral universe, those beings and entities hitherto excluded and to dissolve what he calls the 'indefinite claim of difference' or 'inexpressible ground of exclusion' that bars others from occupying 'our realm of justice' (*Claim* 378). For our purposes, the poetic act may bring into the jurisdiction of a natural contract the hitherto excluded third—the world-wide world—grounded in what Serres calls the 'rights of symbiosis' in which the claims of human beings and the claims of nature are equally pro-

1 Stanley Cavell, *The Claim of Reason: Wittgenstein, Skepticism, Morality, and Tragedy* (Clarendon and New York: Oxford University Press, 1979), 353.

2 Percy Bysshe Shelley, *A Defence of Poetry, Shelley's Prose, or The Trumpet of a Prophecy*, ed. David Lee Clark (Albuquerque: The University of New Mexico Press, 1954), 276–97, 278. William Wordsworth, Preface, 608.

tected (38). The idea of a natural bond reinforced or constructed by means of empathic *poesis* brings us around to Clare, whose poetry erases the grounds of exclusion and affirms that nonhuman beings are granted a rightful place in our realm of responsibility and justice. While such poems as 'To a Fallen Elm', 'The Mores', 'Emmonsales Heath', 'The Lamentations of Round Oak Waters', and 'The Lament of Swordy Well' enact paradigmatically the verbal act of acknowledgement as a response to nature's suffering and explicitly show how we may recalibrate our orientation to nature by moving from a technology of knowing to a poetics and an ethics of acknowledgment, I will discuss here one of Clare's poems that appears to theorize the distinction between knowing and acknowledging, 'The Landrail'.

'The Landrail' at first appears to be a simple descriptive poem describing the elusive habits of this bird, also known as the Corn-Crake, that many hear but few ever see.[1] According to Thomas Bewick's *British Birds*, 'Its well-known cry is first heard as soon as the grass becomes long enough to shelter it, and continues till the grass is cut; but the bird is seldom seen, for it constantly skulks among the thickest part of the herbage, and runs so nimbly through it, winding and doubling in every direction, that it is difficult to come near it'.[2] In the natural history letters, Clare remarks the 'mysterious noise' from the grass in summer and says, 'I have followed it for hours and all to no purpose; it seemd like a spirit that mockd my folly in running after it'.[3] The poem formulates the elusiveness of the bird thus: 'Tis like a fancy every where / A sort of living doubt / We know tis somthing but it ne'er / Will blab the secret out' (234).[4] The boys who can associate other birds' sounds with an objective knowledge of their haunts and habits are held in thrall by the land rail's mysterious cry:

1 With the advent of mechanized mowing and harvesting machinery in the early twentieth century, and especially since the second world war, the corn crake (*crex crex*) population has precipitously declined, and it is now listed as an endangered species; thus, the rarity of its appearance is more severe now than it was in Clare's day, except in Ireland.

2 Thomas Bewick, *A History of British Birds* (Newcastle, 1826), vol. 2, 130–31.

3 John Clare, Letter to Messrs Taylor and Hessey, III. *John Clare*, ed. Robinson and Powell, 467–69, 467.

4 Clare, John. 'The Landrail', *John Clare*, ed. Robinson and Powell, 233–35.

Boys know the note of many a bird
In their bird nesting rounds
But when the landrails noise is heard
They wonder at the sounds

They look in every tuft of grass
Thats in their rambles met
They peep in every bush they pass
And none the wiser get (234)

Unable to see the land rail anywhere, the human intruders see only its remainders; weeders and mowers by mere chance stumble upon its nest as they work:

Yet accident will often meet
The nest within its way
And weeders when they weed the wheat
Discover where they lay (234)

They know the blotched color and roundness of the eggs, dropped into 'simple holes that birds will rake / When dusting on the ground' (235). Yet, the bird itself remains 'A mystery still to men and boys / Who know not where they lay / And guess it but a summer noise / Among the meadow hay' (235).

Clare's poem draws an opposition between knowledge and acknowledgment, reminiscent of Keats's negative capability. The boys 'know' the note of other birds, but the land rail leaves them instead with doubts and uncertainty, not knowledge. Nonetheless, the bird they cannot see is present to them in song and in the visible traces discovered by accident when mowing or weeding. Cavell's attempt to resolve the problem of skepticism is apposite here. For Cavell, if skepticism insists that 'we cannot know the world exists, its presentness to us cannot be a function of knowing. The world is to be accepted; as the presentness of other minds is not to be known, but acknowledged'.[1]

The insistence of the poem on the presence of the land rail sug-

1 Stanley Cavell, 'The Avoidance of Love: A Reading of *King Lear*', *Must We Mean What We Say: A Book of Essays* (2002; rpt. Cambridge and New York: Cambridge University Press, 2005), 267–353, 324.

gests a similar effort to accept, to acknowledge, without any troublesome reaching after facts. Although only deducible from traces, its presence seems palpable and-during breeding season-nearly ubiquitous: 'tis heard in every vale / An undiscovered song / And makes a pleasant wonder tale / For all the summer long' (234). Its undeniable but 'undiscovered song' invokes a sense of wonder in those who hear, but the boys pursuing the land rail's song meet inevitably with disappointment: 'They peep in every bush they pass / And none the wiser get' (235). And 'If heard in close or meadow plots / It flies if we pursue / But follows if we notice not / The close and meadow through' (234). As far as the poem allows, the land rail always lies, in Clare's idiom, just outside of their knowledge, its presence felt only in the 'undiscoverd song' or the traces of its nest, hardly a nest.

The poem itself functions as another such trace, a second-hand record or report of having heard and of hearing the song of the land rail: 'We hear it in the weeding time'; 'We hear it in the summers prime'; 'And now I hear it in the grass' (233). This anaphoric repetition—'we hear', 'I hear'—and the shift from the iterative (recurrent) to the simple present invite the reader into a participatory relation to the action in the poem. Like the bird's song, the words on the page, the words' sounds, invoke a 'sort of living doubt', but at the same time invite us say with the poet 'We know tis something'. In Keats's terms, the poem invites us into that moment 'when a man is capable of being in uncertainties, mysteries, doubts, without any irritable reaching after fact and reason'.[1] Keats calls this 'half-knowledge', but it is a kind of knowledge here that goes beyond knowing towards what Cavell calls acknowledging, in the sense of 'making connections, seeing or realizing possibilities' without relying upon the claims of reason to establish beyond certainty the existence or identity of a thing (*Claim* 353). In a prose fragment, Clare alludes to such a division when he comments that 'Knowledge gives a great number of lessons for nothing like Socrates she is not confined to Halls or colledges or forum[s] but like him accompany us in our walks in the

1 John Keats, Letter to George and Tom Keats, 21, ?27 December 1817, *John Keats*, ed. Elizabeth Cook, The Oxford Authors (Oxford and New York: Oxford University Press, 1990), 369–70, 370.

fields and attends us in our homes'.[1]

'The Landrail' thus suggests that acknowledging, not knowing, may be sufficient cause for us to approach the world, the earth—here in the guise of the landrail—with a sense of wonder and mystery that affirms the earth's presence even as it does not claim to know, and hence to possess, the world. In contrast to poems such as 'The Mores' and 'Lamentations of Swordy Well', 'The Landrail' does not elicit the moral dimension of acknowledgment, and Clare was not self-consciously advancing a philosophical position in the poem. Moreover, we know from Gilbert White, Wordsworth and Clare how boys tended to act upon their knowledge of birds: they robbed their nests, captured them in traps, or shot them for food, fun, or science. Possession in the form of violent taking, as Cavell observes of Shakespeare's *The Winter's Tale*, runs hand in hand with knowing: 'The violence in masculine knowing, explicitly associated with jealousy, seems to interpret the ambition of knowledge as that of exclusive possession, call it private property' (*Disowning* 10). Acknowledgment, in contrast, entails an acceptance, even an intimacy, a coming into the presence of another,

As Cavell concedes, acknowledging a person or thing does not guarantee or demand certain actions; rather it demands a self-conscious moral relationship that means if we neglect our responsibilities we do so with some consciousness, some moral sense, of deliberately choosing wrong over right. In asking us to take a moral position about the other, about nature, the poetics of acknowledgment does not necessarily advance or recommend a plan of action–moral, political, or otherwise. Cavell recognizes that our sympathy may be withheld from the suffering other, even though we may acknowledge that suffering and the claim it entails. We may acknowledge that pain and that claim, but nonetheless let it 'go unanswered' (263): 'the concept of acknowledgment is evidenced equally by its failure as by its success. It is not a description of a given response but a category in terms of which a given response is evaluated' ('Knowing' 263–64). In this sense, poetry may or may not make something happen. Questioning

1 John Clare, '[Knowledge]', prose fragment, *John Clare*, ed. Robinson and Powell, 482.

a claim of moral rightness involves determining 'what position you are taking, that is to say, what position you are taking responsibility for' (*Claim* 268). Thus, reading Clare's poetry does not necessarily put us in a position to act, nor does it outline a politics of action; it does however model a disposition for a certain moral relationship to nature and puts us in a position to recognize the need for action and to reflect upon the fact that our decision to act or not to act, to act for ourselves or to act for another, has moral implications and often material consequences. That is, Clare's poetry offers us an ecopoetics of acknowledgment or recognition that signifies a moral disposition toward the natural world, a call of conscience to respond meaningfully to the human and nonhuman other; we may ignore or reject, attend to or accept, the poem's implicit invitation that we adopt such a disposition as our own.

If George Perkins Marsh is right that 'Only crisis awakens human beings to the need to act responsibly and preserve what is left',[1] then it may take a moment of 'chastened awakening', as in cases such as the Minamata disaster, the Bhopal tragedy, the Chernobyl accident, or the Deepwater Horizon blowout to move us to a greater sense of the urgency and value of ecopoetics and our stake in a healthy environment. In response to catastrophic environmental disaster, we may, if we are persistent, purposive, and persuasive, own up to our negligence and attend to and emulate Clare's disposition to the world and engage in an ethics of care towards the place(s) in which we are environed. Or we may not—as we may remain 'none the wiser yet', and Clare's or Wordsworth's, or Gary Snyder's or Mary Oliver's poetry, may fall on deaf ears. If we do pay attention, we may in such moments own up to our responsibilities, like Leontes, motivated by both guilt and concern for ourselves and for our others.

Our poets have shown how perhaps the first step or first sign of acknowledgment takes place in the wake of accident, error, rash judgment, and downright bad behavior. This audience will be familiar with Wordsworth's 'Nutting' and the passages in *The Prelude* where a violation of a bond with the natural world invokes a highly

1 George Perkins Marsh, *Man and Nature*, The John Harvard Library (1864; rpt. Cambridge, MA: Belknap Press of Harvard University Press, 1965), 40.

self-conscious sense of guilt from the poet. From 'Nutting' and *The Prelude* to Coleridge's 'Rime of the Ancient Mariner' it is a short distance to Aldo Leopold's 'Thinking Like a Mountain', a touchstone of environmental writing from his Sand County Almanac, published in 1949. In this influential essay written in the wake of the Kaibob Deer irruption of 1924, Leopold recounts an epiphanic episode in his life as he stares into the dying eyes of a wolf that he and his companions have killed for sport. Leopold's exhortation that we must learn to think like a mountain—that is to think in terms of the symbiotic relationships between predator and prey, life and death-may be seen as a kind of ecocentric clarification of the more general, but related and anticipatory exhortations we find in Wordsworth's 'Nutting' and Coleridge's 'Rime'. All three accounts involve an act of violence against nature—as hazel grove, as albatross, as wolf—that results in a scene of admonishment and instruction in one form or another. Lawrence Buell has described such acts as 'a performance of chastened awakening to a deeper grasp of environmental relationships'.[1] In his 'In Quest of the Ordinary', Stanley Cavell reads the killing of the Albatross as the consequence of the Mariner's unconscious sense that nature has some claims upon him.[2] Each of these acts may be read as a kind of *felix culpa*, wherein the human agent in the very act of severing ties with the natural world, or denying its claims upon him, learns to recognize if not nature's moral agency (though there sometimes is that), then humanity's moral obligation or responsibility to and for the nonhuman earth partners with which he is bound. In each case, human agents move tragically beyond conventional knowledge toward an anagnorisis of their connection to the mystery and otherness of the natural world, without, however, achieving some objective knowledge or mastery over that otherness. A prerequisite for such chastened feeling, in Paul Woodruff's terms, is the condition of reverence that embodies those ideals that we hold in awe, and of which, shen we fall short, lead to feelings of shame. Woodruff pulls

1 Lawrence Buell, *The Future of Environmental Criticism: Environmental Crisis and Literary Imagination* (Malden, MA and Oxford: Blackwell, 2005), 105.

2 Stanley Cavell, 'In Quest of the Ordinary: Texts of Recovery', *Romanticism and Contemporary Criticism*, ed. Morris Eaves and Michael Fischer (Ithaca and London: Cornell University Press, 1986), 183–239, 193.

no punches when he gives the alternative: 'if you do not have the capacity to be awestruck in the sight of the majesties of nature you are missing part of the usual human endowment' (9).

Conclusion

In his blessing of the nightingale and its nest, in his expression of his wonder at the mystery of the land rail, Clare has recorded a humble testimonial to the power of acknowledgment to displace knowledge, for a kind of intuitive intimacy to displace violent possession, in our quest for coming to terms with the natural world—our quest for the ordinary, as Cavell calls it. In our contemporary environmental crisis, we are everywhere faced with skepticism—about the sentience of natural beings other than humans, about the actuality of global warming, about the extinction of species, about the limitations of resources. We face a politics of denial even in the face of hard scientific evidence that, to invoke Buell again, 'there is no space on earth immune from anthropogenic toxification' (*Future* 41). It is not that we lack knowledge about environmental ills, but that we fail to acknowledge and act upon that knowledge. It is not that we know too little about the natural world or cannot overcome our skepticism about its very existence, but that we fail to acknowledge nature and our responsibility to coexist symbiotically with it; as Shelley said, we fail 'to imagine that which we know' (*Defence* 293). Given the distance from Clare's world and ours—given the degree of degradation human systems have wrought upon the earth, a degree unimaginable by Clare (or Wordsworth and Thoreau for that matter), we cannot turn to his poetry for a plan of action. What we can do is turn to Clare's poetry—and to that of other similarly disposed writers—for a key to a certain turn of mind and feeling, a feel, a disposition or habitus, that predisposes us to acknowledge the earth, to acknowledge the natural world, as a legitimate partner or member of the moral community and to recognize that we ourselves are, in Aldo Leopold's words, not master and 'conqueror of the land-community', but 'plain member and citizen of it'.[1] As Clare's ecopoetics of acknowledgment dem-

1 Aldo Leopold, 'The Land Ethic', *A Sand County Almanac: With Essays on Conservation from Round River* (New York: Ballantine Books, 1966), 237–64, 240.

onstrates, the price of that citizenship is to turn to the natural world, see it, acknowledge it in all its beauty and mystery, and, ideally, help others to do the same.

Here is Clare in 'Second Address to the Rose Bud in Humble Life' articulating the poet's duty to the worldwide world:

Long may live my artless beauty
Long thy sweetness I may tell
Tis thy poets humble duty
Thus to see and wish thee well
Tis thy poets latest blessing
When fates hazards race is run
That thy life no pains expressing
End as sweet as it begun[1]

Wendell Berry has said that the measure of a powerful ecologically centered writing is 'the health of the place'; the lasting impact upon the place, he believes, is 'one of the indispensable standards of what you write' (50). The preservation of the Lakes is a monument to the ecopoetic force of Wordsworth's poetry and *Guide*; and the respect we are gaining for Helpston, the Clare house, and the existing fields and lands around Clare's home place are a living testimony to the force of his own work—the result of Clare's special disposition to nature, his protest against the forces breaking his world apart, and his acknowledgment of life—from beetles, crickets, dragonflies and crickets to Swallows, martins, bats, owls and the famed nightingale.

So, can Clare's poetry save the earth? Drawing upon Immanuel Kant's (1785) distinction between actions performed from a sense of duty and those performed from inclination, the deep ecologist Arne Naess argues that moral duty is a less reliable basis for ecology than inclination, because moral duty requires people act against their interests; moral duty is most pronounced when a benevolent act goes against ones inclination. Benevolent acts performed out of inclination constitute the beautiful; as he puts it, 'A person acts beautifully when acting benevolently from inclination. ... Environment is then

1 John Clare, 'Second Address to the Rose Bud in Humble Life', *John Clare*, ed. Robinson and Powell, 43–44, 44.

not felt to be something strange or hostile which we must unfortunately adapt ourself [sic] to, but something valuable which we are *inclined to* treat with joy and respect'.[1] Hence, Naess advocates that we develop inclination rather than moral obligation. Inclination, he believes, comes from developing an identification with nature. As I hope I have shown above, Clare's poetry involves both inclination and identification. His work makes us see and feel Clare's sense of beauty and joy, not merely by description or mimesis, but through acts of sympathetic imagination that may awaken us to our own acts of acknowledgment. Whether Clare's poetry makes a difference ultimately depends upon cultivating sympathetic and imaginative readers, for readers are the actors in the present theatre of the world, and we can choose to take from Clare's work a call to action—or not. It's up to us. We must decide, and, with Keats in *The Fall of Hyperion*, we can hope that poetry may play a role in shaping a favourable disposition to the natural world: 'sure not all / Those melodies sung into the world's ear / Are useless'.[2]

1 Arne Naess, *Ecology, Community, and Lifestyle: Outline of an Ecosophy*, trans. David Rothenberg (1989; rpt. Cambridge: Cambridge University Press, 1993), 85.

2 John Keats, 'The Fall of Hyperion', *John Keats*, ed. Elizabeth Cook, The Oxford Authors (Oxford and New York: Oxford University Press, 1990), 291–304, 295.

James Castell

The Society of Birds in *Home at Grasmere*

It is Keats of course who famously writes to Benjamin Bailey in a letter of 1817 that 'if a Sparrow come before my Window I take part in its existence and pick about the Gravel'.[1] The connection has been drawn many times between this animal episode and the even more famous description of his 'poetical Character' that this self-defined 'camelion Poet' offers later to Richard Woodhouse—a 'poetical character' to be distinguished, of course, 'from the wordsworthian or egotistical sublime; which is a thing per se and stands alone' (I, 386–7). As many of his most savage detractors and loyal supporters have been happy to point out, Wordsworth's poetry is more than willing to 'pick about the Gravel' but it is far less likely to have a dramatic capacity to transpose itself into the existence of a bird. Yet, birds remain a frequent literal and figurative presence in Wordsworth's verse and, in this paper, I want to think about and with the birds in *Home at Grasmere*, the opening book of what should have been his poetic and philosophical magnum opus *The Recluse*.

With a certain resistance to dramatic transposition and with an openness to the sort of poetic relations that his blank verse establishes, I want to argue that Wordsworth might make as much of a contribution to the history of Western thought concerning man's relationship with animals as any chameleon poet. Firstly then—with a brief excursion through some criticism—I want to establish the significance of both a gap and a relation between poet and animal in *Home at Grasmere*. Then I want to show how the blank verse itself comes to think a very particular sort of bridge between poet and birds in one

1 John Keats, *The Letters of John Keats, 1814–1821*, ed. Hyder Edward Rollins, 2 vols (Cambridge: Harvard University Press, 1958), I, 186.

specific episode. Finally (and more briefly) I want to consider some more traditional philosophical thought alongside the poem.

Home at Grasmere is still frequently considered a failure. After all, *The Recluse* was never finished and the single book that we do have of its first part is fragmentary. Responses to the publication of this book in 1888 welcomed an addition to the Wordsworthian canon but confidently positioned it as an inferior supplement to *The Prelude*.[1] Many of the most significant recent critics have taken a similar stance. For Jonathan Wordsworth, the poem in its dedication to 'celebrating the paradise of common day, was especially likely to over-rate the literary power of ordinariness'.[2] For Geoffrey Hartman, the poem is 'often embarrassing as well as exuberant' because the poet fails 'to depart from common-sense perception or the corporeal understanding' to 'the fire of the imagination.'[3] Even where other critics have not seen the poem itself as a failure, it is often because they spot significant displacements that imply—even where they don't quite add up to—failures on behalf of the poet.[4]

Duncan Wu offers a particularly interesting hypothesis concerning 'the second half' of *Home at Grasmere*. As a form of response to Coleridge's accusations that he was aloof from the 'the mass of suffering, sinful humanity', Wu argues that Wordsworth embarks upon a 'lengthy self-justification' to try 'to persuade the reader that he is capable of sympathizing with every peasant and dog in the neigh-

1 See Appendix I in William Wordsworth, *Home At Grasmere: Part First, Book First, of 'The Recluse'*, ed. Beth Darlington (Ithaca: Cornell University Press, 1977), pp. 455–462. Unless otherwise stated, all future references to this volume will be by line number to the MS. B reading text or by page number.

2 Jonathan Wordsworth, *William Wordsworth: The Borders of Vision* (Oxford: Clarendon Press, 1982), pp. 138–9.

3 Geoffrey Hartman, *Wordsworth's Poetry, 1787-1814* (New Haven and London: Yale University Press, 1964; repr. 1975), p. 172.

4 See Bruce Clarke, 'Wordsworth's Departed Swans: Sublimation and Sublimity in *Home At Grasmere*', *Studies in Romanticism*, 19 (1980), 355–374; Raimonda Modiano, 'Blood Sacrifice, Gift Economy and the Edenic World: Wordsworth's "Home At Grasmere"', *Studies in Romanticism*, 32 (1993), 481–521; William A. Ulmer, 'The Society of Death in *Home At Grasmere*', *Philological Quarterly*, 75 (1996), 67–83. Ulmer makes a similar point when he states that 'Once celebrated for healing natural supernaturalism, more recently Wordsworth's *Home at Grasmere* has been read for its tensions and disruptions' (67).

bourhood'.[1] To illustrate this, he quotes a charming if undeniably bald passage where the speaker of the poem earnestly asserts how he begins to inscribe upon his heart

> A liking for the small grey Horse that bears
> The paralytic Man; I know the ass
> On which the Cripple in the Quarry maimed
> Rides to and fro: I know them and their ways.
> The famous Sheep-dog, first in all the vale,
> Though yet to me a Stranger, will not be
> A Stranger long; nor will the blind Man's Guide,
> Meek and neglected thing, of no renown. (723–32)

For Wu, it is precisely 'Wordsworth's desperation to prove his good-will towards these humble creatures' that 'gives away the absence of genuine kinship between them'. He argues that when Wordsworth 'tries to convince us that he is one of them, the tone of Miltonic grandeur collapses into bathos.' As such, the failure to show 'genuine kinship' between the speaker and the animal life in Grasmere vale is symptomatic of a more general poetic problem. In many respects, this is a repetition of the old Coleridgean objection of a disproportion between high theme and low subject matter: to write so bathetically about donkeys and guide dogs is to fail to live up to what is expected of a writer who (as Coleridge put it) 'had more materials for the great philosophic Poet than any man I ever knew'.[2]

Taking my lead from Wu's perceptive observation, I want to suggest, however, that Wordsworth's failure to show genuine kinship in his poetic encounters with animals might indeed be important 'material' for the 'great philosophic Poet' that Wordsworth *was*—famously not quite the same as the 'great philosophic Poet' that Coleridge was hoping him to be. Part of the perceived failure of animal kinship may have something to do with what Wordsworth leaves out of the frequently cited MS. B and future versions of the poem. An earlier manuscript, MS. R, includes drafting of a number of passages from *Home*

1 Duncan Wu, *Wordsworth: An Inner Life* (Oxford: Blackwell, 2003), p. 139.
2 Samuel Taylor Coleridge, *Table Talk*, ed. Carl Woodring, 2 vols (London: Routledge, 1990), I, 309.

at Grasmere interleaved with a copy of Coleridge's 1796 *Poems*.[1] On the same pages as lines from the end of the above passage, we find drafting that will later come to form the Wanderer's claim in *The Excursion* that 'Happy is He who lives to understand! / Not human nature only, but explores / All Natures':

Happy is he who lives to understand
for this
Observes explores ~~to the end~~ that he
may find
The law & what it is & where begins
The union & disunion that which makes
all [?the]
Degree or kind in every shape of being
The constitution powers & faculties
do
And habits of enjoyments that assign
its
To every class ~~their~~ offic or abode
Through all the mighty commonwealth
of things
Up from the stone or plant to sovereign
man [2]

This drafting provides valuable insight into the process of Wordsworth's thinking about the ontological and epistemological stakes in this famous 'mighty commonwealth of things'. While there is clearly a transcendental impulse here, this passage should complicate—in its stressing of the simultaneous importance of 'union &

1 For a description, see *Home at Grasmere*, pp. 139–40. Both Sally Bushell and Andrew Bennett have recently discussed this interleaving at length and with differing conclusions: see Andrew Bennett, *Wordsworth Writing* (Cambridge: Cambridge University Press, 2007); Sally Bushell, 'The Making of Meaning in Wordsworth's Home At Grasmere: (Speech Acts, Micro-Analysis and "Freudian Slips")', *Studies in Romanticism*, 48 (2009), 391–421.

2 *Home at Grasmere*, p. 189. For ease of reproduction, I have omitted a jagged line above 'And habits' and an underwritten 'u' (showing that 'enjoyments' was corrected from 'enjuyments'). *The Excursion* quotation refers to the reading text in *The Excursion,* ed. Sally Bushell, James Butler and Michael C. Jaye (Ithaca: Cornell University Press, 2007), IV, 335–7.

disunion'—the desire to find anything like 'genuine kinship' with other natures. In later versions, the importance of separation as well as relation is emphasised further when the easy negation of 'disunion' is crossed through and replaced with 'partition' (*Home at Grasmere*, p. 197). This is a powerful poetic assertion of interest in the resemblance and difference in the 'constitution powers & faculties / And habits of enjoyments' making up the very structure of 'degree or kind in every shape of being'. In contact with the animal life of the preceding *Home at Grasmere* work, this passage considers zoological observation, metaphysical speculation, and epistemological imagining in the question of understanding 'other natures'. Perhaps this is why Wordsworth rehearses at least two and possibly three verbs in the first and second line of the drafting: 'understand' and 'observes' come before 'explores' which is finally settled on for later versions.

Awareness of 'union and partition' is the more general law of many of the social relations in *Home at Grasmere*. This manifests itself in characteristically Wordsworthian doublenesses and contradictions. For example, after claiming so confidently that the Sheep-dog 'will not be / A Stranger long', he states thirty lines later that animals must be

> Strangers to me and all men, or at least
> Strangers to all particular amity,
> All intercourse of knowledge or of love
> That parts the individual from the kind (754–7)

'Stranger' is a particularly complex word in this poem about homecoming. This is demonstrated in the most frequently discussed episode of the poem when the principal human figures are compared to a pair of mating swans with a logic that simultaneously binds humans and animals together and requires their mutual exclusion from each other's pairing: 'They strangers, and we strangers; they a pair, / And we a *solitary* pair *like them*' (my italics, 340–1). This is a relationship of shared solitude that requires shared estrangement. Hence my title—the society *of* birds—which indicates both a relation to birds (something more like humans, poets, or literary critics being in society with birds) and the independence of avian society from external social relation (the society existing exclusively, inaccessibly even, *between* birds). This is one reason why this poem about relation and communication in verse is so consistently and enthusiastically preoccupied with animals, even though the main subject of Wordsworth's philosophic song is undeniably 'of what in man is human or divine' (909). As he says himself, animals must necessarily take a 'subordinate place, / According to [their] claim, an underplace in my affections' (765–6). But, it is precisely this 'underplace' of animal life that becomes essential for thinking poetically about the nonhuman world of Nature and the role of man as a 'poetical animal' within it.[1]

The swans are often seen as the avian centre of *Home at Grasmere*. However, I want to focus on the other major bird episode in the poem where the significance of versified contact with the familiar strangeness of birds comes most sharply into focus. The speaker of the poem invokes 'the aid of verse to describe the evolutions' that a group of 'aquatic fowl' 'sometimes perform, on a fine day towards the close of winter'.[2]

> They show their pleasure, and shall I do less?
> Happier of happy though I be, like them
> I cannot take possession of the sky,
> Mount with a thoughtless impulse, and wheel there,
> One of a mighty multitude whose way
> And motion is a harmony and dance
> Magnificent. (286–92)

Much influential work has emphasized the problematic nature of Wordsworth's sense of ownership in *Home at Grasmere* but, here, the speaker explicitly states that he '*cannot* take possession of the sky'.[3] The thoughtlessness of the birds' 'impulse' to motion and soci-

1 The phrase 'poetical animal' is William Hazlitt's. See *The Complete Works of William Hazlitt,* ed. by P. P. Howe, 21 vols (London: J.M. Dent, 1930), v, 2.

2 This prose from *The Guide to the Lakes* (1823) was also used as an epigraph for the poem 'Water Fowl' when it was published in Wordsworth's 1827 *Poetical Works*. See *Home at Grasmere*, p. 54, and William Wordsworth, *The Prose Works of William Wordsworth,* ed. W. J. B. Owen and Jane Worthington Smyser, 3 vols (Oxford: Clarendon Press, 1974), I, 183–4.

3 My desire to emphasise Wordsworth's humility before the waterfowl is not to downplay the general importance of ownership and possession in this poem.

ety becomes a 'harmony' and a 'dance' from which man is irrevocably separate, excluded even. But, it is also a harmony and a dance that the very human motion of the verse participates in and even comes to drive. The unusual intensification of 'happier of happy' and the cumulative alliteration of 'mount', 'mighty multitude', 'motion' and 'magnificent' amplify the spiraling pleasure of the birds themselves and the blank verse too. The resistance of the birds to poetic appropriation inspires a bird-like circling in the poetry but this goes beyond verse mimesis and becomes a means of prosodic argumentation. The speaker continues:

> Behold them, how they shape,
> Orb after orb, their course, still round and round,
> Above the area of the Lake, their own
> Adopted region, girding it about
> In wanton repetition, yet therewith—
> With that large circle evermore renewed—
> Hundreds of curves and circlets, high and low,
> Backwards and forwards, progress intricate,
> As if one spirit was in all and swayed
> Their indefatigable flight. (292–301)

The repetition of 'orb after orb' and 'round and round', the near-tautology of 'curves and circlets', and the complementary antitheses of 'high and low' and 'backwards and forwards' come to 'gird' this syntactically wheeling passage with a 'wanton repetition' comparable to the circling of the waterfowl. Yet, such 'wanton repetition' is also clearly meant to become sublime repetitiousness when allied to the 'progress intricate' in both 'their' and the verse's 'indefatigable flight.' Such progress through repetition hinges on what appears to be a turn in the verse-sentence at 'yet therewith', but this turn even wheels back upon itself and becomes a continuation of the circling—however 'evermore' expanded. Possessed by such repetition, the syn-

---

In fact, Wordsworth's interest in this theme is unequivocally stated from the outset: 'The unappropriated bliss hath found / An owner, and that owner I am he. / The Lord of this enjoyment is on Earth / And in my breast. What wonder if I speak / With fervour, am exalted with the thought / Of my possessions, of my genuine wealth / Inward and outward?' (85–91)

tactically wheeling pleasure of the lines goes some way to transcending the human speaker's inability to take possession of the sky and the bird's animal experience, but simultaneously its continual circling never quite allows such possession to be consummated.

Kenneth Johnston has spoken of how that phrase 'wanton repetition' 'is apt for the whole style of "Home at Grasmere"': 'everything about it is circular: its arguments tautological, its syntax redundant and repetitious, its imagery full of rounded reflections which reinforce the circling tensions of its structure.'[1] As such, Wordsworth's impassioned reasoning and engagement in verse extends into almost every aspect of this poem's features. Take for example the lively climax to the description of the waterfowl—a number of figurative comparisons which themselves could be seen as repetitions of the real birds:

> see them now at rest,
> Yet not at rest, upon the glassy lake.
> They cannot rest; they gambol like young whelps,
> Active as lambs and overcome with joy;
> They try all frolic motions, flutter, plunge,
> And beat the passive water with their wings.
> Too distant are they for plain view, but lo!
> Those little fountains, sparkling in the sun,
> Which tell what they are doing, which rise up,
> First one and then another silver spout,
> As one or other takes the fit of glee—
> Fountains and spouts, yet rather in the guise
> Of plaything fire-works, which on festal nights
> Hiss hiss about the feet of wanton boys. (768–81)

In this phenomenal piling up of figures, simile, anthropomorphism, metonymy, and metaphor jostle with the prosodic joy of 'frolic motions', fluttering, plunging and the final festal onomatopoeia of plaything fire-works hiss hissing 'about the feet of wanton boys'. The birds 'gambol'—itself a one-word verbal metaphor because

1 Kenneth R. Johnston, *Wordsworth and the Recluse* (New Haven; London: Yale University Press, 1984), p. 88; Kenneth R. Johnston, '"Home At Grasmere": Reclusive Song', *Studies in Romanticism*, 14 (1975), 1–28 (8).

normally used for quadrupeds—in figures that circle repetitiously around them: at once 'whelps', 'lambs', 'fountains', 'spouts', 'fire-works' and 'wanton boys'. The unrest of their movement—that is, as Wordsworth acknowledges, impossible to possess—is brought into human and poetic society by continual figurative revision and re-revision. It is known without being tamed in poetry that is led by the passion of repetition; poetry where, as Wordsworth put it in the 'Note to the Thorn', words might be seen 'not only as symbols of the passion, but as *things*, active and efficient, which are of themselves part of the passion.'[1] Human song is animated into a particular versified society with the birds that it describes and even perhaps to its own animal life. We might even say—without overly subscribing to the Romantic ideology of organic form—that this is verse that comes close to fulfilling Wordsworth's aspiration elsewhere in *Home at Grasmere* to create 'An art, a music, and a stream of words / That shall be life, the acknowledged voice of life' (621–2).

This is why Wordsworth's qualification in the MS. R drafting immediately following 'Happy is he who lives to understand, / Not human nature only, but explores / All natures' need not necessarily be seen as bathetic limitation:

about our daily life
And yet ~~a~~ some thing hangs ~~cleaves~~
Which is not satisfied with this & he
Is a still happier Man Who for these heights
Of Speculation not unfit descends
At Nature's call to walk in humbler
[?ways]
~~[?From] universal truth to [?partial ?truth]~~
Luxuriates & [?finds] [?&] [?] repose
From universal truth in [?partial ?]
Hath individual objects of regard
Among the inferior kinds not merely those
Which he may call his own & which depend
Upon his care, from which he also looks

1 William Wordsworth, *'Lyrical Ballads', and Other Poems, 1797-1800,* ed. Karen Green and James Butler (Ithaca and London: Cornell University Press, 1992), p. 351.

For signs & tokens of a mutual bond
But others far beyond this narrow sphere
Which for the very sake of love he loves [1]

This passage—that later comes to be voiced in the dramatic form of *The Excursion* as a disagreement—argues specifically for attention to be paid to both domestic and wild examples of the 'inferior kinds'. What interests me most, however, is the simultaneous recognition of an opening out—'far beyond this narrow sphere'—and a shutting down—from universal to partial truth—that must occur in any literal or figurative, living or poetic encounter with the other natures of animal life. This is a descent—and one that loves for the very sake of love—that Wordsworth's poetry frequently makes into the airy ontological gulf between Nature and human Life and that his verse comes to continually half-surmount without ever quite overcoming.

At the end of the first book of *On the Parts of Animals*, Aristotle advises that we 'must not recoil with childish aversion from the examination of the humbler animals' because 'in certitude and in completeness our knowledge of terrestrial things has the advantage' over 'the scanty conceptions to which we can attain of celestial things'.[2] Just as consideration of terrestrial animals worthily counterbalances the excesses of human metaphysical speculation for Aristotle, birds provide some opposition perhaps to our tendency to associate animal encounters purely with low terrestriality and poetic or philosophic failure. In the *Essay Concerning Human Understanding*, for example, Locke highlights how waterfowl in particular transcend the elements and 'link the Terrestrial and Aquatique together'. Even more than most birds, they illustrate the remarkable proximity of links in the great chain of being.[3] In *Home at Grasmere*, waterfowl also become a link

1 *Home at Grasmere*, pp. 197–9. Once more, for ease of reproduction, I have replaced a diagonal strike-through with a horizontal one ('a'). I have also omitted the underwritten 'to our' under 'thing', the underwritten 'whicde' under 'which', and the underwritten 'butual' under 'mutual'. I have also omitted the large cross over the whole of this passage that signifies its removal from the MS. B version of *Home at Grasmere* for later recycling.

2 Aristotle, *The Complete Works of Aristotle: The Revised Oxford Translation*, ed. Jonathan Barnes, 2 vols (Princeton: Princeton University Press, 1984), 1, 1004.

3 John Locke, *An Essay Concerning Human Understanding*, ed. by Peter H.

in the 'mighty commonwealth of things' but only in so much as they allow Wordsworth's verse to think the difference between his 'dim and undetermined sense' of various 'unknown modes of being'.[1] This is why, as Heidegger is desperate to emphasise in the twentieth century, 'of all the beings that are, presumably the most difficult to think about are living creatures, because on the one hand they are in a certain way most closely akin to us, and on the other are at the same time separated from our ek-sistent essence by an abyss.'[2] Far from a homecoming of pure interspecies integration, Wordsworth's verse also shows an acute awareness of the dual claim for kinship and separation with animal life. This is why that figure of the inclusive and excluding circle of animal being is so strikingly at home in both the idiom of Heidegger's philosophy and *Home at Grasmere*. Where, however, Heidegger's ultimate aim is to prise the gap open further, Wordsworth's birds provide a new poetic and philosophical way of thinking it.

Nidditch (Oxford: Clarendon Press, 1975), p. 447. Locke's *Essay* is one of many potential influences upon the zoological dimension of Wordsworth's broader transvaluation of high and low: 'All quite down from us, the descent is by easy steps, and a continued series of Things, that in each remove, differ very little one from the other. There are Fishes that have Wings, and are not Strangers to the airy Region: and there are some Birds, that are Inhabitants of the Water; whose Blood is as cold as Fishes, and their Flesh so like in taste, that the scrupulous are allow'd them on Fish-days. There are Animals so near of kin both to Birds and Beasts, that they are in the middle between both: Amphibious Animals link the Terrestrial and Aquatique together; Seals live at Land and at Sea, and Porpoises have the warm Blood and Entrails of a Hog, not to mention what is confidently reported of Mermaids, or Sea-men. There are some Brutes, that seem to have as much Knowledge and Reason, as some that are called Men: and the Animal and Vegetable Kingdoms, are so nearly join'd, that if you will take the lowest of one, and the highest of the other, there will scarce be perceived any great difference between them; and so on till we come to the lowest and the most inorganical parts of Matter, we shall find every-where, that the several *Species* are linked together, and differ but in almost insensible degrees.' (pp. 446–7)

1 These words are obviously used regarding a very different object in the boat-stealing episode. See William Wordsworth, *The Thirteen-Book Prelude,* ed. Mark L. Reed, 2 vols (Ithaca: Cornell University Press, 1991), I, 721–2.

2 Martin Heidegger, *Basic Writings: From 'Being and Time' (1927) to 'the Task of Thinking' (1964),* ed. David Farrell Krell (New York: Harper Collins, 1993), p. 230. I am grateful to the first chapter of David Farrell Krell's book, *Daimon Life: Heidegger and Life-Philosophy* (Bloomington: Indiana University Press, 1992), esp. pp. 1–5, for having brought together Aristotle's *On the Parts of Animals* and Heidegger's 'Letter on Humanism'.

Luce Irigaray has written touchingly about the importance of animals in her childhood and throughout her life. 'The most precious and also the most mysterious aid has often come to me from birds', she writes.[1] For her, the songs of birds are an important corrective to the excesses of instrumental Western Reason. 'To subdue, to possess, to violate the modesty or intimacy of the other, seems, for [our learned philosophers], a proof of virility, rather than learning to sing to invite, at a distance, the other to come closer.' (198) The generalised claim about 'our learned philosophers' may be problematic but, for me, that final phrase—'learning to sing to invite, at a distance, the other to come closer'—resonates beautifully with the verse of Wordsworth's waterfowl passage. It is this 'learning to sing' that allows us to say with the speaker of the poem that 'No, we are not alone; we do not stand, / My Emma, here misplaced and desolate, / Loving what no one cares for but ourselves' (646–8) because 'Joy spreads and sorrow spreads; and this whole Vale, / Home of untutored Shepherds as it is, / Swarms with sensation' (664–6). Even though the focus is not on the actual song of the waterfowl in *Home at Grasmere*, we might describe the 'harmony and dance magnificent' of their circling through and with the poet's own song as a song of the birds in its fullest sense. 'Society is here', Wordsworth says of Grasmere vale, 'The true community, [...] a multitude / Human and brute' (818–828). The society of birds. A society between the human and the animal, between birds and philosophic song. A society with only the most tenuous breaths of versified relation across a physical, epistemological and ontological abyss.

1 Luce Irigaray, 'Animal Compassion' in Peter Atterton and Matthew Calarco, eds., *Animal Philosophy: Essential Readings in Continental Thought* (London and New York: Continuum, 2004), pp. 193–201 (p. 197).

Nahoko Miyamoto Alvey

'Kubla Khan' and Orientalism: The Roads to and from Xanadu

1.

In 'Coleridge's Dream' (1951), Jorge Luis Borges, musing upon what Coleridge in the preface to the published version of 'Kubla Khan' calls 'a psychological curiosity,'[1] mentions the 'symmetry of souls of sleeping men who span continents and centuries':[2] Kublai Khan (1215–1294) saw a palace in a dream, according to which he built a palace east of Shangdu, while Coleridge saw Kubla Khan's palace in a dream, which he retained only partly in memory and turned into a fragmentary poem. The legend of Kublai's dream palace was recorded in *A Compendium of Chronicle*, written by Rashid al-Din (1247–1318), the minister of Mahmud Ghazan (1271–1304), who ruled the part of the Mongol Empire that forms present-day Iran and commissioned the *Compendium of Chronicle*. Coleridge would not have known the episode, because it was introduced in Europe only in 1836, when Étienne Quartremère translated part of the *Compendium of Chronicle* as *Histoire des Mongols de la Perse*. Comparing Coleridge's fragmentary poem with the ruins of Kublai's palace that were found and reported by Father Jean-François Gerbillon of the Society of Jesus in 1691, Borges concludes with 'the possibility that this series of

1 Samuel Taylor Coleridge, *Poems; Samuel Taylor Coleridge* ed. John Beer (London: Everyman, 1991), 228. All citations from the two versions of 'Kubla Khan' are from this edition, hereafter referred to in the main text parenthetically by version (1797, 1816), and line(s).

2 Jorge Luis Borges, *Selected Non-Fictions*, ed. Eliot Weinberger, trans. Esther Allen, Suzanne Jill Levine, and Eliot Weinberger (New York: Penguin, 2000), 371.

dreams and works has not yet ended,' thinking that 'someone, on a night centuries removed from us, will dream the same dream, and not suspect that others have dreamed it, and he will give it a form of marble or of music' (372).

Borges's essay is at the far end of the new historicist reading of the poem explored by Nigel Leask and followed by Peter Kitson.[1] In order to 'restate *Kubla Khan* in the intellectual climate of the late 1790s' and 'to discover a context of literary *orientalism* rather different from that associated with the 1816 poem' (2), Leask considers the poem in relation to two contemporary travelogues: Sir George Staunton's *An Authentic Account of an Embassy from the King of Great Britain to the Emperor of China...taken from the papers of... the Earl of Macartney* (1797), and James Bruce's *Travels to Discover the Source of the Nile* (1790). Staunton's book is one of the first published accounts of the Earl of Macartney's embassy to the court of the Qing emperor Qianlong (1711–1799; reign 1735–1795) between 1792 and 1794, which failed because of Macartney's refusal to kowtow to the emperor. As Leask convincingly argues, Staunton's book has a special relevance to Coleridge's description of Kubla's palace, in its extensive references to Emperor Qianlong's gardens at Yuanmingyuan in Peking and his summer palace at Jehol in Tartary.

Different as their approaches are, both Borges and Leask look into Coleridge's wide reading in the literature of travel and, interestingly enough, start with John Livingston Lowes's *The Road to Xanadu: A Study in the Ways of the Imagination* (1927; rev. 1951). I also start with Lowes's *Xanadu* and, by examining the patterns of repetition in history, will show the inseparable mixture of information and imagination in the textual and visual representations of that fabled place. In this paper I first take a look at different spellings of the same proper names that appear in travel reports on China, tracing historical and imaginary overland routes to and from Xanadu, and consider whether it was possible to present a sublime vision of China in the 1790s.

1 Nigel Leask, 'The Road to Xanadu Revisited,' Romanticism 4:1(1998):1–21. Peter Kitson, *Romantic Literature, Race, and Colonial Encounter* (London: Macmillan, 2007), 143–213.

2.

Lowes calls attention to a long note to 'Sandu' (Shangdu/Shangtu) in Sir Henry Yule's *Cathay and the Way Thither* (1866; rev. 1913–15), in which Henri Cordier, the editor of the book, identifies the city with Coleridge's 'Xanadu,' and introduces the legend about Kublai Khan's dream plan of the summer palace.[1] In 1264 Kublai renamed Kaiping Shangdu, which means 'upper capital.' The city, located on the plain beyond the Great Wall of China, retained its Mongolian heritage and was thus worthy of the honor. A few years later, when Kublai tried to govern the whole of China after conquering the country by adapting Chinese systems and using the Chinese calendar, he proclaimed that a second capital would be created at Daidu, which overlaps the present Beijing. In 1269 Daidu was made the principal capital, while Shangdu became the summer capital.

The name of the historical city, in which Kublai ascended to the throne and which Marco Polo visited, was introduced in Europe as 'Ciandu,' originally recorded in Latin in Polo's travel reports, while Daidu was known as 'Khanbalik' in Europe. Cordier comments: 'The Ciandu or Chandu of Marco Polo, where stood that magnificent park and palace, his description of which set Coleridge a-dreaming (or dreaming that he dreamt) that wonderful poem which tells how 'In Xanadu did Kubla Khan / A stately pleasure dome decree'' (2:227 n.1). Where did Coleridge (or the narrator of the poem) acquire the spelling 'Xanadu' (*1797* 1)? In early nineteenth-century England, if the original source of information was Marco Polo's Latin texts, the city was spelled Ciandu.[2] Even though there is no mention of Purchas's *Pilgrimage* in a short note at the end of the 1797 manuscript, it is possible to guess from the city's spelling from the first

1 John Livingston Lowes, *The Road to Xanadu: A Study in the Ways of the Imagination*, 2nd ed. (London: Constable, 1951), 358, 585–86. Henry Yule, *Cathay and the Way Thither: Being a Collection of Medieval Notices of China*, 4 vols., ed. Henri Cordier (London: Hakluyt Society, 1913–15), 2:227 n.1.

2 See, for example, John Pinkerton's *A General Collection of the Best and Most Interesting Voyages and Travels in All Parts of the World; Many of Which Are Now First Translated into English*, 17 vols (1808–14), vol. 7 (London : Longman, 1811). Pinkerton's source is 'the accurate edition of [Giovanni Battista] Ramusio' (7: 101).

line that the writer/narrator must have been familiar with the transliteration that spells Kublai's summer capital with a capital X, whether the spelling is correct or not. The method of transliteration, in which Kubkai's summer palace was spelled with an X, was invented by the Jesuit fathers Matteo Ricci (1552–1610) and Nicholas Trigault (1577–1628). According to their system of romanization of Chinese characters, 'Sh' at the beginning of a word becomes 'X,' and 'ng' at the end of a word becomes 'm,' turning 'Shang-du' into 'Xamdu.'[1] So, the narrator must have been someone who read Purchas's *Pilgrims* and/or *Pilgrimage*; or more precisely, someone who followed the tradition of transliteration started by Jesuit fathers in the early seventeenth century.[2]

Much ink has been shed on important differences between the two versions of 'Kubla Khan',[3] but there is one more important change: from 'In Xannadù did Cubla Khan' to 'In Xanadu did Kubla Khan' (*1787* 1, *1816* 1). In the earlier version, the Mongolian tyrant is spelled 'Cubla,' which reinforces a possibility, together with the Jesuit transliteration of the place name, that the writer/narrator must have been a person living in the seventeenth century, who could have known 'Mount Amara' (*1797* 41) either from Purchas or Milton's *Paradise Lost* (1667). On the other hand, in the 1816 version, the Mongolian emperor's name is spelled 'Kubla,' which suggests that the writer/narrator would have lived in the eighteenth century, knowing not only Purchas and Milton but also many travel reports written in the eighteenth century in which the founder of the Yuan dynasty was usually spelled Kublai, Khubilai, or Kubla.

Whether the city was spelled Ciandu, Shangdu, or Xanadu, the name of the city, when pronounced, sounds more or less the same to foreign ears. In oral culture, slight differences in spellings would

1 Miyoko Nakano, *Qianlong: Iconography of his Politics* (in Japanese) (Tokyo: Bungeishunju, 2007), 208–09.

2 Coleridge might not have known the correct transliteration of Xamdu. He read both *Purchas His Pilgrimage* and *Purchas His Pilgrimes*, but, although the editions of the *Pilgrimage* published in 1614, 1617, and 1626 used the correct spelling of 'Xamdu,' in the first edition (1613) and the *Pilgrimes* (1625) the spelling was 'Xaindu' (Lowes 361).

3 See, for example, Jack Stillinger, *Coleridge and Textual Instability: The Multiple Versions of the Major Poems* (Oxford: Oxford UP, 1994).

not matter. The musical quality, for which Coleridge's 'Kubla Khan' has been noted,[1] is a characteristic of oral culture. But once names are written down, there appear many different spellings that reveal the languages and ages in which they were recorded. Coleridge the poet was also an avid reader in print culture, and sensitive to different spellings in different ages, as seen in the two versions of 'The Rime of the Ancyent Marinere' (1798) and 'The Rime of the Ancient Mariner' (1817). We remember that Marco Polo's accounts were not written but dictated to his fellow inmate, Messer Rustichello, while he was imprisoned in Genoa. Polo spoke in Venetian; the text was first prepared in Latin, and then translated into French and other languages. It is tempting to think that Coleridge's 'Kubla Khan' might have been produced in a similar way. The writer of the poem, Coleridge, documented the date of composition both in a prose note in the manuscript and in the preface of the 1816 poem, but he is not necessarily the speaker in the poem; like the narrator in Shelley's 'Ozymandias' (1818), he may have met 'a traveller from an antique land,'[2] who may have been in the person of Samuel Perchas or a traveler living in the eighteenth century when Kublai's 'Shangdu' was superimposed on the Qing dynasty's summer capital, Chengde, and when some British overland travelers headed for the capital of China, whether they reached it or not.

3.

Chengde, which is about 230 kilometers northeast of Beijing and where the Qing dynasty's summer palace was located, has been cited in historical records in Chinese, European, and Japanese languages with many different transliterations.[3] This is partly because the city

1 For example, Leigh Hunt says that 'Kubla Khan' is 'a voice and a vision, an everlasting tune in our mouths' (*The Examiner* [21 October, 1821], 665).

2 'Ozymandias,' 1. References to Shelley's poetry are to *Shelley's Poetry and Prose*, 2nd ed., ed. Donald H. Reiman and Neil Fraistat (New York: Norton, 2002).

3 European transliterations include 'Chengde fu,' 'Chengtehfu,' 'Gé-hol,' 'Geho,' 'Geho-eul,' 'Gehol,' 'Je ho,' 'Je ho eul,' 'Jee-ho,' 'Jehol,' 'Reche changing,' 'Rehe xinggong,' 'Tchen-teu-fou,' 'Tch'eng-te shi,' 'Tchhing tefou,' 'Zehol,' 'Zhe-hol' (Phillipe Forêt, *Mapping Chengde: The Qing Landscape Enterprise* [University of Hawaii P, 2000], xiv).

was renamed a few times during the eighteenth century. In order to avoid confusion, I use in this paper 'Jehol,' by which the city was traditionally known in Europe, rather than 'Rehe' or 'Chengde.'[1] Kangxi (1654–1722), the grandfather of Qianlong, called his hunting lodge at Jehol 'Rehe shangying,' which means 'Upper Camp on the Rehe River.' 'Rehe' means 'warm river,' because the hot springs upstream prevent the river from freezing in winter. Thus as Coleridge describes in the poem, a 'mighty Fountain' was literally 'seething' as if 'this Earth in fast thick Pants were breathing' (*1797* 19, 17, 18), and the river sprung and ran near the royal residence, flowing into the larger Luanhe River that eventually goes into the Bohai Sea.

In 1703 Kangxi decreed the construction of two palaces, which were to be the summer capital of the Qing dynasty.[2] In 1711, when the summer capital was completed, Kangxi selected thirty-six beautiful spots in the Summer Hermit Palace, where he composed poems. Matteo Ripa, an Italian Jesuit father and the first European to visit the palaces and gardens in the summer capital, transliterated the Chinese 'Rehe' as 'Jehol.' The Manchu name for 'Rehe' is 'Zeho,' hence the English variant 'Zehol.' In English, the place was spelled 'Jehol' or 'Zehol,' while in French it was 'Gé-hol.' In the 1790s different spellings coexisted; Aeneas Anderson used 'Jehol,' Staunton 'Ze-hol,' and John Barrow 'Gehol' in the *Travels in China* from which Wordsworth borrowed the spelling when writing about the 'paradise of ten thousand trees, / Of Gehol's famous gardens' in *The Prelude*.[3]

1 The word 'Jehol,' conventionally used by such European scholars as Otto Frank and Sven Hedin, evokes oriental dreams mixed with imperialism. Similarly, the Japanese transliteration of 'Rehe,' 'Nekka,' rings a note of exoticism and imperialism in the historical context of 'Manchuria,' a puppet state created by Japan in the 1930s.

2 Macartney knew this (*An Embassy to China: Being the Journal Kept by Lord Macartney during his Embassy to the Emperor Ch'ien-Lung* 1793–1794, ed., J. L. Cranmer-Byng [1962; rpt. London: Routledge, 2000], 336–41). The book is hereafter referred to as Cranmer-Byng.

3 Aeneas Anderson, *A Narrative of the British Embassy to China, in the Years 1792, 1793, and 1794* (London: Debrett, 1795); George Staunton, *An Authentic Account of an Embassy to China from the King of Great Britain to the Emperor of China…Taken from the Papers of…the Earl of Macartney* 3 vols (London: Bulmer, 1797); John Barrow, *Travels in China: Containing Descriptions, Observations, and comparisons, made and collected in the Course of a Short Residence at the Imperial Palace of Yuen-Min-Yuen, and on a Subsequent Journey through*

While the name of the place went back and forth between 'Rehe' and the Confucian 'Chengde' for the next sixty years till it was finally decided on the latter by Qianlong in 1778, the Qing dynasty adhered to a location of the summer palace beyond the Great Wall of China. Though the location was unlikely as a place for the summer capital from the standpoint of Chinese dynasties, it was excellent, from the viewpoint of the Manchu who were invaders, as a meeting place of China, Manchuria, and Mongolia. The Qing dynasty's summer capital was constructed according to the same state-building policies of the non-Chinese dynasties, especially Yuan, founded by Kublai Khan; and it also realized, for the first time in Chinese history, the Chinese cultural landscape beyond the northern boundary of the Great Wall. Jehol was, in a sense, an eighteenth-century Manchurian/Chinese revival of Kublai's summer capital, the ruins of which Gerbillon saw at the end of the seventeenth century.

The first Briton to visit Kangxi's summer capital at Jehol was John Bell, a Scottish diplomat and merchant, who joined the Russian embassy to Isfahan and the first Russian envoy to perform the kowtow to the Chinese emperor.[1] Bell's *Travels from St. Petersburg in Russia to Diverse Parts of Asia* (1763), which must have been based on the detailed journals he kept during his travels, was remarkably accurate despite the long interval between his travels and the date of composition. In July 1719 Bell joined L. V. Ismailov's embassy to China, crossing the Urals, Siberia, and Mongolia, territory not previously described by a British writer, and arrived in Peking on 18 November 1720. On 18 August 1721, Bell was ordered to be escorted to 'Jegcholl' by a mandarin and some military officers.[2] On the following day he left Peking early in the morning, arriving in Jegcholl on August 21.[3]

---

the Country from Pekin to Canton (London: Cadell, 1804). William Wordsworth, *The Prelude* (1805), 8.123–24. References to Wordsworth's *The Prelude* are to *The Prelude 1799, 1805, 1850*, ed. Jonathan Wordsworth, M. H. Abrams, and Stephen Gill (New York: Norton, 1979).

1 Anthony Cross, *By the Banks of the Neva: Chapters form the Lives and Careers of the British* (Cambridge: Cambridge UP, 1997), 126–27.

2 John Bell, *Travels from St. Petersburg in Russia to Diverse Parts of Asia*, 2 vols, (Glasgow: Foulis, 1763), 2:214.

3 On September 3, Bell returned to Peking, 'being three days on the road' (2:326). It took two or three days from Peking to Jegcholl, just like Ciandu, which was

He was shown 'all the buildings and gardens of this charming place, which is certainly worthy to be the delight of so grand a monarch, and is infinitely superior, in beauty and magnificence, to the palace at Pekin or Czchanzchumnienne' (2:245).[1]

Bell's *Travels from St. Petersburg in Russia to Diverse Parts of Asia* was published in Glasgow four years after Johnson's *The History of Rasselas, Prince of Abissinia* and was warmly received. It was published again in Dublin in 1764, in Edinburgh in 1788 and 1806, translated into French and Russian, and last reprinted in volume 7 of Pinkerton's *Voyages and Travels*. Bell was so preoccupied with trade and mission that he did not seem to have thought about the historical and cultural aspects of 'Jegcholl' in relation to Kublai's summer palace. From the 1760s on, however, Bell's *Travels* showed to the British reading public an overland route different from Marco Polo's and traversed by a Briton fifty years ago, a ground route to the Qing Empire's capitals crossing Eurasia.

Between Bell and the Macartney embassy, though abortive, there were some attempts by the East India Company to go overland to the capital of China across the Himalayas as a way around the restrictions of Canton. In the 1760s, both the Company and China were concerned with the invasion by the Hindu Gurkhas of the Newar states, which were closely associated with Lhasa in terms of race and religion.[2] China monitored the Gurkha-Nepali situations carefully, as most of the Mongols in the Qing Empire were Lamanists, and Kangxi had established a protectorate over Tibet. The Company was disturbed by a sharp decline of the trade between Bengal and Tibet that they had just begun in order to redress the imbalance of the China trade. The Gurkhas, seeing the British military presence in the area, sent an embassy to the sixth Tashi Lama (Panchen Lama),[3]

'three days journey north-eastward' (Pinkerton, 103).

1 This is probably Yuanmingyuan before the renovation, known as the 'Old Summer Palace' in Europe.

2 For the relationship between British India and Tibet, I am indebted to Alastair Lamb, *British India and Tibet, 1766–1910*, rev. ed. (London: Routledge, 1985), hereafter referred to as *British India and Tibet*.

3 The Tashi Lama is second only to the Dalai Lama in spiritual authority in Tibetan Buddhism. The correct term is Panchen Lama, but Tashi is used in this paper because the British referred to this authority as 'the Tashi Lama' until the end of

who was respected both in Mongolia and China, and was much more influential than the Incarnation at Lhasa. The Tashi Lama wrote to Hastings, and the letter reached Calcutta in March 1774; Hastings took this chance to establish diplomatic contacts with Tibet (Lhasa), and decided to send a friendly mission to the Tashi Lama (*British India and Tibet* xii, 7).

In May 1774 George Bogle, a young Scot, was sent to 'the Teshu Lama' in order to 'open a mutual and equal communication of trade' between Tibet and Bengal, investigate the relations between Tibet and China, gather information about the countries between 'China and Kashmir,' and seek improvement in English trade and diplomacy with China.[1] In December 1774 Bogle reached Tashihumpo, the seat of the Tashi Lama, and subsequently remained in Tibet for five months. Bogle found that the incarnate head of Tibetan Buddhism had considerable influence on the Chinese emperors, who were 'of Tatar religion, of which the Lamas are the head' (Markham 207). A warm friendship Bogle established with the Tashi Lama led to the latter's promise that he would intermediate between the British and the Chinese court. The Tashi Lama, however, was well aware of the difficult situation in which Tibet found itself. He wrote to Hastings: 'this country…is under the absolute Sovereignty of the Emperor of China, who maintains an active and unrelaxed control over its all affairs, and as the forming of any connection or friendship with Foreign Powers is contrary to his pleasure, it will frequently be out of my power to dispatch any messengers to you.'[2] Still, the Tashi Lama tried to

---

the nineteenth century.

1 *Narratives of the Mission of George Bogle to Tibet and of Thomas Manning to Lhasa*, ed. C. R. Markham (London: Trübner, 1876), 5–8. Hereafter the book is referred to as Markham. For Bogle's mission, see Kate Telscher, *The High Road to China: George Bogle, the Panchen Lama and the First British Expedition to Tibet* (New York: Farrar, 2006).

2 *Bogle and Hamilton Letters, Journals and Memoranda*, ed. Alastair Lamb, vol. 1 of *Bhutan and Tibet: the Travels of George Bogle and Alexander Hamilton, 1774–1777* (Hertingfordbury: Roxford, 2002), 12 [in Bogle Papers Tashi Lama to Hastings, received 22 July 1775]. Hereafter the book is referred to as Lamb. Although Bogle's letters and travel reports were not published until 1876, Hastings approached Johnson regarding the possibility of publishing Bogle's mission to Tibet, sending a letter to Johnson with a copy of Bogle's journals and copies of some of the letters from the Tashi Lama (Lamb 346–47 [Extract from

acquire passports for Bogle when he at last decided to accept the repeated invitation from Qianlong to visit him in Peking (Markham 208). Bogle writes:

> I propose to write him that I shall prepare myself either to go by land over Tatary, if he thinks it possible to procure me passports, otherwise to go by sea to Canton in the full confidence of his sending me some person from himself to Canton with passports, so that I might get to Peking while the Lama is with the Emperor…. If I succeed in procuring passports, I shall then be a situation to urge any points at the Court of Peking with the greatest advantage. But even if I should be disappointed, I do not think it is possible for me to fail in procuring a channel of communication with the Court of Peking, and in finding some person stationed at Canton through whom representations can be made. (Markham 208—09)

Having made a series of attempts to reinforce the success of the first Bogle mission, in 1779, Hastings was ready to dispatch the second Bogle mission in order to send a British embassy to Peking by taking advantage of the relationship between the Tashi Lama and the Chinese emperor and a warm friendship between the Tashi Lama and Bogle. Bogle was instructed to 'endeavour by means of the Lamas of Tibet to open a communication with the Court of Peking, and, if possible, to procure leave to proceed thither.'[1] The mission, however, miscarried due to the Tashi Lama's departure for Peking and his unexpected death by smallpox in Peking in 1780. Thus Bogle's hope of 'one day or other getting a sight of Peking' was not realized (Markham 203).

One more plan to send an envoy from Bengal to Peking via Tibet was proposed in 1787 by Lieutenant Colonel Cathcart. Though the 'newly discovered communication thro' Thibet from Bengal' was considered 'too long and hazardous to be entered upon, as well as very doubtful in the result,'[2] Cathcart submitted an alternative plan

---

Warren Hastings to Dr. Samuel Jonson, Fort William, August 7, 1775]).

1 Lamb 13 [Home Miscellaneous, vol.219, f373; Bengal General Consultation of 19 April 1779].

2 Appendix B, 'Instructions to Lt. Col.Cathcart, Nov. 30th, 1787,' H. B. Morse, *The Chronicles of the East India Company Trading to China 1635–1834*, vol.2

that after reaching Peking by way of Canton he should send Captain Agnew home through Tibet (Lamb 7). The mission, however, failed due to the death of Cathcart on the voyage to China. Still, the overland Tibetan route to China haunted the British mind. On the way to Peking, Macartney, having been Governor of Madras and knowing Hastings's policy toward Tibet, considered seriously the overland route via Tibet as a possible means of communication; in March 1793, off the coast of Sumatra, in a letter to Henry Dundas, he mentioned that he had just asked Cornwallis, then Governor-General of India, to communicate with him 'not only by way of Canton but also by Tibet,' and proceeded to write: 'I propose to try that way also from Peking in order to let you know, if possible, the sooner of my arrival at the Capital, and what may be the likelihood of my success there.'[1]

At the time of writing this letter, however, Macartney was unaware of a radical change in the Nepali-Tibet situation that was to rule out the Tibetan route and jeopardize his own mission to China. In 1788 the authorities in Lhasa, remembering the promises of friendship from Hastings, asked the British for help against the Gurkhas, but Cornwallis did not respond properly.[2] In the second crisis in 1791, while the Gurkhas sought the Company's assistance, the authorities in Lhasa, both Tibetan and Chinese, requested British neutrality. Although the mediation of the Company was offered to both parties, there were enough grounds for suspicion that the British helped the Gurkhas against the Chinese and Tibetans (*British India and Tibet*, 20). Early in 1792, Qianlong sent a powerful force to Tibet, and decisively defeated the Gurkhas.

Little did Macartney know, when he was on the way to meet the emperor at Jehol, that the Chinese were very angry that the British had fought against them in the recent war in Nepal. He noted in his diary on 16 April 1793: 'I was very much startled with this intelli-

---

(1926: rpt. London: Routledge, 2000), 162.

1 Lamb 289 [Macartney to Dundas 25 March 1793, n. 45 CO/77/79 (a collection of miscellaneous letters relating to the Macartney Mission, preserved in the Public Records Office, London)].

2 Lamb, 289 n.47 [Home Miscellaneous, vol. 608, f.33; Bengal Consultation of 6 Jan. 1789 and 9 March 1789].

gence, but instantly told them that the thing was impossible and that I could take it upon me to contradict it in the most decisive manner.'[1] Staunton considered 'the viceroy of canton, [who] lately arrived at Zhe-hol from Tibet, where he had commanded the Chinese troops' as 'a declared enemy of the English,' expressing the standard view of the Embassy by his conditional language: if the Embassy intended for China in 1787 [the Cathcart mission] had reached the court of Peking, it 'would have probably prevented any misunderstanding' between Britain and China, and 'had any person from the King of Great Britain been accredited in China, in 1789 or 1790, by whose means the government of Bengal might have been requested to exert its influence, at an early period...the Emperor would have preferred such a method of attaining his purpose' (2:208, 209, 229, 230).

It cannot be denied that the failure of the Macartney embassy lies not in the British involvement with the Nepali-Tibet affairs but in the Chinese emperor's inability to form any diplomatic relations with foreign powers on terms of equality.[2] Even after the failure of the Macartney embassy, however, there were still some attempts to go across the Himalayas to Peking. Thomas Manning, an English scholar and friend of Charles Lamb, tried to explore the interior of China. Lamb wanted to dissuade his friend from cherishing the idea of visiting Independent Tartary. In a letter dated 19 February 1803, Lamb writes: ''Tis all the poet's *invention*. ...Read no more books of voyages (they are nothing but lies.)'[3] It may be too much to say that

1 John Barrow, *Some Account of the Public Life and a Selection of the Unpublished Writings of the Earl of Macartney*, 2 vols. (London: Cadell, 1807), 2:203—04.

2 See, for example, 'An Edict from the Emperor Ch'ien-Lung to King George the Third of England,' cited in Cranmer-Byng, 336–41.

3 *The Life, Letters, and Writings of Charles Lamb*, ed. Percy Fitzgerald, 7 vols., (London: Moxon, 1876; rpt. Freeport: Books for Libraries, 1971), 2:211. The 'poet' Lamb mentions here is Chaucer. Manning arrived in Canton in 1806, and having failed to enter China from Canton or Macao, and then from Cochin China, he made his way to Calcutta in 1810 with the aim of approaching China by way of the Himalayas and Tibet. Although unable to get through to China, Manning reached Lhasa in 1811, and met the Dalai Lama (Markham, clv–clxi, 213–94). Manning later joined Lord Amherst's Embassy as an interpreter, and proceeded to Peking (Henry Ellis, *Journal of the Proceedings of the Late Embassy of China: Comprising a Correct Narrative of the Public Transactions of the Embassy, of the Voyage to and from China, and of the Journey from the Mouth of the Pei-Ho to the Return of Canton* [London: Murray, 1817], 89, 93).

accounts on China are all poetic invention and lies, but Lamb's letter reminds us that indirect information and wild fantasy sneak into even eighteenth-century materials.

Visions and information, direct and indirect, past and present, are inseparably mixed even in the drawings and paintings by William Alexander, a member of the Royal Academy who accompanied the Macartney Embassy as a draftsman. Alexander provided many drawings for Staunton's *An Authentic Account of an Embassy from the King of Great Britain to the Emperor of China* (1797), which, taken chiefly from the papers of the Earl of Macartney, was considered as an official account of the Embassy to China, and consisted of two volumes with engravings and a third huge folio volume of forty-four plates. The frontispiece of the first volume features a portrait of Qianlong based on a drawing by Alexander, which, Staunton recollects in the main text, 'was made under unfavourable circumstances'; 'the person, dress, and manner, are perfectly like the original; but the features of the face, which were taken by stealth, and at a glance, bear a less strong resemblance' (1:233).[1] The 'unfavourable circumstances' were caused by the Chinese court's convention that only the court painters appointed by the emperor could paint the emperor, which was probably the reason that prevented both Alexander and Thomas Hickey, who joined the Embassy as 'painter,' from accompanying the ambassador to Jehol.[2] Alexander, however, was ordered to make drawings of the events and landscapes in Tartary in order to paint the historical moment of the meeting of the British ambassador and the Chinese emperor.

What was available to Alexander was verbal information from those who had witnessed the audience and the sketches and drawings made by Lieutenant Henry William Parish, who, in addition to commanding the twenty Royal Artillerymen escorting the ambassador, was

1 The portrait can be seen in the Eighteenth Century Collections Online (ECCO).

2 There was no record why the artists were not included in the members who went to Jehol, and Cranmer-Byng says that 'for some reason Macartney decided not to take his artists to Jehol' (314). Alexander kept a journal from which is known that those who remained in Peking included Hickey and Barrow (quoted in Cranmer-Byng 342).

required to make sketches. Alexander made use of Parish's sketch, 'Preparations for the Audience of Lord Macartney by the Emperor of China at Jehol,' and sketch map of the scene,[1] when he prepared plate 25 of the folio volume, 'The Approach of the Emperor of China to his Tent in Tartary to Receive the British Ambassador' (fig. 1).[2] The painting with the same title, which was based upon the engraving, has an inscription in Alexander's hand that reads: 'Emperor's arrival at the Tent in Vun shiu yuen or garden of 10,000 trees on the morning of the British Ambassador's introduction. From a drawing by Capt. Parish. Roy: Art' (Legouix 14).[3]

In representing important historical events or exotic landscapes before the invention of photography, painters and draftsmen tended to be faithful to reality as much as possible, or at least tried to reconstruct 'reality' from whatever they would have got from second-hand information, whether verbal or visual. It was not the case with some of Alexander's drawings and paintings. Like Marco Polo's stories or the narrator's in 'Kubla Khan,' Alexander's paintings are a complex mixture of vision and information, present and past. Plate 25 does not correspond to Parish's sketch that presents small circular tents on either side of the Imperial tent (Legouix 14). Nor does it match Staunton's description: 'Several small round tents were pitched in

1 Susan Legouix, *Image of China: William Alexander* (London: Jupiter, 1980), 14. They are preserved in volume 3 of the India Office Library collection.

2 I am grateful to the General Library of the University of Tokyo for permission to reproduce Alexander's engravings, 'The Approach of the Emperor of China to his Tent in Tartary to Receive the British Ambassador' (Plate 25) and 'A View of Poo-Ta-la or Great Temple near Zhe-hol in Tartary' (Plate 27 [fig.3]). I am also thankful to Mr. Yoshiaki Kimura in the Technical Support Section of the University of Tokyo for his technical assistance.

3 Alexander's plate can be also compared with 'Wan-shu Yuen: Pi-shu Shang-chang, in 1909' (fig.2). I am grateful to the Institute for Advanced Studies on Asia (former Institute of Oriental Culture) for permission to reproduce the photographs 'Wan-shu Yuen: Pi-shu Shang-chang, in 1909' (fig.2) and 'General View of P'u-t'o-tsung-cheng Miao, in 1909' (fig.4 upper) in Tadashi Sekino and Takuichi Takeshima, *Nekka:Explnation* [*Jehol: The Most Glorious and Monumental Relics in Manchukuo*] (Tokyo: Zaiho P and the Institute of Oriental Studies, 1937), 'General Views of P'u-t'o-tsung-cheng Miao' (fig.4 lower) and 'Rear Part of P'u-t'o-tsung-cheng Miao' (fig.5) in Tadashi Sekino and Takuichi Takeshima, eds., *Nekka* [*Jehol: The Most Glorious and Monumental Relics in Manchukuo*], 4 vols. (Tokyo: Zaiho P and the Institute of Oriental Studies, 1934).

Figure 1

Fig. 46 [illegible]

Figure 2

front, and one of an oblong form immediately behind, the latter was intended for the Emperor, in case he should choose to retire in from his throne'; one of the small tents was for the British embassy, while they were waiting for the arrival of the Emperor, and some of the other tents were for 'the several tributary princes of Tartary, and delegates from other tributary states, who were assembled at Zhe-hol on the occasion of the Emperor's birthday; and who attended, on this day, to grace the reception of the English Embassador' (1:225).

Alexander groups together one circular and one rectangular tent, the composition that is strongly reminiscent of the engraving based upon Giuseppe Castiglione's design of an earlier audience ceremony by the same emperor thirty years ago: 'The Emperor Giving a Victory Banquet in Peking to the Officers and Soldiers who Distinguished Themselves in Battle' (1770), executed by Jacque Philippe Le Bas in Paris (Legouix 15). The engraving is one of the sixteen-scene set of etchings, entitled *Conquests of the Emperor Ch'ien-lung*, and commemorates the Jüngar campaign, depicting the arrival of the emperor at a victory banquet in Peking in April 1760. Louis XV not only approved Qianlong's request to have his colonial campaigns represented in European line engraving in 1765, but also ordered the additional printing for himself, which suggests that he considered Qianlong's conquest of Central Asia as parallel to his own colonial project (Forêt 122–23). In 1772 the plates, together with two hundred impressions of each design, were sent to China. Although the emperor strictly ordered that no impressions should be left in Europe, a considerable number of impressions were distributed there,[1] and moreover, the smaller-scale set copied from the original was published in 1785 (Legouix 15). Alexander must have seen either an original set or a smaller-scale set. In seeking an effectively stage-managed framework in which to present an important historical moment in British history, Alexander does not employ much of the information obtained from verbal and visual descriptions of the English witnesses on the spot. Instead he borrows Castiglione's design, which captures the procession of the emperor turning toward the imperial tent. Unlike the ear-

1 Miyoko Nakano, *Roads to Xanadu* (in Japanese) (Tokyo: Seido, 2009), 145–46.

lier audience scene in which the Qing Empire's political and cultural triumph over conquered subjects is shown against the backdrop of the metropolitan residence garden, however, a huge but coarse imperial tent in the rural landscape in Alexander's engraving emphasizes the unsophisticated ethnicity of the Manchu dynasty.

Figure 3

Plate 27, 'A View of Poo-Ta-la or Great Temple near Zhe-hol in Tartary,' has an inscription in the lower left margin: 'drawn by W. Alexander from a Sketch by H. W. Parish' (fig.3).[1] The Potala temple at Jehol was modelled upon the real Potala (the seat for the Dalai Lama). Qianlong built it between 1767 and 1771 in order to respect Lamaist Buddhism and to symbolize the Manchu imperial claim over Tibet and Mongolia. Compared with the photographs of Potala taken and obtained by Sekino's research expedition (fig.4, fig.5),[2] it is obvious that Alexander's painting conflated Chinese, Mongolian,

1 Legouix compares Alexander's engraving with Parish's sketch (65).

2 Fig.4, which has two photographs with the upper one taken in 1909 and the lower one in 1934, and fig.5, which was taken in 1934, show the old Potala (Putuo Zongcheng Temple) before the Chinese government renovated much of the Qing's summer capital area including the temple. The Mountain Resort was listed as a UNESCO world heritage site in December 1994.

and Tibetan elements, adding decorative elements and placing lofty mountains in the background. This is typical of Alexander's romantic and exotic landscapes which hc visualized without ever seeing them.

Figure 4

Figure 5

4.

Was it possible to present a sublime vision of China in the 1790s? If so, how was it possible to do so by using the contemporary Qing emperor, Qianlong, who was known as a man of letters composing an incredibly large number of poems and enjoying personal relationships with Jesuit missionaries while Catholicism was officially forbidden, in whose long reign China's boundaries reached her greatest extent, encompassing Mongolia, Tibet, Nepal, and Taiwan, and who gave a cold reception to the Macartney embassy?

The creativity of the contemporary Chinese emperor was known in Europe when Father Amiot translated Qianlong's poem on tea into French in 1770,[1] and his prose translation was translated into English by Sir William Chambers. Chambers prefixes Amiot's transliteration of 'part of a poem written by Kien-long, reigning emperor of China, in praise of drinking tea' to *An Explanatory Discourse by Tan Chet-*

1 Jean Joseph Marie Amiot, *Éloge de la ville de Moukden et de ses environs; poeme composé par Kien Long. On y a joint une Pièce de vers sur le Thé compose par le même Empereur* (Paris: Tilliard, 1770).

Qua of Quang-cheu-fu, Gent., the appendix to the second edition of the *Dissertation on Oriental Gardening* (1773), and puts his translation from 'the French copy' in a footnote.[1] Chambers frames the explanation 'into a Discourse supposed to be pronounced by Chet-Qua, then in England' (113), but the name of the Chinese emperor, 'Kien-Long,' must have attracted considerable attention, as William Mason in *An Heroic Postscript* (1774) satirizes Chamber's translation: 'Did China's monarch here in Britain doze, / And was, like western kings, a King of Prose' (33—34).[2] After Lord Macartney's mission, however, the image of Qianlong started to be ridiculed and trivialized more cruelly. In 1792 Peter Pindar, who was immensely popular and regarded as 'redoubtable Peter' by Wordsworth in 1796,[3] published *Odes to Kien Long, the Present Emperor of China*, and in 1794, translated Qianlong's poem on tea into an ode in *Pindariana; or Peter's Portfolio*. Satire became more bitter in T. J. Mathias's *The Imperial Epistle from Kien Long, Emperor of China to George the Third, King of Great Britain ... in the year 1794. Translated into English Verse from the Original Chinese Poetry* (1795).

In the final years of the eighteenth century, it would have been very difficult to present a sublime vision of China associated with the aging Qianlong. In the summer or fall of 1797, when Coleridge retired to a farm house between Porlock and Linton and fell asleep over a copy of *Purchas His Pilgrimage* (as he claimed in the 1816 preface) or *Purchas His Pilgrimes*,[4] someone far back in history would have

1 *An Explanatory Discourse by Tan Chet-Qua of Quang-cheu-fu, Gent.* (London: Griffin, 1773; rpt. New York: AMS, 1993), 118–21.

2 William Mason, *An Heroic Postscript to the Public, Occasioned by Their Favourable Reception of a Late Heroic Epistle to Sir William Chambers, Knt, & c.* 4th ed. (London: Almon, 1794). Mason puts a footnote to 'King of Prose': 'Kien-Long, the present Emperor of China is a poet. M. de Voltaire did him the honour to treat him as a brother above two years ago. ...I am...vain enough to think, that the Emperor's composition would have appeared still better in my heroic verse' (8).

3 *Early Letters of William and Dorothy Wordsworth: 1787-1805*, ed. E. de Selincourt (Oxford: Clarendon, 1935), 156.

4 Lowes says that the 1617 folio of *Purchas His Pilgrimage* is one of Coleridge's favorite books, while Coleridge might have borrowed from Wordsworth the 1617 edition of *Perchas His Pilgrimes*, the third volume of which has a detailed account of Kubla Khan (48, 361). It is not certain which edition of the *Pilgrimage* Coleridge was reading before falling asleep nor whether recollec-

been called up from the book, from the Yuan summer palace. The ruins of the Mongol summer palace were located not far from the new summer capital of the Qing dynasty, Jehol, where, surrounded by lakes, rivers, springs, woods, and hills, Kangxi and Qianlong spent three or four months almost every year, leaving the Forbidden City and going beyond the Great Wall of China, and this was where Lord Macartney was received in audience. Although Coleridge would not have known, two days after the audience, Macartney was visited by 'a genteel young Tartar,' who had two names, Manchu and Chinese, and who told him that 'the present Emperor is descended from Co-be-li, or as we call him, Kublai Khan' (Cranmer-Byng 130). It would have been easy to superimpose Kublai's summer capital in the wilderness on the Qing dynasty's summer residence in Jehol. In Coleridge's case, 'that deep romantic Chasm' issues a mighty fountain, fusing Mongol, Manchu, Chinese, and English into a romantic vision, in a way similar to Alexander's engravings (*1797* 12). The vision receded into darkness with the visit of a person on business from Porlock, who might have been a messenger informing Coleridge of Britain's failed attempts to go overland to China.[1]

Comparing traditional accounts of Jehol in both Western and Chinese sources, the landscape of Coleridge's poem is remarkable in two respects. First is the second verse paragraph depicting a 'savage Place' (*1797* 14). It is true that the same mechanism of court gardens as a political tool worked in Louis XIV's Versailles and the Qing emperors' summer residence (Forêt 121—22), but the summer palace at Jehol is unique in the history of Chinese gardens, in its use of a 'savage' place, a huge mountainous district dotted with artificial palaces, temples, and lakes. Though what Forêt calls the 'Chengde Studies' from the eighteenth century on has not yet given a full picture of the Jehol residence (139—52), Coleridge's poem, together with Tadashi Sekino's view of Jehol, stands out in seeing the summer residence in its surrounding natural district. Sekino, who conducted a

tions of *Pilgrimes* were mixed with those of *Pilgrimage*. The famous passage of the Old Man of the Mountain in the *Pilgrimes*, which Lowes mentions (361) and in which Aloadine's pleasure house is described in a similar way to Kubla's summer place in the poem, does not evoke the image of Qianlong at all.

1 Suggested by Professor Matthew Schneider in a private conversation.

three-week research at Jehol and produced an extensive four-volume photographic survey entitled *Nekka* [*Jehol: The Most Glorious and Monumental Relics in Manchukuo*] in 1934, observes the quality of wholeness in the inclusion of human constructions inside natural landscape. Sekino admits an important aspect of the court garden shared by both China and Europe, the preference of 'artificiality' to 'the reproduction and preservation of natural beauty,' but emphasizes the fact that 'the Imperial Park in Jehol was so planned as to preserve the natural features, harmonizing them with artificial beauty,' arguing that though 'Yüan-ming-Yüan' is the 'only garden in China' comparable to 'the Jehol Park,' the former 'lacked in natural mountains,' was 'much smaller' in scale'; he concludes that ' The beauty of artificial hills and ponds of the Yüan-ming-Yüan might be superior to that of Jehol Park, but the harmonious combination of artificial and natural beauty of the one could not stand in comparison with the other' (*Nekka: Explanation* 14–15).

Coleridge appreciates this wholeness by connecting the first verse paragraph of Chinese courtly gardens and the second depicting a 'savage Place' that presents another kind of sublime from the first verse paragraph. Although Coleridge connects those two sections by an antithetical 'But,' they complement each other to form an organic whole, which is crystallized in the remarkable image at the end of the third verse paragraph, 'A sunny Pleasure-Dome with Caves of Ice!' (*1797* 12, 36).

The second section, presenting a sublime landscape of untamed nature, contains another element that has not been included in the traditional cultural geography of the frontier capital of the Qing dynasty: a woman. The political and cultural landscape of Jehol has not acknowledged women's presence, with male court officers, landscape painters, and priests surrounding male emperors and male visitors from other countries. The women of the Kangxi and Qianlong emperors, even if they accompanied the court into Jehol, were rarely heard or seen or depicted. On the other hand, Coleridge's poem presents two women, a 'Woman wailing for her Dæmon Lover' and 'an Abyssinian Maid,' whose vision can emulate the legendary Tartar tyrant's magnificent palace (1797 16, 39).

Both Macartney and Wordsworth seem to have comprehended the intrinsic wholeness of the Tartary frontier landscape. Macartney's view of the gardens in the summer palace is recorded in Barrow's *Travels in China*. Unlike Barrow who did not go to Jehol, Macartney was deeply impressed by 'the western garden,' one of the gardens that the Macartney embassy was specially invited to visit: 'If any place in England can be said in any respect to have similar features to the western park, which I have seen this day, it is Lowther Hall in Westmoreland,' which Macartney considers 'the finest scene in the British dominions' (90). In *The Prelude* (1805), the garden where Macartney had an audience with Qianlong is introduced as the 'paradise of ten thousand trees, / Of Gehol's famous gardens,' which was selected from 'widest empire, for delight /Of the Tartarian dynasty' and built 'Beyond that mighty wall' of China (8.122–23, 125–26, 127). Wordsworth specifically mentions that this oriental 'paradise' is set in a wilderness far beyond the protection of the Great Wall of China, the symbol of Chinese civilization, and declares that his paradise, where he 'was reared,' is 'lovelier far than this paradise' (8.145). Wordsworth's lines are a poetic response not only to Coleridge's poem, but also to Macartney's comment on Qianlong's garden in Jehol. Wordsworth rejects both Coleridge's view and Macartney's comparison.

In 1815 Shelley was composing 'Alastor' without knowing Coleridge's 'Kubla Khan.' In the poem, a solitary 'Poet' travels overland to Ethiopia, where he is assisted by an 'Arab maiden' but does not gain a vision he wants; he then proceeds to go across Central Asia to Kashmir, where in a 'vision,' he meets a 'veiled maid' who rejects him and disappears (50, 129, 149, 151). The narrator in 'Kubla Khan' at least saw that 'sunny Dome! Those Caves of Ice!' in a vision (*1797* 47), but the unnamed Poet in 'Alastor' wanders frantically in search of the lost vision in Central Asia, where no Briton had ever been, and dies unfulfilled, not being able to go beyond Kashmir. In January of 1816, the year when the Amherst embassy failed, Shelley's *Alastor; or the Spirit of Solitude; and Other Poems* appeared, and in May Coleridge's 'Kubla Khan' was published for the first time in *Christabel; Kubla Khan: A Vision; The Pains of Sleep*. With the subtitle and a long preface, the poem, which was about the poet's creativity that may surpass the Asian tyrant's creativity in 1797, looked more like a poem about the poet's creative failure.

Saeko Yoshikawa

Wordsworth in the Guides

Introduction

Wordsworth's public reputation was well-established by the late 1830s. Stephen Gill tells us that 'for the first time in English history a writer's home had become a place of general pilgrimage while its saintly incumbent was still alive'.[1] How did this 'Wordsworth pilgrimage' relate to the wider history of Lake District tourism? And how and when did Rydal Mount become a tourist attraction? Lake District tourism had begun in the late eighteenth century as a quest for the picturesque, but in the nineteenth century this was gradually replaced by interest in literary associations. In this change Wordsworth played an important role, while concurrently the reputation of Wordsworth and Rydal Mount was influenced by the main stream of Lake District tourism. By tracing representations of Wordsworth and Rydal Mount in guide-books to the Lake District, my article will consider the reciprocal relationship between the popular reception of Wordsworth and the changing style of Lake District tourism in the first half of the nineteenth century.

1. The First Appearance of Wordsworth in the Guides

It was around 1820 that Wordsworth began to appear extensively in the guides, apparently owing to the publication of *The Excursion* in 1814.[2] Although it suffered severe reviews, and although sales of the

1 Stephen Gill, *Wordsworth and the Victorians* (Oxford: Clarendon, 1998), 11.
2 David Higgins points out that 'the growing interest in Wordsworth around 1820 is apparent not only in reviews of his new volumes, but also in the appearance of a number of articles that offered general assessments of his work

expensive first edition were slow,[1] *The Excursion* was well-esteemed in the public sphere and parts of the poem were widely read through extracts in reviews.[2] As the poem was set in the Lake District, and was rich in description of Lake scenery, it was quite natural that *The Excursion* was also referenced in guide-books. As early as 1816 we find this comment in Thomas Hartwell Horne's *The Lakes of Lancashire, Westmorland, and Cumberland*:

> ... we passed, on our left, Rydal Mount, the residence of the admired author of The Excursion, who has happily described, in some of his poems, the peculiar beauties of the neighbouring Lake and mountain scenery. (27)

This is the first mention of Rydal Mount in a guide to the Lake District, and Wordsworth is introduced as the author of *The Excursion.* Horne quotes passages from the poem to describe Grasmere and the church, boating on Windermere, the church at Bowness, the sparkling waves on the agitated water, and so on. He has a flair for quoting beautiful lines from Wordsworth fit for his own accounts of the scenery, cultivating a new way of using Wordsworth to describe Lake District scenery, as well as attracting new readers of *The Excursion.*[3]

Horne was followed by John Robinson's *Guide to the Lakes, in Cumberland, Westmorland, and Lancashire* (1819) and T. H. Fielding and John Walton's *A Picturesque Tour of The English Lakes* (1821),

and "genius"'. See *Romantic Genius and the Literary Magazine: Biography, celebrity, politics* (London: Routledge, 2005), 92. This is also apparent in the appearance of many guide-books drawing on Wordsworth around 1820 and onwards.

1 Of the first 500 copies, 120 remained unsold in 1819, when Robinson's guide was published. See W. J. B. Owen, 'Costs, Sales, and Profits of Longman's Editions of Wordsworth' (*Library 5th series*. 12 (1957): 93–107), 97.

2 Within the first five years of its publication in 1814, *The Excursion* was reviewed in 17 periodicals, of which only two or three were completely unfavourable. Most reviews include extracts from the poem. Even those who could not afford to buy the expensive volume could enjoy some extracts in these reviews. See Dan Kenneth Crosby, 'Wordsworth's *Excursion*: An Annotated Bibliography of Criticism' (*Bulletin of Bibliography*, 48.1(1991): 33–49. Generally speaking, *The Excursion* was received positively. See William S. Ward, 'Wordsworth, the "Lake" Poets, and their Contemporary Magazine Critics 1798-1820", *Studies in Philology* 42 (1945): 87–113.

3 I have revised this part of my paper since the conference presentation. I am grateful to Professor Tomoya Oda for the Thomas Hartwell Horne reference.

which not only introduced Rydal Mount as the residence of the author of *The Excursion*, but also extended the range of quotation from Wordsworth beyond this poem to include 'To Joanna' in describing Helm Crag and the effect of mountain echoes, 'The Brothers' for Ennerdale, 'Fidelity' in writing of Helvellyn, and 'The Idle Shepherd Boy' for Dungeon Ghyll. Robinson and Fielding's association of these poetic descriptions with the actual landscape is not necessarily based on precise research. Their purpose was not to locate the settings of Wordsworth's poems, but to capture 'the peculiar beauties of the lake and mountain scenery'.

Robinson was also the first to refer to Hawkshead Grammar School where Wordsworth was educated. When we consider that earlier biographical references to Wordsworth can be found only in Coleridge's *Biographia Literaria* (1817) and a brief note in *A Biographical Dictionary of Living Authors of Great Britain and Ireland* (1816), it is remarkable that Wordsworth's school at Hawkshead was pointed out in general tourist guide-books as early as 1819.[1]

Wordsworth was, however, not the main figure in these three guides. Containing several quotations from Hutchinson, Gilpin and Radcliffe, they were chiefly intended for picturesque travellers. Writings of the so-called 'Lake School' were not yet the trend.

2. Rydal Mount and its Gardens as Tourist Attractions

Rydal Mount attracted tourists in ever greater numbers in the 1820s and 1830s,[2] as references to the house and the poet increased in various publications. Particularly significant among these was a poem by Maria Jane Jewsbury, a close friend of the Wordsworth family from 1825.[3] In summer that year she was invited to stay at Rydal

1 See Walter E. Swayze, 'Early Wordsworthian Biography', *Bulletin of the New York Public Library* 64 (April 1960): 169–195.

2 Stephen Gill finds in Sarah Hutchinson's letter to her sister Mary Wordsworth, 16 August 1820, a reference to a gentleman who visited Rydal Mount 'in veneration of Wm.' to ask if he could 'see the Study'. Gill comments that this gentleman was 'the bell-wether to what became a considerable flock of pilgrims who for the next thirty years trod the path to Rydal Mount'. See *William Wordsworth: A Life* (Oxford: Oxford UP, 1989), 348.

3 Maria J. Jewsbury, an admirer of Wordsworth, sent him a fervent letter in May 1825 with a volume of her poems, *Phantasmagoria*, dedicated to him. From that

Mount, and wrote her impressions of the house and gardens in 'A Poet's Home':

> Low, and white, yet scarcely seen
> Are its walls, for mantling green;
> Not a window lets in light,
> But through flowers clustering bright;
> Not a glance may wander there
> But it falls on something fair: —
> Garden choice, and faery mound,
> Only that no elves are found;
> Winding walk, and sheltered nook,
> For student grave, and graver book;
> Or a bird-like bower, perchance,
> Fit for maiden and romance. (15–26)

First published in *The Literary Magnet* in 1826, this poem was to be widely quoted in guide-books, biographical writings, and literary magazines.[1] It helped to create a popular image of the poet's house as a 'green-mantled' habitation with exquisite gardens. Following this poem several others by female poets describing Rydal Mount and gardens were to appear in the 1820s and 30s.[2] These poems, circulating widely, encouraged new waves of tourists to glimpse Rydal Mount from the road or even to try a visit.

Edward Baines could have been one such tourist. In the summer of 1828 he visited Rydal Mount with a friend from Ambleside who knew Wordsworth. Unfortunately the poet himself was away, but the family welcomed them.[3] He recorded this visit in his guide, *A Companion to*

---

time until her untimely death in 1833, she was a close friend of Wordsworth and his daughter, Dora. On 23 May 1825 she visited Rydal Mount for the first time, and in July she was invited to stay with them for ten days.

1 For example, *The Athenaeum* (1826), *Memoir of the life and Writings of Mrs. Hemans* (1839), *Visitor* (1848), George Mogridge's *Loitering Among the Lakes* (1849), *Black's Picturesque Guide* (1850 and onwards), Christopher Wordsworth's *Memoirs* (1851), *Hudson's Complete Guide* (1853 and onwards), David Richardson's *Flower and Flower Garden* (1855) are among them.

2 Felicia Hemans's 'To the Author of the Excursion and the Lyrical Ballads' (1826), L. E. Landon's 'The Residence of Wordsworth' (1838), Lydia Sigourney's 'Grassmere and Rydal Water' (1841) are among them.

3 Wordsworth, with his daughter Dora and S. T. Coleridge had set out for the

the Lakes of Cumberland, Westmoreland, and Lancashire (1829):

> [Wordsworth's] youngest son accompanied us into the gardens in front of the house, which command two distinct views, each of them amongst the most delicious at the Lakes. ... I was informed that the walk which commands this prospect was constructed by Mr. Wordsworth himself and his sons. (266)

This passage not only informs readers that the gardens command 'delicious' views. It also suggests that tourists may be welcomed by Wordsworth and his family in the gardens of their own making. Later travelogues and guide-books followed the convention of praising the prospects from Rydal Mount, as if the gardens offered new picturesque 'stations' replacing those recommended on the established routes. And visitors were alerted to a garden tour conducted by the poet or his family.

Baines offered his account as personal experience, while *Leigh's Guide to the Lakes and Mountains of Cumberland, Westmoreland, and Lancashire* (1830) informed readers, seemingly more objectively, that Rydal Mount was open to the public:

> Rydal Mount, the residence of Mr. Wordsworth, the celebrated author of "The Excursion," and other poems ... is delightfully situated, commanding prospects of Windermere and Rydal Lakes. The grounds are laid out with great taste. Strangers may obtain permission to go on the mount in front of the house, from which there is a charming view. (43)

The guide-book recommends Wordsworth's residence as an attraction for 'strangers', with all the appearance of authority. Permission may be obtained. Written anonymously, *Leigh's Guide* tried to keep a neutral voice, giving the impression that its information and descriptions were objective and precise. A pocket-sized practical guide, it sold well and went through four editions by 1840, doing much to make Rydal Mount popular as a tourist destination in the 1830s. One such tourist was recorded in Edward Quillinan's diary in 1836, trying to snatch a sprig of laurel from the gardens (Gill [1998] 10). Originally

---

Continent on 22 June, and although back in London on 6 August, he did not come back to Rydal Mount until 27 August.

praised as a 'station' from which to enjoy spectacular views, as years passed, Rydal Mount gradually attracted visitors because of its gardens made by the poet.

And as Rydal Mount became a popular tourist destination, quotations from Wordsworth's poems became standard in more and more guide-books. Writers and compilers vied with one another to find fresh extracts from *The Excursion* and other poems to accompany their accounts of places in the Lake District. Along with Wordsworth, other Lake writers like Scott, Southey, Coleridge, De Quincey and John Wilson also began to be cited.[1] From the 1830s onwards, interest in literary associations consistently accompanied the more familiar picturesque attractions.

3. Literary Associations of the Lake District

A touristic fashion of searching for Wordsworthian associations in the Lakes became more evident in the 1840s. There were three factors that contributed to the emergence of this 'Wordsworthian tourism'. First, the poet's own *Guide to the Lakes*, since its 1820 edition, had been often referenced and quoted in guide-books and travel-articles in magazines, with the final version published in 1835. The *Guide* was popular, quoted extensively, and regarded as authoritative.[2] Although not completely exempt from the influence of the picturesque,[3] Wordsworth's *Guide* was influential in creating a new mode of tourism in the Lake District. Trying to appeal less to the eye of the reader than to their mind, Wordsworth offered his own poetic descriptions of scenery. Following this, other guide-books

1 Scott and Southey appeared earlier than the rest. Felicia Hemans and Harriet Martineau were to be added to the list later.

2 The 500 copies of 1822 edition were sold within a year, and the next edition appeared in 1823 which sold 1000 copies (Owen 103). William Ford, in *A Description of Scenery in the Lake District* (1839), expressed his obligation to Wordsworth's *Guide*, and Mackay in *The Scenery and Poetry of the English Lakes* (1846) deemed it 'the most approved of all'. Editions of *Hudson's Complete Guide to the Lakes* (1842–1864), comprised of Wordsworth's *Guide* along with lots more quotations from his poems and Sedgwick's essays on geology, were also used by tourists and guide-book writers.

3 See for instance, J. B. Nabholtz, 'Wordsworth's *Guide to the Lakes* and the Picturesque Tradition', *Modern Philology* 61 (1964): 288–97.

began to use literature more than painting as a guide for directing the tourist where to go, what to see, and how to appreciate it.[1] Yet more quotations from Wordsworth, both from his poems and guide-book, appeared as a consequence.

The publication of *Yarrow Revisited and Other Poems* in 1835 was another factor that encouraged new waves of 'Wordsworthian tourism'. This volume enjoyed a good sale,[2] and in *Allison's Northern Tourist's Guide* in 1837, Rydal Mount was introduced as 'the seat of W. Wordsworth, Esq. the admired author of "Yarrow Revisited," a sweet volume'.[3] *Yarrow Revisited* included poems set in the Lake District, rich in description of local scenes, affording more material to be extracted in guide-books. Two poems set in Cockermouth offered fresh biographical information about Wordsworth himself. Hence 1837 saw the first mention to Cockermouth as Wordsworth's birth-place in a tourist guide. Although the Wordsworth House at Cockermouth would have to wait another thirty years to become a tourist destination, it is remarkable that it was mentioned in a general guide-book as early as 1837.

The third, and probably the most important, event in the 1830s was the appearance of De Quincey's articles, 'Lake Reminiscences, 1807–1830' in *Tait's Edinburgh Magazine* (January 1839 to October 1840). These decisively encouraged interest in 'Wordsworth as a resident in the Lake District'. De Quincey gave a gossipy account of Wordsworth's poetic life, associated with the Lake scenery, and *Black's Picturesque Guide to the English Lakes* (1841) immediately adopted these new materials provided by De Quincey.

First published in 1841, *Black's Guide* was popular and went through more than twenty editions, constantly revised and up-dated, during the nineteenth century. In spite of its title, *Black's Picturesque Guide* places more emphasis on literature. It was the first guide to the Lake District that deliberately foregrounded literary associations, and especially Wordsworthian associations of the Lake District. Almost

1 See Ian Ousby, *The Englishman's England* (London: Pimlico, 2002), 140–43.

2 The first 1500 copies were sold within a year, and additional 500 copies were printed in the same year (Owen 105).

3 *Allison's Northern Tourist's Guide to the Lakes, of Cumberland, Westmorland, and Lancashire*, 7th edition (1837), 136.

all the chapters quote from Wordsworth. Lines from *The Waggoner* (1819) were quoted for the first time to describe Helm Crag's peculiar crests, likened to an 'ancient woman' and 'astrologer', and these lines remained a popular quotation in later guide-books along with references to the 'Famous Swan'. From 'An Evening Walk' came the lines that describe the Rydal Waterfalls. 'The Yew-Trees' were cited for the famous yews in Borrowdale and Lorton Vale. 'The Wishing-Gate', 'There was a boy' and many new poems from *Yarrow Revisited* also made their first appearance in *Black's Guide.* Later guide-books recycled many of the quotations to which *Black's* first gave currency. If Lake District places had inspired Wordsworth's poems, the poems were now being assiduously mapped back onto the landscape.

Widening the range of quotation from Wordsworth was not the only unique point of *Black's Guide.* Apart from Rydal Mount, previous guides had made little reference to biographical information about the poet. Drawing on De Quincey's articles, *Black's* provided biographical and anecdotal accounts of Wordsworth's life to arouse the curiosity of tourists, and encouraged them to view and visit his houses at Rydal and Grasmere.

Today Dove Cottage is an indispensable tourist destination for Wordsworth's admirers and also for all kinds of tourists to the Lake District. But in Wordsworth's time it was little known until De Quincey's 1839 article gave a description of it. *Black's Guide* took it up:

> To this cottage at Town End, which is now partially hidden from those on the highway, by the intervention of some later built cottages, Wordsworth brought his bride in 1802. Previous to his departure to fetch her, he composed his Farewell, in which these lines occur, —
>
> 'Farewell, thou little nook of mountain ground,
> Thou rocky corner in the lowest stair
> Of that magnificent Temple, which doth bound
> One side of our whole vale with grandeur rare;
> Sweet garden-orchard, eminently fair,
> The loveliest spot that man hath ever found!' ([1841] 20 f)

Intriguingly, *Black's Guide* focuses on the alluring line, 'The loveliest spot that man hath ever found', now used as a catchphrase by the Wordsworth Trust Website to attract web browsers and, hopefully, visitors.[1]

Cockermouth and Hawkshead were also introduced in *Black's Guide*. Although Hawkshead had been mentioned in earlier guides because of the famous grammar school, and Wordsworth's attendance noted, it was again De Quincey's article that drew wide attention to the remote market town. Consulting the article, *Black's Guide* gives this succinct yet intriguing description:

> Hawkshead is a small but ancient market-town at the head of the valley of Esthwaite. … St. Michael's Church, a structure of great antiquity, is placed on a rocky eminence immediately over the town, commanding fine views of the adjacent country.
>
> '… the grassy churchyard hangs
> Upon a slope above the village school.' ([1841] 118)

This is the first quotation from 'There was a boy' in any of the guides. Then, after referring to Wordsworth's school, the guide remarks that 'allusion is frequently made to "The antique market-village, where were passed / My school days"', quoting here from Book One of *The Excursion*, though without citing the source. These quotations, along with that from 'Farewell' for Dove Cottage, suggest that the anonymous compiler of *Black's Guide* was well-informed about Wordsworth's poems, his biography, and the topography of the District.

The introduction to *Black's Guide* emphasizes that it is intended as a companion for touring and for subsequent recollection—a notably Wordsworthian formula:

> In directing the steps of the tourist we have … availed ourselves to a considerable extent of the literature of the district … These quotations … will not only contribute to elevate the feelings and improve the heart, while the reader is contemplating the scenes

1 In the following editions of *Black's Guide* (from 1844 onwards) only the title 'Farewell' was mentioned without quoting any line from the poem. The citation of the poem was to be retrieved in *Black's Shilling Guide to the English Lakes* (1853).

> which are portrayed, but will also form a spell by which, in coming years, he may recall the pleasures of the past, and revisit, in imagination, the scenery over which we are now about to conduct him. ([1841] 3)

Recollection in tranquillity—here we see in almost every sentence how Wordsworth's poetic vision shaped the way visitors now encountered and remembered landscape. It has often been claimed that Wordsworth informed modern attitudes to the natural world and the environment. Equally important, I would like to suggest, was the mediating role of the guides in conveying Wordsworth's poems and his vision to a wide public. *Black's Guide* served as a guide to literature of the Lakes and a guide to the Wordsworthian way of enjoying the natural world.

4. Literary Tourism and the Railway

Charles Mackay was an enthusiastic literary traveller, whose love for the 'Lake Poets' led him to the Lakes in summer 1845. For him, the Lake scenery was evocative before he actually visited, already known and loved in the works of poets and other writers. His purpose was to trace the footsteps of Wordsworth, Southey and Coleridge. His guide-book, *The Scenery and Poetry of the English Lakes* (1846), recording his impressions of this tour, is offered particularly to 'the lover of poetry' and 'the admirer of nature' who can now travel more easily by steam boats and trains. As the title of the book suggests, this is a guide not only to the Lake scenery but also to the poetry of the 'Lake School' on which he gives extensive comments.

Mackay visited Rydal Mount, now firmly established as a tourist's attraction, with a letter of introduction. Following the usual routine, he admired the views of Windermere and Rydal Water from the gardens. As the engraved illustration of Rydal Mount shows, however, the focus of interest has now fundamentally altered from landscape prospect to the poet's domestic life. The engraving offers an idealized image of the house embraced by hills and trees, with three figures in the foreground on the spacious lawn of the mount: two women and a man standing as if in conversation. There are also two smaller figures in the background, near the house. The impression is that Rydal Mount is a sociable space where people gather together, converse and enjoy the gardens—the first 'Wordsworth conference'! Mackay portrays himself as a literary enthusiast, recounting his two hours' conversation with Wordsworth, 'upon poets, poetry, criticism, hill-climbing, autograph-hunting, on Southey, and various other matters'(42). Conversation with the poet-laureate is now a possible attraction; Mackay remarks on another 'enthusiast in literature, who, like [himself], [has] come to pay his respects to the bard' (44). And his book invites others to join them.

During his conversation with Wordsworth, Mackay was recommended to follow a foot-road, the so-called coffin-path, passing behind Rydal Mount to Grasmere as 'very favourable to views of the lake and the vale, looking back towards Ambleside' (21). The horse-road along the western side of Rydal Water, under Loughrigg Fell, was also recommended by Wordsworth as exhibiting 'beauties in this small mere of which the traveller who keeps the high road is not at all aware' (21–22). So the poet-in-residence in the Lakes, now the poet-laureate of England, dispensed authoritative advice to the tourists he had attracted, complementing the taste for landscape he had him-

RYDAL MOUNT.

self created. On one occasion, in trying to find the 'Wishing Gate', Mackay bought a new copy of Wordsworth's *Guide to the Lakes*[1] at Ambleside to help him locate it. That Wordsworth's *Guide* was actually marketed to and on sale for tourists in Ambleside is a highly significant indicator of its influence.

As Mackay predicted, when the Kendal-Windermere railway opened in 1847 more and more tourists began to flow into the Lake District. Responding to the new mode of travelling, several new guide-books appeared in the late 1840s. These were pitched for the new waves of tourists, enabled to come here by railways. Of these not a few seem to have been, like Mackay, literary tourists eager to visit those places consecrated by the Lake Poets' writings. The introduction to *Sylvan's Pictorial Handbook* (1847) remarks:

> Independently of the natural beauty of the English Lake district, it has associations which will ever make it hallowed ground. … Southey and Wordsworth, Coleridge and Shelley, Professor Wilson and De Quincey, Wilberforce, Mrs. Hemans, and, last but not least, Harriet Martineau, all of whom by their writings have illustrated the beauty of the scenes with which they were so intimately connected, and which, for years to come, will cause thousands of votaries to make pilgrimages to their shrines. (2)

Although Wordsworth expressed misgivings about inundations of tourists brought by rail,[2] the fact was that the packed trains carried many literary pilgrims and so-called 'votaries' of the poet himself. William Howitt comments on the coincidence of the opening of the railways and the growing interest in natural beauty and poetry:

> It is curious that steam, mechanism, and poetry, should have been brought simultaneously to bear in so extraordinary a degree on the public spirit and character. The love of poetry and nature, of picturesque scenery and summer-wandering, no sooner were generated … than lo! steamers appeared at the quays, and rail-

1 This is Hudson's adapted edition, *A Complete Guide to the Lakes* (1842 or 1843), where reference to the 'Wishing Gate' is added.

2 See his two sonnets on the projected Kendal and Windermere Railway: 'Is then no nook of English ground secure' and 'Proud were ye, Mountains, when, in times of old'.

> roads projected their iron lines over hill and dale.[1]

The opening of the railway extended the range of travel. Up to now Furness Abbey had not been so popular among the tourists, but since a railway station was built close to the abbey it became a great object of attraction.[2] Wordsworth's new sonnets on the abbey published in 1845 promptly appeared in the guides. The river Duddon was also now more accessible. Travellers could get off the train at Broughton-in-Furness and then walk up the river toward Ulpha and Seathwaite. Accordingly, Wordsworth's Duddon Sonnets, published twenty some years before, began to be quoted extensively in the guides.[3]

For these lovers of poetry and nature, *Sylvan's Pictorial Handbook* was packed with literary quotations and illustrations:

> The increasing demand for illustrated guide books to aid the tourist in his rambles, together with the increased facilities of railway communication, has suggested a want which the present work is intended to supply; ... The object therefore of the present "Pictorial Hand-Book" has been as far as possible to give a pleasant gossiping account of all the objects worthy attention on the routes ... with such pictorial representations of them as shall place the volume on a level with the demand of the age for cheap illustrated literature; (1–2)

As Wordsworth feared, the railway initiated the age of mass-tourism; they came to Windermere by train, from where they enjoyed rambling with one illustrated guide or another. Helped by the illustrations, literary 'votaries' could easily find the shrines they sought: Dove's Nest—the house of Mrs. Hemans, Southey's Greta Hall, and Wordsworth's Rydal Mount; and places hallowed by poetry: Furness Abbey, Langdale Pikes, the Bowder Stone, Dungeon Ghyll, Airey Force and Lodore Waterfall. Literary tourism in the Lake District was now well-underway.

1 William Howitt, *Visits to Remarkable Places: Old Halls, Battle Fields, and Scenes Illustrative of Striking Passages in English History and Poetry* (1840), 203–204.

2 *The Church of England Magazine* 16 (1844): 353.

3 Although Wordsworth's Duddon sonnets were mentioned in *Allison's* (1837) and *Black's* (1841), it was in Mackay (1846) that some lines from the sonnets were quoted for the first time in a guide.

Conclusion

By the mid-nineteenth century a 'station' meant the platform at which one stepped down from a railway carriage and entered the Wordsworth Country. No longer seeing with Gilpin's picturesque eye, tourists were now more familiar with the Lake scenery as it was seen by Wordsworth in the guides. Mass tourism, and especially Wordsworthian tourism, was a flourishing local industry. After Wordsworth's death in April 1850, the road between Rydal Mount and the poet's grave at Grasmere became a major route for literary pilgrims. It would not be long before Dove Cottage opened its doors to tourists, making its own mark in the modern Lake District guides that Wordsworth, we can now see, had himself done so much to invent.

Daniel Robinson

Mary Robinson and the Della Crusca Network

When Mary Robinson returned from her self-imposed continental exile at the beginning of 1788, the poetry of the *World* was all the rage. The sensational and fictional poetic romance between Della Crusca and Anna Matilda, carried on in the columns of John Bell's innovative newspaper the *World*, was at the height of its popularity, with readers speculating feverishly on the identities of the two rhapsodic poets, who eventually turned out to be Robert Merry and Hannah Cowley. This exchange gave Robinson a context in which to begin her career as a professional writer, particularly as it established the kind of poet she was going to be—an exuberant and formally innovative (if not always profound) virtuosa. For Robinson, as for the so-called Della Cruscans, style is substance. And throughout her poetic career, from 1788 to her death in 1800, Robinson never shakes this influence.

Robinson's sojourn had been partly for convalescence and partly to escape her creditors and the infamy of the gossip pages. Years before, Robinson had been a successful actress but had achieved celebrity primarily as the mistress of the young Prince of Wales. She caught his attention playing the role of Perdita in Garrick's adaptation of *The Winter's Tale* and forever would be known as Perdita—literally, 'the lost one'—but obviously with an entirely different connotation than in Shakespeare's play. Now, back in England, in poor health and dire straits, disgraced and humiliated by the fashionable set that considered her a washed up celebrity prostitute, Robinson was in serious need of a profession—and not the oldest one. Preoccupied—obsessed even—as her poetry would be with literary fame, Robinson could not resist Bell's promise 'to transmit to Posterity all the POETRY which shall hereafter appear in the WORLD' (2: 144).[1] Robinson was willing to work for her poetic immortality as a professional writer, even if she had to start by earning pennies contributing newspaper verse.

The most important choice of Robinson's literary career is her participation in the professional network around Bell. When Robinson returned to London, the success of this network already had been established with the popularity of Della Crusca's poetry. I call this network, therefore, the Della Crusca network because Merry's pseudonym was its public avatar. The Della Crusca network afforded Robinson a crucial opportunity for exchanging her previous celebrity for poetic fame. In October, inspired by the success of Bell's anthology, Robinson published her poem 'Lines Dedicated to the Memory of a Much-Lamented Young Gentleman,' her first publication in over a decade. Signing the poem 'Laura', with deliberate Petrarchan resonance, Robinson made her first serious foray onto the literary scene and began to re-appropriate and proliferate versions of her public self, displacing her past as actress and courtesan, while also envisioning other possible contexts for her poetic identity. Merry provided her a model for doing so: after a few years abroad, he had repatriated himself in the newspaper as Della Crusca and had become famous. Merry's success showed Robinson how to parlay form into fame—which is the subject of the book I have just finished writing for Marilyn Gaull's series at Palgrave Macmillan.

My book, entitled *The Poetry of Mary Robinson: Form and Fame*, examines how Robinson formalizes her self-representations in specific instances of self-conscious poetic virtuosity. I also highlight Robinson's maneuverings, her affiliations, and her opportunism figured around her associations with Merry and Coleridge as poetic bookends, but also with publishers Bell and Daniel Stuart as professional ones. I am particularly interested in Robinson's use of pseudonyms, which I call avatars because they are neither characters nor costumes nor disguises but, rather, versionings of her poetic identity. What makes Robinson's avatars unique is the way she continued to use them to proliferate various refractions of her professional self even after she publicly claimed them.

1 *The Poetry of the World*, 2 vols (London: John Bell), 2, 144.

The much maligned Della Cruscans partly were responsible for the 'gaudiness and inane phraseology of many modern writers' (to quote a familiar writer). Intertextual and self-conscious, this poetry is also profoundly ludic (if I may be oxymoronic) in a way that it is not usually given credit for being. I propose thinking of the Della Cruscans not as a coterie of pretentious poets, as most people consider them to be, nor of 'Della Cruscan' as a 'school of poetry', as many contemporary detractors feared it was to become; but, rather, as a network of writers, signatures, texts, intertexts, and media. Moreover, crucial to the idea of this network is the space in which it exists and the medium through which it proliferates: originally, for the Della Cruscans this is the newspaper, a kind of textual heterotopia where different actors—the writers and the poems themselves—cross temporal, textual, and aesthetic boundaries. We should read Della Cruscan poetry, then, in its original context, as the work of social actors networking with one another. As poets such as Southey, Coleridge, and Wordsworth also understood, newspaper poetry served a purpose much like that of the comics section in today's newspapers. These poems are meant to be amusingly consumable and literally disposable.

At the beginning of the Della Crusca–Anna Matilda phenomenon, Bell was central to this network because he provided the media: his editors, chief among them his partner Edward Topham, selected and printed the poems in the newspaper, collected and re-published them in handsome anthologies, with Bell ultimately offering solo book deals to those writers—Merry, Cowley, Robinson—who proved to be the most popular. So, from a professional point of view, Robinson's publishing with Bell during 1788–1792 is networking in today's sense. Bell would go on to publish Robinson's poetry in the *World*, in the *Oracle*, and in four editions of his anthology of Della Cruscan verse, *The British Album*. Bell also would publish four books of her poetry as well as her first best-selling novel. Although she made little money from these books, these publications rehabilitated Robinson's image to such a great extent that in 1791 the *Monthly Review* hailed Robinson as 'the English Sappho' in tribute to her poetical talents—a title she jealously would guard until her death in 1800. At the beginning of her career, Robinson employed her Della Cruscan avatars

'Laura', 'Laura Maria', 'Oberon', and 'Julia' as a means of effacing 'the celebrated Perdita,' as she was euphemistically known, and of transforming 'Mrs. Robinson' to 'the English Sappho'. Through this network Robinson gained access not only to a publisher, with whom she could attempt to make money, but also entrée to a world of fellow writers and readers who already were having fun with the poetry of the *World* and its avatars.

I like to say that by taking the Della Cruscans too seriously we risk not taking them seriously enough. The much-maligned and misread poetic correspondence between Della Crusca and Anna Matilda is actually a comically amoebean competition between the two poets, in which the man is motivated by his sexual frustration and the woman by her poetic frustration, as she continues to exhort him to control himself and to write better poetry. Poem after poem records their adoration of and admonitions to one another—while Bell's editor Topham facetiously puffs them as the greatest poets who ever lived. When read as playful popular culture, particularly in their newspaper context, these poems are hilarious. For this reason I object to the way literary history uncritically has taken the side of satirist William Gifford, who eviscerated the Della Cruscans for not being great literature—a straw man argument if you ask me. Today, we ought to be familiar enough with popular culture to understand its *modus operandi* as it seeks to entertain and to make money. Moreover, we should not overlook the fact that Merry and others in the network knew very well that his pseudonym 'Della Crusca' was a centuries-old inside joke. In fact, the original Accademia della Crusca had ludic origins: its name means literally 'academy of bran', deriving from a circle of friends who playfully joked that they were a '*brigata dei crusconi*' ('brigade of coarse bran'). For the sixteenth-century Della Cruscans, the name was a bread-making metaphor for their aim of purifying the Italian language and of preserving the Florentine poetic diction of Dante, Petrarch, and Boccaccio. The flour is good language, the bran is bad. Although they were serious about their goal, as the publication of their *Vocabolario* attests, the name is playfully self-deprecating, even burlesque. And they too used facetious avatars—all of which pertained to various aspects of the making of bread.[1] In fact, Bell's partner and Merry's Cambridge chum Edward Topham created the Della Crusca pseudonym as a multi-layered inside joke. The signature literally means 'man of bran' and, by allusion to this well-established history, 'bad poet'.

The avatar, moreover, originally was exclusive to the *World*, a kind of branding of Merry's poetry as the property of Topham and Bell. Since the poetry of the *World* was a network of avatars, Robinson naturally made her first contribution with a pseudonym—'Laura', which allows Robinson to write as Petrarch's Laura alive and subjectified, as a lyric agent rather than a lyrical object. Robinson obviously understood the punning relationship between *Laura* and *laurel.* Temporarily effacing her own identity and her much-discussed sexual past, Robinson thus was able to remake herself as an unstained avatar of poetic authority and legitimacy. At the same time as she is inserting herself in the Della Crusca network, she is inserting herself into an intertextual network of literary tradition.

The Laura avatar was networking in several other ways. The allusion was a specific invitation to Della Crusca, who assiduously employed Petrarchan tropes in his poems, and presented Laura as an erotic and poetic competitor to Cowley's Anna Matilda. But also, in choosing this particularly resonant avatar, Robinson alludes to *World* contributor Miles Peter Andrews's love poem 'To Laura' signed 'Arley'. Robinson knew Andrews from her days in the theatre, so her choice of pseudonym is her attempt to resume the connection and her assumption of the role of Arley's beloved.[2] The 'Laura' Arley addresses, as its headnote indicates, was an actress he loved but who has died—thus the allusion to Petrarch's deceased Laura. Robinson as Arley's Laura thus takes on the persona of an adored but deceased young woman—but this time she is an actress, a cunning figurative reference to and effacement of her past. In fact, the real Laura of Arley's poem is probably the celebrated actress Mary Ann Yates, who

1 Frances A. Yates, *Renaissance and Reform: The Italian Contribution* (London: Routledge, 1983.), 18

2 *Memoirs of Mrs Mary Robinson*, ed. Hester Davenport, *The Works of Mary Robinson*, gen. ed. William D. Brewer, 8 vols, (London: Pickering & Chatto, 2009–10), 7, 236.

had recently died. Yates, Andrews, and Robinson all were affiliated with Drury Lane and thus with the network around David Garrick and thus also with Sheridan, who controlled the political content of the *World*. Robinson even appeared on stage with Yates, as she recalls in her *Memoirs*.[1] So, Robinson's first avatar, like her later ones, is variously shaded with winking references. Moreover, by assuming the sobriquet Andrews gives to Yates, Robinson asserts her literary survival in the overwriting of her previous public identity, Perdita.

Robinson's second appearance as Laura in the *World* similarly displays her poetic networking with former associates. 'To Him Who Will Understand It' appeared 31 October 1788, with the Laura signature; its title recalls Arley's 'Elegy. To the Lady Who Will Best Remember It'.[2] Robinson's *Memoirs* provide an account of the poem's composition as an impromptu social performance. As such it is a pretty vigorous pastiche, if not all-out parody, of Della Crusca and Anna Matilda's style, down to the octosyllabic couplets that most frequently characterize their poetic exchanges. It has all the requisite expressions and tropes of Della Cruscan popular culture—the farewell to England, the 'mournful Philomel', the arduous escape from heartbreak, and the refuge in, of all places, Italy. Like Merry's 'Adieu and Recall to Love', Della Crusca's first poem, Laura's ironic renunciation of passion and its 'throbbing Pulses' playfully emphasizes the throbbing:

> Nor will I cast one thought behind,
> On *Foes* relentless—*Friends* unkind;—
> I feel, I feel their poison'd Dart
> Pierce the Life Nerve within my Heart,
> 'Tis mingled with the Vital Heat
> That bids my throbbing Pulses beat....[3]

Although autobiographically resonant, in the columns of the *World* this poem is practically an erotic invitation for correspondence with

1 *Memoirs*, 7, 244, 374.

2 *Poetry of the World*, 2, 57–59.

3 Mary Robinson, *Poems*, ed. Daniel Robinson, *The Works of Mary Robinson*, gen. ed. William D. Brewer, 8 vols, (London: Pickering & Chatto, 2010), 1, 53, lines 73–84.

Della Crusca. Robinson certainly intended for this poem to be read in the newspaper series knowing that in her previous poem Anna Matilda had complained that Della Crusca's proposed sojourn in Italy invariably would result in his infidelity.

Receiving no response from Della Crusca, Robinson's Laura made another, more blatant attempt to catch his attention. Her poem 'The Muse' appeared 13 November 1788, with a taunting editorial headnote, possibly written by herself: 'Of Poetical Trifles, where is there, even from DELLA CRUSCA, any Writing with more shew of Facility, and more beautifully Finished than much of the following?' This says a lot about the ludic characteristics of this kind of writing—it is supposed to demonstrate a degree of *sprezzatura* but with some refined polish as well. These are, after all, 'poetical trifles'. Laura invokes the muse by invoking Della Crusca with a playful allusion to Anna Matilda's first poem to him, 'The Pen', with its invitation to 'thrill' Anna Matilda's 'bosom' with his comically phallic 'golden quill'; however, Laura, in a move characteristic of Robinson, takes command of Della Crusca's instrument herself:

> O! LET me seize thy Pen Sublime,
> Which paints in glowing dulcet Rhyme
> The melting Pow'r, the magic Art,
> Th' extatic raptures of the Heart....[1]

Laura's claim to Della Crusca's pen is perhaps a bit more earnest, and less playfully erotic, than Anna Matilda's poem, which is downright bawdy; but her poem goes on to provoke Anna Matilda by identifying the source of Anna Matilda's phrase 'golden quill' as actually belonging to Shakespeare (sonnet 85) and by proposing that she and the Muse figured as Della Crusca share a 'sweet converse'.[2]

With this, Laura finally received a response, not from Della Crusca, but 'Leonardo'. Here, the Laura avatar becomes fully initiated and inscribed within the Della Crusca network, for, as it turns out, the Leonardo avatar is Della Crusca in disguise. This is part of the fun of this poetic network, in which one pseudonym can serve as

1 *Poems*, 1, 53, lines 1–4.
2 *Poems*, 1, 54, line 49.

a disguise for another pseudonym while combining as an avatar for Robert Merry. When Leonardo's poem, written by Merry, appeared, Topham hailed Leonardo as the latest disciple of 'the Della Crusca school'—another inside joke because Topham undoubtedly knew it was Merry. In 'To Laura', a sympathetic Leonardo urges her to avoid Italy and to remain in England, where she can learn fortitude—perhaps in his company as he offers his friendship. Laura is not so easily seduced, however, and her response impugns Leonardo as a feckless lothario:

> AND dost thou hope to fan my Flame
> With the soft breath of FRIENDSHIP'S Name?
> And dost thou think the thin disguise
> Can veil the *Mischief* from my Eyes?[1]

Rejecting Leonardo's impropriety, Laura suggests that he pursue love elsewhere that he may again feel the 'Throb Divine' of poetic inspiration—that is, erotic fascination.[2] Here she quotes directly Della Crusca's phrase from his second poem to Anna Matilda (21 Aug. 1787), slyly indicating her suspicion that Leonardo and Della Crusca are one in the same.

Laura's poetic union with Leonardo/Della Crusca moves forward, but not without the intervention of a jealous Anna Matilda, who unmasks Leonardo as Della Crusca in a comic harangue. Incensed by his poems to Laura, Anna Matilda disavows her love for Della Crusca and in jealous fashion directs her hostility towards Laura, comically implying alcoholic dissipation. And to emphasize the playful nature of all of this, I should point out that, in the same column, just below Anna Matilda's signature, Topham facetiously printed the following: 'Mrs. Cowley is now at Paris; and all who know her talents, must wish, that she may not lose her moments in inactivity'. Videogamers call these self-reflexive, winking gestures 'Easter eggs'.

As I hope I have shown, the poetry of the Della Crusca network is meant to be amusing. But there is serious play going on here, and it includes real literary ambition—particularly on the part of Robinson.

1 'To Leonardo', *Poems*, 1, 55, lines 1-10.
2 *Poems*, 1, 56, line 46.

Robinson's contributions to this exchange show a fiercely competitive poet at work, employing the formal tools at her disposal to demonstrate her own metrical virtuosity. And she skillfully employs her formal choices in the service of the ludic mode and of visceral effects. Today few readers appreciate is that Della Cruscan poetry counteracts pure sentimentality in favor of a disorienting range of effects—what one pre-Gifford reviewer of *The Poetry of the World* actually calls an 'orgasm'.[1] Exactly. This orgasm comically winks at sensibility and weeps at sexuality. This is a poetry about *frisson* for its own sake, while knowingly and self-reflexively deploying the tropes of Sensibility essentially for a cheap thrill. If Della Cruscan poetry has a redeeming quality, it is its burlesque of Sensibility. This is why I think of the Della Cruscans as post-Sensibility.

For Robinson, this poetry is also an opportunity to showcase her metrical skills—remember Coleridge later remarked to Southey, 'Ay! that woman has an ear!'[2] In her final contribution to the Della Crusca-Anna Matilda-Laura triangle, 'To Anna Matilda', Robinson heightens the competition with her own considerable poetic ambition. As one might expect, Laura's poetic address to Anna Matilda is mischievous and downright catty. While Della Crusca and Anna Matilda sing to one another and while Topham puffs them into outrageous immortality, Robinson seems more intent on actually earning it. 'To Anna Matilda', moreover, is Robinson's first venture into the metrical experimentation of the irregular ode. So, when she comes to do poetic combat with Anna Matilda, Robinson's Laura must demonstrate her facility in working in the irregular ode. In other words, her success in the duel is contingent upon her constructing elaborate stanzaic units with varying rhyme schemes and meters. This poem may be ludicrous, as Robinson surely intended it to be, but it does show Robinson more carefully constructing formal variation than, say, in her supposedly improvisational composition of 'To Him Who Will Understand It'. She will perform similar metrical gymnastics in her subsequent odes—including her final ode, more than ten years

1 *English Review*, XII (August 1788), 126-36 (127).

2 *Collected Letters of Samuel Taylor Coleridge*, ed. Earl Leslie Griggs, 6 vols (Oxford: Clarendon, 1956–71), 1, 562.

later, 'To the Poet Coleridge', which matches many of the metrical moves Coleridge makes in 'Kubla Khan', to which Robinson directly responds. As I argue, this formal virtuosity is the hallmark of her poetry and is likely the reason Coleridge shared his poem with her sixteen years before he published it.

My book concludes with another look at the poetic exchange between Robinson and Coleridge ten years later—but not according to a teleology of Romanticism—but rather through lens of the Della Crusca network.[1] Robinson's poetic response to 'Kubla Khan' is characteristic of certain strains in Robinson's poetry from the beginning of her career. Her 'extatic' praise of Coleridge strongly echoes her 'Ode to Della Crusca', from 1791, which celebrates the poetic achievement of Della Crusca's *Diversity* and his bold assertion of metrical variety. Many of the qualities critics since Lowes have found in 'Kubla Khan' likely would have been imperceptible to Robinson and Coleridge, both of whom I suggest would have seen the poem as an irregular ode in the Della Cruscan vein. Robinson at least saw it as a poem about *frisson* and, for lack of a better word, pleasure—the enjoyment of fanciful poetry and bewitching lyrical metrics. What happens to 'Kubla Khan' if we read it as part of Robinson and Coleridge's playful, quasi-private rekindling of a Della Cruscan poetic romance? Well, Coleridge's simile 'As if this Earth in fast thick Pants were breathing' that precedes the forcing of his 'mighty fountain' might seem a lot less Freudian and more playfully erotic as well as more carefully crafted—as Robinson's reading of the poem suggests that it was. Perhaps this is why Coleridge did not share 'Kubla Khan' with anyone other than Robinson for several years: although Coleridge intended us to see the poem as dropping from the heavens, to Coleridge the poem may have seemed a relict of Della Cruscanism. When he had put enough distance between the poem and its Della Cruscan associations he finally published it. It was then that he set about mythologizing the circumstances of the poem's composition. But he did not need to mythologize the poem for Robinson because

1 In the book I thus revise (and correct) my reading from many years ago: Daniel Robinson, 'From "Mingled Measure" to "Ecstatic Measures": Mary Robinson's Poetic Reading of "Kubla Khan"', *The Wordsworth Circle*, 26 (1995), 4–7.

she knew as well as he did the pleasure of—and the price poets pay for—feeding on honeydew and drinking the milk of Paradise. At the end of her life, her praise for Coleridge is similar to her promise to Della Crusca nearly a decade earlier: she will celebrate his 'matchless numbers' by actually matching them and thereby claim for herself her share of poetic fame. As for Coleridge, although in 1816 he calls it a 'psychological curiosity', in 1800, when he shared it with Robinson, 'Kubla Khan' was good enough for a playful poetic correspondence but it may have seemed to him too Della Cruscan to publish.

Erica Levy McAlpine

Keats's Might: Subjunctive Verbs in the Late Poems

In the following well-known lines—some of the last he wrote before dying of tuberculosis in February 1821—John Keats turns the benign word 'hand' into a haunting visual effect:

> This living hand, now warm and capable
> Of earnest grasping, would, if it were cold
> And in the icy silence of the tomb,
> So haunt thy days and chill thy dreaming nights
> That thou would wish thine own heart dry of blood,
> So in my veins red life might stream again,
> And thou be conscience-calm'd—see, here it is
> I hold it towards you—[1]

Keats's posthumous fragment has been read variously. The hand is of course the physical, fleshy part, but it is also the poet's script—the inky poem on the page.[2] It is also a dark marriage proposal to Fanny Brawne, a too-late offering of the poet's hand to the woman he loved, straight out of the tomb.[3] The hand may also suggest a clock:

1 John Keats, 'This Living Hand,' in *John Keats: The Major Works*, ed. Elizabeth Cook (Oxford: Oxford University Press, 1990), p. 331. All subsequent citations from Keats's poetry will come from this edition and will be cited parenthetically.

2 Posthumously published in 1898, nearly 80 years after the poet's death, the poem feels, to its audience, like a hand from the tomb. On Keats's interest in describing deteriorating bodies as well as the possibility of 'after-fame' and his anticipation of it, see Andrew Bennett, *Romantic Poets and the Culture of Posterity* (Cambridge: Cambridge University Press, 1999), pp. 139–157.

3 For the possible reasons behind Keats's reprimand, 'and thou be conscience-calm'd,' see the poet's letters to Fanny Brawne written between March and August of 1820 (particularly the letter composed on the 5th of July). Quoted in

starting out presently—'*this* living hand, *now* warm and capable'—the poem suddenly shifts forward into a world beyond the speaker's death and even beyond the reader's, only to turn time back again at the end: 'here it is / I hold it towards you—.'[1] But I would like to point out, as others have, that this poem never actually shifts in time.[2] Rather, Keats writes most of it in the conditional ('would...were... might'), suggesting the possibility of his speaker's death, but not its actuality.[3] The hand that reaches out in the last line isn't the dead hand conjured up in the second through seventh lines, but the living hand of the first. In this way, Keats's strange fragment conforms to what Jack Stillinger has called the 'typical' structure of the English Romantic lyric: it 'begins in the real world, takes off in a mental flight to visit the ideal, and then—for a variety of reasons...—returns home to the real.'[4] And yet the 'icy silence of the tomb' hardly constitutes an 'ideal' world. On the contrary, the 'earnest grasping' of the living hand as well as its reaching outward at the poem's end seem to be what the poet idealizes; the possible death of the speaker, though written only conditionally, feels more like grim reality.

Using subjunctive and conditional syntax, Keats inverts in this and other late poems the basic relation between real life and poetic reverie that so much of his earlier work develops; the power of what is not

---

The Major Works, pp. 526–534.

1 See Andrew Bennett, *Keats, Narrative and Audience: The Posthumous Life of Writing* (Cambridge: Cambridge University Press, 1994), pp. 11–14, and Brooke Hopkins, 'Keats and the Uncanny: 'This Living Hand,'' in *The Kenyon Review* 11, 4 (1989): 28–40.

2 For further discussion of this poem, see, in addition to Bennett and Hopkins, Jonathan Culler, *The Pursuit of Signs: Semiotics, Literature, Deconstruction* (London: Routledge and Kegan Paul, 1981), pp. 153–154, Lawrence Lipking, *The Life of the Poet: Beginning and Ending Poetic Careers* (Chicago: University of Chicago Press, 1981), pp. 180–184, Timothy Bahti, 'Ambiguity and Indeterminacy: The Juncture,' in *Comparative Literature* 38 (1986): 218–223, and Richard Macksey, 'Keats and the Poetics of Extremity,' in *MLN* 99 (1984): 853–854.

3 Perhaps for this reason, Susan Wolfson calls the poem a 'surrealism.' Susan Wolfson, *The Questioning Presence: Wordsworth, Keats, and the Interrogative Mode in Romantic Poetry* (Ithaca: Cornell University Press, 1986), p. 368.

4 Jack Stillinger, *The Hoodwinking of Madeline* (The University of Illinois Press: Chicago, 1971), pp. 101–102. See also Jack Stillinger, *Romantic Complexity* (Chicago: University of Illinois Press, 2006), p. 153.

real in 'This living hand' stems not from fantasy or idealization (as in early Keats) but from its technical source, its grammar of potentiality. As such, what is most threatening about the dead hand in lines two through seven, what gives it a vividness so palpable that we mistakenly imagine that *it* is the poem's final, outstretched hand rather than the living one, is the fact that it exists only as a possibility. *If* the hand *were* dead, *we would wish* to die so that it *might live* again—a proposition more frightening than if the hand were dead from the start. For a reader who recalls Keats's assertion of the power of 'negative capability' (of 'being in uncertainties, Mysteries, doubts'), the threat of what might be, but isn't yet, and indeed might never be, is more powerful than the knowledge of what is.[1]

In this essay, I aim to equate the grammatically hypothetical reality of 'This Living Hand'—which is, in fact, a vivid un-reality—to the reveries and fantasies of the poet's earlier works, which achieve their escapes through myth, fantasy, and dream, rather than through grammatical flourish. Some of these early settings of reverie include the dream in *Endymion* and arguably the entire poem; the fantasy at the end of 'On First Looking Into Chapman's Homer'; the romance and intertextuality of 'Isabella'; the dreams in 'The Eve of St. Agnes'; and others. My argument is that 'This Living Hand,' along with many of Keats's other late poems, including some of the odes and sonnets to Fanny Brawne, retain in their subjunctive and conditional grammar a spark of that early-Keatsian impulse towards reverie that has been explored, and sometimes attacked, by his critics.[2] I am suggesting

1 Keats writes in a letter to his brothers George and Tom Keats on the 21st of December, 1817: 'at once it struck me, what quality went to form a Man of Achievement especially in Literature & which Shakespeare possessed so enormously—I mean Negative Capability, this is when man is capable of being in uncertainties, Mysteries, doubts, without any irritable reaching after fact & reason—.' Quoted in *The Major Works*, p. 370.

2 See Marjorie Levinson, *Keats's Life of Allegory: The Origins of a Style* (Oxford: Basil Blackwell, 1988), pp. 227-254, Bennett, *Keats, Narrative and Audience*, pp. 61-81, Morris Dickstein, 'The World of the Early Poems,' in *John Keats, Modern Critical Views*, ed. Harold Bloom (New York: Chelsea House Publishers, 1985), pp. 49–66, Harold Bloom, 'Keats: Romance Revised,' *John Keats, Modern Critical Views*, ed. Harold Bloom (New York: Chelsea House Publishers, 1985), pp. 105–126, and Nicholas Roe, *John Keats and the Culture of Dissent* (Oxford: Oxford University Press, 2007), pp. 202–212.

that in spite of the late poetry's self-conscious interest in the actuality of experience, the subjunctives and conditionals prevalent in these poems—wherein Keats depicts the world as it 'would' or 'might' be—are in fact related to what Marjorie Levinson calls the 'swooning' voice of early 'Johnny Keats.'[1] Hypothetical syntax provides Keats with a new form of escape at a time in his life when he is most aware of the suffering reality has to offer. (Keats himself articulates this idea best in 'Ode on a Grecian Urn,' whose characters, despite their seeming happiness, thrive on their perpetual state of promise alone.) When Keats leaves behind his early poetics of romance and dream to write about experiential life, his escapist impulse doesn't disappear: it seeks a subtler venue—and finds one in the intricacies of grammar.

Consider the middle stanza of 'To Autumn,' Keats's last, and seemingly most experiential ode:

> Who hath not seen thee oft amid thy store?
> Sometimes whoever seeks abroad may find
> Thee sitting careless on a granary floor,
> Thy hair soft-lifted by the winnowing wind;
> Or on a half-reap'd furrow sound asleep,
> Drows'd with the fume of poppies while thy hook
> Spares the next swath and all its twined flowers:
> And sometimes like a gleaner thou dost keep
> Steady thy laden head across a brook;
> Or by a cyder-press, with patient look,
> Thou watchest the last oozings hours by hours.
> (324, lines 2–22)

Keats describes autumn more delicately, perhaps, than any other poet by revealing it in terms of its 'store' rather than its self.[2] Here autumn

1 Levinson, *Keats's Life of Allegory: The Origins of a Style*, p. 195.

2 In doing so, he also asks us to compare the season to the poet, who, according to his letters, should similarly be capable of 'filling some other Body.' Keats, 'Letter to Richard Woodhouse,' in *The Major Works*, p. 418–419. In an earlier, but related letter to J. H. Reynolds on the 3rd of February, 1818, Keats writes: 'Poetry should be great & unobtrusive, a thing which enters into one's soul, and not startle or amaze it with itself but its subject.' Keats, 'Letter to J.H. Reynolds,' in *The Major Works*, p. 377.

is simply a series of its own effects—a phantom presence. And yet autumn's effects do not actually take place in the poem. The conditional phrasing of the stanza's second line removes any presence of the actual season. 'Sometimes whoever seeks abroad *may* find/thee,' Keats writes; he means: 'it is *possible* that a person *might sometimes find* traces of you in the following autumnal effects—.' Such a grammatical inversion not only deprioritizes the speaker's impressions (he never mentions 'I'—only 'whoever'), it also transforms the season into a kind of poetic supposition. Of course we know that Keats experiences actual autumn—his letter to J. H. Reynolds on the 21st of September 1819, describing the occasion of his writing this poem, makes that clear enough—but his poetic autumn vacillates between possibility and truth.[1] The 'flowers' and 'oozings' of Keats's second stanza occupy a purely aesthetic, potential realm—a little different from the 'bowery clefts' and 'leafy shelves' of Keats's early reveries because autumn's effects are imagined as part of a human, rather than poetic, world, but similar in their ultimate separateness from it.

The middle stanza of 'To Autumn' presents possibility in its simplest form. 'May find' is a 'potential subjunctive' verb, introducing a scenario that is viable but lacks certainty. The opening verb in 'Bright Star' is also subjunctive, but it operates differently:

> Bright star, would I were stedfast as thou art—
>   Not in lone splendour hung aloft the night
> And watching, with eternal lids apart,
>   Like nature's patient, sleepless Eremite,
> The moving waters at their priestlike task
>   Of pure ablution round earth's human shores,
> Or gazing on the new soft-fallen mask
>   Of snow upon the mountains and the moors—
> No—yet still stedfast, still unchangeable,
>   Pillow'd upon my fair love's ripening breast,
> To feel for ever its soft fall and swell,
>   Awake for ever in a sweet unrest,
> Still, still to hear her tender-taken breath,

1 While the second stanza is subjunctive, the first and third stanzas remain present indicative.

And so live ever—or else swoon to death—
(325)

Although nearly forgotten by the poem's end, the grammar of Keats's first line dominates the poem. The 'optative subjunctive' phrase 'Would I were stedfast as thou art' (optative because it represents action that exists only as a wish or a prayer) places the poem's final quatrain and couplet in an alternate reality. The last six lines invoke a wished-for, rather than plausible, world, in which the speaker of the poem is blessed with the lifespan of a star.[1] But what is unusual about the poem—since its content is standard fare for a love sonnet—is its syntax. Its initial subjunctive seems to set up an 'if/then' structure that never materializes. We expect, after 'would I were,' a series of 'then I would' phrases: for instance, 'then I would be able to live with my beloved forever'; or, 'then I would be able to write more poems'; etcetera. But Keats instead proceeds by negation ('*Not* in lone splendour hung aloft the night...'), denying in lines two through eight all that the stars actually do with their lives in an attempt to emphasize the devotion he would show by his own choice. He would, were he so 'stedfast,' focus on his girl alone. The failure of the poem's syntax to follow through on its initial promise constitutes a kind of technical flirtation, a grammatical tease. It matches the twist that Keats works into his second line, wherein the phrase 'hung aloft the night' confirms the surprising fact that his speaker uses the words 'bright star' literally (to refer to an actual celestial body) rather than as a metaphor for the lady, who might have supposed, upon reading the poem's first line, that *she* was the one being called 'star.'

'Bright Star' thus proceeds idiosyncratically.[2] Rather than finish-

1 He would, he claims, spend the entirety of his years in such a world doting on his lady's breasts. Christopher Ricks calls the poem's treatment of Fanny's breasts its single flaw; he argues that Keats, usually so adept at demonstrating embarrassment poetically, should have shown more embarrassment here. Christopher Ricks, *Keats and Embarrassment* (Oxford: Clarendon Press, 1984), p.112.

2 Two of Keats's more conventional uses of the optative subjunctive appear in the odes: '*That I might drink*, and leave the world unseen,/And with thee fade away into the forest dim' (Keats, 'Ode to a Nightingale,' in *The Major Works*, p. 286, *my italics*); 'O, for an age so shelter'd from annoy,/ *That I may never know* how change the moons,/ Or hear the voice of busy common-sense!' (Keats, 'Ode on

ing off the 'would I were'/'then I would' pattern, the poem's final lines merely extend the fantasized supposition. They pick up, after a seven-line hiatus of little import to the poem's overall plot, right where the first phrase left off: 'yet still stedfast.' The grammar here is tenuous. Keats advances almost paratactically at the end, even though his punctuation and formality of tone suggest something more strategic. This kind of violation of grammar—within an already-sophisticated grammatical mode—allows the poet to pursue pointless or experimental sympathies that are more obvious in his early poems.[1] But now lapses in grammar, rather than excursions into dream or reverie, constitute escape; Keats suggests that what occurs within the 'skip' between lines two and nine, is primarily aesthetic—poetry meant purely for pleasure. The late sonnet, 'The day is gone, and all its sweets are gone' operates similarly. Beginning, like 'Bright Star,' with an independent clause, its dependent second through ninth lines skip, proceeding by delay:

The day is gone, and all its sweets are gone!
  Sweet voice, sweet lips, soft hand, and softer breast,
Warm breath, light whisper, tender semitone,
  Bright eyes, accomplish'd shape, and lang'rous waist!
Faded the flower and all its budded charms,
  Faded the sight of beauty from my eyes,
Faded the shape of beauty from my arms,
  Faded the voice, warmth, whiteness, paradise,
Vanish'd unseasonably at shut of eve,
  When the dusk Holiday—or Holinight—

Indolence,' in *The Major Works*, p. 284, *my italics*).

1 No other Romantic poet so often risks his grammar in such a way; even Shelley, the most imaginative of Keats's contemporaries, is strict in his usage. An important exception can be found in the ninth section of Wordsworth's 'Immortality Ode': 'not indeed / For that which is most worthy to be blest— / Delight and liberty, the simple creed / Of Childhood, whether busy or at rest, / With new-fledged hope still fluttering in his breast:— / Not for these I raise / The song of thanks and praise; / But for those obstinate questionings / Of sense and outward things, / Fallings from us, vanishings.' Wordsworth's uncharacteristic grammatical ellipses here are similar to Keats's; it is likely that the younger poet admired this poem—and this passage, in particular. William Wordsworth, 'Immortality Ode,' in *The Major Works*, ed. Stephen Gill (Oxford: Oxford University Press, 1984), p.301, lines 137–146.

Of fragrant curtain'd Love begins to weave
  The woof of darkness thick, for his delight;
But, as I've read Love's Missal through to-day,
He'll let me sleep, seeing I fast and pray.
  (327)

The second line of this sonnet introduces a series of 'vanishings'[1] that offer only a pretence of grammatical order. Lines two, three, and four are not really complete thoughts or phrases (since they lack verbs) but rather a list of images. It is significant that this list ('lips,' 'hand,' 'breast,' 'breath,' and so on) is, like the appositional phrases at the end of 'Bright Star,' sexual; by setting these impressions off at a grammatical distance, Keats leaves them 'poetical,' reserving them for pleasure rather than for thought. The lines that follow these three do so mischievously: 'Faded... Faded... Faded... Vanish'd.' Each of them begins by breaking the iambic pentameter with a trochee. We know Keats is writing about the disappearance of the day's 'sweets,' but he avoids using verbs, leaving his syntax somewhat ambiguous. Does he simply mean 'Faded *[is]* the flower.../ Faded *[is]* the sight,' and so on? If so, where is the noun that should precede 'Vanish'd'? —Or is it implied, too? (As in: '[*All these things*] Vanish'd unseasonably at shut of eve.') Alternately, we might read: '*[So]* Faded the flower.../*[So]* Faded the sight.' But taking the syntax this second way, lines ten through twelve would appear to be written in the wrong tense—they should say, in that case, 'When the dusk Holiday.../of fragrant curtain'd Love *began* to weave,' rather than 'begins.' Neither syntax works fully. And yet Keats conscientiously maintains the poem's rhyme scheme and meter; it is certainly a finished piece. I am picking so closely at the grammar here neither to suggest any failings in Keats's sonnet nor to imply that disambiguating his syntax would be important to our understanding of his meaning (the gist is clear). I want, rather, to point out that Keats banishes here, as he does in 'Bright Star',[2] his poet's concern over grammar so that he can dip, by means of technique, into the pleasure-world that his early poetry occupies in content alone.

1 See note on Wordsworth, above.
2 And in another late sonnet, 'I cry your mercy—pity—love!—aye, love.'

But not all of Keats's late subjunctives are so grammatically complex. In addition to 'potential' and 'optative' forms, Keats uses 'jussive subjunctives' to suggest possibility more plainly. Look at the end of 'To Fanny':

> Ah! if you prize my subdued soul above
> The poor, the fading, brief, pride of an hour:
> Let none profane my Holy See of Love,
> Or with a rude hand break
> The sacramental cake:
> Let none else touch the just new-budded flower;
> If not—may my eyes close
> Love on their last repose! (331)

Arranged like a prayer, Keats's 'Let…' clauses construct a potential world of happiness with Fanny out of what appears to be his fear of her indifference.[1] '*If* you love me,' Keats implies, '*let no one else* have or even touch you.' By writing it conditionally rather than in the present imperative (i.e. '*please* love me' and '*do not allow somebody else* to have or even touch you'), Keats makes a separate realm of experience out of a mere possibility. He uses the same form at the end of the poem 'What can I do to drive away' (sometimes called 'Ode to Fanny'), except he writes in the first person (meaning that his verbs are 'hortatory' jussives):

> O, let me once more rest
> My soul upon that dazzling breast!
> Let once again these aching arms be placed,
> The tender gaolers of thy waist!
> And let me feel that warm breath here and there

1 See Keats's letter of admonishment to her on the 5th of July, 1820. In it he writes: 'You may have altered—if you have not—if you still behave in dancing rooms and other societies as I have seen you—I do not want to live—if you have done so I wish this coming night to be my last. I cannot live without you, and not only you but chaste you; virtuous you. The Sun rises and sets, the day passes, and you follow the bent of your inclination to a certain extent—you have no conception of the quantity of miserable feeling that passes through me in a day.—Be serious! Love is not a plaything—and again do not write unless you can do it with a crystal conscience.' Keats, 'To Fanny Brawne,' in *The Major Works*, p. 533.

To spread a rapture in my very hair,—
O, the sweetness of the pain!
Give me those lips again!
Enough! Enough! it is enough for me
To dream of thee! (329)

Keats's imaginative capacity for pleasure in these lines approaches the reveries he creates in the grammatical skips of the two sonnets we just looked at. And yet here, he is more explicit about his fantasy's potentiality, much in the same way that he is explicit in his early poems about his idealization of poetic escape. By continually using the words 'once more' and 'once again,' Keats reminds his reader and himself that what he is writing is not actual but a mixture of memory and fantasy. He also returns here to the heroic couplet, the form so many of his earlier poems use to describe alternate or mythopoetic worlds. The world here is not mythopoetic, but it is alternate: as he admits in the poem's last line, what he has just described is nothing but a 'dream.'

Although Keats's jussive subjunctives are less subtle in their forays into the world of imagined possibility than his potential and optative forms (which set up longer passages of writing that appear to be present indicative—and therefore actual—even when they are not), these jussives are importantly related to what Keats considers one of poetry's primary tasks—to instruct (not morally, but in matters of sympathy and the imagination). Nowhere in Keats is this task better prescribed than in *The Fall of Hyperion: A Dream,* although it is interestingly not Keats, but his poetic interlocutor, Moneta, who does the prescribing.[1] *The Fall's* opening lines express Keats's longstanding belief in poetry's capacity for occupying potential realities:

Fanatics have their dreams, wherewith they weave
A paradise for a sect; the savage too
From forth the loftiest fashion of his sleep
Guesses at heaven: pity these have not
Trac'd upon vellum or wild Indian leaf
The shadows of melodious utterance.

1 Keats eventually abandons this unfinished poem, right about the time that he composes 'To Autumn' in September of 1819.

For poesy alone can tell her dreams,
With the fine spell of words alone can save
Imagination from the sable charm
And dumb enchantment.
(291, 1:1–11)

Keats seems to be comparing his late poetic project—to 'save/ Imagination from the sable charm/and dumb enchantment'—to the dreams of fanatics and the guesses of savages. And yet according to these lines, what separates poetry from fantasy is not its content but its capacity for favourable expression: among the poet, the fanatic, and the savage, only the poet can turn dreams into aesthetically-pleasing language. The idea hearkens back to Keats's early poetics; and indeed, he goes on to write, 'Who alive can say "Thou art no Poet; may'st not tell thy dreams"?' And yet whatever Keats suggests in these lines about the merits of escapist poetry is revised later by his pronouncement of poetry's ultimate purpose, which comes in the form of Moneta's harsh reproof against him and the rest of the 'dreamer tribe':[1]

Thou art a dreaming thing;
A fever of thyself—think of the Earth;
What bliss even in hope is there for thee?
(295, 1:168–170)

To which the poet replies, still with some hope:

sure not all
Those melodies sung into the world's ear
Are useless: sure a poet is a sage;
A humanist, Physician to all Men.
(295, 1:187–190)

Moneta's response in the lines that follow is the dictum that guides all of Keats's later work:

1 Keats, 'The Fall of Hyperion,' in *The Major Works*, p. 296, line 198. See Bloom's *The Visionary Company*, wherein he calls these lines, and what follows them, 'the finest moment in Keats's poetry' and the 'culmination of Keats's work.' Harold Bloom, *The Visionary Company*, revised and enlarged edition (Ithaca: Cornell University Press, 1971), pp.426–427.

—Art thou not of the dreamer tribe?
The poet and the dreamer are distinct,
Diverse, sheer opposite, antipodes.
The one pours out a balm upon the world,
The other vexes it.
(296, 1:198–202)

Whether Keats himself is a poet or dreamer becomes the complex question surrounding this poem (the title of which claims that the poem itself is a dream and thus the product of a dreamer). Moneta, who ministers over the dead Saturn and in doing so becomes a figure for poetry's altruism, reminds Keats of the poet's power to heal—if he would only, to use a phrase of Walter Jackson Bate's, 'confine his imagination to the concrete and living world.'[1] Her name, which derives from the fourth principle part of the Latin verb *moneo, monere,* meaning 'to warn; to instruct,' suggests her role in the poem: to instruct the poet of his sympathetic duty to compose poetry that can be a balm to the world, rather than an escape from it (which would be a balm for the poet alone).

But Keats is ambivalent about Moneta's admonishment (and perhaps this ambivalence is one reason why the poem remains unfinished). Reading *The Fall* as a kind of commentary on the ideas I am putting forth in this essay, we might expect that most, if not all, of the poet's subsequent work (which includes 'To Autumn' and all of the poems to Fanny) would be firmly rooted in actual experience, with no traces of escape. But Keats only partially heeds Moneta's call, emphasizing in his last poems poetry's capacity for dwelling in possible worlds that are neither completely lodged in experience nor too far from it. Keats's choice to abandon idle dreaming, only to replace it with a more subtle form of dreaming, demonstrates his unresolved ambivalence about what it is that gives poetry its might. This ambivalence with respect to Moneta's message—that poetry is more powerful than dreaming—reflects Keats's earlier ideas about the strength

1 Bate, *The Stylistic Development of Keats*, p. 173. See also Geoffrey Hartman, 'Spectral Symbolism and Authorial Self in Keats's Hyperion,' in *The Fate of Reading* (University of Chicago Press: Chicago, 1975), pp. 60–61. Hartman considers Moneta to be a kind of instructive authorial figure who is like Keats's 'poetical character' in its capacity to assume other forms.

in negative capability. The fact that Keats is content with his own uncertainty about the source of poetry's power is a manifestation of the capability of the poet that Keats valorises in his letters. He is able to maintain this uncertainty by his attraction to subjunctive verbs and conditionals, which allow him to retain his dreaming in spite of his late call to realism. His solution is to describe experience in terms of its potential, thus replacing the 'vex' of escapism with the might of possibility.

Poetry's ability to instruct forward becomes its lasting power for Keats. This idea can be found in his early poetry, but the windows into potential worlds are much more obvious there. In the late poems, Keats achieves the transition from actual to potential almost invisibly. From Keats's early to his late poems, the world changes from being limiting to containing and potentiating the imagination in all its power. Moneta is the figure who returns him to this task, and Keats undertakes it syntactically in nearly all of his last poems, which have the special capacity for transforming the actual into the potential, and which, like their short-lived poet, have become symbols of glimpsed possibility.

Huey-fen Fay Yao

'Old Romance' and New Narrators: A Reading of Keats's 'Isabella' and 'The Eve of St Agnes'

'Isabella, the Pot of Basil' (1818) and 'The Eve of St Agnes' (1819) are significant poems in Keats's poetic development. In them we are aware of the poet as a narrator writing in an innovative way. In his influential book *The Hoodwinking of Madeline* (1971), Jack Stillinger argues that Keats is anti-romance in these two poems.[1] Indeed, in 'Isabella' and 'The Eve of St Agnes', Keats uses sophisticated narrative skills as he questions the nature and function of 'old Romance' ('Isabella', line 387; 'The Eve of St Agnes', line 41). I shall argue that, in 'Isabella', he uses digressions to show his authorial intention and presence. He also employs rhetorical devices, such as repetitions, parallelism, and questions, in order to create a dramatic effect. In this way, Keats differentiates himself from the old romancer Boccaccio, whom he tries to challenge. In 'The Eve of St Agnes', I shall suggest that Keats's modernity as a narrator shows in his use of a fluid narrative perspective. Keats presents a narrator whose identity is ambiguous and whose point of view constantly shifts. This makes the narrator's presence ambivalent and his role indeterminate.

In 'Isabella', Keats alerts the reader to his status as a modern narrator by using digressions. Critics have different views concerning the grouping of digressions. Miriam Allott does not use the term 'digression' to indicate Keats's intentional change of the subject. Instead,

1 See 'Keats and Romance: The "Reality" of *Isabella*' in Jack Stillinger, *The Hoodwinking of Madeline and Other Essays on Keats's Poems* (Urbana: University of Illinois Press, 1971), 31–45, especially 31, 37; and 'The Hoodwinking of Madeline: Skepticism in *The Eve of St Agnes*' in *Hoodwinking*, 67–93.

she uses the term 'insertions' and she says that there are four 'insertions' in 'Isabella'. They are stanzas 12 to 13, 16 to 20, 49, and 55 to 56.[1] Yet Susan Wolfson has a different grouping. For Wolfson, stanzas 12 to 13, 19 to 20, 49, 55 to 56 and 61 are digressive stanzas.[2] In my view, there are two kinds of digressions—the major and the minor digressions—and they perform different roles. The major ones, which include stanzas 19, 20, and 49, clearly display Keats's proclamation of his stance as a contemporary poet. The poet's authorial presence, the first-person point of view, is strongly to the fore in these stanzas. The minor digressions, stanzas 12 to 13, 16 to 18, 55 to 56, and 61, have their own functions: these include foreshadowing, reinforcement of the plot, and emotional intensification. Like the major digressions, they 'intrude' into the text and indirectly underline Keats's status as a modern teller. I will use stanzas 19, 20, 49, 12 and 13 to illustrate my point.

In 'Isabella', Keats, implicitly or explicitly, shows his authorial intention and assurance in his digressions. By doing so, Keats demonstrates autonomy as a modern writer. In his published Preface to *Endymion* (1818), Keats explicitly discloses his belated anxiety of influence as a young poetic novice. But in 'Isabella', he implicitly demonstrates a kind of authorial assertiveness.[3] This kind of authorial confidence appears as an apology, but, paradoxically, this apologetic modesty accentuates his confidence as a modern poet.[4] Take the first major digressions, stanzas 19 and 20, as an example:

> O eloquent and famed Boccaccio!
>   Of thee we now should ask forgiving boon,
> And of thy spicy myrtle as they blow,
>   And of thy roses amorous of the moon,

1 See *The Poems of John Keats*, ed. Miriam Allott (London: Longman, 1970), 332 notes to lines 89–104.

2 See Susan Wolfson, 'Keats's *Isabella* and the "Digressions" of "Romance"', *Criticism*, 27 (1985), 249–50.

3 See Kurt Heinzelman, 'Self-interest and the Politics of Composition in Keats's *Isabella*', *Journal of English Literary History*, 55, 1 (1988), 174.

4 Michael LaGory has a similar view to mine. He suggests that Keats's invocation to Boccaccio is 'an expression of personal identity'. See Michael LaGory, 'Wormy Circumstance: Symbolism in Keats's *Isabella*', *Studies in Romanticism*, 34, 3 (1995), 337.

And of thy lilies, that do paler grow
  Now they can no more hear thy ghittern's tune,
For venturing syllables that ill beseem
The quiet glooms of such a piteous theme.

Grant thou a pardon here, and then the tale
  Shall move on soberly, as it is meet;
There is no other crime, no mad assail
  To make old prose in modern rhyme more sweet:
But it is done—succeed the verse or fail—
  To honour thee, and thy gone spirit greet;
To stead thee as a verse in English tongue,
An echo of thee in the north-wind sung.
  ('Isabella', 145–60)[1]

In stanza 19, he purposely diverts from his storytelling of the opposition between the capitalist brothers and the young lovers. But he interpolates his invocation to Boccaccio: 'O eloquent and famed Boccaccio! / Of thee we now should ask forgiving boon' (145–46). In this way, he breaks the sequence and alerts the reader to his authorial presence.[2] His addressing to Boccaccio exhibits his attempt to distance himself from the old romancer. That is to say, in addition to the conventional request for Boccaccio's pardon, Keats conveys a sense of his own poetic voice and introduces his design. In this respect, his syllables are 'venturing' (151) not only because he wishes to redo an Italian romance but also to 'stead' (159), to substitute, Boccaccio's narrative in the English tongue (159). Moreover, he expects that his new fashioning will make the old romance sweeter (156). Keats shows an assertive authorial autonomy in these digressive stanzas and his daring spirit displays his purpose.

Yet when adapting the old romance to his new tale, Keats encounters difficulty: there is the question of inclusion. But such a difficulty accentuates his status as a contemporary writer. In stanza 49, another

1 *John Keats: Complete Poems*, ed. Jack Stillinger (1978; Cambridge, MA: Harvard University Press, 1982). All quotations of Keats's poems are taken from this edition, with line numbers in parentheses.

2 John Barnard discusses those authorial interpolations as gaps between Boccaccio and Keats. See John Barnard, *John Keats* (1987; Cambridge: Cambridge University Press, 1993), 78.

major digression, the story swerves. It abruptly breaks off from the narrative of the graveyard scene and the poet poses questions:

> Ah! wherefore all this wormy circumstance?
> Why linger at the yawning tomb so long?
> O for the gentleness of old Romance,
> The simple plaining of a minstrel's song!
> Fair reader, at the old tale take a glance,
> For here, in truth, it doth not well belong
> To speak: —O turn thee to the very tale,
> And taste the music of that vision pale.
> ('Isabella', 385-92)

Keats seems perplexed; he affects to hesitate about the ways in which he should recount the story. Hence he initiates a debate within himself between what is expected in the old romance and in the new story: 'Ah! wherefore all this wormy circumstance? / Why linger at the yawning tomb so long?' (385–86). This creates a dramatic effect and emphasizes Keats's self-consciousness. First he acknowledges the simplicity of old romance because he notes in it 'the gentleness of old Romance' (387) and 'the simple plaining of a minstrel's song' (388). As he indicates in stanzas 19 and 20, he questions the nature of 'old Romance' and wishes to challenge its conventions in stanza 49. He then considers his story may not be appropriate for the modern reader because he wishes to include the grotesque details, the 'wormy circumstance'. He therefore reveals his doubts by saying 'in truth, it doth not well belong / To speak' (390–91). This statement, I would suggest, is an affected apology. Keats still desires to include the grotesque details in his modern romance. He wishes to differentiate his romance from Boccaccio's old tale as he asks his 'fair reader' (389) to 'taste the [his] music of that vision pale' (392).

Keats's authorial intention and narrative skills as a modern story-teller are further substantiated by the rhetorical devices, such as repetitions, parallelism, and questions, which he employs in his minor digressions. I will take stanzas 12 to 13, the first minor digressions, as an example. These two minor digressions foreshadow the plot. In the story, the narrator is like the Greek chorus.[1] He comments on and anticipates the plot while narrating the story. At the outset of the story, the narrator concentrates on the love between Lorenzo and Isabella. Their love story continues for eleven stanzas and Keats veers in stanza 12. He poses a rhetorical question: 'were they unhappy then?' (89), and this way alerts the reader that something is going to happen to the young lovers:

> Were they unhappy then? —It cannot be—
> Too many tears for lovers have been shed,
> Too many sighs give we to them in fee,
> Too much of pity after they are dead,
> Too many doleful stories do we see,
> Whose matter in bright gold were best be read;
> Except in such a page where Theseus' spouse
> Over the pathless waves towards him bows.
> ('Isabella', 89-96)

He invokes unhappy lovers to describe their happy love. That is to say, he uses the classical allusions of the sad and abandoned lovers, Ariadne (95-96) and Dido (99), to describe Isabella. In this way, Keats aptly hints that their love is going to face an imminent catastrophe.

This foreshadowing of the coming disaster for the young lovers is more elaborated in stanza 13:

> But, for the general award of love,
> The little sweet doth kill much bitterness;
> Though Dido silent is in under-grove,
> And Isabella's was a great distress,
> Though young Lorenzo in warm Indian clove
> Was not embalm'd, this truth is not the less—
> Even bees, the little almsmen of spring-bowers,
> Know there is richest juice in poison-flowers.
> ('Isabella', 97–104)

In this stanza, the first two lines, 'the general award of love, / The little sweet doth kill much bitterness' (97–98), strongly suggest that

1 I hold the same view as Heinzelman. See Heinzelman, 174.

the lovers will face a challenge. Their love is too happy and it cannot stay forever. This foreshadowing is further reinforced in the last two lines: 'Even bees, the little almsmen of spring-bowers, / Know there is richest juice in poison-flowers' (103-04). From these descriptions, the reader is made aware of the impending tragedy for the young lovers—and yet also that there is something of value ('richest juice') in what will ensue.

Though it is the first abrupt transition, stanza 12 displays the importance of the narrator's role and his technique as a modern writer. On the one hand, the reader is made aware of the author's voice. Instead of a statement, Keats poses a question, 'Were they unhappy then?', which may produce an unsettling feeling in the reader. It is especially abrupt for the reader to see the incongruity in the narrative sequence as this stanza is the first digression. Keats, as noted, repeats this technique in stanza 49. On the other hand, the use of the two other rhetorical devices, parallelism and repetition, intensifies the questioning and further complicates the rough transition. Though Kurt Heinzelman contends that the qualifiers, 'too many', 'little' and others in stanzas 12 and 13, are 'mawkishly overdetermined play of quantifying signifiers' (180), I would argue that the stylistic strategies, the repetition of 'Too many' and the parallel structure in lines 90 to 93, reinforce the sense of the question. A look at stanza 12 can illustrate my point about the function of the rhetorical devices:

> Were they unhappy then? —It cannot be—
> *Too many* tears for lovers have been shed,
> *Too many* sighs give we to them in fee,
> *Too much* of pity after they are dead,
> *Too many* doleful stories do we see,
> ('Isabella', 89–93; italics mine to emphasize the repetition and parallel structure)

The reader will be conscious of the mounting intensity reflected in stanza 12 and be impressed with the question.

In 'Isabella', digressions reflect Keats's modern consciousness. But in 'The Eve of St Agnes', it is the freedom and fluidity of narrative perspective that make Keats an original narrator.

In 'The Eve of St Agnes', the narrator's identity, presence, and narrative perspective are ambiguous. Though Robert Kern argues that the narrator assumes a traditional all-knowing stance of narrating and participating in the story,[1] other critics have complex ideas of the narrator's identity and role. Wolfson calls the narrator, not the poet-narrator Keats, but 'Keats's narrator'. And she does not specify any point of view.[2] James Chandler says that the poem 'offers no explicit persona, no first-person singular narrator to whom to attribute motives or ideas'. Yet he observes that in stanza 5, it is 'a first-person plural'.[3] These latter two critics summarize the common problems when reading this narrative poem. 'The Eve of St Agnes' is unlike *Endymion.* In *Endymion*, we can see that Keats the narrator merges with the protagonist Endymion. Neither is it like 'Isabella' since in that poem we constantly perceive the authorial intrusions and the narrator's sympathy for the heroine Isabella. Rather, in 'The Eve of St Agnes', the authorial subjectivity and presence become very fluid. We cannot say that it is Keats the poet-narrator or Keats's narrator. Neither can we pin down the narrative perspective, that is, is the narrative told in the first-person point of view? The third-person one? Is it the singular viewpoint? Or the plural one? Is the narrator omniscient or does he adopt a limited narrating stance? Moreover, can we allege that the narrator is covert and present or is he implied and invisible?

From the first stanza, the narrative perspective seems very fluid. In the first line, 'Ah, bitter chill it was' (1), we can be aware of Keats's or Keats's narrator's point of view. The narrator uses 'Ah', an interjection, to tell us what he thinks of the cold. It thus conveys a dramatic sense since he tries to make the reader feel the cold by uttering his thought. Wolfson argues that this word 'Ah' is a romance convention and is melodramatic.[4] But, I would suggest that, as dis-

1 Robert Kern, 'Keats and the Problem of Romance', in *Critical Essays on John Keats*, ed. Hermione De Almeida (Boston: G. K. Hall, 1990), 79. This article was originally published in *Philological Quarterly,* 58 (1979), 171–91.

2 See Susan Wolfson, *The Questioning Presence: Wordsworth, Keats, and the Interrogative Mode in Romantic Poetry* (Ithaca: Cornell University Press, 1986), 289, 295.

3 See James Chandler, 'Romantic Allusiveness', *Critical Inquiry*, 8, 3 (1982), 484.

4 Wolfson, *Questioning*, 289.

cussed, this exclamation shows the narrator's participation in the story. Nevertheless, after the utterance of 'Ah', the narrative perspective seems to shift from the implicit first-person singular narration to the third-person omniscient one. That is to say, from line 2, the narrator presents a wintry scene of the shivering owl, the limping hare, and the silent sheep flock in an objective way.

But in stanza 5, the narrator's perspective changes. It is the only place where we can clearly see the narrator's point of view. In this stanza, the narrator does not use the first-person singular but the first-person plural, 'us' (41), as though he wished the reader to identify with him. This shift of perspective, nevertheless, happens imperceptibly.

The fluidity of perspective and the narrator's indeterminate role are fully revealed in the gazing scene. In stanza 22, the narrator's perspective alters again. This time the narrator has the third-person singular omniscient viewpoint. He is asking Porphyro to be ready for his intention, the surreptitious gaze, as he says: 'Now prepare, / Young Porphyro, for gazing on that bed' (196–97). In his *Keats, Narrative and Audience* (1994), Andrew Bennett contends that 'The central narrative impulsion that draws together the frictions of Keats's fiction is Porphyro's desire for the vision of Madeline (her sight and the sight of her; Porphyro's visual vision of Madeline and her visionary vision of him; his seeing and her unseeing eyes; he unseen and she seen).'[1] Though Bennett has a good discussion of the paradoxical relationship between Porphyro's and Madelines's seeing and vision, he does not take the narrator's role into consideration. Within this framework, I would suggest that in the gazing scene, we cannot clearly perceive whether the narrator sides with Porphyro, the voyeur, or not. The narrator seems to present the scene as the tone sounds neutral. But it is difficult to state with confidence that the narrator simply narrates the scene. We must remember that though it is Porphyro who wishes to gaze Madeline 'all unseen' (79), it is a gaze of the desiring eye. We also need to note that the narrator assumes the third-person omniscient perspective and his omnipresence, naturally, guarantees him the gaze as well, though he appears invisible. Perhaps the narrator's gaze

1 Andrew Bennett, *Keats, Narrative and Audience* (1994; Cambridge: Cambridge University Press, 2006), 97.

is also a gaze of the desiring eye. In other words, it is hard to say that the narrator has no desire involved in this scene. There is an ambiguity in this scene and the narrator's role is indeterminate.

In stanza 28, the ambiguity in narrating stance appears once more. We are unable to say clearly that the narrator is third-person omniscient and objective perspective or the third-person limited viewpoint. It is also hard to say that he adopts the first-person narration. The narrator addresses to Porphyro and seems to identify with Porphyro: he sees Madeline via Porphyro's eyes. In this respect, two perspectives are combined: the first and the third ones. For instance, when he utters 'And 'tween the curtains peep'd, where lo!—how fast she slept' (252), we know that the narrator and Porphyro are both looking at the sleeping Madeline. The following idea can explain the narrator's narrating stance: 'It frequently happens that "this" is selected rather than "that", "here" rather than "there", and "now" rather than "then", when the speaker is personally involved with the entity, situation or place to which he is referring or is identifying himself with the attitude or viewpoint of the addressee.'[1] In this scene, there is the context of 'this, here, and now' and the narrator seems to merge with Porphyro and thus he can see how deeply Madeline sleeps. But Marian Cusac argues that the 'lo', the exclamation, has the similar function as 'ah' (1, 118).[2] She seems to see that the narrator's perspective is the first-person point of view and offers no alternative perspective. Though I agree with her observation as it accords with my earlier discussion of the narrator's stance when he utters the word 'Ah', I suggest that the exclamation 'lo' creates a problem for the reader. When referring to the objectivity of narration, we cannot be sure of the narrator's stance in this scene but are confused by it. The narrator appears very elusive in this scene.

In 'Isabella' and 'The Eve of St Agnes', Keats uses different narrative skills to highlight and express his modern consciousness, a

1 John Lyons, *Semantics* (Cambridge: Cambridge University Press, 1977), 677, quoted in Sylvia Adamson's 'Subjectivity in Narration: Empathy and Echo', in *Subjecthood and Subjectivity: The Status of the Subject in Linguistic Theory,* ed. Marina Yaguello (Paris: Ophrys, 1994), 197.

2 Marian Hollinsworth Cusac, 'Keats as Enchanter: An Organizing Principle of *The Eve of St Agnes*', *Keats-Shelley Journal,* 17 (1968), 117.

consciousness aware of the poet's role in shaping meaning and of narrative's dependence on perspective. In 'Isabella', he uses digressions to narrate a story. As a narrator, his voice and presence are manifestly perceived. There is a strong subjectivity in his narrative. But in 'The Eve of St Agnes', Keats adopts the opposite stance. The narrator's identity is ambiguous. His voice is not distinctly heard and he has a fluid narrative perspective. In this way, his presence and role are indeterminate. These techniques make Keats a different narrator from the old romancer. Keats thus makes his romances new and unconventional.

Anthony John Harding

The Fate of Reading in the Regency

The first part of my title is meant as a modest tribute to Geoffrey Hartman, whose extraordinary intelligence as a reader of poetry was generously shared at many of these conferences in the 70s and 80s. An entirely inimitable blend of wisdom, great learning, and wit; yet always in subtle ways admonishing us that behind the good fellowship and play of mind, there might be something life-changing at stake.

Hartman's book *The Fate of Reading* appeared in 1975, at a time when the study of literature as something that might have its own, intrinsic history—related to, yet distinct from, social and cultural history—appeared to be under attack. Without ever losing sight of the many relations literature has with psychology, philosophy, history, and material culture more broadly considered, Hartman resisted the competing calls to subsume literary studies under one or other of these newly authoritative disciplines: 'through a genuinely reflective history writing', he wrote, '[the critic] protects the very concept of art from the twin dangers of ideological appropriation and formalistic devaluation'.[1] Uncannily prescient about the damage that the culture wars would do to the academic status of literary studies, Hartman reaffirmed the principle that whatever the psychological limitations, religious biases, or political adhesions of the artist, the artwork has its own way of surviving them, its own way of being in the world; believing, with Coleridge, that 'art is the most conscious form of anti-selfconsciousness yet devised' (259).

The rest of my title indicates the intention to focus on the decade

1 Geoffrey H. Hartman, *The Fate of Reading and Other Essays* (Chicago: University of Chicago Press, 1975), xiii.

1811–1820, and on three writers in particular: Jane Austen, William Wordsworth, and Percy Bysshe Shelley. This is partly because I've become interested in this period as the transition into what has been called 'second romanticism', but it's also in response to the growing consensus of recent scholarship that this was the period when modern notions of literary studies, and the concept of a literary canon as something that readers might be guided by—or engage in debate about—began to come into focus.[1]

At the beginning of his essay, Hartman actually traces the idea of 'society born a second time, of the world of letters' to the late Victorians: 'The world of art and letters, of culture, is now [in the late Victorian period] seen as a *commonwealth* accessible to all through the key of literacy, and spreading therefore into the homes and consciousnesses of ordinary people' (249). But if this was the assumption on which Arnold, Ruskin and their contemporaries proceeded, it derived much of its authority from the arguments and counter-arguments that were first advanced during the Romantic period: and particularly, during the second decade of the nineteenth century.

Some years ago at this conference I suggested that one important legacy of the 1790s was a greatly increased attention to both the general social value, and the benefits to the individual, of reading. A fairly uncontroversial claim: but I was interested in seeing what authors in that period had to say on the subject, particularly what might be new or distinctively romantic about this new focus on reading, and how it differed from the attitudes of, say, David Hartley and Adam Smith. For the generation that came of age in the 1790s, William Godwin's idea that literature could be an important instrument of social progress was clearly crucial, though it's important to

1 See among others Alan Richardson, *Literature, Education, and Romanticism: Reading as Social Practice, 1780–1832* (Cambridge: Cambridge University Press, 1994); David Simpson, *The Academic Postmodern and the Rule of Literature: A Report on Half-Knowledge* (Chicago: University of Chicago Press, 1995); Clifford Siskin, *The Work of Writing: Literature and Social Change in Britain, 1700–1830* (Baltimore: The Johns Hopkins University Press, 1998); Lucy Newlyn, *Reading, Writing and Romanticism: The Anxiety of Reception* (Oxford: Oxford University Press, 2000). The term 'second romanticism' is from Virgil Nemoianu, *The Taming of European Romanticism* (Cambridge, MA: Harvard University Press, 1984), 27–9.

remember that for Godwin, this meant not just what we now call 'literature' (belles-lettres—poetry, drama, fiction), but publications in the sciences as well. Also crucial was the fact that many of the emerging generation of writers either were members of Dissenting communities for some portion of their lives, or at least lived among family or friends who were Dissenters: Godwin himself (he studied at the Hoxton Academy), Anna Laetitia Barbauld, Mary Wollstonecraft, Helen Maria Williams, William and Dorothy Wordsworth, Samuel Taylor Coleridge, Charles Lamb, William Hazlitt. The attitude of critical and morally-engaged attention that influential Dissenters (such as Joseph Priestley) enjoined, towards both the biblical text *and* the current state of society, helped to form the concepts of reading as a means of social and moral improvement that lay behind such works as Wollstonecraft's *Historical and Moral View of the French Revolution*, Wordsworth's 1800 Preface to *Lyrical Ballads*, Coleridge's *The Friend*, and Hazlitt's *Essay on the Principles of Human Action*.[1]

If we move ahead a decade or so, questions about reading as social practice and as the individual's route to self-development seem just as current, just as much at the forefront of writers' preoccupations, between 1811 and 1820 as they were between 1791 and 1800—in ways that make the term 'Fate of Reading' somehow more appropriate as a title. The emergence of a widely-circulated and influential periodical press is itself evidence of a growing public interest in the direction of people's reading: we could say, an interest in becoming better able to discriminate between what literature is healthful or essential, and what may be passed over or positively condemned. But the periodical press also posed a new kind of challenge to writers who

1 Some material from this paper was used in the article 'An Ethics of Reading: A Conflicted Romantic Heritage', *Keats-Shelley Journal* 57 (2008):45–65; see particularly 47–9, 53–61. John Beer has recently argued that the early 1790s marked the beginning of a 'crisis of the word', a phrase that encapsulates some key aspects of the change I've just referred to: the radical challenges to the credibility and authority of the Bible, and the sense of a threat to those social structures that were thought to give stable meanings to certain crucial words, such as 'honour', 'virtue', 'sensibility'. See *Romanticism, Revolution and Language: The Fate of the Word from Samuel Johnson to George Eliot* (Cambridge: Cambridge University Press, 2009), 21–2, 32.

hoped to build a closer relationship with their own audiences, communicating with them through a kind of dialogue between mind and mind, as if with a circle of intimates, as Coleridge certainly wanted to do in *The Friend*, rather than first having to appeal to the cultural gatekeepers or janissaries of the literary marketplace. When he uses the phrase 'the anxiety of authorship',[1] Coleridge means the simple fact that an author whose books were sold in bookshops (rather than by subscription, for instance) could have no idea what individuals were reading his work; but for him and for other writers of the time, the considerable influence of the literary reviews added greatly to the author's anxiety about finding the right kind of reader. In 1814, the print run for each issue of the *Edinburgh Review* was approximately 13,000, and for the *Quarterly* about the same.[2] In what follows, then, I'll be referring quite often to the literary reviews, as they were themselves an integral part of the story about the fate of reading during the Regency.

On 30th April 1811, Jane Austen wrote to her sister Cassandra: 'We have tried to get Self-controul, but in vain'.[3] *Self-Control* is a novel by Mary Brunton, published in 1810, in which the heroine, with all the usual attributes of such heroines, is particularly distinguished by the virtue named in the title. Her heroic dedication to self-control enables her to fend off the sexual advances of her would-be seducer, Hargrave. Austen's verdict on this novel, when she did finally manage to read it, was characteristically acerbic: 'my opinion is confirmed of its' being an excellently-meant, elegantly-written Work, without anything of Nature or Probability in it' (*Letters*, 234 [letter no. 91]). Behind the nicely calculated sarcasm of that comment, we can perhaps detect some anxiety: the anxiety of an as-yet-

1 S. T. Coleridge, *Biographia Literaria*, ed. James Engell and W. Jackson Bate, 2 vols, *Collected Coleridge*, Bollingen Series LXXV, vol. 7 (London and Princeton, NJ: Routledge and Kegan Paul and Princeton University Press, 1983) 1:233.

2 Newlyn, *Reading, Writing and Romanticism*, 9. For a detailed analysis of the power of the *Edinburgh Review* see William Christie, *The Edinburgh Review in the Literary Culture of Romantic Britain: Mammoth and Megalonyx* (London: Pickering and Chatto, 2009), 44–55 and *passim*.

3 *Jane Austen's Letters*, ed. Deirdre Le Faye (Oxford: Oxford University Press, 1995), 186 (letter no. 72).

unpublished author, wanting to get the measure of her rivals, who are competing for the same readership. Austen's first published work, *Sense and Sensibility*, was still in press with Egerton at the end of April, and was not to appear until October. That novel, too, represents the risks of behaving without what society considers common prudence, though it also examines the possible *costs* of making self-control one's chief guiding principle. No wonder Austen was anxious about Mary Brunton.

The 30th April letter goes on to say that Austen would like to hear Mrs. Knight's opinion of Brunton's novel. Mrs. Catherine Knight was the very wealthy widow who with her late husband had adopted Austen's brother Edward in 1783, and who in 1797 transferred to him the Godmersham Park and Chawton estates. 'I *should* like to know what her Estimate is', Austen wrote, '—but am always half afraid of finding a clever novel *too clever*—& of finding my own story & my own people all forestalled' (*Letters*, 186). Austen clearly saw Mrs. Knight's reaction to her own work as important, too, and not just because of the family connection: after all, Mrs. Knight was representative of the rather small class of people who could afford actually to *buy* novels, and might be persuaded to do so if they considered a particular novel worth owning. 'I think she will like my Elinor', Austen wrote on 25th April (*Letters*, 182–3 [letter 71]).

Recent work on Austen has thoroughly demolished the old idea that she wrote merely as a pastime, and did not particularly care about sales figures. She was serious about making at least a modest amount of money. She wrote to her brother Francis in a characteristically bantering tone, 'whenever the 3d appears [that is, *Mansfield Park*], I shall not even attempt to tell Lies about it [conceal her authorship].—I shall rather try to make all the Money than all the Mystery I can of it.—People shall pay for their Knowledge if I can make them' (*Letters*, 231 [letter no. 90]). At the beginning of the Regency, then, Jane Austen, behind all the banter, is more serious than ever about writing publishable novels that might make her a little income, contributing to the household finances. As Margaret Anne Doody puts it, 'In bringing her works into line with the new era—putting them into their Regency walking dress, as it were—Austen underwent a sort of personal and authorial revolution. That revolution made her publishable'.[1] But Austen also cared about how she would be read, and about the future of reading as a social practice: indeed, I think one could claim that she cared about the fate of reading in the Regency, and not just because she wanted people to buy *her* books. Like Jane West, Mary Brunton, and other predecessors, she wanted readers of her work to think intelligently about their own conduct and that of other people. Her comments on the work of other novelists show she was modestly confident that she could do something rather different from what others were doing in prose fiction; something that engaged a reader's rational mind, faculty of moral judgment, and sensibility, with a considerable spicing of wit and playfulness. There is certainly wit in the portrayals of *Mansfield Park*'s Mrs. Norris and Lady Bertram, and of both Mr. Elton and his bride in *Emma*; and in all these instances, the wit has a keen edge of moral and social critique.

Much has been written in recent years about the degree to which Austen participated in the religious revival of the early 1800s, particularly that strand of it known as Evangelicalism and identified with such figures as Hannah More, Jane West, and William Wilberforce.[2] John Beer's *Romanticism, Revolution and Language* places Austen alongside Coleridge and Wordsworth in the context of this revival, which he suggests was urged on by 'a sense of crisis, following the French Revolution, and an accompanying fear that the whole of civilization was under threat' (168.) He suggests too that 'she herself became more serious, sharing the desire of men such as Coleridge, Wordsworth and Southey for a stronger grasp of principle' (165). I certainly do not want to minimize that serious part of what Austen wanted to do. After all, she accepted that novels like Brunton's were

1 Margaret Anne Doody, 'The short fiction', *The Cambridge Companion to Jane Austen*, ed. Edward Copeland and Juliet McMaster (Cambridge: Cambridge University Press, 1997), 86.

2 See in particular Sarah Emsley, *Jane Austen's Philosophy of the Virtues* (New York: Palgrave Macmillan, 2005); and Karen Valihora, *Austen's Oughts: Judgment after Locke and Shaftesbury* (Newark, DE: University of Delaware Press, 2010). Mark Canuel's comment that 'the account of Fanny's reading practices suggest that she is trained to read the very novel into which she is written' is also relevant here—'Jane Austen and the Importance of Being Wrong', *Studies in Romanticism* 44.2 (2005):149.

at least well meant, and in such figures as the Edmund Bertram of *Mansfield Park*, she indicates her general approval of public efforts to reform contemporary manners and morals, particularly through reform of the Church. But it is the Edmund Bertrams and Edward Ferrars who will carry out the public side of such work, just as it's Mr. Knightley who will keep order, and dispense appropriate welfare support, at Donwell Abbey and its surrounding communities; while the *medium* through which such questions are raised is almost exclusively the consciousnesses of the women who love them: Fanny Price, Elinor Dashwood, and Emma Woodhouse. And what is on the agenda in all these novels is not just the virtue of these women, but their *happiness*. Austen surely knew that she would not awaken her readers' interest merely with characters who were paragons of prudence and religion. Following the agonies of Fanny Price as she watches Edmund fall for the sophisticated teasing of Mary Crawford, or Emma's mistaken attempts at 'charity' and her blunders as she flirts with the complaisant and charming Frank Churchill, the reader is always aware that it's not just the moral virtue of these heroines that is at stake—important though such virtue undoubtedly is—but their eventual earthly happiness.[1] 'By the Affections we are excited to pursue Happiness, and all its Means, fly from Misery, and all its apparent Causes'—so wrote David Hartley, whose work was dedicated to putting forward the doctrine of 'ultimate, unlimited Happiness to All'.[2] The relationship between the affections and happiness was much dwelt upon by eighteenth-century thinkers such as Hartley, and in this respect Austen was thoroughly grounded in earlier thought.

Consider the career of Anne Elliot in *Persuasion*. Anne has broken off her engagement to Captain Wentworth because 'She was persuaded to believe the engagement a wrong thing—indiscreet, improper'.[3] Anne believed she was being prudent, or rather was per-

1 Sarah Emsley points out that Emma's notion of charity is a cover for her own pride, 'charity conceived of as condescension' (*Jane Austen's Philosophy of the Virtues*, 133).

2 David Hartley, *Observations on Man, His Frame, His Duty, and His Expectations*, 2 vols (London, 1749), 1:iii; 2:438.

3 Jane Austen, *Persuasion*, ed. Janet Todd and Antje Blank (Cambridge:

suaded to think so. A significant reflection then follows: 'No second attachment, the only thoroughly natural, happy, and sufficient cure, at her time of life, had been possible to the nice tone of her mind' (30).

The reader follows her pilgrim's progress through several stages and levels of unhappiness. When her sister goes off with Charles to the great house where Captain Wentworth will be amusing the guests, we read Anne's reflection: 'what was it to her, if Frederick Wentworth were only half a mile distant, making himself agreeable to others!'—meaning, of course, the very agreeable Henrietta and Louisa (62–3); and the unspoken cry, 'what was it to her' clearly invites the reader to conclude that it was, in fact, enormously painful.

Persuasion also puts emphasis on the sensible management of literary taste. Anne's conversations at Lyme with Captain Benwick, a man 'of considerable taste in reading, though principally in poetry', are quite crucial. They discuss Scott and Byron. This encodes much of Benwick's character and current mood: that is, melancholic, dark, and regretful. Anne 'ventured to recommend a larger allowance of prose in his daily study', though ironically reflecting, as she parts company with Benwick, that her own lack of patience and cheerfulness hardly meets the moralists' standards (108).

In the last few chapters, when Mrs. Smith refers to the rumour of Anne's imminent engagement to Mr. William Elliot, saying 'I hope and trust you will be very happy' (212), Anne makes her intentions clear: 'he is nothing to me' (213). And at this point Mrs. Smith resolves to disclose what she knows of Mr. Elliot's real character—something she has refrained from disclosing before, because she feared that to do so might compromise Anne's chance of happiness.

When considered from a Godwinian perspective (that is, from the perspective of groups such as the Joseph Johnson circle of the early 1790s with its hopes for the abolition of privileges of rank and wealth), the explorations of human happiness that are offered in *Sense and Sensibility*, *Mansfield Park*, *Emma*, and *Persuasion* may seem, at best, a poor compromise with social convention and the long-standing ties between property ownership and political power. Nor did they win Jane Austen a very large readership, in her own life-

---

Cambridge University Press, 2006), 30.

time. *Pride and Prejudice*— even though it was said by Annabella Milbanke to be 'the fashionable novel', and went into a second edition—was printed in a first edition of (probably) 1,000 copies, then a second edition of only 750, and earned Austen a mere £110, since she had made the mistake of selling the copyright to Egerton.[1] The largest edition of an Austen novel was the first printing of *Emma*: 2,000 copies, which however did not sell out (Fergus, 18). In reference to Austen's sales, William St. Clair uses the phrase 'modest success'.[2] But such novels as *Emma* did win a small victory for Austen: the respect of some contemporary reviewers not only for her own work, but for the novel as a genre. Walter Scott, writing in the *Quarterly* in 1816, famously commented that the new 'style of novel', of which *Pride and Prejudice, Sense and Sensibility*, and *Emma* were examples, avoided

> those pictures of romantic affection and sensibility, which were formerly as certain attributes of fictitious characters as they are of rare occurrence among those who actually live and die. The substitute for these excitements ... was the art of copying from nature as she really exists in the common walks of life .... We, therefore, bestow no mean compliment upon the author of *Emma*, when we say that, keeping close to common incidents, and to such characters as occupy the ordinary walks of life, she has produced sketches of such spirit and originality, that we never miss the excitation which depends upon a narrative of uncommon events, arising from the consideration of minds, manners, and sentiments, greatly above our own. In this class she stands almost alone; for the scenes of Miss Edgeworth are laid in higher life, varied by more romantic incident, and by her remarkable power of embodying and illustrating national character. But the author of *Emma* confines herself chiefly to the middling classes of society .... [her world] affords to those who frequent it a pleasure nearly allied with the experience of their own social habits.[3]

1 Jan Fergus, 'The professional woman writer', *Cambridge Companion*, ed. Copeland and McMaster, 22.

2 William St. Clair, *The Reading Nation in the Romantic Period* (Cambridge: Cambridge University Press, 2004), 365.

3 [Walter Scott], review of *Pride and Prejudice, Sense and Sensibility*, and *Emma*, *Quarterly Review* XIV (March, 1816). William Galperin has recently pointed out,

Perhaps even more significantly, no less a figure than Archbishop Whately, reviewing *Persuasion* and *Northanger Abbey* just a few years later, wrote that

> The time seems to be past when an apology was requisite from reviewers for condescending to notice a novel ....
>
> For most of that instruction which used to be presented to the world in the shape of formal dissertations, or shorter and more desultory moral essays, such as those of the Spectator and Rambler, we may now resort to the pages of the acute and judicious, but not less amusing, novelists who have lately appeared .... Among the authors of this school there is no one superior, if equal, to the lady whose last production is now before us .... her's is that unpretending kind of instruction which is furnished by real life; and certainly no author has ever conformed more closely to real life, as well in the incidents, as in the characters and descriptions.[1]

The eventual result of such positive judgments appearing in the respectable pages of the *Quarterly*, and the growth of Austen's reputation in the Victorian period thanks partly to the refashioning of Austen as a model Victorian woman in the biography written by her brother, was that the term 'Regency' has become indissolubly associated with a well-defined type of prose fiction, now considered a genre in its own right, in which marriage is the expected destination, the male characters are generally expected to behave like gentlemen, the female ones like ladies, and there is lavish description of at least one of the stately homes of England. As Austen herself might have said, 'elegantly-written Work, without any thing of Nature or Probability in it'. These expectations, these stereotypes, are now in turn imposed on Austen's own work, so that it becomes difficult to keep clearly in view just how much Austen did in fact question and

however, that when Scott detects a new realism in Austen's work, he ignores the extent to which the work is actually oppositional to this contemporary trend in that it creates 'incompetent or perplexed' narrators—*The Historical Austen* (Philadelphia: The University of Pennsylvania Press, 2003), 6.

1 Archbishop Richard Whately, '*Northanger Abbey* and *Persuasion*', *Quarterly Review* XXIV (January, 1821); reprinted in *Northanger Abbey*, ed. Claire Grogan (Peterborough, ON: Broadview, 1996), 260, 262–3, 265.

undercut the prevailing assumptions of her own time.

According to an entry in Mary Shelley's journal for 14 September 1814, on that date Percy Shelley brought home a copy of *The Excursion*, and they read some of it together:

> 'Talk & read the newspapers. Shelley calls on Harriet who is certainly a very odd creature—He writes several letters—calls on Hookham and brings home Wordsworths Excursion of which we read a part—much disapointed [*sic*]—He is a slave—'.[1]

The term 'slave' here is no casual insult, but a term that both of them at this time would have used with fairly precise meaning, referring to one who has subdued and shackled his mental powers to the preservation of existing institutions (including religion), and the existing state of society. To those who admire both Wordsworth and Shelley this might still seem unnecessarily harsh, since Wordsworth most certainly wanted to criticize and change the existing state of society, and at this time felt himself to be in some sense the heir of John Milton. Poetry—or rather, poetry of Miltonic scope and seriousness—was the only literary form that could deliver the kind of meditation on enduring human values that a nation exhausted and corrupted by nearly twenty years of war desperately needed. The 'enlightened Critic', Wordsworth remarks in the 'Essay, Supplementary to the Preface' of *Poems*, 1815, seeks in such poetry 'a reflexion of the wisdom of the heart and the grandeur of the imagination'.[2]

Yet such a poet, publishing a work belonging to what Wordsworth calls the 'higher departments of poetry' ('Essay', 165) in the decade following the 1811 Regency Act, could not but be aware of enormous difficulties in reaching the unprejudiced, yet educated and culturally-equipped readers that such work might deserve. Francis Jeffrey, expecting poets to uphold neoclassical standards in subject-matter

1 Mary Shelley, *Journals*, ed. Paula R. Feldman and Diana Scott-Kilvert, 2 vols (Oxford: Clarendon Press, 1987), 1:25. At this point, Mary was still Mary Godwin. She and Percy Shelley were staying in an Oxford Street hotel, having arrived at Gravesend the previous day after their cross-Channel trip from the Netherlands. They had sailed from Marsluys on 11 September.

2 'Essay, Supplementary to the Preface', *Literary Criticism of William Wordsworth*, ed. Paul M. Zall (Lincoln, NE: University of Nebraska Press, 1966) [158–87], 161.

and versification, and preferably to favour the Whig line in politics, had heaped abuse on Wordsworth's entire poetic enterprise after the appearance of *Poems in Two Volumes* in 1807: William Christie, indeed, remarks on Jeffrey's 'preoccupation, not to say obsession, with Wordsworth throughout the early years of the nineteenth century' (60). Wordsworth risked no further published volumes of poetry until 1814, when *The Excursion* appeared in an expensive, handsome format which, as Paul Zall suggests, 'marked Wordsworth's declaration of independence from Jeffrey and the public for which [Jeffrey] stood'.[1] Despite the implicit claim made by its format, *The Excursion* received mostly negative reviews, the *Edinburgh* once more being particularly scathing—though William Hazlitt, writing in *The Examiner*, did express some 'limited admiration' for the poem. Hazlitt detected in it evidence of genuine creative power, and felt that Wordsworth was rivalling Milton in poetic seriousness, even if his choice of materials—in Hazlitt's words the 'Objects (whether persons or things) which he makes use of as the vehicle of his sentiments'—failed to reach the level of sublimity demanded by the Miltonic scope of the poet's aims.[2]

It is pertinent to my topic that in Book IV of *The Excursion*—the Wanderer's long discourse offering consolation, moral correction, and brotherly advice to the Solitary—the Wanderer counsels the Solitary to compensate for his solitude by reading the right kind of book, much as Anne Elliot was later to recommend a more healthful literary diet to Captain Benwick. No specific authors are mentioned (and we should be wary of confusing the voice of the Wanderer, sustained by a firm faith in a benevolent natural order, with that of Wordsworth himself). Since, however, the Wanderer later gives back to the Solitary the latter's copy of *Candide*—which he has found in a nook, left there, as the Wanderer puts it, 'Among more innocent rubbish'—with the comment 'You have known lights and guides better than these', he is presumably recommending authors other than Voltaire.[3]

1 Paul M. Zall, 'Introduction', *Literary Criticism of William Wordsworth*, xi. On the extent to which the *Edinburgh* was associated with Whig orthodoxy, see Christie, 52–4.

2 Beer, 133, quoting William Hazlitt, *Works*, ed. P. P. Howe, 4:124–5.

3 *Poetical Works*, ed. E. de Selincourt and Helen Darbishire, 5 vols (Oxford:

In other words, long before Carlyle advised readers 'Close thy *Byron*; open thy *Goethe*' (*Sartor Resartus*, chapter 9), the Wanderer tells the Solitary, 'Close thy *Voltaire*, open thy *Milton*'. The interesting point, however, is the context in which the activity of reading is recommended. The Poet has just responded to the Wanderer's advice to get up early and walk on the fells—'climb once again, / Climb every day, those ramparts'—with corresponding enthusiasm:

> 'How divine,
> The liberty, for frail, for mortal, man
> To roam at large among unpeopled glens
> And mountainous retirements, only trod
> By devious footsteps; regions consecrate
> To oldest time!
> ... what a joy to roam
> An equal among mightiest energies ....'
> (*WPW* 5:124; Bk IV.493–494; 5:125; Bk IV.513–518, 531–532)

The Wanderer then reminds the Solitary that the forms and images he sees around him in Langdale should remind him of his 'native glen', establishing a continuity in his life that remains in spite of the traumatic rupture he feels it has undergone – the loss of his two children and then of his beloved wife; a tragic personal loss, followed, several years later, by the return of hope and human feeling at the dawn of the Revolution, feelings that were to become embittered when his revolutionary hopes were crushed by the Terror and the rise to power of Napoleon.

> 'Compatriot, Friend, remote are Garry's hills,
> The streams far distant of your native glen;
> Yet is their form and image here expressed
> With brotherly resemblance. Turn your steps
> Wherever fancy leads ....
> You dwell alone;
> You walk, you live, you speculate alone;
> Yet doth remembrance, like a sovereign prince,

Clarendon Press, 1949), 5:141; Bk IV.1009, 1017.

For you a stately gallery maintain
Of gay or tragic pictures. You have seen,
Have acted, suffered, travelled far, observed
With no incurious eye; and books are yours,
Within whose silent chambers treasure lies
Preserved from age to age ....'
(*WPW* 5:126; IV.550–554, 558–566)

This is recognizable to us as a programme of psychological healing, through the stimulation of the sufferer's own active mental resources, stored up in his own past experience, his native curiosity, and his love of nature: 'remembrance'. Like the concluding stanza of the 'Intimations' Ode, the passage reassures the reader that, though much is taken, much abides; and strength and comfort are to be gained by realising that – though time has passed and one's powers of response may alter ('not the same / As those with which your soul in youth was moved' [IV.555–556])— there *is* still continuity, as well as change and loss. The lines 'Turn your steps / Wherever fancy leads' echo Wordsworth's description of his own explorations, in 'Tintern Abbey'—though *he* was led by 'Nature', not 'fancy'. From these sources, renewal will come: the forms and images of nature, experienced since childhood, though in different places and with different kinds of response; after that, the storehouse of memory; and, after that, a modest amount of reading—but only of the right kinds of regenerative books. It is clear that the healing process is to consist mainly of regenerating the Solitary's own innate ability to respond to the outside world with warmth of feeling.

Even in the Victorian period, when *The Excursion* attained the status of a best philosophy for many devoted readers, there were some, such as Harriet Martineau, who—perhaps confusing the Wanderer with his creator—thought that Wordsworth was naive or self-deluding about the ability of sublime landscapes to affect the moral temper of those living among them.[1] In this part of *The Excursion*, however, there is a mature and chastened sense that neither nature nor books will heal

1 See Harriet Martineau, *Letters to Fanny Wedgwood*, ed. Elisabeth Sanders Arbuckle (Stanford: Stanford University Press, 1983), 114 (letter dated 15 May 1851).

the wounded mind until the mind is prepared to receive what nature and books can give. There is a striking example of this, indeed, at the very beginning of the crucial dialogue between the Wanderer and the Solitary. Upon leaving the Solitary's cottage, the three companions follow a path that seems to lead upwards to the fell, but instead ends in an enclosed space, a 'hidden nook', with the way barred by 'the smooth surface of an ample crag, / Lofty, and steep, and naked as a tower' (*WPW* 5:76; Bk III.41–42). The forbidding and (it seems) unexpected appearance of this 'crag, / Lofty, and steep' might associate this scene with the episode in *The Prelude* in which the poet recalls the crag that seemed to stride after him as he rowed the stolen boat away across the lake.

The Wanderer is however struck by the sight of a strange grouping of rocks: a pair of upright rocks, supporting a bare, horizontal slab, on which a holly bush has somehow found enough of a crevice to put down roots and flourish. The Wanderer is immediately drawn to this picture, and his highly active imagination reads it as a type or symbol of something greater:

> 'Among these rocks and stones, methinks, I see
> More than the heedless impress that belongs
> To lonely nature's casual work: they bear
> A semblance strange of power intelligent,
> And of design not wholly worn away.
> Boldest of plants that ever faced the wind,
> How gracefully that slender shrub looks forth
> From its fantastic birthplace!'
> (*WPW* 5:77 [Bk III.80–87])

The Solitary answers that for *him*, this combination of rocks and bush represents not *design*, but nature's complete, blind indifference to human affairs—or what Thomas Hardy was later to call 'crass casualty'. Thus, in his more sombre moods, the chance assemblage of rocks merely provokes his pessimistic and saturnine side:

> 'But if the spirit be oppressed by sense
> Of instability, revolt, decay,
> And change, and emptiness, these freaks of Nature

And her blind helper Chance, do *then* suffice
To quicken, and to aggravate—to feed
Pity and scorn, and melancholy pride ....'
(*WPW* 5:79 [Bk III.137–142])

This exchange, and the Solitary's narrative and Wanderer's response to it, can be seen as an enquiry into the ways in which the accumulation of life-experiences lends a sober colouring to the mind, to all the intellectual powers, and hence determines the way in which that mind then *reads* the world around it—'the self-same cause / Different effect producing', as the Solitary says (*WPW* 5:79 [Bk III.154–155]). This is why *The Excursion* is not an epic but a metrical novel, to use the term Wordsworth himself uses.[1] It seems appropriate, then, to apply to *The Excursion* the principle that Wordsworth suggested to Francis Wrangham, in writing of *The White Doe of Rylstone*: 'Throughout [the poem], objects ... derive their influence not from properties inherent in them, not from what they are actually in themselves, but from such as are bestowed upon them by the minds of those who are conversant with or affected by those objects'.[2] And in a letter to Coleridge about *The Excursion*, he wrote: 'One of my principal aims ... has been to put the commonplace truths, of the human affections especially, in an interesting point of view; and rather to remind men of their knowledge, as it lurks inoperative and unvalued in their own minds, than to attempt to convey recondite or refined truths' (*Middle Years*, Part ii, 238). This emphasis on awakening the dormant, neglected, undervalued knowledge that readers *already* possessed, by offering commonplace truths, and shunning high-coloured description (of the kind found in *Childe Harold*), still spoke to such readers as Charles Lamb, and to a few others. David Hartley had argued that 'the actual View, or the mental Contemplation, of rural Scenes' could not help but bestow 'Health, Tranquillity, and Innocence' (*Observations on Man*, 1:420). But this particular route to

1 'Preface' to *Poems*, 1815, *Literary Criticism of William Wordsworth*, ed. Zall [139–57], 141.

2 *Letters of William and Dorothy Wordsworth*, ed. E. De Selincourt, 2nd edition, III: *The Middle Years*, Part ii: *1812–1820*, rev. Mary Moorman and Alan G. Hill (Oxford: Clarendon Press, 1970), 276 (W.W. to Francis Wrangham, 18 January 1816).

happiness no longer seemed persuasive to an audience that had been battered and perhaps secretly excited by years of reading about military defeats and victories. And the use of Miltonic periodic sentences to narrate the life-stories of ordinary people and their reactions to everyday objects can only have seemed incongruous, to those whose literary tastes were guided by the reviews in the *Edinburgh*. The only real precedent in the blank-verse long poem, Cowper's *The Task*, had appeared to set itself far more modest ambitions.

The lukewarm reception of *The Excursion*, and the distracted state of the public mind—at least that was how Wordsworth seems to have read things—meant that in private Wordsworth was resigned to winning only a few attentive readers during his own lifetime. As he remarked in a letter to his brother Christopher in 1816, referring to the recent publication of an *Ode* celebrating Bonaparte's defeat: 'The state of the public Mind is at present little adapted to relish any part of my poetical effusion on this occasion.—There is too much derangement in the taxation of the Country; too much real distress, and above all too much imaginary depression and downright party fury. But all this I disregard as I write chiefly for Posterity' (*Middle Years*, Part ii, 292). By 'imaginary depression', Wordsworth must have meant the depression or enfeebling of the imaginations of his potential readers; a recognition that the end of the war had *not*, for most people, brought an appetite for new intellectual enterprises, but only a grim sense of the long-term damage done to the militarized and overtaxed nation; of exacerbated social and economic problems.[1]

Nevertheless, in the Preface to the two-volume 1815 edition of his *Poems*, and still more in the supplementary Essay, Wordsworth tried to guide the more receptive reader towards achieving the right frame of mind in which to approach his work. Allowing for some (understandable) querulousness about the contemporary state of public taste, and particularly the role of the periodical press, both the Preface and the Essay tell us much about the fate of reading in the Regency.

In mid-decade, Wordsworth clearly believed that reading, at least

1 Nevertheless, when *The White Doe of Rylstone* appeared, it was published in a relatively expensive quarto, 'To express [his] own opinion of it', as he told Sir Humphry Davy— Benjamin Robert Haydon, *Diary*, ed. Willard Bissell Pope, 5 vols (Cambridge, MA: Harvard University Press, 1960–1963), 2:470.

the philosophically reflective reading that his own 'unostentatious' and 'pure' style demanded, was in retreat before the twin juggernauts of a public preoccupied with material concerns—a result of the catastrophic state of the postwar economy—and a literary climate, fostered by the periodicals, that favoured high-coloured, exotic narrative over Miltonic seriousness and the produce of the common day. Coleridge, in an early number of *The Friend* (14 September 1809), had complained about critics who demanded that his weekly essays offer something more topical than discussions of how a human life should be lived. 'My Themes must be *new*, a French Constitution; a Balloon; a change of Ministry'.[1] In 1815, Wordsworth was also attempting to say something about how a human life should be lived, and was even using a rather novel means of saying it; but he too felt the gatekeepers of the literary realm were an obstacle to building the audience his poetry was meant to address.

Writers who took a more radically oppositional stance against 'social and hereditary privileges' (Coleridge, *The Friend* 1:447), and refused to accommodate their work to the demands of the marketplace or to booksellers' notions of what was saleable, were equally concerned about the fate of reading; but less inclined than were Wordsworth or Coleridge to write 'chiefly for Posterity'. This sense of urgency, the wish that his writing might bring about social and political change *for his generation*, characterizes virtually everything Percy Shelley wrote.

Shelley's aim—and in this respect he is surely not totally different from Wordsworth—is in some sense to have his words overleap the barriers of everyday, utilitarian, leaden discourse, to awaken in the reader the dormant power to envision our world in a more fully human way. Both poets carried the legacy of William Godwin's empowering belief that 'the collision of mind with mind', through the medium of literature, was one of the engines of advancement

1 S. T. Coleridge, *The Friend*, ed. Barbara E. Rooke, 2 vols, *Collected Coleridge* Vol. 4, Bollingen Series LXXV (London and Princeton, NJ: Routledge and Kegan Paul and Princeton University Press, 1969), 2:73. On Coleridge's view of the literary life, as set forth in *Biographia Literaria*, see particularly James Vigus, 'Teach yourself guides to the literary life, 1817–1825', *Charles Lamb Bulletin* ns140 (October, 2007):154–6.

towards social justice. Godwin held that literature was one of the 'causes by which the human mind is advanced towards a state of perfection'[1]—though he did recognize that, as literature at that time reached only a small percentage of the population, it was necessarily limited in its effects. However, while Wordsworth was brought by his philosophy of a 'love of humankind' to a reconciliation with Christian beliefs, Shelley—following his first reading of Lucretius in 1810—embraced a 'Lucretian' view of the discourses of his time, by which I mean that he saw parallels between his own poetic vocation and Lucretius' desire to free men from the confining bonds of religious worship and superstitious beliefs.[2] The epigraph to *Queen Mab* is from Lucretius: 'I blaze a trail through the pathless tracks of poetry, where no foot has ever trod before. What joy it is to discover virgin springs and drink their waters, and what joy to gather new flowers ... never before wreathed by the Muses around anyone's head! First, I teach of great matters; and I go on to free men's minds from the crippling bonds of superstition'.[3]

The image of the poet as holding a light, a blazing torch, aloft, recurs frequently in *Queen Mab* and elsewhere in Shelley's work. Speaking to the soul of Ianthe, Queen Mab appeals to her, 'And midst the ebb and flow of human things / Shew somewhat stable, somewhat certain still, / A lighthouse o'er the wild of dreary waves' (*Complete Poetry* 2:224; VIII.55–57). Even closer to the Lucretian source are the lines in the *Revolt of Islam* addressed by Cythna to Laon: 'When I go forth alone, bearing the lamp / Aloft which thou hast kindled in my heart'—a direct echo of Lucretius' 'Tam clarum extollere lumen'.[4]

Most relevant to Shelley's concept of the poet's relation to the

1 William Godwin, *Political and Philosophical Writings*, ed. Mark Philp, 3: *An Enquiry Concerning Political Justice, ed. Mark Philp with Austin Gee* (London: William Pickering, 1993), 14–15.

2 See Paul Turner, 'Shelley and Lucretius', *Review of English Studies* n.s. 10 (1959):269 [269–82]; Timothy Webb, *The Violet in the Crucible: Shelley and Translation* (Oxford: Clarendon Press, 1976), 3, 53–5.

3 Donald H. Reiman and Neil Fraistat, eds., *The Complete Poetry of Percy Bysshe Shelley*, 2 vols to date (Baltimore, MD: The Johns Hopkins University Press, 2000–), 2 (2004):522.

4 *Revolt of Islam* Cto II, stanza xliv, lines1055–1056; see Turner, 'Shelley and Lucretius', 271.

reader, however, is the Lucretian idea that the universe results from the 'turbulent interaction' of atoms in 'this multitudinous ocean of matter', making the storm at sea a key image for Lucretius that evokes the 'inescapable turmoil' of human life. Such turbulence could actually be a way of *enabling creativity*, rather than inducing despair, as Hugh Roberts points out.[1] If the collision of atom with atom in the primordial chaos could generate the physical universe, with all of its evident beauties, then the intellectual eddies and currents impelled by the poet's words could similarly bring about new conceptions of the world—that 'collision of mind with mind' to which Godwin had attached such high value.

When Shelley wrote to Thomas Hookham about the printing of *Queen Mab*, his desire to skirt around the obstacles placed in his way by conventional, commonsense assumptions and the everyday use of language took a quite literal form: 'Let only 250 Copies be printed. A small neat Quarto, on fine paper & so as to catch the aristocrats: They will not read it, but their sons & daughters may'.[2] This rather impractical plan can be seen as dramatising, on a small scale, Shelley's hopes for all his work: that it would bypass the paternal presence, the Jupiter-figure in each mind that says 'thus it has always been and shall be evermore', to touch the unprejudiced, youthful mind, releasing the molecules of our fixed mental concepts from their bondage, and restoring the imaginative fluidity that every human being potentially possesses. In the Shelleyan understanding of art, poet and reader both participate in the reinvigorating of language.

This idea of a poet's words as freeing a reader's mind from prejudice and dogma by restoring its own inherent free-flowing creativity makes the elusive language of such poems as 'Mont Blanc', and *Prometheus Unbound* Act IV, easier to grasp. As has often been noticed, when Shelley's speaker in 'Mont Blanc' refers to the 'universe of things' it's simultaneously the poet's mind, the reader's mind, and the universe itself that are all combining together in the act

1 Hugh Roberts, *Shelley and the Chaos of History: A New Politics of Poetry* (University Park, PA: Pennsylvania State University Press, 1997), 251, 256.

2 Quoted in Donald H. Reiman, *Intervals of Inspiration: The Skeptical Tradition and the Psychology of Romanticism* (Greenwood, FL: The Penkevill Publishing Co., 1988), 231–2.

of creation initiated by the sound of the river:

> Thou art pervaded with that ceaseless motion,
> Thou art the path of that unresting sound –
> Dizzy Ravine! And when I gaze on thee
> I seem as in a trance sublime* and strange
> *[Version B: 'vision deep']
> To muse on my own separate fantasy,
> My own, my human mind, which passively
> Now renders and receives fast influencings,
> Holding an unremitting+ interchange
> +[Version B: 'unforeseeing']
> With the clear universe of things around ....[1]

The sense of a chaotic sound (the roar of the torrent) that is at the same time the matrix and source of music recurs in Act IV of *Prometheus Unbound*, when Ione and Panthea have been listening to the Chorus of Hours and Spirits:

> IONE What is that awful sound?
> PANTHEA 'Tis the deep music of the rolling world,
> Kindling within the strings of the waved air
> Aeolian modulations.
> IONE Listen too,
> How every pause is filled with under-notes,
> Clear, silver, icy, keen, awakening tones,
> Which pierce the sense, and live within the soul,
> As the sharp stars pierce winter's crystal air
> And gaze upon themselves within the sea.
> (IV.185–193; Leader and O'Neill, eds., 301–02)

The reviewers, on the whole, were not receptive to the political and philosophical beliefs driving this work, though there were glimmerings of understanding, and even admiration, in a significant number

1 *Percy Bysshe Shelley: The Major Works*, ed. Zachary Leader and Michael O'Neill (Oxford: Oxford University Press, 2003), 121. The text quoted here is that published in *History of a Six Weeks' Tour*, 1817, designated by Leader and O'Neill 'Version A'. 'Version B' (from the Scrope Davies notebook), reads 'vision deep' instead of 'trance sublime'; and 'unforeseeing interchange' instead of 'unremitting interchange' (Leader and O'Neill, eds., 125).

of reviews. By contrast, his skill in versification and ability to enchant the reader did win several admirers, though even the more positive reviews took care to warn *their* readers against the poet's doctrines, liberally sprinkling their reviews with terms such as 'venomous', 'abominable', and 'pernicious'.

A review that may have been at least partly written by J. G. Lockhart praised the power and originality of *The Revolt of Islam*, in terms that suggest the author of the review preferred to encourage the generous feelings and vivid imagination he found in Shelley's work rather than to vilify Shelley as a dangerous atheist.

> Such of our readers as have been struck by the power and splendour of genius displayed in *The Revolt of Islam*, and by the frequent tenderness and pathos of *Rosalind and Helen*, will be glad to observe some of the earliest efforts of a mind destined, in our opinion, under due discipline and self-management, to achieve great things in poetry. It must be encouraging to those who, like us, cherish high hopes of this gifted but wayward young man, to see what advances his intellect has made within these few years.[1]

Adopting similar tones of enthusiasm slightly tempered by caution, an anonymous reviewer in the *London Magazine*—appealing to 'Wordsworth, our great philosophical poet', as an example that Shelley ought to follow—remarked on *Prometheus Unbound*:

> In Mr. Shelley's piece, the deliverance of Prometheus, which is attended by the dethroning of Jupiter, is scarcely other than a symbol of the peaceful triumph of goodness over power .... To represent vividly and poetically this vast moral change, is, we conceive, the design of this drama, with all its inward depths of mystical gloom ... and its fair regions overspread by a light 'which never was by sea or land,' which consecrates and harmonizes all things .... To the ultimate prospect exhibited by that philosophical system which Mr. Shelley's piece embodies, we

1 [John Gibson Lockhart?], review of *Alastor; or the Spirit of Solitude, and Other Poems* (1816), *Blackwood's Edinburgh Magazine* 6 (November 1819):148–54, in *Shelley: The Critical Heritage*, ed. James E. Barcus (London: Routledge and Kegan Paul, 1975), 101.

have no objection.[1]

At the opposite extreme to these generally positive if sometimes rather patronizing reviews, however, stands John Taylor Coleridge, whose review of *The Revolt of Islam* for the *Quarterly* lambasts Shelley not merely for atheism, but for being a heretical apostate from the Church of Wordsworth:

> there is a naiveté and openness in his manner of laying down the most extravagant positions, which in some measure deprives them of their venom ... [Mr. Shelley] is, we are sorry to say, in sober earnest: —with perfect deliberation, and the steadiest perseverance he perverts all the gifts of his nature, and does all the injury, both public and private, which his faculties enable him to perpetrate .... Though we should be sorry to see the Revolt of Islam in our readers' hands, we are bound to say that it is not without beautiful passages, that the language is in general free from errors of taste, and the versification smooth and harmonious. In these respects it resembles the latter productions of Mr. Southey .... Mr. Shelley indeed is an unsparing imitator; and he draws largely on the rich stores of another mountain poet, to whose religious mind it must be matter, we think, of perpetual sorrow to see the philosophy which comes pure and holy from his pen, degraded and perverted, as it continually is, by this miserable crew of atheists or pantheists, who have just sense enough to abuse its terms, but neither heart nor principle to comprehend its import, or follow its application.[2]

Did such reviews actually influence people's choices of reading matter? The consensus seems to be that they did: there was a feeling that an overwhelming number of new books was being published, and authors often expressed the fear that hostile reviews would drive away potential readers, or at least potential *buyers*. De Quincey commented, in relation to the contemporary literary marketplace, that 'a

1 Anon., review of *Prometheus Unbound, with other Poems*, *London Magazine* 2 (September–October 1820):306–08, 382–91, in Barcus, ed., *Shelley: The Critical Heritage*, 244.

2 [John Taylor Coleridge], review of *Laon and Cythna* and *The Revolt of Islam*, *Quarterly Review* 21 (April 1819):460–71, in Barcus, ed., *Shelley: The Critical Heritage*, 124–6.

miserable distraction of choice ... must be very generally incident to the times' (quoted in Vigus, 161); and the result seems to have been that members of the reading public did rely on reviews to guide their choices.

Today, the problem of too much choice has entered a new order of magnitude. One e-reading device (Amazon's Kindle) offers a choice of 400,000 books for purchase, with a further million available free. What may be happening, as e-books gain a foothold, is actually the further withdrawal of the activity of reading from any connection with the public sphere: not a social activity, as it was most of the time for Austen, Wordsworth, and Shelley, but a reactively anti-social one, reading as pure solipsism, the very opposite of the idea of reading as an engine of social transformation that Godwin envisaged.

Ken Johnston

Wordsworth at Forty: Memoirs of a Lost Generation

On the occasion of the fortieth Wordsworth Summer Conference, I wondered what Wordsworth might have been doing at forty, in 1810. Not a banner year, particularly, I supposed. Looking it up, with my anniversary cap on, I found that he was just getting into serious composition of *The Excursion*, which finally appeared in 1814.[1] Still, not a promising piece of data, was my first reaction. Another essay on *The Excursion*? (Not that there have been so many of them.) But I looked at this fact with different eyes, now, than when I first studied *The Excursion*, in my 1984 book on *The Recluse*.[2] Because I suddenly recognized, with considerable excitement, that Wordsworth's re-start on *The Recluse*, out of which *The Excursion* came, fit right in with my own current research preoccupation, which has to do with what I call the 'lost generation' of the 1790s. Or, to give it its full working title, 'Unusual Suspects, Unlikely Heroes. Pitt's Reign of Alarm and the Lost Generation of the 1790s.' Now, the Solitary, the disillusioned antagonist of *The Excursion*, was always going to figure in this study, as a representative case. But I was not prepared for my realization, as I began to study the details of *The Excursion*'s composition and its manuscripts, that Wordsworth was contemplating very nearly the same project, as he resumed composition on *The Recluse*,

1 'A great amount of continuous or methodical composition toward a poem similar to the present *Excursion* cannot have taken place before late 1809 or early 1810 [though some passages for later books and possibly 'some part' of Book II 'were already in existence']. Mark Reed, *Wordsworth. The Chronology of the Middle Years* (Cambridge, Harvard U.P, 1975), 666.

2 *Wordsworth and 'The Recluse.'* Yale U.P., 1984.

after having finished *The Prelude* in 1805.

In a nutshell, my project is about the large number of young writers, men and women, whose writing careers were derailed, detoured or destroyed by their run-ins with the vast security apparatus devised in the 1790s by the Prime Minister, William Pitt the Younger, and his two Home Secretaries, Henry Dundas and William Cavendish, the third duke of Portland. I have found evidence that at least seventy-five people suffered in this way, though I have reduced the number to about a dozen for the book I'm writing. People like Gilbert Wakefield, James Montgomery, Thomas Beddoes, Sr. and others. The best quick vignette I can give for it is the famous story of 'Spy Nozy,' sent down to Somerset from London in summer 1797 to spy on Wordsworth and Coleridge as possible French agents scouting out landing places for an invasion. All a big funny mistake, as we hear about it from Coleridge in *Biographia Literaria* in 1817. No joke (nor mistake) at all, as we read about it in agent James Walsh's report to his controller, John King, in Portland's office. Dead on, in fact: 'this will turn out to be no French affair,' Walsh reported, 'but a gang of disaffected Englishmen.' Period. Case closed.

After-effects or fall-out? No arrests or anything like that, of course—though the local Somerset doctor who sent in the report, the *in-form*-ation, was operating very much under the encouragement of the king's proclamation of May, 1792, that his subjects should report any evidence they thought they might have found, of suspicious activity in their parts. As it says in our tubes and subways and airports today, 'See something? Say something!'

All that happened was that the Wordsworths lost their lease, or rather their chance to renew it, on Alfoxden House, thus contributing to their decamping to Germany with Coleridge the next year. Which, it might be said, was a very 'fortunate fall' for the development of English Romanticism, for it was there, isolated in Germany, thrown entirely back on himself and his own resources, that Wordsworth began the series of sketches of his childhood experiences that gave him the impetus to compose 'The Poem on the Growth of My Own Mind,' which we call *The Prelude*.

But the results for most of my other 'suspects' were not so fortunate. Indeed, many of their lives—or rather, their careers—were ruined. And in all cases there appears a sharp demarcation between the promising 'Before' of their youthful lives, and the sadder-but-wiser 'After' of their later lives. I am not speaking, for the most part, about the more than 100 persons who were *tried* for sedition or treason between 1792 and 1798—more trials for these crimes than ever before or after in British history—and who were usually (two-thirds of the time) convicted and jailed, fined or transported; some even executed. No, I am talking about people, like Wordsworth and his Solitary, who took their disillusionment personally, as it were, escaping back to some place where they could nurse their wounds and sense of injustice in private. Or else went into some other radically altered, downgraded line of work. These were precisely the persons for whom Coleridge said *The Recluse* was intended: 'I wish you would write a poem, in blank verse, addressed to those who, in consequence of the complete failure of the French Revolution, have thrown up all hopes of the amelioration of mankind, and are sinking into an almost epicurean selfishness, disguising the same under the soft titles of domestic attachment and contempt for visionary philosophes.'[1]

That is, *The Recluse* should address the condition of their entire generation. But the people I am writing about were generally not so very selfish, soft, or contemptuous of political philosophy. Coleridge, like Wordsworth in *The Excursion*, seems to throw the blame primarily on this generation's loss of idealism, as if it were a character flaw, rather than the result of the harsh penalties the government, and its hegemonic allies, had been meting out for nearly ten years by the time Coleridge wrote this, in 1799.

In all cases, my 'suspects' suffered some apparently slight penalty—like Francis Wrangham losing his graduate fellowship—not from the state's legal system, but from its *hegemonic* 'overflows.'[2]

1 *Ca.* Sept. 10, 1799; *Collected Letters of Samuel Taylor Coleridge,* ed. E.L. Griggs (Oxford U.P., 1956), I.527.

2 *Hegemonic* signifies the entire range of power exerted by the dominant group in a society over other groups, regardless of their consent: not just political and economic power, but also ideological and cultural power, very often indirectly and unannounced. The term was popularized by the Italian philosopher and politician Antonio Gramsci (1891-1937), who used it to describe the pervasive and often invisible way that bourgeois values permeate modern "democratic"

Yet these penalties and slights fundamentally altered the course of their careers: fellowships denied, university positions withdrawn, church-livings promised but then taken back, inheritances denied, engagements broken, contracts abrogated, and so on and on. (See appendix for a partial list of the sort of things I have in mind.) For the proverbial picture-worth-a-thousand-words illustrating how this unsystematic system operated, see James Gillray's cartoon, 'Smelling out a Rat,' of December, 1791. My adapted caption for it would be, not 'The Long Arm of the Law,' but 'The Long Nose of Hegemony.' All very much like the McCarthy era in 1950s America.

We can sum up this phenomenon with an excellent quotation from William St. Clair's biography of the Godwins and the Shelleys:

> By the turn of the century the men and women who had dominated the intellectual scene in the early years of the decade were widely perceived and portrayed as a conspiracy of disloyal dissenters of the type who had killed King Charles, international atheists and liberals who admired every country but their own, fast-talking theorists intent on tearing down every social institution, agitators who made the poor discontented, sexually loose media people, ambitious fifth columnists awaiting their opportunity, and Irish rebels subsidized by the country's external enemies.[1]

Or, from the other side of the political coin, Henry Tilney's *reassurance* to Catherine Morland, in *Northanger Abbey* (published in 1818 but written in 1798), that they are 'surrounded by a neighbourhood of spies,' so the terrible Gothic horrors she imagines his father General Tilney committing could never occur in England. But General Tilney does turn out to be a monster, not Gothic, but of an all too familiar domestic kind, and the same might be said of the paternal aspect of Pitt's 'security' system, if we read Austen's passage with the right (i.e., wrong) emphasis:

---

societies. I am adapting it a little further, to describe the voluntary ways in which many people in 1790s acted against others, whom they perceived—with direct or tacit encouragement from the government—as enemies of the state.

1 William St. Clair, *The Godwins and the Shelleys. The biography of a family* (The Johns Hopkins U.P., 1989), 196.

> Dear Miss Morland, consider the dreadful nature of the suspicions you have entertained. What have you been judging from? Remember the country and the age in which you live. Remember that we are English, that we are Christians. Consult your own understanding, your own sense of the probable, your own observation of what is passing around you. Does our education prepare us for such atrocities? Do our laws connive at them? Could they be perpetrated without being known, in a country like this, where social and literary intercourse is on such a footing, where every man is surrounded by a neighbourhood of voluntary spies, and where roads and newspapers lay everything open? Dearest Miss Morland, what ideas have you been admitting? (Chapter 24)

Hence I was excited to see, as I began studying the new Cornell edition of *The Excursion*, that Wordsworth was very much turning his compositional thoughts to the same task.[1] He resumes his intended masterwork, *The Recluse*, by trying to recall and recuperate the 'lost generation' of his 1790s young manhood. *The Excursion*, in Books II–IV, where he began—since Book I was adapted from 'The Ruined Cottage' of 1797–98—has good drive and forward motion, which it loses progressively in Book V and after, as Wordsworth returns it to Grasmere and tries to make his tales of his neighbours bear the weight of his reflective meditation, that they are apt materials for 'the Mind's *excursive* Power' (IV.1259) to work upon redemptively.

But in Books II–IV, the poem has a *plot*: it sets up the drama of the recuperation of a member of the 'lost generation' of the 1790s: The Solitary, the title-figure of Book II (followed by his 'Despondency' and its 'Despondency Corrected' in III and IV). Notice how those titles echo and parallel—in reverse—the titles of the final books of *The Prelude*, which Wordsworth had just completed: 'Imagination, How Impaired and Restored.' They set us up to witness—if we were to read these two large poems consecutively, as Wordsworth wrote them—how a representative man of this activist generation fell into enthusiasm for the French revolution, as an escape from personal grief and despair (the deaths of his wife and children), then fell out of it,

1 *The Excursion*, ed. Sally Bushell, James A. Butler, Michael C. Jaye, David Garcia. Cornell U.P., 2007.

first into selfishness and dissipation, then to escapism (to America), and finally to the mountain valley where The Wanderer and The Poet find him, and hope to redeem him, or at the very least, cheer him up in some significant way.

The figure of the Solitary has long been identified, since Wordsworth so fingers him in the Fenwick note of 1843, with Joseph Fawcett, a preacher in Old Jewry Street in London whom Wordsworth heard in 1791. Wordsworth's description of Fawcett, both in poem and in note, is not exactly true to life, and Hazlitt was the first to roundly declare that Wordsworth had unfairly libeled Fawcett for his 'dissipation.' Wordsworth speaks of Fawcett in the Fenwick note in a disapproving, condescending tone. 'The chief of these [persons] was, one may *now* say [Wordsworth's emphasis] a Mr. Fawcett, of 'shewy talents [but] he had not strength of character to withstand the effects of the French Revolution, and ... the wild and lax opinions which had done so much toward producing it, and far more in carrying it forward in its extremes.' 'Poor Fawcett [fell] into habits of intemperance, which I have heard (though I will not answer for the fact) hastened his death.' Wordsworth concludes, that 'there were many like him at the time which the world will never be without, but which were more numerous then for reasons too obvious to be dwelt upon.' The emphasis on 'now' is evidently Wordsworth's own, in the sense of, 'one may now safely say,' at a distance of some thirty years (1814–1843). As if it wouldn't have been possible to say this in 1814 when *The Excursion* was published.

Even setting aside Wordsworth's stuffy censure, one might well ask, exactly how much strength of character would have been necessary to withstand the effects—the attractions, the repulsions, the events—of the French revolution? Quite a bit, I would say, since thousands, nay, millions, were swept away by it, either in enthusiasm or horror. As Wordsworth so famously had already said of himself, 'bliss was it in that dawn to be alive, but to be young was very heaven!' Wordsworth is here *personalizing* or *psychologizing* the Solitary's investment of his hopes in the revolution. But he was certainly not alone in doing that.

More to my point, he also says, of the original model or models for the Solitary, something that is often skipped over, that he was based on a Scotch pedlar in Grasmere, 'a character suitable to my purpose, *the elements of which I drew from several persons with whom I had been connected, and who fell under my observation during frequent residences in London at the beginning of the French Revolution.*' (PW, V.374; italics added) That is, a very large swath of such persons was on Wordsworth's mind, in describing various facets of the Solitary's character and experience. Rather than being based on one or two originals, he is in some respects an amalgam of many aspects of the group I call 'unusual suspects.'[1]

Latterly, beginning with E. P. Thompson, in *The Making of the English Working Class*, the claims of John Thelwall to have contributed something to the creation of The Solitary have been urged, and Thelwall is now pretty generally regarded as a tributary source for his character. But since Thelwall is also the best candidate for the source of *The Recluse*'s topic sentence, 'On Man, on Nature, and on Human Life,' from his very similar long poem (to *The Excursion*) *The Peripatetic* of 1793—which might be said to be an *Excursion* before the Fall—his presence in *The Excursion* is even more palpable, anticipating its entire structure of ambulatory conversation. Henry Crabb Robinson, who is usually a reliably straight shooter, declared firmly that Wordsworth had borrowed without acknowledgement from Thelwall.[2]

However, my point is not to argue Thelwall's claims over Fawcett's, but to argue that Books II–IV of *The Excursion*, the best part of the whole poem, are shot through with Wordsworth's recollections of many of his contemporaries, friends and colleagues from the time—including above all Wordsworth's sense of himself. Hazlitt said *The Excursion* had three speakers in one voice, a sort of Trinity-plus-One, the three being the Wanderer, the Poet, and the Pastor, and the One, the God-head as it were, being Wordsworth. But Wordsworth is also

1 'The Solitary is founded on rationalistic liberals [particularly Fawcett, but] ... John Thelwall and Gilbert Wakefield, among others, must have contributed to the portrait.' (Carl Woodring, *Wordsworth*. Harvard U.P., 1968, 183), cited in George Myerson, *The Argumentative Imagination: Wordsworth, Dryden and religious dialogues* (Manchester U.P., 1992), 54.

2 *The Excursion* (Cornell U.P., 2007), 9.

behind, or in, some of the expressions of the Solitary's enthusiasm and disillusion with the French revolution—as many close parallels indicate, between his expressions and those we know, that his contemporaries could not know, from Wordsworth's descriptions of himself in Books IX–X of the 1805 version of *The Prelude.* If one reads some of these passages aloud, even a trained Wordsworthian's ear is hard pressed to say whether they are from *Excursion* Books II–IV or *Prelude* Books IX–X, except for the difference in pronouns. In *The Excursion*, then, Wordsworth was re-doing *The Prelude*, but with a new slant or perspective on it, third-person rather than first-person.[1]

I find many 'hooks' and parallels in the things Wordsworth says about the Solitary that set him up as a prime 'unusual suspect' of the type I am writing about. I will roughly categorize them for my purposes here as *inter-textual*, *extra-textual*, and *con-textual.* I do not have space to detail all the ways in which things that are true of the Solitary are also true of one of more of my 'unusual suspects,' so I will focus instead on one of each type.

Inter-textual: Gilbert Wakefield

Wordsworth introduces the Solitary with a quotation—very unusual in itself, for there are very few quotations from other works in *The Excursion.* He says the Solitary has come back to 'live and die / Forgotten,—at safe distance from "a world / Not moving to his mind"' (II.331–32). That is, he suffers the disillusionment particular to intellectuals when they find out that their wonderful ideals for social change are not going to come about as easily, nor even with the same form and content, as they had hoped.

The internally quoted lines, which Wordsworth emphasizes as 'serious words' are from George Dyer's 1802 poem, 'On the Death of Gilbert Wakefield. Meditated in a Garden, near a Churchyard, at the Close of the Year.' But they are not identified in the 1814 text; they were traced later in the 19th century by Nowell Smith, one

1 It seems to me that it may have been about this time that he decided, or began to consider, not publishing 'the poem on the Growth of my own mind' (*The Prelude*) in his lifetime. For why start out all over again with essentially the same story, when you have just told it in first-person terms?

of Wordsworth's best early editors. It's a Thomas Gray or William Collins elegy, or perhaps more like Coleridge's 'Monody on the Death of Chatterton.' That is, a lament for a special individual, whose death symbolizes the loss of something important and significant beyond the person himself.

Dyer's full statement says, 'When man, quite wearied with a world, perhaps, / Not moving to his mind, a foolish world, / Seeks inward stillness, and lies quiet down.' Dyer remembers that he and Wakefield 'together … did hail / The star of Freedom, rising on a world / Of slavery-goaded men: we lived to see / France rise to something of the new-born man … .' Bliss was it in that dawn, all over again.

But now Wakefield is dead, prematurely at age forty-five, from a typhus fever contracted during his two-year prison sentence for seditious libel in the harsh Dorchester gaol, a couple of months after his release. Dyer, who is only a journeyman poet at best, nevertheless has an elegant line, regretting not just Wakefield's death, but the world's particular loss, in that it will never be able to read Wakefield's *reflections on the meaning* of his arrest, trial and imprisonment—just the sort of perspective Wordsworth is taking in the character of the Solitary. 'He seem'd / Destin'd to live, *the cool grey chronicler / Of years now passing* …' (Dyer, 11–13; my italics). 'The cool grey chronicler': that's good, I think. Although Wakefield was anything but 'cool,' being one of the liveliest, not to say angriest, types of that special literary job-description popular at the end of the 18th century, the controversialist or polemicist. I give you Tom Paine as the full development of the type. Or Christopher Hitchens today. Maybe not nice guys, but they make you think.

It is, I think, as some people now say, 'huge,' that Wordsworth should allude this specifically to Wakefield at this point in his reviving *Recluse/Excursion* poem. It is in the nature of inter-textual studies that much is made of apparently very little, and that is what I am doing here, with these seven words from Dyer's elegy. For Gilbert Wakefield was not just anybody. He was, rather, the last victim of Pitt's reign of terror, or alarm, whichever you want to call it. His trial and conviction for seditious utterance in 1798–99, for attacking Richard Watson, Bishop of Llandaff, for his *Address to the People of Great Britain*, supporting Pitt's new, desperate war-funding measures—with which we are all now very familiar: the income tax and budget financing based on deficit projections—was the last trial of the 1790s, the last in an unbroken sequence of twenty trials per year, on average, between 1792 (Paine's trial *in absentia*) and Wakefield's. And it was, furthermore, seen in exactly that light at the time. Charles James Fox remonstrated that it signaled the end of the liberty of the press in England. And Fox was right: there were no more trials for sedition or treason for five years after Wakefield was convicted. Not because nobody had any more seditious thoughts, but because everyone was afraid to express them. One comes upon what seems like a startling 'gap' in Howell's and Cobbett's massive edition of the *State Trials* at this point. And when the trials resumed, they tended to be trials of desperate individuals hatching desperate plots, a far cry from the organized movements of the London Corresponding Society or the Society for Constitutional Information, or the many other organized bodies in London and the provinces active earlier in the decade. Which of course was exactly the government's successful intention, to drive the plotters underground so they could be more easily isolated, criminalized and dealt with more harshly and efficiently.

But there is more. For why should Wordsworth allude textually to Wakefield's disillusionment and death at just this initiating point in setting up the anti-hero whom he hopes to redeem? Because Wordsworth knew what only a handful of people reading *The Excursion* (and that was about the size of its original reading audience, unfortunately) could have known: namely that he too, the William Wordsworth who is the author of the poem we are reading, and not just a typological character called the Solitary, was the author ('By a Republican') of just such an attack on the same Bishop of Llandaff, his unpublished *Letter to the Bishop of Llandaff* of 1793. The perfectly preserved, unique copy in Wordsworth's own hand of which is safely preserved in the vaults of the Wordsworth Library in Grasmere. If he had published that in 1793, it is safe to say that we would not be celebrating him today, or not in the same way. Just as, if he and Francis Wrangham had published their imitation of Juvenal's eighth satire in 1796, they would very likely have been hauled up before the magistrates under the provisions of the newly passed Gagging Acts of December, 1795. He would, perhaps, have made the cut as one of the more interesting 'unusual suspects' I am studying: young writers who started out strong, but who in one way or another were side-lined, officially or (much more often) unofficially, and who were never able to, as we sometimes lamely say, 'realize' their potential.

And yet, let him who has eyes to see and ears to hear, let him read. For those who care to know it, either about Wakefield or about Wordsworth's peculiar *almost shared* fate, signalled in a very small voice here, it is true, but signalled all the same—this little *homage* of Dyer upon Wakefield is simultaneously Wordsworth's homage to him: someone who dared to do what I *almost* dared to do, and paid the consequences for it—which I did not, which allows me now to honour him by way of representing what is, in fact, the entire intention of my poem, as enunciated by my friend Coleridge, 'a poem on those who, in consequence of the complete failure of the French revolution, have thrown up all hopes of the amelioration of mankind,' etc., etc.

Or, as I would add in the case of Wakefield and most of my other 'unusual suspects': who lost their chances for the career they wanted because of the unappealable injustices they suffered. Or as Wordsworth says forthrightly in Book IV, he seeks to restore 'the loss of confidence in social Man, / By the unexpected transports of our Age / Carried so high, that every thought—which looked / Beyond the temporal destiny of the Kind— / To many seemed superfluous' (IV.262–66). That is to say, he seeks to re-adjust thoughts which went *too far*. He was, we know, consciously preparing *The Excursion* to be the 'necessary' book of philosophic-political recovery for the approaching post-war era. Hence his allusion to the Solitary-as-Wakefield is richly ambiguous, both in itself and its buried connection to Wordsworth-as-Wakefield.

Extra-textual: Francis Wrangham

Francis Wrangham is not in *The Excursion*, but Wordsworth sent Wrangham a complete late draft of the poem just before publication, expressing the hope that he would like it. Just a friendly gesture? Maybe. But his friendship with Wrangham, which went back to their days at Cambridge, included two factors that are very salient to what *The Excursion* is about—that is, the business that Wordsworth is undertaking in it. Their co-authored imitation of Juvenal's eighth satire in 1795 could've got them in a lot of trouble, with its attack on the specious nobility of the so-called noble classes, naming plenty of names, including Wordsworth's nemesis, James Lowther, Lord Lonsdale, who had refused to pay the Wordsworth children the money he owed their father. But his successor had made good on most of the amount, and was now Wordsworth's nominal patron, and lord of the manor in Westmoreland. Indeed, *The Excursion* is dedicated to Sir William Lowther, so it would never do to publish words like these on his predecessor:

> Must honour still to Lonsdale's tail be bound?
> Then execration is an empty sound.[1]

But Wrangham kept pestering Wordsworth to publish the thing for years, especially after the defeat of Napoleon in 1815—as if 'that wild stuff we wrote in the '90s' could now safely be trotted out again—and he kept it up well in the 1820s. Wordsworth's first refusal, in November 1806—when he was just starting to make some exploratory probes at composing what became *The Excursion*—is nervous, vehement and a bit flustered:

> I would most willingly give them up to you, fame, profit, and everything … if it were unknown to everybody that I ever had a concern in a thing of this kind; but I know several persons are acquainted with the fact and it would be buzzed about; and my name would be mentioned in connection with the work, which I would on no account should be.[2]

'Which I would on no account should be.' That is to say, more clearly: I very much want this not to be the case, not to happen.

But, far more than his saying he 'now' could identify Fawcett as an

1 Wordsworth, *Early Poems and Fragments, 1784-1797*, ed. Jared Curtis and Carol Landon (Cornell U.P., 1998), 808.

2 *LMY*, 89; Nov. 1, 1806.

original for the Solitary, Wordsworth *never* thought it was time good enough or safe enough to publish this piece of collegiate verse. It was only published in full in 1997, in the Cornell Wordsworth, edited by Jared Curtis and Carol Landon, though it was pretty fully available in DeSelincourt's edition of the *Poetical Works* (1940–49).

Yet Wordsworth also knew that Wrangham had already suffered for his youthful liberal idealism, been seriously disillusioned, that is, *with consequences*, as the Solitary, like Wordsworth, had not. (I mean material consequences, as distinct from emotional consequences—not that both cannot be severe.) Wrangham lost his college Fellowship, and with it his long-desired academic career, a career that he was perfectly cut out for. He won several literary and translation prizes, which were very important keys to careers then. Both the 1895 *Dictionary of National Biography* and that of 2004 state that Wrangham lost his fellowship because of his sympathy for the French revolution, and that is substantially why he did lose it. But of course he *didn't* lose it for that reason, technically. Nobody ever said, 'you're too liberal, you can't have the fellowship.' Instead, in a way that perfectly exemplifies what I call the 'hegemonic' punishment of this young generation of liberals, Wrangham lost his fellowship through the smooth operation (i.e., the clever manipulation) of his college's academic machinery. The graduate fellowship committee that was to award him the fellowship took it back because they said he wasn't as well qualified for it as another candidate, to whom they did give it. Even though this other candidate (John Vickers) wasn't technically eligible for the fellowship because he already held a church living (i.e., a job) worth more than the amount of the fellowship. But the committee told him to resign that fellowship and then re-apply for this one, which they promptly awarded him. I mean, it stinks to high heaven! And yet, I'm sorry to say, it is a perfectly recognizable bit of academic shenanigans, of the sort we still have with us from time to time. The committee that awards the fellowships says you're not qualified? Then that's it, you don't get it. Wrangham tried to appeal the decision, but it was fruitless, since the Vice-Chancellor, Isaac Milner, was in on the fix from the get-go, as part of his general policy to purge liberals from the faculty and student body and make

Cambridge University safe from reform.

So Wordsworth was asking for Wrangham's approval of a poem that he knew would touch very close to home, and open up old wounds, when Wrangham read about the Solitary, for he was still—always—sore about the injustice he had suffered, and would also have recognized the allusion to Wakefield.

And yet, as in the case of Wakefield, there is more, going from the extra-textual back to the inter-textual, a parallel between Wordsworth's small but undeniable *homage* to Wakefield, and Wrangham's 'revenge,' such as it is, upon Cambridge and its Vice-Chancellor for denying him the career he wanted. Wrangham didn't make a public remonstrance at the time: what's a young college grad to do? But he certainly didn't accept it quietly: 'I was *virtually exiled* from the University, to which I had certainly done no discredit; my academical prospects wholly blasted, and the regular avenues to professional emolument and dignity obstructed – apparently forever.'[1] Wrangham never forgot the injustice done him in his youth. Indeed, he came to see it as a kind of curse on him and his family. He could not, for example, get a fellowship for his son at Cambridge, lamenting 'that if he could not do more for his son than he had done for himself, the young man had no chance of election.' What we can't do for our children hurts more, in a way, than things we have to suffer ourselves.

He fell first into a hand-to-mouth existence, prepping students for university. He was finally rescued by a church living in his native Yorkshire that his father managed to secure for him. He became semi-famous as 'Archdeacon Wrangham,' a lifelong doer of good social works in his diocese, and as a collector of books, insofar as one can become famous in that line. He published several compendia of local and national history, the most well known of which was his six-volume *British Plutarch* of 1816. This is where, submerged

---

1 Michael Sadleir, *Archdeacon Francis Wrangham* (Oxford U.P., 1937), 57. Henry Gunning, longtime registrar of the university, looking back at Wakefield's case from the perspective of sixty years, declared the faculty's decision "unstatuable" (i.e., impossible to reconcile with the statutes governing that fellowship), showing that it had been held to "absolutely binding" at two other colleges. (*Reminiscences of the University* [London: George Bell, 1854], 14, 21.)

in a long footnote to his life of Sir Francis Bacon, Wrangham takes his 'revenge' for the injustice he had suffered a generation earlier. He concocts a little historical romance, developing the idea of the curse on him into a historical myth in which he protests the injustice he suffered some twenty years earlier. He tells of the trials and travails of one 'Wraynham or Wrayngham' (probably not a real relation, just a similar-sounding name) who was thrown into the Tower for making an accusation of bribery against the then Lord Chancellor. Later, when Bacon himself was put on trial, and ultimately disgraced, the same charge was used as 'a well-founded complaint and true in every particular!' But too late for poor Wraynham, who was ruined, dead, and his family reduced to beggary by then. Wrangham's note continues on up the present, taking up the mantle of Wraynham's sufferings, 'from which after the long lapse of nearly two centuries they [i.e., his ancestors] are *but just* under the providence of God beginning slowly to emerge [i.e., now, in 1816; italics added].' Michael Sadlier, Wrangham's only biographer, says (in 1937), Wrangham's 'elegant diction has a characteristic undertone of half-humorous astringency, not unconnected, one suspects, with Wrangham's own unhappy experience of a Lord Chancellor's sense of justice.'[1] But Sadlier's own diction is too tentative by half, or even by whole. Yet it is characteristic of the way these 'unusual suspects,' these members of the 'lost generation' of the 1790s have been handled by posterity, their injustices recycled and thereby redoubled over time. One 'suspects'?? One knows that Wrangham was sore as hell about what had happened to him. But he also knew he could do nothing about it. And he also knew he had still to be careful how much he protested—there were his sons' prospects to consider, for example. And so he 'revenges' himself in an extremely small way, turning the injustice he suffered not only into a parallel with that of his with his supposed ancestor, Wraynham, but also suggesting that now, thanks to him, Francis Wrangham, he and his family are beginning to emerge from this cloud of disgrace and injustice. A tiny 'revenge' for a very substantial wrong!

These are the kinds of (im)-balances that I find everywhere among

1 Sadleir, 2

my 'unusual suspects': they lost much more than they were ever able to gain back, like the victims of McCarthyism. Yet they inflect the shape of the 'English Romanticism' that we think we know, with other dimensions that we can barely see.

Speaking of nearly invisible dimensions, we may hear Wrangham speaking out more loudly to Wordsworth in his poem on the deaths of Saul and Jonathan in 1820, a standard trope for the theme of lost friendship between men. But he is still speaking in code, for instead of the name of the person he is addressing, he prints only asterisks. But it sounds like it could be 'Wordsworth': the word fits the meter, and extends the implied alliteration of W's.

> O ***, thou alike in weal and woe
> Found *trusty*, might I *utter unbetray'd*
> The name, which springs to my impatient lip,
> How would I syllable it forth! But thou
> Hast that within thee (should this mystic verse
> E'er meet thy conscious vision) – that, with throb
> Answering to mine, will recognize and seize
> Each *veil'd allusion*, as in *fond disguise*
> *Cautious it shadows forth* our early hours.
> A halo-glory crowns each blessed spot
> Visited by our steps in youth's sweet prime,
> … Conversing … of Granta's amaranth bowers,
> And with many a studious friend *with hooks of steel*
> Link'd to our common heart!
> (*Poems*, 1820; italics added)

They are separated now, but the speaker marks his friend's 'brightening fame,' which was very much Wordsworth's case, finally, ca. 1820. But Wrangham would always have to wonder if he was 'trusty' enough for Wordsworth, because he, like Thelwall and Coleridge and Southey and others, knew potentially damaging details from the poet's radical youth. And his ominous hush-hush diction, italicized here, betrays or highlights the thought.

Con-textual: The Solitary in the United States of America

In the last one hundred lines of Book III ('Despondency'), Wordsworth sends the Solitary off to America, specifically the new United States, 'to fly, *for safeguard* to some foreign shore,' 'an Exile, *freed from discontent*' (III.843–46; italics added). Here again we can see ways in which Wordsworth's account of the Solitary's life and career is a wide collocation and summary of many different persons in his 'lost generation,' his 'portrait of an age' to be renovated, restored and rehabilitated. Neither Fawcett or Thelwall went to America, of course, no more than did Wordsworth. But many of my 'unusual suspects' of the 'lost generation' did, whose history has been very thoroughly documented by Michael Durey, in his *Transatlantic Rebels and the early American Republic* (University of Kansas Press, 1997). And they went for reasons that Wordsworth's language neatly—or ambiguously—alludes to: for safety, or out of discontent with impossibility of personal political life in England in the late 1790s.

The important, expectable references are there, and easy to identify, even if not named as such by Wordsworth in his text. William Godwin, for example, who is my paradigmatic 'unusual suspect' (as Thelwall is the paradigmatic *usual* suspect) was never arrested, but his career was derailed anyway, hegemonically, so that for a number of years he could only write and publish under pseudonyms. He makes his standard cameo experience in *The Excursion* as in *The Prelude*, as the 'wild theory' man (II.275), referring to *Political Justice* of 1793. So too does Tom Paine, the archetypal usual suspect, even more than Thelwall (except that he absconded from trial in late 1792, never to return to England again), in six lines which sketch the salient arc of his 1790s writings in England.

> There arose
> A proud and most presumptuous confidence . . .
> Not alone in rights,
> And in the origin and bounds of power,
> Social and temporal . . . .

That would be the Paine of *Rights of Man*, Parts I and II (1791 and

1792). But when this presumptuous confidence applied itself to 'laws divine, / Deduced by reason, or to faith revealed' (240–55), Wordsworth is speaking of the Paine of *The Age of Reason*, which added blasphemy and apparent atheism to his political 'crimes' of treason and sedition and libel, and lost him many erstwhile supporters, both in England and even more in America.

The whole going-to-America thing for the Solitary hardly makes sense, or makes only a very weak kind of sense, if we take it thematically—as I suppose I did when I first read it—merely as a reference to the failure of the American 'experiment,' one generation on: 1776–1806, paralleling what Coleridge called 'the complete failure' of the French Revolution. But it makes much more sense, has much more *point*, if we read it in the knowledge of the many persons, including Wordsworth's his own muse Coleridge, who, despairing at the possibility of change in England in the 1790s, contemplated emigration to the new United States, including thousands upon thousands who did so emigrate, and mostly never came back.

Others left because the climate in Britain had become just too toxic for them to work and live, most famously Joseph Priestley, whose invaluable house and laboratory were burned to the ground in the infamous Birmingham riots of 1791, who left for Pennsylvania in 1794. And where he went, others were to follow, including Wordsworth's closest friends Coleridge and Southey, who planned to build their 'Pantisocratc' community on the banks of the Susquehanna River near Carlisle and Harrisburg, the present capital of Pennsylvania, where Priestley's elegant Georgian house and laboratory still stands, as a museum in a state park. All I will say here is to re-insist on what I have said elsewhere (in Nick Roe's collection, *Coleridge and the Sciences of Life*) that the Pantisocracy plan was, no more than the Spy Nozy story in its actuality, a joke, despite all the fun that has been had with it, from the laughter of the Bristol conservative establishment in 1797 down to our present academical days. Poets farming on the banks of the Susquehanna (what a funny-sounding name!), writing poetry in the afternoon and swapping their wives round in the evening! What a laugh! Well, I have to say that, from the other side of the pond (as we say), the idea of a persecuted minority fleeing to American shores to practice their religion or their politics or, for that matter, their poetry, does not seem like a joke at all. It seems more like the history of my country, from the Pilgrims to the Mormons, and with many stripes and types in between—and since. Not to be too solemn about it, of course, because it was rather a hare-brained scheme. But the point is that several highly intelligent and talented young people worked seriously on the idea for a couple of years, and they were not play-acting. Many of these self-exiles or absconders became very successful citizens of the young United States, senators, governors, professors (like Priestley, at the University of Pennsylvania), and so on.

No less a historian than G. M. Trevelyan, hardly a radical, has opined that, if convictions had been returned for any of the defendants in 1794, a wave of executions and other severe penalties would've been released, very much parallel to the similar government-sponsored terror in France. We know the government had hundreds of arrest warrants ready and signed, to put to use in expectation of a 'Guilty' verdict. John Horne Tooke, the third defendant tried, along with Thelwall and Hardy, was in no doubt that the government wanted 'our blood, blood, blood!' That may sound a bit histrionic, but not if you're on death row, where they were, standing accused of a capital crime. But the statement accurately reflects the amount of tension at the time, which many people, like our Solitary, and like Coleridge and Southey, contemplated escaping from, or actually did emigrate away from.

All this is to say, that the lines on America in *The Excursion* are not just a summary typology of what happened to people like The Solitary, but have very specific reference to people that Wordsworth knew well, in person or by sight, those 'several persons with whom I had been connected, and who fell under my observation during frequent residences in London at the beginning of the French Revolution.' Indeed, to leave out the American 'option' for disillusioned liberals and radicals of the time would be to distort the whole picture. But, that said, the Solitary does not fare well there, unlike Priestley, or Robert Merry, or Alexander Calender, or Charles Pigott, or many others. Instead, in somewhat the same spirit as Dyer's lines on Wakefield, he finds the New World unsuited to his mind: 'a motley spectacle / Appeared, of high pretensions … / Big passions strutting on a petty stage' (III. 905–07).

Yes, America was a rough, raw country in 1810. The seat of government had moved from Philadelphia to Washington, the District of Columbia, only ten years earlier, and it was still a swampy mess. In fact, Wordsworth did all his composing of *The Excursion* during the term of James Madison's presidency, 1808–1817, which is an unusual perspective in which to see the poem. But a revealing one, since England and America were back at war then, in what Americans call the War of 1812, but which was rather, in the bigger picture, one of the many international sites of conflict during the so-called Great War of 1803–1815, often called the first 'world war' for that reason.[1]

This seems to have been the America that Wordsworth was thinking about at the time, when he has the Solitary say, 'Let us, then, … leave this unknit Republic to the scourge / Of its own passions.' (922–24) And he returns directly to the setting of *The Excursion* (so far as it can be determined), described in a very interesting MS variant captured in the Cornell edition: 'the expanse of unappropriated earth' (948, MS 71). Interesting, because this is almost exactly the same phrase Wordsworth had used to describe Grasmere in his *Recluse*-attempt of 1800, 'Home at Grasmere,' *before* completing *The Prelude*, when he tried recasting Grasmere as a 'centre … come from whereso e'er you will,' that could be seen, at least in imagination, as a centre of imaginative energy capable of competing in quality if not in quantity with other world centres like London, Paris, or indeed Washington, D.C.

> Society is here:
> The true community, the noblest Frame
> Of many into one incorporate;
> … a multitude
> Human and brute, possessors undisturbed
> Of this recess, their legislative Hall,

1 I can't resist the illustrative anecdote of the two old generals, one American, one British, who had got on to the topic of times when the two partners in this so-called "special relationship" had not treated each other very well. 'After all', says the American, 'you burned Washington!' 'What?? Never!,' splutters the old Brit. 'Joan of Arc, yes, I admit it. Regrettable. But never Washington!'

Their Temple, and the glorious dwelling-place
(818–20, 825–28)

Interesting, that is, because this is exactly the strategy he will use to bring *The Excursion* to a conclusion. This 'expanse of unappropriated earth,' though it does not appear in the published poem, is the pivot point on which Wordsworth, not the Solitary, turns, to propose that the tales he tells of its inhabitants in Books V–IX have enough of the variety of 'human life,' its tragedies and triumphs, to restore his lost 'confidence in social Man.' But the Solitary, to his credit, and hence also to Wordsworth, as his creator, does not quite buy it, but says he'll think about it.

And so, I think, should we. Tracking the many traces of Wordsworth's 'lost generation' we can find, with diligence, in Books II–IV of *The Excursion,* is a promising way to go about it, allowing us to say that we can now see more of its intentions and dimensions than Wordsworth was able to say, for whatever reasons, in 1810 or 1814.

Appendix: biographical consequences for some members of the 'lost generation' of the 1790s.

1) death by execution or from the effects of imprisonment (William Orr, Joseph Gerrald, Gilbert Wakefield);

2) imprisonment or transportation (James Montgomery, the 'Scottish Martyrs');

3) abscondment, flight, immigration or self-exile (Paine, Priestley, Helen Maria Williams, William Cobbett, Robert Merry, Alexander Callender);

4) arrest, detention, and long periods of being 'held for questioning' in defiance of, or during the frequent abeyance of, the right of habeas corpus (John Thelwall, Thomas Spence, Daniel Isaac Eaton, William Drennan);

5) financial penalty or material ruination, including permanently damaged career prospects (William Frend, Elizabeth Inchbald, Francis Wrangham, David Williams, Thomas Beddoes, Sr.);

6) episodes of continuous government and/or vigilante harrassment (Robert Bage, Robert Burns, Thelwall);

7) psychological damage or physical harm, temporary or permanent (John Tweddell, Charles Lloyd, George Burnett, William Wordsworth, Joseph Ritson, Beddoes, Sr.);

8) effective silencing and discouragement of literary production (Bage, Mary Hays, Montgomery, Eliza Fenwick, Anna Barbauld);

9) extended periods of orchestrated public criticism, ridicule and (unprosecuted) libel (Mary Wollstonecraft, Sydney Owenson,Charlotte Smith);

10) pseudonymous, anonymous, or long-delayed publication (Godwin, Mary Robinson, Thomas Holcroft, Wordsworth);

11) extended periods of unexplained silence or disappearance (Tweddell, George Crabbe, Wordsworth);

12) significant change in choice of literary topics, and/or in rhetorical and formal means of expression (Burns, William Blake, Drennan, William Roscoe);

13) significant revision or outright erasure of 'juvenile errors' (Wordsworth, Coleridge, Amelia Alderson Opie),

14) very long-term or virtually permanent damage to career and reputation (Wollstonecraft above all, but also Priestley, Merry, Drennan, Thelwall);

15) little discernible effect, pro or con, one way or the other (George Dyer, Joanna Baillie);

16) voluntary, sincere changes of mind and political opinion (Robert Southey, Wordsworth, Coleridge, Archibald Hamilton Rowan, James Mackintosh);

17) dramatic, calculating adoption of contrary conservative and/or outright pro-government positions (Lloyd, Charlotte Dacre, Humphry Davy);

18) public recantation of former opinions, and/or informing on or otherwise besmirching the reputations of former liberal colleagues (Coleridge, Mackintosh);

19) direct monetary reward from officialdom for such changes or actions (Davy, John Wolcot, James Gillray).

Richard Gravil

Is *The Excursion* a 'metrical Novel?'

In the final paragraph of his bewildering preface to *The Excursion*, Wordsworth famously denies having any intention of 'formally announcing a system', even in *The Recluse* itself, let alone in 'this intermediate poem'. He hints that the reader may be able to 'extract a system for himself' if the poet succeeds in conveying 'clear thoughts, lively images and strong feelings', but, again, this claim is made not about *The Excursion*, but about 'the whole poem', namely *The Recluse*, and it is that ghostly entity whose ambitious, appetizing and never-to-be-fulfilled 'Prospectus' his final paragraph introduces.[1] Approaching that digressive instalment, *The Excursion*, in the expectation of finding the exposition of a philosophy of life must, therefore, be self-defeating.

What, though, if we look instead for palpable life experiences and for a variety of perspectives on those experiences, offered through subtly differentiated fictional minds, whose role is to act as lenses upon our world? This being a poem composed of ambulatory dialogue between four characters, designed to tell the story of the conspiracy between three of those characters to reform the fourth, it seems appropriate to engage our critical faculties in adjudicating between perspectives, suspending judgment as to which perspectives

1 The Winter School talk from which this essay is drawn rashly attempted to answer five questions: what was *The Recluse* and how did it develop? What (had it been writeable in 1799/1800) would a finished *Recluse* have argued? How does the quasi-dramatic medium of the only completed portion of the whole affect its message? What traces remain in the poem of the influence of its Godfather, John Thelwall? And, given that his prospectus promised a version of paradise regained, just what did Wordsworth understand by paradise? This essay addresses only the third of those questions; all five will be addressed in *A Guide to Wordsworth's 'Recluse'* (forthcoming, 2011).

carry the author's imprimatur, and prepared to question what we are told, rather than assuming that our role is merely to be borne upon a palanquin (I borrow Wordsworth's own 1815 trope for the passive reader) into realms of transcendental revelation. Is its design, perhaps, more *maieutic* (in the Socratic and Kierkegaardian sense)[1] than we have generally given it credit for?

Such a question is not as strange as it may sound, if we remember both Wordsworth's own compositional practice before he wrote *The Excursion*—his radical experiments with voice and character in the years 1798 to 1807—and what happened to the long poem very soon after Wordsworth, in, perhaps especially, Adam Mickiewicz's *Pan Tadeusz* (1834), *Clough's Amour de Voyage* (1858) Browning's *The Ring and the Book* (1868) and Barratt-Browning's *Aurora Leigh* (1857).[2] He has explored the potentialities for ironized speakers, limited points of view, and (especially germane to the *telling* of the Solitary) the merits of the twice-told tale, of which *Hart-Leap Well*—a poem associated in *Home at Grasmere* with the burden of *The Recluse*—is so remarkable an instance. And in the Preface of 1815 he himself numbered 'the metrical Novel' among the poetic genres.[3]

What works Wordsworth had in mind by 'that dear production of our days, the metrical Novel' is hard to say. W. J. B. Owen's wonderfully laconic note on the matter reads (in its entirety): 'Crabbe's tales? Scott's narrative poems?' (189, n. 4.). The recent success of Byron's *The Giaour* (1813) and *The Corsair* and *Lara* (1814) might also contribute to Wordsworth's hint of derogation in 1815 ('that dear production of our days') except that these are tales, and whatever he means by 'the metrical Novel' it is apparently *not* synonymous with Epic,

1 Maieusis = 'midwifery' is the term Kierkegaard (following Socrates) uses for the role of the work of art in aiding the birth of new structures of thought or feeling in the reader.

2 For several dozen examples of the verse novel's recent florescence, c. 1980–2001, beginning with Vikram Seth's *The Golden Gate* and Walcott's *Omeros* see John Lennard's introduction to Ralph Thompson, *View from Mount Diablo: an Annotated Edition* (Humanities-Ebooks and Peepal Tree Press, 2009), 12–14), *View from Mount Diablo* being a major instance.

3 W. J. B. Owen, ed. *Wordsworth's Literary Criticism* (Routledge 1974) 176 (also *Prose Works* [Clarendon] 3: 27). I am grateful to Anthony Harding for reminding me of Wordsworth's use of this phrase—see page 164 above.

or Tale, or Romance, which he lists in the same sentence as exemplifying other modes of the narrative genre. Since Landor's *Gebir* is also no more than a 'tale', and works like *Madoc* and *Thalaba* are more often styled 'epics' or 'romances', one might conclude that the primary instances of 'that dear production of our days, the metrical Novel' are in fact Goethe's 9-Canto *Herman and Dorothea* (translated by Holcroft and printed in Bristol by Biggs and Cottle) and *The Excursion* itself. Indeed Holcroft's summary of the impact of Goethe's work upon its translator rather suggests this conjunction: Goethe's poem may have a more eventful plot than Wordsworth's, but like *The Excursion* it offers 'No artful denouement, no crouded incidents, nor any prolonged suspence' (*sic* and s*ic*). In reading, Holcroft continues, 'the mind is always kept alive, it is never so hurried as to lose the power of reflection' and the soul 'is never tortured by compassion: its feelings are pure, mild and in unison with the dignified tone of the narrative'. In its characterisation—a point often made pejoratively in critiques of *The Excursion*—'all strong contrasts are avoided' [1]

Charles Lamb, in his review, described *The Excursion* as a conversation poem, not in the Coleridgean sense of quasi-conversational monologue but based upon actual, if somewhat archangelic, conversation. It is a conversation between four subtly differentiated figures, a lapsed Calvinist, the Wanderer, to whom Wordsworth gives his own childhood and experience of nature: the Solitary, a lapsed lay preacher and revolutionist, in whom Wordsworth expresses his own experience of revolutionary sympathies and his own moral crisis; a Poet, who is less Wordsworth than either of these; and a Pastor. The Wanderer is Wordsworth as he might have been had he not gone to Cambridge. The Solitary is Wordsworth as he might have been if had not had the love of Dorothy and Coleridge to fall back on in Somerset. The Pastor is (perhaps) Wordsworth as he might have been if he had followed the family expectations that he would take holy orders, bearing somewhat the same relation to his author as Childe Harold to his.

And the Poet? The Poet contributes least to the argument of this poem and most to its hermeneutic challenge. He overflows with sym-

1 J. W. von Goethe, *Herman and Dorothea* [1799]; tr. Thomas Holcroft (Bristol, 1801),vii, viii.

pathy at the tale of Margaret, with ecstasy at the sight of Blea Tarn, with uncritical friendship whenever he comments on the Wanderer, and with boyish enthusiasm whether talking about the British Empire in Book 6, or demonstrating his rowing prowess in Book 9. Whoever he is, he seems not to be the poet who wrote *The Prelude*, claimed the lake district as his mountain playground, found the Alps an insufficient challenge, and who in climbing Snowdon found himself 'as chanced, the foremost of the band'. For which reason I capitalise Poet throughout this essay when referring to the character rather than to the poet.

Our very first encounter with this Poet finds him, as compared with the possessor of Wordsworth's stout legs, curiously enfeebled:

> Across a bare wide Common I was toiling
> With languid feet which by the slippery ground
> Were baffled; nor could my weak arm disperse
> The host of insects gathering round my face....(1, 21–24)1

Book 1 presents this feeble figure as a willing acolyte to a hale and hearty Wanderer, whose wisdom he will never seriously question throughout the 9 books of *The Excursion*, only once hinting that his friend might have spoken to the Solitary more understandingly. In Book 2, bizarrely, he needs the Wanderer as a guide to the modest heights of Lingmoor Fell, which he seems never to have seen and by which he seems quite overcome (2: 343–7). This introduction in *The Recluse* part 2 of a fictionalized Poet, the 'I' in the poem, as its primary narrator creates problems that Wordsworth, had he ever progressed with 'The Recluse Part First' or embarked on 'The Recluse Part Third', would have had somehow to resolve. Since, in *The Excursion,* most of Wordsworth's formative life-experience and much of his 'philosophy' have been gifted to either to 'The Solitary' or 'The Wanderer', how could 'The Poet' of *The Recluse* ever establish the existential ground from which to argue whatever it was that he was to argue?

One can summarise the poem's 'plot' easily enough. It is designed, all agree, as an exercise in group therapy: two counsellors, one quali-

1 All quotations from *The Excursion* are from *The Poems of William Wordsworth: Collected Reading Texts from The Cornell Wordsworth*, ed. Jared Curtis (Humanities-Ebooks, 2009) volume 2.

fied by holy orders, the other by life experience of the kind depicted in Book 1, attempt to cure the Solitary of what they regard as a cynical view of life and a tendency to self-indulgent spleen, and re-educate him to the point where he can be safely invited to take tea at a vicarage. Critics have adapted well to these parameters, writing in psychotherapeutic mode, pointing out, for instance, how at certain points the Solitary shrinks from exhortations, which, symptomatically, he tends to see as criticism, while at others he shows signs of responding well to conversational openings and begins to play a more active part in discussion(!).

But why is this poem routinely read as if its *overt* signals are to be trusted? It tends to be assumed that the Solitary is indeed a cynic, even a misanthrope. According to Kenneth Johnston he exhibits 'a settled depression .... that he nurses with excruciating misanthropic care. ...The Solitary's principled philosophy, based on the authority of his own life experiences, is that human life is without meaning, that human efforts to give it meaning are pretentiously laughable, and that we are better off dead.' He is egotistical, and his idealism is suspect (Johnston, 264).[1] Sally Bushell notes astutely how this effect is partly contrived as composition proceeds: Book 5 is carefully edited to make the Solitary seem more cynical or sarcastic than in draft: 'he is no longer really allowed to speak on behalf of others [i.e. sympathetically to the lives of peasants], rather he is represented as being virtually incapable of doing so.' But Bushell adds her own negative perceptions to those insinuated by the poet: his memory, she says, is 'dysfunctional' and his apparent sympathy for the old man whose funeral is narrated in Book 2, is unconvincing; the Solitary 'abuses' the old man in death by appropriating the narrative for himself rather than making it a memorial for the old man; his egotism is 'blatant and unattractive' (220, 229).[2]

Is he really as bad as that? And come to that, is the Wanderer as good as that? Wordsworth's four-person strategy has never really been taken as an invitation to scrutinise all four characters as unknown

1 Kenneth R. Johnston, *Wordsworth and 'The Recluse'* (Yale University Press, 1984), 264).

2 Sally Bushell, *Re-Reading 'The Excursion': Narrative, Response and the Wordsworthian Dramatic Voice* (Ashgate, 2002), 220, 229

entities, about whose qualities we are to make up our own minds. When Blake stages a conversation between a clod and a pebble in *Songs of Innocence & Experience* most modern readers would recognise that while the poem seems to invite us to decide whether we agree with the clod's thesis or with the pebble's antithesis, it may be nudging us towards generating our own synthesis or towards some other way of escaping the presented dichotomy.

Yes, 'The Solitary' is unhappy, and restoring him to 'contentedness & even cheerfulness of mind' is one goal of Wordsworth's poem.[1] But something we can hardly miss is that Wordsworth projects into the Solitary his own experience, his own despair, and his own skills of argument. He also expresses through the Solitary his own bereavements and his own anxiety—his own poignant knowledge of what it is like to lose two children, and his all-too-vivid imagination of what it would have been like to lose a beloved wife as well.[2] The main burden of the Solitary's great monologue in Book 3 is the crisis autobiography of lines 427–998, perhaps the most compelling passage in all of Books 2–6 of *The Excursion*, or indeed of Books 2 to 9. The story is a powerful compressed reprise, with variations, of Wordsworth's own crisis autobiography in Books 7–11 of *The Prelude*, including a transatlantic journey Wordsworth never made, and a contempt for native American life that he did not feel.[3] The verse is sustainedly interesting and engaging because of existential passion, its historical and geographical sweep and its forward drive (after the tale of Margaret and her ruined cottage there is little of that in *The Excursion*). What we discover in Book 3, along with glimpses of transatlantic history

1 See *The Fenwick Notes of William Wordworth*, ed. Jared Curtis, revised and corrected (Humanities-Ebooks, 2007), 215.

2 Lines drafted for the Solitary in 1813 were first published as 'Maternal Grief' in 1842; they now appear in proper proximity to 'Surprized by Joy' in *The Poems* (2009), vol. 3, 49–52. Somewhere in the background of these lines is the deeply painful poetry John Thelwall wrote on the death of his child Maria, of which Wordsworth said to Haydon that because of their harrowing subject matter and inconsolability 'one cannot read them but with much more pain than pleasure'. To Haydon, January 1817, *LMY* 2: 361.

3 See Kenneth R. Johnston, 189–93 above, on the Solitary's experience of that 'unknit republic', the USA. It had yet to be knit, Wordsworth was in the habit of observing to visitors to Rydal Mount—a little callously but not unprophetically—by civil war.

in the Age of Revolutions, is that the Solitary's crime is to be miserable—and that he has ample cause to be miserable. We are required (and enabled) by the poetry to engage with his sorrows. Given this experience, compared with the tranquillity of the Wanderer and of the Pastor, and the relative non-entity of the poem's (fictive) Poet, the Solitary has struck many readers, from Francis Jeffrey onwards, as the centre of attraction and interest. His ineffectual mentors in the poem try to counter his sceptical opinions with an admixture of Natural Religion and Anglicanism. It is not clear that either of these antidotes is supposed to work, or that their proponents, the Wanderer and the Pastor, are not at times, at least, 'straw men'.

When Wordsworth speaks of adopting 'something of a dramatic form' for tthese exchanges, we may well mutter 'not half enough'; not least because in a drama one looks for vividly differentiated characters, with idiolects of their own, and Wordsworth's characters *in this poem* do sound all-too-alike, and are too little prone to speaking in terms of pointed asperity, or sarcasm, or impatience, or any of the feelings which (as Paul H. Fry has aptly noted in *The Poetry of What We Are*) we are from time *told* they express, but which rarely dislocate the steady and stately progress of the verse.[1] The anxiety of reading *The Excursion* stems in part from losing one's sense of who is speaking; because if one does, it becomes necessary to go back or forward to the next speaker interchange, and thus, in all probability, lose one's tenuous grasp on the unfolding syntax of an *Excursion* sentence—sentences which frequently induce rapid-eye-movements as we try to keep one eye one where we are while the other goes in eager (indeed desperate) search of a full stop. Introducing each speech with the name of the speaker, as in drama, or even closet drama, would have been one way to relieve this anxiety, though it would have accentuated the fact that each of them is (rather too often) given sentences that are not capable of being spoken—that is, capable of being *read aloud* and made comprehensible by the known laws of English intonation.

1 Occasional signals of spritely interchange—'A pause ensued'; 'Then said I, interposing'—are swamped by pedestrian iambic transitions: '"Methinks", persuasively the Sage replied', or 'The grey-haired Wanderer steadfastly replied'.

If, however, we chose to not assume that *The Excursion* is a dogmatic poem, but preferred to read it as a quasi-dramatic contest of ideas, in which there is pointedly *no outcome*, how differently might we experience it? What quiet signals might we reappraise as triggers to sceptical reading procedures, that in reading it as dogma we overlook as accidentals? One could start by observing that in the great opening book, otherwise known as *The Ruined Cottage*, the Wanderer who upbraids the Poet for a too-emotional response is himself misty-eyed. We could also note how that same Book closes with an invitation to ask ourselves whether we are persuaded by The Wanderer's stoicism; or whether, though we admire it, we do so without being able to share it; or whether his response shows all too clearly why this character has gone through life without any close attachments. If we *do* notice this invitation, as readers have done in the hermeneutic history of 'The Ruined Cottage', we may also notice that in the wider structure of Books 2 to 4 the same issue is writ large and the Wanderer's representativeness questioned more complexly.

The business of Books 2 to 4 (before the scene moves to a churchyard and the Pastor is introduced as a foil to the Wanderer, contributing an alternative kind of moral authority) is devoted to the introduction of the Solitary, who is, ostensibly, to be salvaged. We all tend to assume that Book 1 takes place in Somerset, a long way from home for a Scotch Pedlar to be found; if so, the two friends are somehow wafted overnight to somewhere in the vicinity of Elterwater.[1] Be that as it may, the Wanderer leads the Poet knowingly from some unspecified but drearily flat part of the country, towards Blea Tarn (resisting the Poet's desire to turn aside for a country fete and perhaps to enjoy some further dalliance with the frank hearted maids of rocky Cumberland alluded to in *The Prelude*) where he is to meet a kind of moral exemplum, whose character deficiencies the Wanderer prejudges in what he calls a 'brief communication' whose 269 lines (2: 63–332) turn out to be far from brief, and highly problematic.

We would almost certainly assume, if reading Jane Austen, that if we are told at some length that a man we have not yet met has wasted

1 The dislocation is perhaps a fraternal echo of the locational shift between Parts 1 and 2 of *Christabel*.

his talents, married for money, been driven into misanthropic retirement by disappointed expectations, become jealous of those who have prospered in the eyes of the world, and spent his days caring for nobody and nothing—we would suspect, I suggest, that the *purveyor* of this dismal record will be shown to be lacking in some essential qualification for the weighing of human experience. We might anticipate that, some chapters hence, we will be shown aspects of the supposed misanthrope's nature that require us to reassess what we have been told, so as to value him quite differently. The fact that *The Excursion*, while on a wholly different scale from that of *Hart-Leap Well*, is by the same poet who gives us the tale of Sir Walter's hunting feats from at least two, and arguably three, radically different perspectives, would surely, if we passed directly from one poem to the other, suggest to us that something similar might apply in this case.

The presentation of The Solitary in Books 2 and 3 is indeed, like *Hart-Leap Well*, a twice-told tale. The more inward and engaging verse of 3: 488–998 tells ostensibly the same life story but with wholly different emphases from the Wanderer's professedly friendly but markedly prejudicial sketch in Book 2. The second narration throws considerable doubt on numerous aspects of the Wanderer's version—not least his cynical, indeed libellous, interpretation of the Solitary's marriage. Moreover, it gains immensely from offering us what the modern reader has been trained to expect and to value in Wordsworth, namely passional self-disclosure, rather than reflections *ab extra* of the kind specified for 'The Recluse' by Coleridge. The general effect of the Solitary's autobiography (which shadows Wordsworth's own) raises a question as to why the Wanderer, if he is as wise as he is said to be, so 'rich in love and sweet humanity', and if he has truly transcended the narrow dogmatism of his background, has gone out his way in Book 2 to prejudice the Poet and the reader against his unfortunate friend in this fashion. It also supports the Solitary's dignified and impressive self-judgement in lines 277–80 where he finds:

> Reviewing my past way, much to condemn,
> Little to praise and nothing to regret
> (Save some remembrances of dream-like joys
> That scarcely seem to have belonged to me)…

But I anticipate. As we arrive at Blea Tarn and the Solitary's Cottage, where the Wanderer is to introduce the Poet to his friend the Solitary, we are conscious that the Poet's own judgment has already been sharply ironized. The Poet's rapturous response to his first glimpse of Blea Tarn, and its little valley, a spot where human kind, he imagines, are 'uncalled upon to pay / The common penalties of mortal life' (2: 387–8) has been interrupted by a funeral procession. Irony indeed. Seeing this procession, the Wanderer jumps precipitately to the conclusion (almost as if he desires this outcome) that the Solitary, the object of their visit, is dead. The Poet then pauses, as they approach the cottage, to delight in a miniature garden 'plainly wrought by children's hands', and invites the Wanderer to share his pleasure. This supposedly 'high-souled and tender-hearted man' however, looks about him 'carelessly' (445). He is much more engaged and animated by the Poet's discovery of a damp and discarded copy of Voltaire's *Candide,* on which he casts 'an eye of scorn' and which he finds well suited to its owner—his *scorn* for both the book and its supposed owner is registered more strongly than any grief he might be supposed to feel at the loss of his friend. If he grieves at all, it is implied, it is because, if the Solitary is dead, their walk has been wasted and (the language is surely revealing of a suspect egotism) their 'errand hath been *thrown away*':[1] 'Grieved shall I be—less for my sake than yours' (whose time has been wasted) 'And least of all for him who is no more' (490–3).

We now meet the unlamented Solitary:

> He saw us not, though distant but few steps;
> For he was busy, dealing, from a store
> Which on a leaf he carried in his hand,
> Strings of ripe currants; gift by which he strove,
> With intermixture of endearing words,
> To soothe a Child, who walked beside him, weeping
> As if disconsolate.— (2: 528–34)

The impression, if we give it its novelistic weight, quite undercuts the

1 One thinks of the narrator of 'We are Seven', and his impatience with this animistic child: of their rewarding dialogue he says ''twas throwing words away'.

account of a man said to be both loveless and narcissistic. While we absorb this new information (the first information about him that is derived, as it were, from empirical observation) we also witness the striking contrast—dramatized by our Poet—between the Wanderer's greeting of the Solitary and the Solitary's greeting of the Wanderer.

> Glad was my Comrade now, though he at first,
> I doubt not, had been more surprized than glad.
> But now, recovered from the shock and calm,
> He soberly advanced; and to the Man
> Gave cheerful greeting.—Vivid was the light
> Which flashed at this from out the Other's eyes;
> He was all fire: (538–42)

The scene is heightened by the fact that the reader is aware, as the Solitary is not (in a conspicuous instance of 'dramatic irony') of the manner in which the Wanderer has hitherto represented his supposed 'friend' to the Poet. 'He was all fire' may be critical, or it may imply a wholeness, an undividedness, preferable to the sober cheer of the Wanderer. The Poet draws no explicit conclusion, but he does seem a little disconcerted by the Wanderer's surprise.

One might suppose that the first concern of the Wanderer would be his friend's state of mind, but the Solitary's interesting self-diagnostic remark on the funeral

> —'The hand of Death,'
> He answered, 'has been here; but could not well
> Have fallen more lightly, if it had not fallen
> Upon myself.' (569–72)

is wholly disregarded by the Wanderer who embarks instead on an impersonal discourse on funerals in general (574–619).

So we have here in adjacent episodes, a telling contrast between the way the Solitary adapts his customary language to comfort a child, and the markedly solipsistic, unbending, almost Asperger's-like, discourse of the Wanderer. The Poet registers little of this, and what he does notice is selective and partisan. Nonetheless the Lawrentian adage about story-telling applies: we may be *told* that the

Solitary's face wears 'a faint sarcastic smile / Which did not please me' and that there is some 'carelessness' in the Solitary's response to the Wanderer's harangue; but we are *shown* that while the Solitary comforts a child and interrupts his own discourse to offer his guests hospitality, the Wanderer speaks and acts with apparent indifference to what the Solitary might be feeling (620–663). Listening to Mr Collins in *Pride and Prejudice* we may wonder whether his adulation of Lady Catherine is shared by the author. The Poet's inexhaustible adulation of his Pedlar friend can begin to have the same effect.

To entertain his guests, the Solitary somehow conjures a wholesome 'pastoral banquet' from his simple domestic economy. Such a banquet, in a novel by Dickens, or indeed in *Guilt and Sorrow*, would signify that the provider is more concerned with the comfort of others than his own, though this unpoetical Poet seems mainly impressed by the disorder. While they eat, the Solitary offers the poem's very first instance of responsiveness to the sublime in nature, a deeply felt paean to the wild concert of the winds as they rage about the Langdale Pikes. The Wanderer interrupts, seemingly indifferent to such nature notes; instead, he recalls the Solitary to his threatened tale of the death of the old man, whose funeral procession has been witnessed. Once again, what we hear belies what we have been told about the Solitary. This man, supposedly dead to all human concerns outside himself, displays in his narration (lines 758–929) joy, grief, respect, anger, a discriminating mind, and a remarkable capacity for sublime experience (whose fountains, we all know, are within). He might perhaps be criticised for his sharp judgement on the housewife in whose service the old man almost met his death on the hills—but when the Poet later meets this lady, he corroborates the Solitary's judgment (as indeed does the poet himself in the *Fenwick Notes*).

Now it is true, as Sally Bushell complains (229), that when the Solitary becomes caught up in a vision of the heavenly city in a cloudscape above Hartsop (one of the great 'set pieces' in *The Excursion*), he momentarily forgets the plight of the Old Man he has helped to rescue. Yet in the parallel scene of Book 1, when the Wanderer turns away from the fate of Margaret to contemplate the soothing beauties of speargrass, he commends his own parallel forgetfulness. The

Solitary's forgetfulness is brought about by his 'vision', as we know because he reproves himself for it. He forgets the old man once more when narrating his vision to his visitors, and he again reproves himself. (Could a proneness to self-criticism be one of the failings from which the Solitary is to be redeemed?). The amnesiac power of this 'vision', it should be noted, derives not from indulgent enjoyment of atmospheric effects but from the conviction that what he has seen is 'the revealed abode / Of Spirits in beatitude', spirits that include his wife and their children. He cries out '"I have been dead," … "And now I live! Oh! wherefore do I live?" / And with that pang I prayed to be no more'. This cry within a cry undoubtedly expresses an acute and disabling despair, which can avail a man nothing, and which he would be better off if he could overcome, but it is no basis for dismissing the man as a misanthrope.

Book 2, having climaxed with this emotive revelation, closes with a small and revealing power-play. The Solitary, not unnaturally some might feel, reaches for a drink, but the Wanderer, dominating as always—he began this Book over-ruling the Poet's desire desire to linger at a country fair—insists that they all go forth into the sun where, in Books 3 and 4 ('Despondency' and 'Despondency Corrected') the Solitary's life is to be unfolded. In a curious landscape setting, cut off from distant views, backed by a 'moist precipice', and littered with standing stones, dialogue resumes, focused at first, as seems appropriate, upon the chosen scene. The Wanderer offers a superstitiously antiquarian reading of the surrounding rocks, as 'a chronicle … / Of purposes akin to those of Man / But wrought with mightier arm than now prevails' (3: 93–5), to which the Solitary very sensibly rejoins that on the contrary they 'doubtless must be deemed / The sport of Nature aided by blind Chance' (129–30). He takes evident pleasure in his guests' enjoyment of the scene, but confesses—self-diagnostically—that the spot, with its arrangements of rock suggestive of pagan ritual or the decay of civilizations can come to seem 'fraught with depression rather than delight' and, as it were, feed the spleen of someone sufficiently depressed already. It is an interesting remark, and much to his credit, as perhaps is his half-envious depiction of the busy botanist and geologist capable of escaping themselves in their obsessions, just as the children of *Prelude* Book 6 lose themselves in their play. This Prelude motif is positively recalled by the Poet (who at this moment does seem plausibly aligned with the poet) at lines 199–211.

One major issue in The Excursion (being an instalment of 'The Recluse') is, properly enough, the matter of reclusiveness, and modes of withdrawal from society. It is never made clear, however, whether the eponymous recluse of 'The Recluse' is the poet, the Poet, or the Solitary. Our Solitary is called 'the pale recluse'; the Poet, like the poet of 'Home at Grasmere, denies that his own retirement is at all reclusive; yet 'The Recluse' itself is billed as enshrining the reflections of a poet living in retirement. This eddying suggests an anxiety that will not quite be stilled, and the matter is overtly thematized in Book 3. As the Solitary's autobiography gets under way, the Poet's slighting reference to the self-secluding 'Brotherhood / Of soft Epicureans', at line 355, provokes in the Solitary a sympathetic defence of the monastic and contemplative spirit. The Solitary's lines as Sally Bushell and others have shown, are a very slightly amended version of passage written in Wordsworth's own voice in 'The Tuft of Primroses' and intended originally for that part of *The Recluse* preceding *The Excursion*.[1] 'What motive … drove the Hermit to his cell?' the Solitary asks himself (374–6). His answer evinces the true voice of feeling and a passion that is thoroughly Wordsworthian. Hermitude, he opines, craves 'a life of peace, / Stability without regret or fear'. The monastic ideal he defines as:

> The life where hope and memory are as one;
> Earth quiet and unchanged; the human Soul
> Consistent in self-rule; and heaven revealed
> To meditation, in that quietness! (3: 86–94, 404–10)

One notes the extraordinarily convoluted self-reflexivity: the Poet has slighted the reclusive spirit, despite his own ecstatic contemplation of the idyllic retreat of Blea Tarn, and despite the poet's similar celebra-

1 See Sally Bushell's exemplary commentary on this passage and its revisionary history, *Re-Reading*, pp 70ff.

tion of epicurean retirement in *Home at Grasmere*, and despite the sequestering impulses Wordsworth himself shows at Furness Abbey and in the Skating spot of time. He is rebuked by the Solitary in terms first composed by the poet in his own voice as 'The Recluse'. There is no better encapsulation of the slipperiness of this work, its refusal to ease the reader's way to final judgements on character, its tendency to place such judgments, when offered, in a sceptical light.

A fine modern critic once wrote of the verse letter to Sarah Hutchinson that while it may not be as fine a poem as 'Dejection: an Ode' it is only in the letter that we catch 'the full throb of Coleridge's unhappiness'. In Book 3 lines 427–998, despite the quasi-fictional disguise, Wordsworth amply meets that demand for the confessional in poetry. The lines in which the Solitary first speaks of his wife are steeped in dramatic irony: he does not know that he is upbraiding the Wanderer for the skewed manner in which he has told of the Solitary's marriage (nobody seems ever to have suspected the Solitary of suspecting his friend in this fashion), but we are surely meant to note the point and to draw appropriate conclusions:

> Towards that tender-hearted Man he turned
> A serious eye, and thus his speech renewed.
> "You never saw, your eyes did never look
> On the bright Form of Her whom once I loved.—
> Her silver voice was heard upon the earth,
> A sound unknown to you; else, honored Friend,
> Your heart had borne a pitiable share
> Of what I suffered, … (3; 486–93, my italics)

The domestic ties were, to Wordsworth, of paramount importance. What does it say about the Wanderer that he discounts the Solitary's bereavement, as compared to his political disillusionment, in his overall assessment of his friend's despair? Is this an editorial oversight, or does it dramatise that the Wanderer really *is* what Coleridge (who had his own way of escaping domestic commitments) ludicrously supposed Wordsworth to be, and demonstrably was himself—namely a *spectator ab extra*? It is certainly the Wanderer, rather than the Poet, in this poem, who repeatedly reminds us of Coleridge's peculiarly un-Wordsworthian specification for *The Recluse*, that it should emanate from a man whose 'principles were made up' and who was prepared 'to deliver upon authority a system of philosophy'.

It is tempting to linger on what remains of Book 3, if only to illustrate more of the relative vitality of the Solitary's discourse, when compared with his companions', but a more complex novelistic experience impends in the discussions of Book 4. Here, it has to be said, though we are promised 'Despondency Corrected', correction never arrives, unless we construe 'corrected' as synonymous with upbraided. In the early part of the book 'correction' takes the form of misplaced dogmatism, wearying abstraction, and mounting unintelligibility of the kind that Jeffrey very properly castigated in the Wanderer's discourses.[1]

But lines 467–1292 of Book 4 do have a remarkable unity, some genuine exchanges, and an increasing reciprocity of concern between the three figures. The passage begins unpromisingly with what appears to be the Wanderer's considered view of what would cure the Solitary. 'Trust me' he begins (an ill-advised opening phrase): 'the languor of the Frame / Depresses the Soul's vigour.' And the antidote? It is to 'Rise with the Lark! ... Climb every day, those ramparts' and eschewing more mental pursuits

> roll the stone
> In thunder down the mountains: with all your might
> Chase the wild Goat; and, if the bold red Deer
> Fly to these harbours, driven by hound and horn
> Loud echoing, add your speed to the pursuit:
> So, wearied to your Hut shall you return,
> And sink at evening into sound repose." (4: 480–504)

Is it possible that Wordsworth, who found the Baron d'Holbach shallow, who was used as philosophical sounding-board by Coleridge,

1 Coleridge, Mme de Staël told Crabb Robinson in 1813 had 'no idea of dialogue' (*Henry Crabb Robinson on Books and their Writers*, ed. Edith J Morley. 1938, : 132) and the same is manifestly true of the Wanderer. Were these harangues based in some degree (like Peacock's in *Headlong Hall* and *Nightmare Abbey*) on Coleridge's famous monologues? Were they, just possibly, a shade satirical, an instance of the ludic Wordsworth, an unsuspected satire on the monologic forays of his friend into misty transcendental seas?

and who dismissed Emerson's essays as 'what passes for philosophy at Boston' (*LY*, 4: 231), could offer this kind of stuff and expect us to take it seriously? Surely not; and so, quietly, but in *a mode proper to quasi-dramatic art*, the Poet, in the poem, says likewise. He is provoked by the Wanderer's strangely inept homily into offering a sort of antistrophe in which a palpably different kind of nature enjoyment is offered.

The style of this antistrophe is neither the Wanderer's, nor precisely recognizable from *The Prelude* as Wordsworth's own, but if Shelley had already exclaimed to the West Wind (as he would do five years later) 'be thou me—impetuous one!' we would all, if we met these lines from *The Excursion* running wild in the deserts of Arabia, cry out 'Shelley'![1] In lines 508–537 the Poet proclaims the joy of surrendering to the elements: 'to have a Body ... / And to the elements surrender it / As if it were a Spirit!'. 'How divine'—he exclaims ecstaitically—to 'roam at large [in] 'regions consecrate / To oldest time! and, reckless of the storm / That keeps the raven quiet in her nest, / Be as a Presence or a Motion—... / An Equal among mightiest Energies.'

Nor does this energising interchange end there. As befits a work in which some measure of interaction, some clash of character is intended, the result of the Poet's intervention is that the Wanderer himself is raised, for the first time since the close of Book 1, into something resembling poetry. Thanks to the Poet's outburst—his 'be thou me, impetuous one!'—the Wanderer now responds to what the Solitary has previously remarked about pagan belief systems (3: 322–30). In short, the eloquent dissertation on pagan mythology now uttered by the Wanderer—which will be of such importance to Shelley and Keats—is, as it should be in a novelistic work, brought about by encounter with the utterances of those with whom he is supposed to be in dialogue. For the first time in Books 2–4, the Wanderer does something other than hector, or disapprove. Kindling as he speaks, he pursues at an altogether deeper level than in his 'early to bed, early to rise' homily, this conversational theme of the mind's ennobling

1 Waterloo seems to have released in Wordsworth a strangely Shelleyan mode of poesy, which comes out in some of the odes of the period.

interchange with nature. In lines 558–883, kindred to some of the most remarkable of Wordsworth's manuscript musings in 1797/98, he lives up, at last (though not without subsequent relapses), to his billing as an inspired autodidact.

Nevertheless, there is little evidence of futher rapprochement between the Wanderer and the Solitary. The Wanderer finds his friend guilty of 'An infidel contempt of holy writ' (2: 264) which may be true, and judges him dead to all personal and social concerns, which is clearly false. The Wanderer's pious enthusiasm for providence, rules, and piety, as 'the only support' for mortal life, makes him a prejudiced witness on the first point, and the narrative of Book 2 has exposed the latter to be a mistaken judgement. Whatever we are told by the ineffectual Poet about the relative dependability of the Wanderer and the Solitary, nothing in the Solitary's attitude towards others, approaches for complacency and impertinence (in both senses), the remark of the Wanderer at the close of the tale of Ellen in Book 6. The strategy of these church-yard books, with their empirical presentation of humankind's struggle with existence, is to invite the reader to weigh both the content of the stories themselves, and the variant responses of the characters in the poem to the characters in the Pastor's tales—indeed to use the responses of the characters in the poem to help focus our own responses (rather as one uses literary criticism).

Ellen is an unmarried mother who loses her child, and throughout her ordeal is exploited unfeelingly by her employer (another parishioner). This is how the little graveside seminar responds:

> The Vicar ceased; and downcast looks made known
> That Each had listened with his inmost heart.
> …
> —I noted that the Solitary's cheek
> Confessed the power of nature.—Pleased though sad,
> More pleased than sad, the grey-haired Wanderer sate;
> Thanks to his pure imaginative soul
> Capacious and serene, his blameless life,
> His knowledge, wisdom, love of truth, and love
> Of human kind! He was it who first broke
> The pensive silence, saying, 'Blest are they

Whose sorrow rather is to suffer wrong
Than to do wrong, although themselves have erred.
This Tale gives proof that Heaven most gently deals
With such, in their affliction.' (6: 1074–94)

Such what, exactly? The Poet may be impressed, but the reader may properly wonder whether the Wanderer's is in any sense an adequate or even a tolerable comment, and ask, also, whether the author of *Lyrical Ballads*, or *The Ruined Cottage* (to which 'the Poet' alludes in lines omitted from my quotation), can possibly have supposed that it was—any more than he can have supposed that early to bed, early to rise, is a self-sufficient philosophy. There is a conspicuously disconcerting jolt, another of those lacunae which we are surely intended to register, between the eulogy in lines 1086–89 to the Wanderer's 'imaginative soul' and 'love of human kind', and the egregiously inapposite quality of the judgement that follows.

Perhaps I exaggerate the poem's disruptions, trying too hard to rescue the poem from its apparent complacencies. Yet nothing in the poem's textual conduct requires us to identify more closely with the Pastor or with the Wanderer, or with the Poet (whose role seems to be in part to accentuate the poet's absence from his text, or his dispersal within it) more than with the Solitary. One can confidently assert of the Solitary that it would be very desirable that he were less miserable, and less isolated, and that he found a wider sphere than Blea Tarn in which to engage his evident gifts. It is also true that in his bitterer moments this man who has lost his wife and two children, is inclined to think night preferable to day and death to life; but the last words of the poem are given to a Pastor who wishes the elect to be wafted away, the rest of us consigned to perdition, and time to conclude its weary course. Both perspectives are equally far from the radiance of Wordsworth's 'Prospectus'. Perhaps, after all, for all the apparent dogmatism at least two of the speakers in the poem, or the expectation of didacticism that we bring to it, its real intention is just as open-ended as those early poems, such as *Simon Lee* or *We are Seven* or *The Mad Mother*, poems that resolutely shirk their duty to arrive at or even imply a conclusion, and that very deliberately leave the reader in what *Goody Blake* calls 'a sad quan-dary'.

The Excursion ends by wondering overtly (now, surely, in the poet's own voice)[1] whether two books of counselling from the Wanderer, and two books of communing with the dead, followed by a sunset sermon on Loughrigg Terrace *have had any beneficial effect* on the Solitary's frame of mind. James Montgomery wondered in his review whether Wordsworth's next instalment of *The Recluse* would be 'the third part of the whole Poem, or a second part of this second part' and Wordsworth himself confessed to 'a wish, & I might say intention' to somehow resume this colloquy, accompanying the Solitary into his native glens where some religious ceremony amid the scenes of childhood might restore his faith and thus accomplish what all these 'effusions and addresses had been unable to effect'[2] but as Sally Bushell has observed, there is no obvious place in the documented scheme of things for a sequel to *The Excursion*.

What was to have followed the joint labours of the Wanderer and the Pastor to set forth a viable philosophy of life, from their respective positions, was a final 'Part', in an unknown number of books, in which the Poet expounded his own position on all these matters. Since *The Excursion*, as Wordsworth said in the preface, dwelt upon 'an existing state of affairs', we may surmise that *The Recluse* Part 3 would have provided the prophetic dimension of the work. It would have fleshed out the restorative arguments of *Prelude* 12–14, *Home at Grasmere* and the '*Prospectus*'—the coming of that 'milder day' foreseen in *Hart-Leap Well*—and done so in (and on) his own terms. It is not wholly impossible that Wordsworth did conceive of narrating in his own voice, in Part 3 of *The Recluse*, an energizing return of the Solitary to his roots, parallel to that which Wordsworth himself experienced. In such a narrative there would have been ample opportunity for the poet to return to the kind of experience narrated of himself in *The Prelude*, or indeed in *Tintern Abbey*, but this time with the specific intention of deriving from this data the clearest possible understanding of where our native strengths lie, and in what conditions our

1 The poet merges with the Poet while rowing his elfin pinnace upon Grasmere.
2 Robert Woof, ed. *William Wordsworth: the Critical Heritage* (Routledge, 2001), 436; *The Fenwick Notes*, 215

being best thrives. It is possible, that is to say, that in *The Recluse, Part Third*, Wordsworth would have offered an authoritative argument in which his readers would have been, as Keats put it, 'bullied' into accepting a particular philosophy. But in *The Excursion* that is manifestly not the case.

Instead, in the final puzzling Book, the Wanderer and the Pastor, though billed as tactical allies, come to express contrary views of human life and possibilities, polarized between the natural Quakerism of the one and the abject Pietism of the other. Put briefly, the Wanderer—suddenly rejuvenated (as a character he is as apt to flit from one philosophical premise to another, as one might expect from someone whose lines are crafted at very different stages of this poet's progress)—preaches by and large an Alfoxden vision of 'the one Life', and of how we have all of us 'one human heart'. He invokes that active principle which circulates through all things and is 'the Soul of all the worlds', which nameless 'something far more deeply interfused' (seemingly inspired by Lucretius, Virgil, Newton and the *philosophes*) underwrites the humanist faith of *Tintern Abbey* and the ascent of Snowdon. In this faith, all man needs to listen to is what emerges from himself, and the only law he needs to obey is 'the law of life, and hope and action'. From this radical humanist premise the Wanderer develops a view of human life as progressive, offering a sort of vision of permanent revolution: a programme consistent with the *Prelude* thesis that our real home is 'the world which is the world of all of us', and that our desire is for 'something evermore about to be'. The Pastor, contrariwise, ventriloquizes the Coleridge-ordained conclusion that human endeavour avails nothing without divine intervention. The 'system' Coleridge desired Wordsworth to 'deliver' was not evolutionary, after all, but redemptive. The poem was to have 'affirmed a Fall in some sense, as a fact … attested by Experience & Conscience … and not disguising the sore evils under which the whole Creation groans, to point out however a manifest Scheme of Redemption from this Slavery' (Griggs, 4: 574–5).

Believing in neither the fall nor the necessity for grace, Wordsworth himself *could not* have offered such an argument. To pastiche it he constructs a dramatized Pastor, who obliges by moralizing most depressingly on a Grasmere sunset with cloudscape in a manner we are (surely) invited to contrast with the reading offered of the 'celestial city' by the Solitary in Book 3. The Book 3 cloudscape is lent to the Solitary by the poet himself, or—more exactly—is compounded from one cloudscape seen by Captain Luff of Patterdale and another jointly experienced by William, Mary, and Sir George and Lady Beaumont.[1] This vision was, the Solitary says, 'too bright and fair / Even for remembrance' yet it was 'By earthly nature … wrought / Upon the dark materials of the storm'. He perceives it, appropriately for an erstwhile priest, in terms of the celestial city of the prophets, now home to his wife and their children. The Book 9 sunset as described by the poet is another piece of entirely natural supernaturalism: vivid tongues of cloud are bathed in the last red beams of the declining sun, their 'prodigal communion' received into the bosom of the steady lake. But the eye altering alters all. Viewing the sunset as a revelation of 'the pomp / Of those who fill thy courts in highest heaven, / The radiant Cherubim;' the Pastor prays that 'We, thy humble creatures' may eventually join 'the elect', 'divested at the appointed hour / Of all dishonour, cleansed from mortal stain.' Let our days end, he prays; 'Conclude / Time's weary course!'; remove 'The sting of human nature' out of mercy to 'thy wretched sons'; let humanity reach its quietus. 'The way is marked / The guide appointed, and the ransom paid…'. Even if we fail to compare the two cloudscapes, the one appropriately expressive of the Solitary's sense of loss, and the other viewing nature through a Calvinist lens, it is not possible to miss how starkly Wordsworth is characterising (if not exactly ironizing) Coleridge's theological posture. In converting natural beauty into a dubious typology of his creed the Pastor also denigrates human being, and—and a point missed by those who misconstrue Book 9 as monolithic utterance—denies the ameliorative vision the Wanderer has advanced throughout this book. It is not impossible to imagine, at some future point in *The Recluse*, further colloquy between Wanderer, Poet and Solitary, but it is very hard after this performance to see the Pastor being invited.[2]

1 *Fenwick Notes*, 201.
2 For somewhat fuller discussion of the structure of Book 9, see my *Wordsworth's Bardic Vocation* (Palgrave 2003) chapter 10.

Of course, there is no reason to associate the phrase 'metrical Novel' with indeterminacy or lack of closure, even if that is the quality we find in some of the greatest of Victorian endings. Nor can we know whether *The Recluse, Part Third* had it been writeable, would itself have attained closure. But the frustration of closure in the present work is clearly integral to the plan of there being a further instalment of *The Recluse*. To read *The Excursion* expecting to find in it not only an end but a conclusion, seems to me a wilfully impoverishing procedure. *The Excursion* does not offer a stable position or even an attempt at consensus. Its climax—to repeat myself—is a polarized debate between a rejuvenated Wanderer who tells us that humanity *can become whatever it wishes to become*, and that nature earnestly desires mankind to realize its birthright of genuine liberty; and a Pastor who embodies Coleridge's demand that Wordsworth should articulate a desire for redemption, specifically and unambiguously through the intervention of the supernatural, since liberty, as we were peremptorily told in *France an Ode*, is not compatible with forms of human power.

Reading *The Excursion* as a novel, with the skepticism we properly bring to bear on characters and on narrators, may lead to suspend judgement on the Wanderer's construction of the Solitary and the Poet's construction of the Wanderer, and to question whether, because the Wanderer and the Pastor seem intent on reforming the Solitary, they both proceed on the same premises; or whether the poem's 'intention' is to depict one as right and the other wrong, or both (in the presence of a Poet who for most of Book 9 is tactically silent) as unreliable. There being no figure of indisputable authority in the present poem, and there being no further poem to offer a resolution, the adjudication between the religious perspectives offered in the poem, as much in Books 2–4 as in Book 9, is—as Lamb contentedly implies and as Coleridge and Montgomery lamented[1]—left for the unguided reader to decide.

1 Lamb welcomed what he 'ventured' to call 'a sort of liberal Quakerism'; Montgomery complained that the absence of a firmly enunciated creed leaves us 'wandering in darkness, and still crying, – "What shall I do to be saved?"' Woof, *Critical Heritage*, 411, 434.

Seamus Perry

Wordsworth's Pluralism

I want to come at the subject of Wordsworth and pluralism here through the contrary experience of two of his most remarkable Victorian readers: John Stuart Mill and Matthew Arnold; both of whom play important roles in the establishment of pluralism as a political and a literary idea in the nineteenth century. By *pluralism* here I purposefully mean something quite inclusive: the fundamental belief (it can hardly be a proven observation) that the world at large is characterised not by some underlying or overriding unity but, rather, by an incorrigible manyness and plenitude. The world is not deeply structured by some master-truth into an organisation or hierarchy: it is, rather, a place of proliferation and multiplicity without any dominantly central restraining rule – 'more like a federal republic', as William James puts it, 'than like an empire or a kingdom'. His memorable description of this exciting and prolific place appears in his *A Pluralistic Universe*:

> Pragmatically interpreted, pluralism ... means only that the sundry parts of reality *may be externally related* … Things are 'with' one another in many ways, but nothing includes everything, or dominates over everything. The word 'and' trails along after every sentence. Something always escapes. 'Ever not quite' has to be said of the best attempts made anywhere in the universe at attaining all-inclusiveness.[1]

James obviously approves that the universe should be this way. The good pluralist has a corresponding ethical preference within the human world for a plurality or diversity or multiplicity of persons

1 William James, *A Pluralistic Universe* (1909; Lincoln, NA, 1996), 321–2; 321.

and creeds and behaviours: generally, the merit or attractiveness of a social arrangement is proportional to the amount of plurality or diversity or multiplicity that it encourages or allows. Many later commentators testify to the ubiquity of such a view, and indeed subscribe to it themselves, as does Isaiah Berlin: 'no one today', he once said (he was writing in 1975) 'is surprised by the assumption that variety is, in general, preferable to uniformity – monotony, uniformity, are pejorative words'.[1] Bernard Williams glosses Berlin's position sympathetically: 'if there are many and competing genuine values, then the greater the extent to which a society tends to be single-valued, the more genuine values it neglects or suppresses. More, to this extent, must mean better'.[2] Differentness is better than sameness, and individuality better than commonness: these remain, of course, wholly normal ideas today, and, apart from anything more salubrious, the stuff of much uplifting contemporary political discourse.

Pluralism has some claim to be the most successful of the political ideas to emerge from the nineteenth century; and this is, to be sure, a noble kind of inheritance. But celebrating plurality as simply some untroubled and self-evident good may make it seem more banal than it has the capacity to be, and, particularly, may reduce its fruitfully paradoxical and self-questioning life as a concept. Returning to Wordsworth, whom I take to be a key figure at the beginning of the history of nineteenth century pluralism, may prove salutary here: for his dealings with the idea revolve powerfully upon the fruitful difficulties that plurality properly brings with it, and so help return the concept to something of its original complexity.

(i)

After Wordsworth's, John Stuart Mill's must be one of the most famous childhoods in English letters; and it is the antitype of Wordsworth's. Mill was brought up by his father, the zealous Utilitarian James Mill,

1 'The Apotheosis of the Romantic Will' in Isaiah Berlin, *The Crooked Timber of Humanity: Chapters in the History of Ideas*, ed. Henry Hardy. (London: John Murray, 1990) 207–237, 207.

2 'Introduction' to Isaiah Berlin, *Concepts and Categories: Philosophical Essays*, ed. Henry Hardy, intro. Bernard Williams (London : Hogarth Press, 1978) xi–xviii, xvii.

as an educational experiment. He began learning Greek when he was three; by the time he was eight, he had read Herodotus and Xenophon, and six of the dialogues of Plato; then he started Latin, putting Virgil, Horace, Ovid, Lucretius, Livy, and others, under his belt by the time he was twelve, at which age James Mill began an intense instruction in philosophy and political science. Additionally, he took a daily constitutional with his father, summarising as they walked the books he had mastered the day before, which included mostly works of history and exploration. It is both an heroic and a monstrous story, which Mill relates in the posthumously published *Autobiography* with all his customary evenness and determination to be fair; but, as he recognises in that work, such an upbringing at once equipped him for a thoughtful life superbly while, at the same time, leaving him wholly ill-equipped for a human life at all. Mill emerges from his training as a young man with a clear ambition in life: to apply Benthamite principles of utility to the problems of the age and so to improve the world; but one morning he awakes in low spirits, and

> In this frame of mind it occurred to me to put the question directly to myself: 'Suppose that all your objects in life were realized; that all the changes in institutions and opinions which you are looking forward to, could be completely effected at this very instant: would this be a great joy and happiness to you?' And an irrepressible self-consciousness distinctly answered, 'No!' At this my heart sank within me: the whole foundation on which my life was constructed fell down.[1]

The chapter is called 'A Crisis in my Intellectual History': Mill self-consciously places his confession of dejection within the context of of two great Romantic crisis poems by Coleridge, 'in whom alone of all writers I have found a true description of what I felt': 'Dejection' ('A grief without a pang, void, dark, and drear, / A drowsy, stifled, unimpassioned grief') and 'Work Without Hope' (*Autobiography*, 76; 77). Something must be radically wrong with his view of things, he comes to realise: 'unless I could see my way to some better hope than this for human happiness in general, my dejection must continue'

1 *The Autobiography of John Stuart Mill* (1873), ed. A.O.J. Cockshut (Krumlin, Halifax: Ryburn, 1992), 74.

(*ibid.*, 80). At this point in the narrative he reads Wordsworth properly 'for the first time'. Mill had 'looked into' *The Excursion* a few years before without it making much impact; but now he turned to the two-volume poems of 1815 and the poems spoke to him momentously: 'They seemed to me the very culture of the feelings, which I was in quest of', he recalls; 'And I felt myself at once better and happier as I came under their influence' (*ibid.*, 81).

What was it that Mill found restorative in Wordsworth? It is in large part the vivid example he offered of someone who pulled themselves out of loss. Wordsworth writes in *The Excursion* of 'Despondency Corrected' and so readily occupied a restorative role within Mill's life; and Mill writes with special appreciation in the *Autobiography* about the Intimations Ode, which (although he thinks it bad philosophy) manages to find hope within the embers left once the enjoyments of young life have passed away.[1] In the *Autobiography*, Wordsworth's healthy influence effects the discovery of what Mill calls 'the common feelings and common destiny of human beings' (*ibid.*, 81); but at the time he wrote with a slightly different emphasis on the nature of Wordsworth's mind: there, Mill praises instead the 'extensive range of his thoughts and the largeness and expansiveness of his feeling' and the 'extreme comprehensiveness and philosophic spirit which is in him'. Wordsworth is, Mill writes, 'the direct antithesis of what the Germans most expressively call one-sidedness'.[2] What Wordsworth principally effects in the young man is a kind of catholicity, a loosening of Utilitarian zeal, a movement into what Mill calls elsewhere 'enlarged experience'. Wordsworth enters Mill's life in the Autumn of 1828 as something like a force for tolerance: post-Wordsworth, Mill wrote to Carlyle that he had become unable to '*deny* anything but Denial itself' (to Thomas Carlyle, 12 January 1834; *Earlier Letters*,

1 Notes survive for a talk that Mill gave about Wordsworth around this time, in 1828; and there he mentions, as well as the 'Ode', 'Tintern Abbey' and 'The Solitary Reaper'. See Karl Britton, 'John Stuart Mill: A Debating Speech on Wordsworth, 1829', *Cambridge Review* 79 (1958), 418–420; and, for a fine account, Stephen Gill, *Wordsworth and the Victorians* (Oxford: Clarendon Press, 1998), 48–50.

2 To John Sterling, 20-22 October, 1831. *The Earlier Letters of John Stuart Mill 1812-1848 Part I*, ed. Francis E. Mineka, intro. F.A. Hayek (Toronto: University of Toronto Press, 1963), 81.

205). Wordsworth was a force for tolerance, then; or, to put that same point a different way, an inspiration to pluralism. Wordsworth embodies 'comprehensiveness' – which is to say, a rejection of 'one-sidedness'; and that is an excellence that Wordsworth himself would have recognised, since he himself identified among the excellences that characterise the poet 'a more comprehensive soul, than [...] supposed to be common among mankind'.[1]

Mill would return to the matter of 'one-sidedness' and its opposite, 'many-sidedness', in his great essay *On Liberty* (1859): 'in the human mind', he says there, pessimistically, 'one-sidedness has always been the rule, and many-sidedness the exception'.[2] *On Liberty* is one of the foundational nineteenth century defences of pluralism, including the 'diversity of opinion' (*ibid.*); but also, much more generally, 'diversity', for Mill, is, as he says, 'not an evil, but a good': so, 'there should be different experiments of living ... free scope should be given to varieties of character ... the worth of different modes of life should be proved practically, when any one thinks fit to try them' (*ibid.*, 57). It is better to have a 'plurality of paths' (*ibid.*, 72). The language he uses to defend these positions is, in its first impulse, still utilitarian: Wordsworth does not effect a revolution in Mill's thinking so much as a serious complication of it. In such a utilitarian spirit, he finds ways to encourage diversity: it will facilitate the greater general happiness; the more ideas there are in discursive play, the better the chance that one of them might be right; the more likely that current half-truths will ally themselves to form the whole truth about something; and even if complete error is being propagated then the challenge of working out why it *is* error is improving and salutary. All of these are utilitarian arguments for a diversity of opinion and the (more or less) unhindered freedom to express them in one's choice of life. But Mill employs quite another language, besides, to describe the importance of his ideal pluralistic discursive universe; and if one had to pick a word one might say that this language was that of 'Romanticism':

1 'Preface' to *Lyrical Ballads* (1800), in *The Major Works*, ed. Stephen Gill (Oxford: Oxford University Press, 2000), 603.

2 *On Liberty, with The Subjection of Women, and Chapters on Socialism*, ed. Stefan Collini (Cambridge: Cambridge University Press, 1989), 47.

> It really is of importance, not only what men do, but also what manner of men they are that do it. Among the works of man, which human life is rightly employed in perfecting and beautifying, the first in importance surely is man himself ... Human nature is not a machine to be built after a model, and set to do exactly the work prescribed for it, but a tree, which requires to grow and develope itself on all sides, according to the tendency of the inward forces that make it a living thing. (*Ibid.*, 59; 60.)

This comes from the chapter entitled 'Of individuality, as one of the elements of wellbeing'. The urgency of Mill's language implies something. Iris Murdoch once said that it is a good question to ask of any philosopher, 'What he is afraid of?' And if we ask what Mill is afraid of here, as he stresses the intrinsic (and not the utilitarian) value of human self-realisation, the answer turns out to be: the trend of modern life itself. It is just the nature of democratic government, says Mill, to promote and maintain mediocrity: 'the general tendency of things throughout the world is to render mediocrity the ascendant power among mankind': 'At present individuals are lost in the crowd' (*ibid.*, 66). The crowd is the main enemy in *On Liberty,* and one of Mill's main antagonists is 'public opinion', or what he calls the 'moral police', against which he is quite as concerned to defend liberty as he is against the encroaching powers of government or the state. And the principal agency of the public is the force of custom: what Mill calls the 'despotism of custom' (*ibid,* 70), a subject on which he is very compelling.

> They ask themselves, what is suitable to my position? what is usually done by persons in my station and pecuniary circumstances? or (worse still) what is usually done by persons of a station and circumstances superior to mine? I do not mean that they choose what is customary, in preference to what suits their own inclination. It does not occur to them to have any inclination, except for what is customary. (*Ibid.*, 61.)

The terms of Mill's protest have strong Wordsworthian credentials: for it is against custom — what is called in the 'Advertisement' to the 1798 *Lyrical Ballads,* 'pre-established codes of decision' (*Major Works*, 591) — that the 'experiments' (Wordsworth's own word, from that same 'Advertisement') of *Lyrical Ballads* set themselves; and Wordsworth anticipates — and indeed received — a hostile reaction from readers 'accustomed to the gaudiness and inane phraseology of many modern writers' (*ibid.*). Wordsworth shares too the conviction that 'the present day' represents a particularly stiff challenge to the claims of the individual: 'For', as the 'Preface' to *Lyrical Ballads* puts it, 'a multitude of causes, unknown to former times, are now acting with a combined force to blunt the discriminating powers of the mind, and unfitting it for all voluntary exertion to reduce it to a state of almost savage torpor' (*Major Works*, 599). '[S]ociety has now fairly got the better of individuality', is Mill's complaint: or, as Wordsworth might put it, 'The world is too much with us'; and the metaphor of stuntedness that Mill uses — that the over-socialised man turns out like a pollarded tree — recalls what might seem an exemplarily Romantic sort of imagery: Coleridge, for example, thinks of Samuel Pepys as a pollarded tree, his higher mental faculties snipped off by the remorseless commercialist spirit of his age in which Pepys partook so energetically.[1] The point at stake here would not really be that human beings are defined by their 'common feelings and common destiny', as Mill puts the Wordsworthian lesson he learns in the *Autobiography*, but, rather, that they are defined by being *different* from one another. The counter-thrust to uniformity can come only from some heroic re-assertion of the self: 'One whose desires and impulses are not his own, has no character, no more than a steam-engine has a character'. Enslaved to custom, people do not ask the question that would free them:

> In our times, from the highest class of society down to the lowest, every one lives as under the eye of a hostile and dreaded censorship. Not only in what concerns others, but in what concerns only themselves, the individual or the family do not ask themselves — what do I prefer? (*Ibid.*, 61.)

And this enabling piece of self-interrogation, if asked by everyone, would very likely establish Mill's pluralist world:

1 *Marginalia*, ed. H.J. Jackson and George Whalley (Princeton, NJ: Princeton University Press, 1980-2001), iv.78.

> There is no reason that all human existence should be constructed on some one or some small number of patterns. If a person possesses any tolerable amount of common sense and experience, his own mode of laying out his existence is the best, not because it is the best in itself, but because it is his own mode. Human beings are not like sheep; and even sheep are not indistinguishably alike. (*Ibid.*, 67.)

I admire his defence of the individuality even of sheep, for which I cannot find a precedent in Wordsworth. But while the language of 'common sense' is not especially Wordsworthian either, still, the more general conviction at play here, that a man's life is somehow self-vindicating if it is genuinely his *own,* is something to which *The Prelude* speaks especially. The word 'own' does a lot of unostentatious work in the poem: the poem begins with a liberated heart, 'Joyous, nor scared at its own liberty', and goes on to ring numerous changes upon the word's complex inflections:

> Of genius, power,
> Creation and divinity itself
> I have been speaking, for my theme has been
> What passed within me. Not of outward things
> Done visibly for other minds, words, signs,
> Symbols or actions, but of my own heart
> Have I been speaking, and my youthful mind.
> (*The Prelude, 1850,* iii.173-9)

'What passed *within* me', which the metre might recommend; or 'What passed within *me*'? The striking lines make a claim about inwardness as opposed to the public world of 'other minds' — what passed *within* me — but they also make a claim about the vindication created by a truly authentic *me* — 'my own heart', 'his own mode'. We probably do not think of Mill as a Romantic thinker, but he would fully earn the title according to one highly distinguished and influential scholar of the subject: Isaiah Berlin, with whom I began, both espoused the pluralist values of liberalism and studied the history of their emergence; and he came to consider the Romantic period a moment of central importance in the history of ideas he had to tell, because it was during that age that the truth of pluralism emerged. Summarising on one occasion what he thought of as the Romantic position, Berlin said this:

> The general position is that 'I create as I do, whether I am an artist, a philosopher, a statesman, not because the goal that I seek to realise is objectively beautiful, or true, or virtuous, or approved by public opinion, or demanded by majorities or tradition, but because it is my own'.[1]

(ii)

But you could find much more troubling the pluralism that emerges once individuality is adopted at the basis of things. Matthew Arnold shared with Mill a sense of 'the present time' as especially testing, a uniquely modern form of crisis. Arnold describes what is the trouble with modernity in many places — you could say that it is his main subject as a writer — but he does so perhaps with most forcefulness in his essay on Heine in the first volume of *Essays in Criticism,* where he attributes the epochal break to the work of Goethe, and what he calls Goethe's 'profound, imperturable naturalism', namely this:

> he puts the standard, once for all, inside every man instead of outside him; when he is told, such a thing must be so, there is immense authority and custom in favour of its being so, it has been held to be so for a thousand years, he answers with Olympian politeness, 'But *is* it so? is it so to *me?'* Nothing could be more really subversive of the foundations on which the old European order rested; and it may be remarked that no persons are so radically detached from this order, no persons so thoroughly modern, as those who have felt Goethe's influence most deeply.[2]

If we follow Iris Murdoch's advice once again and ask what Arnold

1 Isaiah Berlin, 'The Counter-Enlightenment', in *Against the Current,* ed. Henry Hardy (London: Hogarth Press, 1979; repr., 1980) 1-24, 16.

2 'Heinrich Heine', in *Lectures and Essays in Criticism*, ed. R.H. Super, with the assistance of Sister Thomas Marion Hoctor (Ann Arbor, MI: University of Michigan Press, 1962) 107–132, 110.

is afraid of, then the answer in Arnold's case is going to be something like: 'unchecked pluralism': a panorama of disorderliness opening up, a realm in which truth has been scattered into as many points of view as there are individuals to have a point of view. Arnold evidently felt that his contemporaries were unable or unwilling to escape a literature merely of the point of view. Robert Browning, for example, 'is a man with a moderate gift passionately desiring movement and fulness', or so Arnold at his most lofty told Clough, 'and obtaining but a confused multitudinousness'. Browning nor Keats, 'will not be patient neither understand that they must begin with an Idea of the world in order not to be prevailed over by the world's multitudinousness'.[1] In the days of pre-modernity you might aspire to write a work of due mastery (a favourite term of praise for Arnold) such as 'An Essay on Man' – though, as it happens, Pope was not one of Arnold's preferences; but what the nineteenth century produced instead was pluralised efforts such as Browning's *Men and Women* — not the unity of Homeric epic but splintered epic such as *The Ring and the Book* — of which G.K. Chesterton finely said that it was 'the great epic of the age', quintessentially modern, because 'it is the expression of the belief that [...] no man ever lived upon this earth without possessing a point of view'.[2] The modern age is marked by an endless proliferation of individualities. For Arnold one of the horrors of Bishop Colenso, the liberal Biblical scholar, was the way his writings unleashed 'a surge of liberal speculation ... amidst the undisciplined, ignorant, passionate, captious multitude' (*Lectures and Essays*, 54): every man for himself. It is what, in *Culture and Anarchy,* Arnold movingly calls 'anarchy' — 'all the multitudinous, turbulent, and blind impulses of our ordinary selves'. There, he hopes that anarchy might not prevail because its plurality might be mastered somehow by 'culture', which will create the 'best self', a mysterious supra-individual state-identity into which we might all be subsumed for the better: 'to make the state more and more the expression, as we say, of our best self, which is not manifold, and vulgar, and unstable,

1 *The Letters of Matthew Arnold to Arthur Hugh Clough*, ed. Howard Foster Lowry (London: Oxford University Press, 1932), 97.

2 *Robert Browning* (London: Macmillan, 1903), 171.

and contentious, and ever-varying, but one, and noble, and secure, and peaceful, and the same for all mankind'.[1]

The question here amounts to more than just different ways of thinking about the pluralism brought about by the new individualism: it becomes a concern within Wordsworth criticism. For where Wordsworth stands for Mill as a voice that resists one-sidedness, for Arnold, contrarily, he is the solution to the plural problems of the age. The 'Memorial Verses' that Arnold writes in memory of Wordsworth in 1850 counts off the deaths of Byron, Goethe, and, latterly, Wordsworth: Arnold makes a grand elegiac gesture by announcing with the death of Wordsworth the death of poetry itself and his own verse – not poetry, therefore, but a sort of posthumous effort at poetry – decorously misses its footing:

> Goethe in Weimar sleeps, and Greece,
> Long since, saw Byron's struggle cease.
> But one such death remained to come;
> The last poetic voice is dumb—
> We stand to-day by Wordsworth's tomb.
> (11.1–5)

The misrhymed triplet come/dumb/tomb is a piece of mordant and deferential wit, dramatising a post-Wordsworthian poetry that is beginning to fray apart. What is just as important about the lines, however, is the insistence of the pronoun: 'We'. As later in the poem, Wordsworth does not only bring good experiences, but he brings them to an 'us': the incorrigible isolation of individual experience is redeemed into the experience of a community, or, in more Wordsworthian phrase, a 'commonalty'. 'Wordsworth's poetry is great because of the extraordinary power with which Wordsworth feels the joy offered to us in nature, the joy offered to us in the simple primary affections and duties ... the extraordinary power with which, in case after case, he shows us this joy, and renders it so as to make us share it'.[2] As he creates the grounds of this shared experience,

1 *Culture and Anarchy and Other Writings*, ed. Stefan Collini (Cambridge: Cambridge University Press, 1993), 166–7; 181.

2 'Wordsworth', in *English Literature and Irish Politics*, ed. R.H. Super (Ann Arbor, MI: University of Michigan Press, 1973) 36–55, 51.

Arnold's Wordsworth works against the modern principle of differentiated lives, instead gathering individuals into an ennobling common experience:

> Wordsworth brings us word ... according to his own strong and characteristic line, he brings us word
>
> Of joy in widest commonalty spread.
>
> Here is an immense advantage for a poet. Wordsworth tells of what all seek, and tells of it at its truest and best source, and yet a source where all many go and draw for it. (*Ibid.*.)

Arnold's own testimony is of something very different from such widest commonalty:

> Yes! in the sea of life enisled,
> With echoing straits between us thrown,
> Dotting the shoreless watery wild,
> We mortal millions live alone.
> The islands feel the enclasping flow,
> And then their endless bounds they know.
> ('To Marguerite. Continued', ll.1–5)

(iii)

Does what I am saying amount to much more than evidence for the truism that people can read a great poet in very different ways? I think so, because both Mill and Arnold read Wordsworth deeply and I should say manifestly well, but oppositely; and that might suggest that something deeply oppositional was going on in Wordsworth before they arrived. That a poet of the point of view should also be a prophet of some universal truth is paradoxical; and the lines from 'To Marguerite' might help us to grasp something of that paradox. Being an island is a matter of being cast into loneliness: 'We mortal millions live alone'; but the line has a quiet sort of oddity for while isolation is the Arnoldian stock in trade, at least it remains a plight that we are all in together. Michael O'Neill puts his finger on this nicely when he observes that 'Arnold's image of isolation is remarkable for its collectiveness'.[1] A lot of Arnold's best poetry dwells on the twinned thoughts that we moderns are all solitaries, each ultimately cut off and unknowable to the other, but at the same time part of some approximate and common enterprise; and such a splicing of individual and common experience seems to me something that has learnt from Wordsworth – the real Wordsworth, that is, rather than the needy recuperative myth of Arnold's late prose.

An example of what is at stake here might be 'The Old Cumberland Beggar', a distinctively Wordsworthian poem, at once about the collectivity of the human lot, but also about the incorrigible individuality of people. The poem begins with a superb evocation of a life being led far away from any public eye: here, as in Arnold, the hallmark of another's individuality is his inscrutability.

> I saw an aged Beggar in my walk;
> And he was seated, by the highway side,
> On a low structure of rude masonry
> Built at the foot of a huge hill, that they
> Who lead their horses down the steep rough road
> May thence remount at ease. The aged Man
> Had placed his staff across the broad smooth stone
> That overlays the pile; and, from a bag
> All white with flour, the dole of village dames,
> He drew his scraps and fragments, one by one;
> And scanned them with a fixed and serious look
> Of idle computation. In the sun,
> Upon the second step of that small pile,
> Surrounded by those wild unpeopled hills,
> He sat, and ate his food in solitude:
> And ever, scattered from his palsied hand,
> That, still attempting to prevent the waste,
> Was baffled still, the crumbs in little showers
> Fell on the ground; and the small mountain birds
> Not venturing yet to peck theft destined meal,
> Approached within the length of half his staff

1 'The Burden of Ourselves: Arnold as a Post-Romantic Poet', *The Yearbook of English Studies* 36 (2006) 111–127, 123.

The poem recognisably relates to a recurrent interest in both Wordsworth's and Coleridge's leftist poems of the later 1790s, in which an encounter across a social division reveals some essential principle of commonalty between speaker and encountered figure: Coleridge's hailing of the young ass as 'brother' would be only the most smokeable example. But Wordsworth's poem, while certainly mindful of that encouraging and progressive paradigm of social connectedness, nevertheless explores a different kind of reality at the same time: his lines are quite shut out, wholly unassertive about what, if anything, is going on inside the beggar's head: 'He travels on, a solitary Man'. That is a desperate state, something about which the poem is absolutely clear; but the hard argument of the poem is that if suffering is the precondition of a kind of individuality, then that might prove worth it: individuality might be a more important attribute of a life than, say, receiving the shelter or food that are offered by the state structures established for the poverty-stricken: 'May never House, misnamed of Industry, / Make him a captive!' The Poor Laws were one of the main objects of reform contemplated by Utilitarians such as Mill's father, and the reason Wordsworth wishes to keep the Old Man out of the workhouse is a firm instinct opposed to the style of arguments that are invoked to justify such an institution — based, as they are, on what David Bromwich calls 'the reductive universalism of political economy'. An uncomfortable and bitter individual life is better than the enforced univeralising of the common, state-owned life. Bromwich's account of the poem is a marvellously attentive and wholly persuasive account of the poem's odd regard for the Old Man's unknown inwardness, and, in being so, a denial, as Bromwich says, of the sentimental view 'that a feeling *about someone* becomes deeper by pretending to be a feeling from *the other person's point of view*'.[1] That we mortal millions live alone need represent no catastrophic challenge to a proper or decent kind of thinking about the shape and terms of our social life: on the contrary, such a realisation can even form a better (because a less self-delusive) condition for that thinking than the assumption that we are all part

1 *Disowned by Memory: Wordsworth's Poetry of the 1790s* (Chicago: University of Chicago Press, 1998), 23; 40.

of one great experience, acquainted intuitively with one another's inmost needs, and able to share one another's pain.

So, when the poem reaches its doctrinal climax we might expect some complication of feeling; and that, I think, is what we find:

> this single cause,
> That we have all of us one human heart.

Wordsworth's primary meaning here is, no doubt, something positively counter-individualist and communitarian, like: 'we are all of us part of the one community of feeling', so one heart beats in time in everyone. That sense is what Gaskell responded to, with great decency of feeling, when she acclaimed these lines as a 'beautiful truth' in a letter to Mary Howitt; but the truth she cited was not quite Wordsworth's: 'That we have all of us a human heart'.[1] That was one of the things that Wordsworth chose not to write, as he chose not to write, say, 'We share between us all one human heart'. The wording that he did choose is great because it has another, contrarian, sense hanging about in the back of its mind: that we each have a heart of our own. Here is a good test for the Wordsworthian axiom enunciated by Clough: 'is it not intelligible that by a change of intonation, accent, or it may be mere accompanying gesture, the same words may be made to bear most different meanings?'.[2] Like Arnold's mortal millions living alone, the line unobtrusively joins the different critical apprehensions of Arnold and Mill, aware at once the value of commonalty and of the value of plurality too.

1 *The Letters of Mrs. Gaskell*, ed. J.A.V. Chapple and Arthur Pollard (Manchester: Manchester University Press, 1966), 12.

2 *Prose Remains of A.H. Clough, with a Selection from his Letters and a Memoir*, ed. by his wife (London: Macmillan, 1888), 313.

Wordsworth from Humanities-Ebooks

The Cornell Wordsworth: a Supplement, **edited by Jared Curtis ††**

The Fenwick Notes of William Wordsworth, **edited by Jared Curtis, revised and corrected †**

The Poems of William Wordsworth: Collected Reading Texts from the Cornell Wordsworth, **edited by Jared Curtis,** *3 volumes* **†**

The Prose Works of William Wordsworth, **Volume 1, edited by W. J. B. Owen and Jane Worthington Smyser †**

Wordsworth's Convention of Cintra, a Bicentennial Critical Edition, **edited by W. J. B Owen, with a critical symposium by Simon Bainbridge, David Bromwich, Richard Gravil, Timothy Michael and Patrick Vincent †**

Wordsworth's Political Writings, **edited by W. J. B. Owen and Jane Worthington Smyser. †**

Other Literary Titles

John Beer, *Coleridge the Visionary*

John Beer, *Blake's Humanism*

Richard Gravil, *Wordsworth and Helen Maria Williams; or, the Perils of Sensibility* **†**

Richard Gravil and Molly Lefebure, eds, *The Coleridge Connection: Essays for Thomas McFarland*

John K. Hale, *Milton as Multilingual*

Simon Hull, ed., *The British Periodical Text, 1796–1832*

W. J. B. Owen, *Understanding The Prelude*

Pamela Perkins, ed., *Francis Jeffrey: Unpublished Tours.* **†**

Keith Sagar, *D. H. Lawrence: Poet* **†**

Irene Wiltshire, ed. *Collected Letters of Elizabeth Gaskell's Daughters* **[in preparation: title t.b.c.]**

† Also available in paperback, †† in hardback
http://www.humanities-ebooks.co.uk
all available to libraries from MyiLibrary.com